Dauntless

VALIANT HEARTS ◇ Book One

Đauntless

DINA L. SLEIMAN

BETHANYHOUSE
a division of Baker Publishing Group
Minneapolis, Minnesota

© 2015 by Dina L. Sleiman

Published by Bethany House Publishers
11400 Hampshire Avenue South
Bloomington, Minnesota 55438
www.bethanyhouse.com

Bethany House Publishers is a division of
Baker Publishing Group, Grand Rapids, Michigan

Printed in the United States of America

Library of Congress Cataloging-in-Publication Data
Sleiman, Dina L.
    Dauntless / Dina Sleiman.
        pages cm. — (Valiant hearts ; book 1)
    ISBN 978-0-7642-1312-0 (pbk. : alk. paper)
        [1. Adventure and adventurers—Fiction. 2. Robbers and outlaws—Fiction.
    3. Nobility—Fiction. 4. Orphans—Fiction. 5. Conduct of life—Fiction.
    6. Middle Ages—Fiction. 7. Great Britain—History—13th century—Fiction.]
    I. Title.
    PZ7.1.S59Dau 2015
    [Fic]—dc23   2014040985

Scripture quotations are from the King James Version of the Bible.

This is a work of fiction. Names, characters, incidents, and dialogues are products of
the author's imagination and are not to be construed as real. Any resemblance to actual
events or persons, living or dead, is entirely coincidental.

Cover design by Paul Higdon
Cover model photography by Steve Gardner, PixelWorks Studios, Inc.

Author represented by The Steve Laube Agency

15 16 17 18 19 20 21   7 6 5 4 3 2 1

To my readers:

My prayer is that you will be strong and courageous. Follow the path God has laid before you, wherever that might lead. Be a doctor, a lawyer, a professional athlete, a wife, a mother, or even a president.

Chase after your dreams, and if a handsome knight in shining armor should happen to come alongside you, headed in the same direction, and you should happen to fall in love . . . then join together and become partners in your quest.

But please remember—you are complete, you are beautiful, and you are dearly loved by God just the way you are.

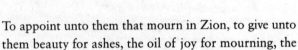

To appoint unto them that mourn in Zion, to give unto them beauty for ashes, the oil of joy for mourning, the garment of praise for the spirit of heaviness; that they might be called trees of righteousness, the planting of the Lord, that he might be glorified.

—Isaiah 61:3

Prologue

I am air.
I am wind.
I am stealthy like a cat.
A wild lynx of the forest.

I whisper my chant as I await my prey, crouched in the branches of a tree, one with it, as I must be. My green tunic and hood, my brown leggings, even my stray wisps of hair blend into the forest about me. The rough flaxen sack, the quiver and bow upon my back, add texture and disguise my feminine shape. Only my trembling hands give me away as human, as other. But I must be dauntless to accomplish this task.

Again I steel my heart. Steady its beating. Will it to turn hard and sharp like the dagger in my belt? Though I have never thrust a blade into human flesh, if needed, I think I could. I fancy myself a fearless leader, but my hands—I glance down and rub them together—my trembling hands always give me away.

Taking deep, calming breaths of maple-scented air, I study the forest across the dirt road from me, picking out the eyes from leaves, bushes, and branches. My "men" remain well camouflaged, as usual, but if I peer closely enough, I can always find their eyes. Tough eyes, strong eyes, yet with echoes of little boys hidden in their depths, begging me to care for them. To somehow, someway, be the mother and father they each have lost, though I am naught but seventeen myself. My men will back me up, protect me with their lives if needed. But I cannot call upon them to do so.

I will do this thing alone. Stealthy like a cat. In and out before they realize. 'Tis always best this way.

In the distance, I hear the first creaks and jangles against the rustling of the leaves. I sigh. One way or another, soon it will be over—until next week, or perhaps tomorrow. I must not think about that now.

I have heard tales of a fellow in Sherwood Forest, not so terribly far away. Robyn of the Hode, they call him, with his own band of men, although I imagine his are actual *grown* men. Oh, a few of mine are large enough. And I've trained them to fight like the guards who once protected me . . . in a stone castle that used to be mine . . . until it was all taken away. Robyn and I, we have that in common if legend holds true.

Yes, I tell myself, *I am ready for this.*

An explosion of bright color bursts onto the scene. Two stalwart knights on white steeds, covered with drapes of purple and red, proudly displaying some inconsequential coat of arms, ride to the front of the retinue. Another knight in a matching surcoat drives the traveling wagon and clicks to his well-trained team. The wagon itself is painted and gilded like an exotic bird swooping through the green and brown world of our forest. A wagon intended for noble travel, with a rare wooden roof and luggage fortuitously secured on top, just as my informer reported.

I await, lest there be more.

But no.

To my great relief, that is all. A rear guard would be my worst enemy. Perhaps a servant or two yet ride along back to hue the cry if trouble approaches, but no guards watch from behind. The quaking in my hands subsides to a slow tremble. If I still believed in God, I might have whispered a thanks. But I do not. I only believe in me. And the children I must protect. Robyn of the Hode might steal from the rich and give to the poor, but we are the poor, and I concern myself only with caring for us.

I ready myself. Stealth and silence. These are my allies. Cunning and the forest. My forest. And timing. Timing is of the utmost. I will rely on these, and I will prevail.

I give my men the signal. The whistling call of a crested lark.

As the wagon approaches, I scramble along my branch at precisely the right moment and hop onto the roof with nary a thud. I hold tight for a moment, but if the occupants sensed a disturbance, they must have thought it naught but a bump in the road. With great haste I rifle through bags and trunks, grabbing up food supplies and useful trinkets, stashing them in the sack upon my back but leaving nothing amiss.

I catch a flash out of the corner of my eye. My men flying through the forest, quiet as phantoms alongside the wagon.

There remains one last chest. A small one. Locked. I know what this means, and I must make my choice in an instant. It may be the difference between meager dinner and feast. Between prison and death. But our funds run low. One never knows when a little one might need a physician. Or we might require quick passage aboard a ship. And so I stash it as well, with not a moment to spare.

Just ahead, there it is.

The most delicate part of this mission. My escape branch—higher than the one I descended from. I must jump to catch it and swing myself up before I am spotted. One fraction of a moment off and all could be lost. I must account for the extra weight upon my back. But I have trained for this.

Moving closer to the front of the wagon, I leap, a cat, at just the right time. I catch the branch and swing myself up, clutching, clinging, indeed like a scared kitten.

The wagon continues down the road, no one the wiser. My branch sways ever so slightly as a servant perched on the rear board stares up into the puffy white clouds while picking at his teeth with a stick. And then they are gone, around the next bend.

Once upon a time I, too, stared into clouds, dreaming they were dragons, or flowers, or . . . or handsome princes who would carry me away.

But I no longer believe in handsome princes. So I climb down the tree and am met by a quiet but hearty round of hugs from my men. They slap me on the back, grinning like the overgrown children they are.

"Good job, Lady Merry," whispers Allen, as Red and Cedric boost me atop their shoulders.

I wish he would not call me that.

Red grunts. "She's heavy today, boys."

"Must have caught us something good!" Henry, only fourteen, nearly shrieks with delight.

We all shush him.

James returns the conversation to a whisper. "I'd say she caught us an awfully big fish."

"I think you shall be pleased," I say with a sly smile. Taking my sack from my back, I withdraw the small ornate chest and display it for them.

They stare in reverent silence.

"But you know what this means." Shrewd Robert, always a step ahead of the others, knows that if gold lies in that chest, we shall have to move camp. I had only stolen anything so substantial once before, and we all agreed if it happened again, we must move on.

"'Tis worth it." Red waves his hand in dismissal. "A great story and an even greater victory!"

"Besides," says Cedric, "'tis high time we start a new adventure."

A new adventure indeed. I will miss this stretch of forest, which has grown to be a friend, but I agree with Cedric. Time for a fresh start. Whispers already circulate through the surrounding villages that ghosts reside in these woods, stealing from passing travelers. The Ghosts of Farthingale Forest. Would anyone believe that ghosts had need of gold?

We have survived for nearly two years here, but we can start again. "Let us get back to camp for now. The chest is locked, and we need to pick it. No doubt the girls and the little ones are anxious for our return."

Being carried through the woods thus, seeing the appreciative smiles of my men, hearing the joy in their voices, makes it all worthwhile. But a piece of me will always long to be back at camp like the other girls, caring for the children, preparing the meals. No, not at camp. In the castle great hall with my mother, embroidering and playing the lute. Waiting for my father to run through the door and catch me in a warm embrace. But those days are long gone, and truth be told, embroidery never made my blood rush like a successful plunder.

I grin in spite of myself.

Chapter 1

Wyndeshire, England
Late August 1216

"I hear tales that the Ghosts of Farthingale Forest might have descended upon our very own Wyndeshire." Lord Wyndemere looked up from sharpening his favorite sword. "What hear you?"

Timothy Grey shivered at the intense stare his employer shot his way. It somehow matched the cold stone walls of the surrounding armory. "No doubt the overactive imagination of some fool villager."

"Perhaps." The lord ran his finger along the glinting blade. "Perhaps not." Light gleamed against his balding head in a manner that intimidated rather than amused. His remaining salt-and-pepper hair and matching beard framed sharp features. Though a fair man, he could be ruthless if crossed. "I shall not tolerate thieves in my realm."

"Of course not, my lord." Timothy continued polishing Lord Wyndemere's gilded shield with a smooth white cloth.

13

"They have plagued those to the east for years. And word has it they might be the ones who stole that chest of taxes headed to the king." The lord performed a thrust and parry, testing the weight and balance of his weapon.

"Ghosts stole the gold? Whatever shall they do with it in the netherworld?" Timothy chuckled at the ridiculous notion.

"Ah, but we, my good lad, are not silly villagers. We understand that the ghosts must employ some human form. A new and most brilliant band of thieves, methinks."

"Stealing gold intended for taxes? Sounds more like Robyn of the Hode than the Ghosts of Farthingale if you ask me." Timothy held the shield to the thin streams of light pouring through the barred windows and spotted a smudge on the upper right corner.

"True, not their typical thievery. But over the past month we have had reports of hams, turnips, even tunics gone missing from these parts, with nary a sound nor a wisp out of place. Either the Farthingale ghosts have moved to town, or we have acquired our own."

"We should await proof before we trouble ourselves with the matter. Nothing has gone missing from the castle thus far."

"Ah, my stalwart Timothy Grey. Always cautious and prudent. Little wonder you have grown to be my most trusted assistant." Lord Wyndemere tousled Timothy's hair as though he were a child and headed out the doorway.

Timothy did not let the abrupt departure halt his polishing. Lord Wyndemere knew his own mind and rarely shared it with others. No doubt some random thought had flitted through his head and launched him on a new mission. Or his stomach had rumbled, sending him in search of a kitchen maid. Or . . . as Timothy considered the comely kitchen maid, he realized his lordship might be thinking of something else entirely.

His face heated, and he focused on his work, banishing disturbing images from his head.

Oh, to be a lord. To jaunt off at the slightest whim. Master of his own fate. Never answering to the beck and call of superiors. But he would not likely know that pleasure. His sisters might receive the courtesy titles of Lady Ellen, Lady Ethel, and Lady Edith, but never him. Never a nobleman's son who had been "blessed" with eight elder siblings. Nine children! Such families were all but unheard of in their corner of England.

Blast the hearty Grey stock.

He would forever be Tiny Little Timmy, runt of the Grey clan. Never mind that he had passed nineteen summers and two yards in height. Never mind that he had mastered both sword and lance and his shoulders had at long last broadened to fill his velvet tunics. No, people would forever go about ruffling his hair, even if they must reach up to do so.

A pox upon his flaxen white-blond hair.

He would never be the strongest. That would be his brother Derek, the valiant warrior off on crusade. Nor the smartest. That would be Frederick, the priest in London town. Nor even the handsomest. That would be Randolph, no doubt somewhere wooing the ladies. He would never give his parents the most grandchildren. Ellen had a twenty-year advantage in that area. And he would never, ever be called Baron of Greyham. No, only his father and someday his eldest brother, Noel, would be called that.

Unless he did something drastic, he would be just plain Timothy Grey for the remainder of his pathetic life. Just a plain scribe. A plain servant. With his plain grey eyes to drive home the point.

At least for the time being he had escaped to help Lord Wyndemere in the armory, but soon enough he would be back to transcribing correspondence at his desk. Thank goodness he was at least smart enough to read and write, to learn Latin and earn some sort of employment. Otherwise he would have rotted at home as the family pet for all eternity.

But as Lord Wyndemere himself so readily admitted, Timothy had grown invaluable to him in a few short years. His steady temperament the perfect complement to the earl's impulsive ways. More and more often his lordship called upon him to help with a variety of tasks. Perhaps in time Timothy might gain favor. Perhaps please the king. Perhaps, just perhaps, if he worked terribly hard and made himself indispensable, he might earn a minor title and a small piece of land to call his own.

He inspected the shield before him to make sure it was perfect. No, it yet required one more round of buffing. So he continued.

Timothy was a patient man. He would do his job, await his opportunity, and then seize it with all his might. Someday he would conquer some foe, unveil some plot, perform some feat so legendary that he could no longer be ignored.

Some feat . . . like capturing the Ghosts of Farthingale Forest.

Merry Ellison surveyed the newly constructed camp. Their little huts were both durable and disguised to blend with the surrounding forest. Small children dashed and squealed through the circle between the dwellings as they played an energetic game of chase. How lovely to see them settled into their new home and behaving as normal, happy children once again.

The trek had taken weeks. They had skirted several large towns and walked through endless forests before coming to this area far to the west of their old camp. Finally the scouts spotted this perfect vale, surrounded on all sides by a ring of hills and with a creek nearby.

Merry took in a deep draught of air, tinged with Scotch pine and meadow flowers. Home again. At long last.

"Lady Merry, Lady Merry!" Abigail nearly crashed into Merry in her enthusiasm.

"Whoa there." Merry caught her by the shoulders as the youngster slid to a halt.

"I've lost my tooth." With great pride, the child held the bloody, hollowed tooth for examination.

"Oh, how . . ." Merry quelled the churning of her stomach. "How wonderful."

"Gilbert tumbled me to the ground, and I bumped my chin and it fell out from right here. Look!" She pointed to the gaping hole in her gum. "But don't you worry. Been loose for weeks, it has."

Merry did take a moment to look—at far more than Abigail's bleeding gumline. The child's blond hair shimmered in the sunshine to match the healthy golden glow upon her skin. Though her tunic was a bit grubby and rumpled, it was made of fine lavender linen.

Each of the children owned several tunics now, as well as warm woolen cloaks, and sturdy shoes. Although they lived a rough life by Merry's former standards, she had never seen the peasant children so plump, healthy, and well-dressed back in their home village. When they first escaped, many of them had been dressed in tattered brown rags.

Little Wren wobbled up beside them upon her chubby toddler legs. "Ma-wee, Ma-wee. Me have teeth!" She grinned with teeth together and gums spread wide to display a row of tiny teeth the color of pearls. Then she began to cough. A rough, croaking cough.

Merry withheld a frown. For the past two autumns, Wren had been struck by a malady of the lungs. Might it be starting again? Merry determined to check her supply of herbal remedies soon. But no need to concern the child now. "Those are lovely, my little Wren. Be sure you let Abigail scrape them clean with a stick each night before bedtime."

"Yes, ma'am." Wren stuck her thumb in her mouth.

Merry doubted many of the children had cleaned their teeth before she took over their care.

Even their huts looked better constructed than the wattle-and-daub homes of the peasant village surrounding her father's castle. Though she had long considered her father a fair and brave man for standing against the king, she now considered their entire social order as fundamentally unjust.

Red poked his head through the doorway of the largest construction project—a wooden fort of sorts, which could serve as a storage facility, group dining hall, meeting place, and even a school when time allowed. "Lady Merry."

Just plain Merry, she grumbled to herself, knowing saying it aloud would accomplish nothing. "Yes, Red."

"The council of elders is ready for you."

Council of elders, indeed. Merry held back a grin at the ludicrous title. When first they had all been orphaned, she appointed this group of "elders" to help her lead. At the time they had ranged in age from thirteen to fifteen. Now, two years later, this esteemed group ranged from fifteen to her own seventeen years of age. She thought giving them an impressive title would instill confidence, and somehow it had. Even for her.

If only her beloved older brother had not gone back to help on that ill-fated night. If only he had stayed with the children as her father instructed. If only . . . Her life was full of *if onlys*. If only her father had not plotted against the king. If only King John was not so epically evil.

She shook her head to clear her thoughts. Focusing upon what could have been served little purpose.

18

But somehow their band of raggedy orphans had managed eight seasons alone in the woods, outside of the law, keeping everyone alive. Even their precious Wren, the infant they had carried into the forest that horrible night.

"God give you good day," she said to Big Charles as she ducked through the low doorway of the hut, and he merely nodded. Charles rarely spoke. Due to his childish mind and huge size, he had been assigned as permanent guard of the camp, a task he performed with admirable diligence.

Inside the dim room with walls of woven branches waited Red, Cedric, James, Allen, Kate, and Jane, all in a semicircle. Merry assumed an air of dignity she did not feel and lowered herself onto a large stump. She pulled back her hood, giving them an unobscured view of her feminine features and hair. Although she had bobbed her brown tresses to chin length long ago, the silken curls would ever give her away as a girl.

She cleared her throat. "Welcome to the first official meeting in our new home."

They cheered.

"Let us begin with reports. Kate, you first, please."

"Supplies are holding." Kate brushed her own straggly brown hair from her eyes with a regal air of authority. These former peasants took great pride in their new positions. "We have plenty for two fortnights, assuming hunting, fishing, and minor raids continue with the same degree of success."

"Fishing and hunting are going well," reported Red.

"Raids upon wealthy townsfolk and manor homes have proven profitable, although I still wish we would leave some sort of token," Cedric said, with an incorrigible wiggle of his eyebrows. "The Ghosts of Farthingale Forest strike again. Perhaps a single wisp of white cloth."

"That would serve no purpose but to demonstrate our

arrogance and leave a trail." Although amused by his wit, Merry glared in his direction.

He sat a little straighter. "I merely jest, Lady Merry. Of course I would never do such a thing. Anonymity is our friend."

"Stealth . . . " Kate opened the chant, and they all joined in. " . . . anonymity, and restraint. These are our allies. These three we shall never betray."

"Excellent." Merry clapped her hands together. "Let us never forget it. This pledge has taken us further than we ever dreamed."

"And now we have an entire coffer of gold coins to guard," said Allen, head of camp security.

That gold had lain heavy upon Merry's mind since the moment she had stolen it. The chest contained much more than she had imagined. A small fortune. She feared she had made a dreadful error that would move the Ghosts of Farthingale Forest from fanciful local legend to notorious thieves worthy of capture. But the deed could not be undone. "When we resume full-scale missions, some of the men must always stay behind to help Big Charles guard the camp. And the time has come to train the boys who have passed ten years of age since our initial formation. How many is that, Jane?"

Jane served as surrogate mother to the younger children. She had a commendable system for organizing them and assigning tasks. "Only three boys have passed their tenth birthdays since the first round was trained, but I believe Sadie fancies herself the next Lady Merry. Methinks she will insist to be trained as well. She's already quite handy with the bow."

"Four, then," said Merry. "Excellent. Allen, you can begin training at once. And do not dare go easy on Sadie."

Years ago, all the older girls besides Merry had chosen traditional female roles. Excitement thrummed through her at the thought of raising up another woman warrior. "Be tough on that girl."

"Yes, sir . . . um . . . I mean, m'lady," Allen stammered, with a blush that colored the center of each cheek.

Authority suited her, and well she knew it. Someday she might choose one of the young men as a husband, to share her position of authority. Perhaps Allen, with his sandy hair and hazel eyes. But she was in no hurry to share her leadership role. And goodness knew, they had no need to bring more children into their group.

"Sir, ma'am, m'lady—it matters little to me, as long as you follow orders." She sent him a pointed look, and everyone laughed.

"I know we don't say it enough, but we are blessed to have you as a leader, Lady Merry." Jane bit her lip, as if she should not express herself so, although Merry had never demanded such a high level of respect that the others could not share their thoughts at will. Old habits were hard to break, she supposed. To them she would ever be the local nobility, despite the fact her father had been officially stripped of title and lands before his execution—or as she preferred to call it, slaughter.

"Thank you for your kind sentiment, Jane, but back to the business at hand. We have a few weeks until someone shall have to venture into Wyndbury with a conspicuous gold coin to purchase supplies. During that time we must establish a story that shall allow us freedom to spend that coin." Such bounty they now possessed, yet near impossible to spend. One wrong move could bring the law upon them.

"In Farthingale, giving presents to the villagers seemed our best strategy," offered James. "Some venison steaks and a few of the pretty trinkets from our raids should do."

"I have a thought." Robert served as her tactical advisor. All eyes turned to him in anticipation. If Robert had an idea, every person in this room would be in for a wild romp.

Chapter 2

Robert paused for effect, and the room fell silent. "Remember the armor we stole from Black Stone Castle? I say we put it to good use and create a new hero, a charitable knight who rides about doing good deeds for the poor. Red would be the right size, and though I hate to admit it, he is a rather handsome lout. When he tries to spend gold coin in town, no one will question it."

Merry pondered that. A new legend that might help them leave the Ghosts of Farthingale Forest back in Farthingale where they belonged. "A most excellent idea." She patted her knees and examined Robert, a dark, wiry boy of sixteen with a thin, crooked nose, but clever as could be and, all things considered, quite attractive.

Ugh! Why must her mind always wander to such ridiculous notions. She was a leader, a warrior. No longer a noble lady free to dream of handsome barons' sons she had met at tournaments and fairs. No, she must train her mind as she had trained her body. To be both tough and restrained.

She returned her considerations to Robert's plan. "Despite the fact that Red is indeed a reasonably handsome lout, he should remain masked. We do not want anyone to recognize him if he is seen with one of us on a different occasion." Yes, Red was handsome, in a rugged sort of way, but he was hardly noble looking.

Jane smiled at Red with admiration shining in her blue eyes, nonetheless. "And we shall need a romantic name for him." She batted her lashes.

"No." Allen shook his head. "Methinks not. He cannot go about calling himself by silly titles."

"We could whisper it in the villages," Merry said. "We are going to have to get them used to a few of us passing through." She scanned her brain for names, but nothing suitable came to mind.

"I still say we should pass ourselves off as a band of traveling tumblers," Cedric suggested with a shrug.

"No!" they shouted in unison. They had voted against his daft schemes—including tumblers, players, and worst of all, traveling minstrels—time and again. No one but Merry and Jane could even manage a musical instrument. And they could never afford to bring such notice to their band of thieves.

Robert tapped his forehead. "A name for our knight. It is coming to me. 'Tis almost here . . ."

His sister, Kate, gave him a little shove. "Oh, please, Robert. Think you that none of the rest of us can have a worthy idea?"

"Fine, then, what say you, Miss Kate?"

"Let's keep it simple. The Masked Knight. Then no one shall expect to see his face."

The council of elders looked at one another and nodded their approval.

"He shall need a horse," said Allen.

"That can be arranged." Merry supposed they could find a place away from camp to stable the noisy creature.

"Perhaps I'll fight in a tournament as such." Red grinned from ear to ear, obviously pleased with the idea and the title.

"You'll never get in without official documents, but no doubt you'll have the village girls swooning at your feet." Robert would come no closer than that to agreeing with his sister.

But there it was again. The allusion to the inevitability of romance in the band's not-so-far-off future.

One could not hold back change. If life had taught her anything, it had taught her that difficult lesson. But she *could* take better charge of her own thoughts and ambitions. Just as she had steeled her heart so many times before beginning a dangerous mission, she must steel her heart against love. She would put her band first and foremost. Focus upon being their leader and protector.

Lady Merry Ellison had no need of a man. Now or ever. She had not been able to rely upon her father, nor her brother. No, she could rely upon no one but herself.

"'Tis down this alleyway," Allen whispered.

Allen, Merry, and Cedric moved through the streets of Wyndbury in dun-colored hooded cloaks, faces turned straight ahead and buried deep within the shadows of the rough flaxen cloth. They could have been any traveler. Any farmer hiding from the cool autumn winds. Any friar passing through town.

Anonymity was their ally.

Even so, Merry's gaze darted about. She would let her marksman's eyes miss no detail. Nor would she miss the cry of hawkers, air thick with the scent of manure and unwashed bodies. She must record every street, every alley, every twist and turn. Recall the market vendors with their faded awnings and mud-daubed shops. Study the thatched rooftops crowding in upon one another and the pathways they could provide. Someday she might have an important mission in this village. Someday she might be called upon to save her friends from the dungeon or worse.

Although she would rather forget the decomposing remains of criminals hanging from stakes on the town walls, along with their stench and all that they suggested, she would not. Rather, their warning would resound like a clanging cymbal within her for weeks to come. On every mission. Each time her men left camp.

Robert had stayed back in case this mission went amiss. And Red could no longer leave the forest without his "Masked Knight" disguise. Today it had been decided that only Merry, Allen, and Cedric would hazard the trip to town.

They rarely risked her on such public missions. No, she was a secret weapon, and her anonymity needed to be maintained at all costs. Peasants seldom traveled more than ten miles outside their villages in a lifetime, but any visiting nobleman might recognize the fallen Lady Merry Ellison.

Allen bumped his shoulder against hers as they passed a small doorway. The sign over top featured a rough painting of dried herbs along with a mortar and pestle.

Cedric stopped and leaned against the wall of the shop while Allen and Merry continued around the corner to an even narrower alleyway that skirted the side of the building. More of a muddy, stinking crack between the buildings than a proper alley. But Merry spied precisely what she needed.

Her heart clenched.

Another window. This one too far back to lead to the main shop. As her eyes adjusted to the dim light, she held a finger to her lips. Allen nodded. They ducked under the window. Merry alone peeked over the ledge and into the dark room. She could just make out the outline of shelves. From the sack on her back she pulled a candle and a piece of flint. Allen made short work of lighting it. She needed to see clearly, or all would be for naught.

As daughter of the castle, she had been instructed in basic healing and herbs. Only she could recognize the medicine needed to soothe Wren's worsening cough. And only she could read any inscriptions upon the bottles with true accuracy. While inside she would stock up on herbal supplies for the winter. No need to risk a physician over this. Although Wren's cough troubled them all and could easily grow out of control, Merry knew how to treat it.

She must succeed. Merry rubbed her trembling hands before taking the candle from Allen. She took deep calming breaths. Steadied her rapidly beating heart. The moment had come.

Merry whistled their signal and listened as Cedric entered the shop with a booming "Hullo there!" in a false accent.

Allen stood watch as she scrambled through the window. With all due haste, she snatched up bottles and supplies, found the remedies for Wren's cough. But she could not locate the feverfew. Where was it? Surely they would need it come winter.

She paused for only a breath and listened as Cedric boomed out ridiculous questions to occupy the shopkeeper. She could afford a moment more. The feverfew must sit on the highest shelf beyond her reach. She tested her weight against the shelves to ensure they would not topple, then climbed up.

Yes! Victory! There it sat, along with other precious remedies. She crammed them into her sack. Snuffing out her candle, she stuffed it in as well, and slung the sack onto her back.

At that moment she heard the shopkeeper say, "Excuse me, please. I need to check my stock."

"No need," Cedric called.

But she could not await the shopkeeper's reply and would not risk another second. In one neat move, Merry, light as a cat, hopped across the floor and somersaulted through the window onto the cold, damp alley.

Allen and she crouched into the shadows as they heard the shopkeeper shuffling through the shelves. "Hmm . . . that's odd," he said. "I could have sworn I had some right here. I don't . . ." His voice trailed off.

Then as always, quickly as they had come, they were gone with nary a trace.

They rounded the corner, and Merry spied Cedric in the market square. But she did not rush her pace. No, hurrying drew eyes, attracted undo attention. She and Allen continued onward as if they had not a care.

Once in the marketplace, they sidled up to Cedric as he tested a shiny red apple for the proper degree of firmness. "Success?"

"Success," Merry assured him.

"These sure are pretty. Wish we could buy us some." Cedric brought the apple to his nose and took a whiff.

Merry could smell the sweet fruit well enough from where she stood. She lowered her voice. "If we had small coins we could have simply purchased the remedies." Until they established Red's Masked Knight story, they could not risk using the gold coins.

"But where would be the fun in that?" Cedric winked.

"Come." Allen took a step toward the city gates. "Time to move along."

Merry turned to join him, and as she did, a retinue of liveried horses trotted through the gates. In the lead rode a balding nobleman with a grey beard and an intimidating demeanor.

"That must be Lord Wyndemere," whispered Allen, who had been involved in the most missions to town. "Just as the townspeople described him."

As Lord Wyndemere passed by, Merry noticed the young man

riding behind him. He turned as if he sensed her eyes upon him, but surely found nothing more exciting to meet his gaze than a band of muddy travelers.

But she had seen him.

And she would not be able to wash the image from her mind. A face she had wished never to encounter again. The familiarity of his features sliced through her, straight to her heart. His flaxen hair. His strong chin. His pale grey eyes. His full, soft lips. *Timothy Grey.*

She dared not move, though she longed to run away. Run far, far away and never return.

"They have struck again." Lord Wyndemere's stern voice cut through the din of the castle's great hall filled with boisterous diners. He tossed a bone to the rush-covered floor and took a sip of mead from his goblet, as if the matter concerned him little.

Two dogs rushed up to grab the bone. They yapped and wrestled over it, but Timothy paid them little heed. Instead, he set his knife next to his trencher of bread with spicy stew and turned his attention to his master, as he knew the man expected. "The Ghosts of Farthingale Forest?"

Lord Wyndemere waved his free hand. "Yes, the ghosts. Who think you? Robyn of the Hode? No, this was undoubtedly the ghosts. Struck closer to the castle than ever this time. The shopkeeper suspects the theft occurred on Tuesday while some odious traveler plied him with foolish questions. But he is not sure, did not even notice items missing until midway through the next day. So stealthy they were that he had to check his full inventory before he could tell for certain."

Tuesday. The day something—or someone—had given Timothy a strange shiver as he rode through the marketplace. How odd. Might he have sensed something? Might God in heaven be preparing him to undertake a mission to discover the thieves? The unusual timing of the situation gave him the courage to be bolder than he might have been otherwise. "I will capture them for you, my lord."

"Well, you had better." Wyndemere spoke as he chewed a large chunk of beef. "Especially if they come anywhere near my castle. Which, by the way, you shall be in charge of while I am gone to court."

"But . . . I . . . that is to say . . ." Shock coursed through him, and Timothy could not manage to construct even a simple sentence. His eyes glanced about the hall. The rows of tables full of soldiers and castle staff. The falcons with their masters. The dogs, now nestled by the huge fire, each with their own bone. The bright banners along the walls. But nothing helped him to make sense of his lordship's astounding proclamation.

"Do not choke on your food, my boy." Lord Wyndemere slapped him hard on the back.

But Timothy had not taken a single bite. The Ghosts of Farthingale Forests fled his mind. Lord Wyndemere was willing to leave him in charge. Of the castle? Of the entire town?

He knew the man had begun to trust him more and more, but in the past he had always left the castle under the charge of his chief guard, or one of the nearby barons, or even Timothy's father in the old days. But never with him. Plain Timothy Grey. Ninth child of the Baron of Greyham. He hardly knew what to say.

So he made due with "Thank you, my lord."

"Not at all. You have earned my trust."

Timothy's mind continued to spin. Lord Wyndemere had no sons. His wife had died in childbirth shortly after they wed. The townsfolk tried to turn the story into a romance—both minstrels and troubadours claiming the earl had never loved again—but Timothy knew better. Lord Wyndemere loved well, and he loved often. He loved whomever he pleased, just never a suitable marriage prospect.

His heir apparent, a nephew, fought for the king in Normandy. Who knew how long the man would last? Timothy's heart sped at the prospect. Might his lordship be grooming him for something great? That minor title he wished for—if nothing else?

Two years ago his existence had lost all meaning. But perhaps it was not too late. Perhaps Timothy Grey would yet find something worth living for.

He took a few bracing sips of sweet mead. He must not let his mind skip ahead of him, must not let it rush to conclusions. No, he prided himself in his patience and stability. What mattered most was that he did a satisfactory job. Consistently. Day after day. Without fail. That was what Lord Wyndemere needed from him. And that was what he would deliver.

"I shall take excellent care of matters, my lord. With all that is within me, I long to deserve your trust."

"You had better. Had you not? I believe capturing the Ghosts of Farthingale would indeed be the perfect way to thank me for this favor."

Timothy could do it. No one knew the forests surrounding Wyndemere as well as the Grey boys. Their manor home lay at the opposite end of those very woods. He had all but lived in them throughout his childhood. Surely he could find any ghosts floating through his favorite stomping grounds.

"Then capture them, I shall."

John could barely stand to look upon the pandering pup, but look he did.

Look. And study. And despise. His stomach churning at the sight. Unable to bear the scent of the spicy stew before him.

How he hated that spoiled, pampered Timothy Grey, who sat upon the raised dais in his deep blue velvet tunic with gold embellishments, as if he were a lord born. Supping at the right hand of the Earl of Wyndemere, the man who failed to acknowledge John's lowly existence. The man who now treated Timothy as if he were a son.

He feigned eating his meal, attempted to speak to his dining companions, but he could not keep his eyes from Timothy. Why did the fool appear confused and happy at once? How he wanted to wipe the silly smile from the idiot's face. Had the earl offered him still more preferential treatment?

Timothy Grey, who penned letters with ink and parchment while John toiled out of doors, who lived in a spacious apartment in the castle proper while John slept in cramped and chilled quarters beyond. Whose skin was as fair and flawless as a maiden's while his own had grown rough, callous, and scarred over the same nineteen years.

He could not tolerate the grand injustice much longer. God in heaven could not expect that he simply stand aside and endure, that he watch it flouted before his face day after day.

He must do something to undermine Timothy Grey. To tear asunder his connection with Lord Wyndemere. Destroy his standing in this castle.

Or better yet . . .

Destroy the detestable oaf himself.

Chapter 3

Merry surveyed the open circle between the huts, which brimmed with activity. As Allen drilled the older "men" at their blunted practice swords, Robert worked with the young boys in agility training. At the moment they practiced shoulder rolls. Front and back. Right and left.

"Tighter," Robert shouted. "Land in that crouched position. Hands always at the ready for battle."

Young Phillip, who had only recently passed his tenth birthday, looked tense, his back too stiff. But Sadie performed the maneuver perfectly.

Just as Merry was about to call out, Robert yelled, "Phillip, curve your spine. Tuck your chin to your neck. Remember, light and flexible, like a cat. Keep that image always in your mind." He strode toward Sadie, still rolling to and fro. "Excellent work, Sadie. I'll have to get Lady Merry to begin training you in the more advanced moves soon."

Merry chuckled to herself. She need not watch so closely. Robert kept matters well in hand. Of her men, he alone had mastered the higher-level tumbling skills, but all were accomplished at fighting with swords, daggers, and bows. Bless her father for humoring her rambunctious nature as a child. She had spent as much time on the training field as in the solar with her mother—until her twelfth birthday, when her parents had deemed her too near marriageable age to continue with such "nonsense." Such nonsense as protecting herself in a ruthless kingdom? If only they could have seen how such nonsense served her years later.

Closer to Merry, some of the little ones attempted the tumbling maneuvers. Abigail imitated a reasonable forward roll. Meanwhile, Wren placed her head upon the dusty ground and got stuck with her plump rear high in the air. After several attempts, she managed to thump over onto her back. Abigail giggled in delight. Perhaps Sadie's interest in fighting would draw more of the girls to the skill.

Merry turned her attention to the swordsmen thrusting and parrying, dodging and striking. Making use of their own agility skills as they ducked and rolled. And making nary a sound as they did so. The Ghosts of Farthingale Forest had not earned their reputation for naught.

The younger trainees would practice with the weighted wooden swords next—building upper body strength being the main goal for them. Before long Sadie's arms would be taut and rippled like Merry's.

Though slight, Merry no longer possessed the soft, supple body of a noblewoman. Such bodies were intended for spoiled ladies of leisure. For catching husbands. Kirtles of silk and velvet had no place in her life. Did she miss them? Perhaps on occasion, but no use dwelling on the past.

The younger combatants now arched their backs, hands upon the ground behind their heads. They rocked back and

Dina L. Sleiman

forth, attempting to either stand or kick over. One of the boys tried to stand, but fell directly upon his bottom. Another struggled to kick over his head, but with no success. Meanwhile, Sadie flipped neatly from feet to hands and back again, upright as oft as upside down. Soon Merry would teach her to add the springing momentum needed to turn the move into an effective battle maneuver, although few of her men had mastered the skill.

Sadie reminded Merry so much of herself at that age. When the traveling tumblers had come to their castle, Merry longed to imitate them, and did so with little effort. It was as if her limbs had been waiting her entire life for her eyes to witness the tricks and her brain to bid them attempt the shapes and patterns. Bless her father once again for keeping the tumblers at the castle the entire season. By the end of her ninth autumn, Merry had surpassed all but the most expert members of the group.

Robert clapped his hands together. "Good work. Now to the board."

A long, thin board stretched between two sturdy wooden boxes, and the children lined up at one end. The first boy stepped onto the contrivance, walking forward with a degree of confidence and then backward, more slowly and with some apprehension.

Wren toddled over to join the line with a huge grin upon her cherubic face.

Robert took the child by the shoulders and turned her away. "Not yet, little one."

Wren stuck her thumb in her mouth. Her face mottled red, and she broke into a wail. Spotting Merry, she ran to her and cried, "Ma-wee, Ma-wee, Wobert mean."

Merry scooped the precious girl into her arms, savoring her softness and warmth. She buried her face into the small one's downy head of russet hair and drank deep of her baby scent. Drawing it into her thirsty soul.

Why must she always hear the "Ma" in little Wrenny's garbled "Ma-wee" so acutely? The child pulled at a special place in Merry's heart, ever reminding her that if her parents had prevailed, she might have had a child this age or older.

They had been prepared to marry her off at fourteen. Not an uncommon occurrence among the nobility. And the boy had been nice enough. A friend of both herself and her brother, Percivale, since childhood. Kind and handsome. In fact, he was even kind enough to recognize the stark terror upon Merry's face and persuade both families that they needed not rush into the alliance, that she required time to grow and come into her own.

In the moment he argued for her, as she watched him defend her, she saw something else. A flash into her future. A picture of him as her husband. Her protector. The father of her children.

And on that night she had rewarded him with a single kiss. Warm, soft, and tingling. The only kiss she had ever shared with a boy. The only kiss she might ever share.

One perfect kiss to last a lifetime.

A memory to be buried deep and treasured, much like their chest of gold.

Wren's crying ceased, and she pressed her face into Merry's shoulder as she sucked her grimy thumb. Naptime was nearly upon them.

Merry breathed deeply again. She had not been ready to marry and start a family at fourteen, but she had hoped to do so someday. Might things have been different if she were married and settled when her father rebelled? She might have been safe, a wife and mother. Although King John could have gone after her husband's family as well. And what would have happened to the village children had she not been there? She nuzzled Wren's tuft of hair.

No, it was for the best that she had not married. Now she must put such childish dreams far behind.

She had hoped for the best when the Charter of Liberties was signed last year, placing the king under the rule of law. With great anticipation she had hurried to the nearest town to read the document, being called the Great Charter or Magna Carta by some. She had even committed its most pivotal lines to memory. "No free man shall be taken or imprisoned or deprived or outlawed or exiled or in any way ruined, nor will we go or send against him, except by the lawful judgment of his peers or by the law of the land." If King John had honored that simple statement, she would now be free. But alas, he had not.

She had dared to hope again when the barons strengthened their rebellion, and when Prince Louis of France joined their cause. But despite all that, King John still ruled with an iron fist. She would hold out vain hopes no longer. This was her life. This camp. These children. And she must accept it.

Merry might bless her father for his kindness during her childhood, but in the end he had let her down. For what? His principles. Sound principles to be sure. To stand strong for justice. To bring down a tyrant. But they had done little good.

Merry would hold to one principle only: Do whatever it takes to protect these children.

She focused again upon Sadie as the girl strutted across the board in her short boy's tunic. Spinning in the center like a wisp on the breeze, leaping and touching her knees to her chest, then continuing backward as though she had been born upon the board.

Merry's own station in life might have sunk considerably, but these children enjoyed opportunities for which they had never dared dream. Although children died daily in peasant villages across England—in castles, for that matter—not a one had perished under her care.

If only they did not have to live outside the law. If only they did not face constant danger.

There she went again. Blast the dreaded *if only*. She must attend to the here and now. Lead these children. Protect and provide. Now that they had settled in, she must find time to continue their training in reading, writing, and mathematics in addition to the battle skills. And she would hope against hope that someday they might find a way to make a true and lasting life for themselves.

The clang of steel reverberated through Allen's arm. Red had passed him of late in height, and apparently in strength as well. But he would keep his wits about him. He could still outsmart and outmaneuver the younger man.

Allen braced his quivering arm and moved on the attack once again. The rhythm of swordplay soothed him. The clatter of steel against steel. The dance between combatants. Merry had insisted they all gain agility as well as strength, and her training had proven sound.

Who would have dreamed that Allen of Ellsworth, born to the peasant class, would someday learn to fight like the fiercest knight in the land?

"Is that all you've got, then?" Red taunted. "I may as well practice with yon little tykes." He nodded to the children training on a board across the clearing.

Allen drew in a deep breath. "Never fear, I always have more."

"So says you. Let us see it."

Allen shored up his strength and determination, preparing the next strike. He studied Red's stance and cadence. The tilt of his sword. The arrogance with which the younger man undertook battle, as if it were a performance more than a survival skill. They circled about one another, stalking like predators, fully engaged in the moment, practice swords or not.

"Such pretty play will not suffice to defeat the nobles of King John." Red thrust his sword Allen's way, toying with him.

Allen batted it aside with his own. "If and when the time comes, we shall be well prepared."

"I for one am sick near to death of waiting." Red hoisted his weapon over his head with two arms.

"Me too," chimed James from where he sat under a nearby tree. "What good are we doing here running practice drills?" He moved toward them.

Allen braced himself as he caught Red's fierce blow against his own sword, and the strike again reverberated through his arm, causing a pounding ache deep in his shoulder joint.

"England needs us," said James. "The barons in the north must prevail, and we could help."

Allen needed to devise a different tactic before Red wore him down with sheer brute strength. And he must not let the others gain a clue about his own weakness. "We cannot abandon them now." He gestured with his head to the nearby children. "We're barely settled in, and we haven't yet stored up enough supplies to last the winter. When the time comes, we shall consider the matter and decide which of us will go and which will stay."

Allen felt obligated to say as much, although he itched to enter a real battle. One that could mean their permanent safety and bring them out of hiding at last.

"The fight in the north will be nothing compared to what we shall endure when Lady Merry discovers our plans." Cedric chuckled. "She's been more fearsome than ever since we returned from town."

Allen darted a glance to Cedric sprawled on the ground staring at the sky, then focused on Red again. "Which is one of many reasons why we shall keep this plan to ourselves for now." He had noticed Merry's turn in mood as well, although he considered it melancholy more than fearsome. Try as he might, he could recall nothing from the mission that should have turned her so.

"Surely she must suspect." James stepped forward but then back again when the fray traveled his direction.

"I'm not sure that she does." Allen deflected another blow. "She's been so focused on this move and keeping the little ones safe. She thinks of naught else."

Cedric sat up. "I for one have no desire to take on that bundle of fury. She may well throttle us before we set foot out of camp."

"She'd be down four warriors either way, so perhaps not," said James.

"Or perhaps." Red poked his sword Allen's way a few times and advanced several paces.

"She shall resist at first." Allen's heart beat wildly now. Over the rush of battle, or the thought of Lady Merry, he could not say. "But she'll come around eventually." Merry might be tough on the outside, but she was not unreasonable, and she had another side as well.

He snuck a quick glance to where she nuzzled Wren. Indeed, she had a soft side Allen's errant heart wished to explore. He quelled the thought before it could fully form. Despite the fact that their world had been turned topside-turvy, that he had learned to read and fight, and that he had taken on the role of priest for their band, a certain God-ordained order to the world must be maintained.

Merry was nobility. He was not. Such matters should be simple.

Allen returned his focus to Red, battle, and the war that raged to the north. He and Red were the best fighters of the bunch, and if he proved to be like his older brother—Allen blinked away the pain that crashed through him at the memory of his family—he would yet grow another few inches. Truth be told, he longed to be a hero as much as any young man, but in the end, he would make the decision that was best for the group. He always did.

Eyes trained on Red, he finally spotted his moment.

Chapter 4

The battle fever in Allen's blood pitched to a new level. Using one of the tumbling maneuvers he had practiced again and again, he dove forward, rolled on the ground, and knocked Red off his feet. Red's weapon flew from his hand. With a bound, Allen was standing again, practice sword denting into the flesh at Red's throat.

"Ho!" shouted James.

"Good show!" Cedric ran over to thump Allen on the back.

"I guess we know at least one warrior who shall be heading north." James grinned.

Allen let up the pressure on Red's neck, and Red stood and brushed himself off. "Do not discount me so soon. I shall best him the next time."

"'Tis what you said the last time." Cedric guffawed.

"Yes, well, let's see how *you* fare against me." Red snatched up his sword and returned to battle stance.

Cedric grabbed his own sword. "Is that a challenge?"

"Of course it is."

Allen put a good-natured arm around James's slender shoulder and drew him out of the way. James was only fifteen, but he had sharp natural instincts for battle, and he had proven to be a quick learner. Soon enough, he would be able to take on any of them. "You shall battle Cedric next. Now, in the spirit of knowing your opponent, what must you remember with Cedric?"

"He always leads to the left, and he gives away when he is about to strike by scrunching his lips together."

Allen squeezed James's shoulder, then let him go. "Exactly—like a girl searching for a kiss."

They shared a chuckle over the comic image of Cedric preparing to strike.

"But keep in mind that with a true opponent you must think on your feet, James. Studying them, surveying them, even as you fight."

James offered a wry expression. "You've told me that nigh on a thousand times."

"And I shall tell you a thousand more." Allen gave James a little shove. He wanted nothing more in the world than to keep these children safe. Having lost one family already, he would not lose another.

He leaned against his sword and mopped sweat from his brow, enjoying a moment of respite while Red and Cedric clashed weapons. The two had become skilled warriors and did not require his attention. Thus, he allowed his focus to wander to Sadie, who flipped neatly back and forth upon the balancing board.

Years ago, he had hidden behind the stables and watched a young Lady Merry perform just such tricks with the band of traveling tumblers—much as he had watched Lord Ellison's soldiers train in the castle courtyard, and as he had watched Merry and her brother, Percivale, play in the forest. But he had always observed from a distance, respecting the separation between the classes.

Those who labor, those who pray, those who fight—his father had drilled that into him again and again. *"We are those who labor, a part of God's great tapestry. His divine plan. Be proud of it, my boy. Embrace it. Never strive against your God-given destiny."*

Had his father suspected that he secretly wished for more? While Allen loved working the fields and watching the grain sprout and grow beneath his nurturing touch—and was willing to play his role in life—something within him always longed to fight and pray as well. To protect his family. To connect with the Divine. Now he filled all those roles and more.

The realization stole his breath away at times.

He turned to study Merry, with her striking features, peachy lips, and softly curling hair the color of roasted chestnuts. As much as his world had changed, there still remained lines he must not cross. Particularly, he must control that lodestone within him that drew him toward her with increasing fervency. Like the other day in town, when the compulsion to rub her trembling fingers in his own, to savor their supple smoothness, had nearly overtaken him. Thank the good Lord that bashfulness had held him back as much as anything else. He might tussle and cavort with the others, offer them embraces of encouragement, but he could not bring himself to give Lady Merry more than the briefest pat.

From the beginning he had supported her in leading the group. Despite his humble upbringing, he obeyed when she ordered him to learn reading and swordplay. Only in the area of their spiritual educations had he noticed a gap, which he happily filled. He had spent much of his childhood dogging the parish priest, asking question after question about the Scriptures and church traditions, and he slid naturally into such a role.

Considering their unfortunate position as outlaws, Allen felt all the more compelled to safeguard their spiritual well-being. He encouraged the others to think of themselves as dissidents and warriors, not thieves. They had been thrust against their wills into this role of renegades, and they did only what they must to survive in a cruel kingdom. Allen held tight to that conviction that eventually a noble ruler would take the throne again, and he longed to take up the sword to assist the noble FitzWalter and his barons from the north in their quest to establish Louis of France as the new and rightful king.

Looking again to Wren cuddled in Merry's arms, he suppressed a desire to feel Merry's arms around him thus and trained his eyes upon Sadie instead. He recalled watching Merry do partner tumbling tricks with the leader of the troupe that had visited Ellsworth Castle all those years ago, a brawny fellow with graying hair. Allen had often thought to try such tricks with her, except that he would never dare to touch her so intimately.

Perhaps he could give a try with Sadie, flipping her about his shoulders and allowing her to balance on his hands. Although it might not be helpful in battle, it certainly would prove entertaining for the others.

But he would put first matters first. And the first matter involved gathering supplies to feed the children this winter.

As he turned to encourage the new trainees, Henry dashed down the hill in a panic, interrupting the day's practice. "Intruders! Intruders in the forest. To the hideaway. Quickly."

The children burst into action. Clearing the circle. Covering the fire pit with leaves. Reinforcing the camouflage. Each having practiced their assigned task to precision.

Allen gathered the training equipment as Merry hustled Wren into the main building. Within moments he waved the last of the children through the door and ducked inside to join them in the shadowy room. He counted the group, taking a moment to peruse their faces.

Their silence unnerved him. This was no way for them to live.

Robert scanned the clearing as he manned the opening. "Methinks 'tis everyone," he whispered, pulling closed the leaf-covered doorway, which would blend with the forest from a distance.

Counting heads for a second time, Allen hoped from the core of his being to discover he had been mistaken. But once again he came up short. Twenty-two. One missing.

His stomach clenched tight. "Gilbert!"

Timothy, riding upon his faithful mount, Spartacus, broke through the dense trees into a wash of sunlight at the top of a rise. He pulled to a stop. Though the earl had been gone three days already, Timothy had been overcome with castle business until this afternoon. He had less than two weeks left to catch the thieves before his lordship returned.

With a crackle of branches, his retinue of three castle guards—Hadley, Bradbury, and White—joined him upon the hilltop and reined in beside him. They were some of the earl's best men—men trusted to maintain the secretive nature of this mission. Timothy did not wish for word to get out that they searched for the ghosts, lest they scare them away. The guards wore surcoats emblazoned with the earl's gold-and-red coat of arms, but at least they'd left their chain mail at the castle, else the ghosts would be frightened off by its noisy jangling for certain.

He took a moment to survey the terrain. A valley with a stream flowing through the center, surrounded by more hills and more trees. To most, the forest looked much the same, yet he recognized this precise location. Frederick had once shoved him to the ground near yon boulder as they fought over who would take credit for the day's kill of a feisty hare. And he had splashed in that very stream on a warm summer's day with Derek and Randolph.

Hadley leaned over his warhorse and sighed. "Which way now, Grey?"

Grey. Not Sir Grey, nor Lord Grey, nor even a polite Mister Grey, as one might expect from a guard of lowly birth. But surely the parish priest would call such prideful thoughts a sin. Once upon a time Timothy had troubled himself with thoughts of love and family, not of power and fame.

He would petition God for forgiveness later, but for now he answered, "Let us continue straight north, as we have been heading. That direction is full of these vales, any one of which could provide an excellent lair for our thieves."

"Any of which might be, or might have been, this exact same valley, for all we know." Hadley snorted back a laugh.

Bradbury managed to remain stoic, but White covered his mouth with his gloved hand to hide a smile.

Hadley continued, "I would swear we've been going in circles for well nigh an hour."

Timothy hardened his gaze and clenched his jaw. He must not waver. He must not let these men undermine his newfound authority for even a moment. "Do you question my good judgment, man? For I feel obligated to mention that, in doing so, you question the good judgment of the Earl of Wyndemere, who entrusted me with this mission."

Hadley cleared his throat. "I apologize. I meant only to jest, as we do amongst ourselves." He jerked his head in the direction of his fellow guards.

Timothy's jaw unclenched. Perhaps he had been too harsh. Soldiers did joke so. Perhaps he should be honored that they treated him as one of their own. "No, I apologize. I misunderstood."

"I must confess." White swept his hand in the direction of the valley. "The terrain all looks much the same to me. But if anyone knows this land, it would be you and your brothers."

"Ah yes." Hadley rubbed his dark-bearded chin. "I had forgotten. Your father is the Baron of Greyham, is he not?"

"Yes, these are our family lands. Our Manor adjoins the forest to the west."

"This all seems rather pointless, though," said Hadley. "If indeed the Ghosts of Farthingale Forest have come here to roost, I suspect they would not be easily spied by a group of noisy soldiers on horseback."

"I have been thinking the same." Before he left, Lord Wyndemere had insisted Timothy bring a contingent of guards on his search. But Timothy had already decided he would need to return to the woods alone and on foot later. "However, we might catch sight of footprints or a fire pit, a piece of fabric, perhaps. Stay alert for anything that could point to human habitation."

"In the meantime, why don't we hunt for a fine stag, as we are supposedly doing?" Bradbury slung his bow over his shoulder and pulled an arrow from his quiver. "What good is a hunting party that catches nothing? It will help to heighten our senses and keep us alert. We can bring home supper, if nothing else."

"Might as well have a bit of fun while we're about it, I say." Hadley grinned.

"Why not? But let us leave the mounts behind for a while." Timothy hopped down to tether his horse, and his men did likewise. He nocked his bow, then led them stealthily down the valley and up the other side.

How he adored this lush world of green and brown. All the vibrant memories it stirred. So different than his shadowy, grey existence at Castle Wyndemere. This forest fed a place deep in his soul. The cool wind grazing his cheek. The fresh scent of leaves and earth. The bright sound of birdsong. The—

A snap of branches to his left drew his attention.

Thinking to spot a rabbit or a deer, he turned and drew back his bow. The guards followed suit. Something stepped through the thicket. As Timothy's fingers twitched to release the bow-string, a child's blue tunic alerted him. "Halt," Timothy commanded his men before tragedy struck.

The small boy took one look at them, and his eyes grew huge. He tossed a bucket of berries into the air and dashed back into the bushes.

Timothy gave chase. What was such a young child doing alone in the woods, leagues from the nearest village? "Wait! Stop! We will not harm you. You are in no trouble with us. Please, let us help you."

Hadley soon caught up to the child and spun him around.

The boy trembled. His chin quivered as if he might cry, but he drew himself up to his full height, which must have been all of four feet, and bit his lip. Judging by his missing tooth, the child could be no more than seven years of age. "I'm sorry, m'lord. Please don't whip me. I've been lost in the forest for ever so long. I didn't mean to steal your berries, I didn't. But I got so hungry, you see."

Timothy did not wish to frighten the boy further, but he also did not wish for the guards to think him weak. "I see no reason to press charges in such a case. Do you agree, men?"

"I suppose anyone might grow hungry when lost in the forest. No harm done," said White.

Hadley and Bradbury nodded their agreement.

"Then never fear, little one. You shall not be tried for thievery under my watch." Timothy crouched down to put himself at the boy's height and ruffled his brown hair. He examined the clean freckled face, the healthy plumpness to the boy's cheeks. Someone must be missing the lad terribly. "Tell us where you hail from, and we shall return you posthaste."

"Might as well," said Hadley. "We've had little enough success *hunting* today."

True enough. Although they had barely begun their hunt for game, their hunt for ghosts had proved fruitless.

"I say, you haven't seen any deer in these woods, have you?" asked White with a wink. "Or perhaps a boar, or for that matter . . . any men?"

The boy appeared more terrified than ever. His voice seemed to strangle in his throat. But he managed to squeak out a simple, "No."

"Of course not." Timothy took the boy's hand in hopes of soothing him. "So where are you from?"

The boy's blue eyes grew larger and larger. A tear slid down his cheek.

"Please do not be afraid of me. You know, I used to play in these woods when I was a child. Got lost a time or two myself. I am from Greyham Manor. Where is your home?"

"I don't . . . I don't remember. I . . . we . . . 'tis just *the village*. The village what I always called home. I never strayed so far before."

Ah. Timothy understood. Many peasants never left their village of origin. They had no need to mention names. Poor frightened child. Probably knew nothing of the basic geography of his own shire. "Allow me to guess, and perhaps you shall recall the name. Perhaps . . . Endsworth or Flotsdale?"

The child remained frightened and confused. "'Tis that way, methinks." He pointed west. "Not so far. I didn't pass nothing in between."

"Ah! Bryndenbury?"

"Yes, yes, that's the one. Bryndenbury. I suppose now that you've said the name, I can find it myself. Thank you for your help. I don't want to trouble you."

"Absolutely not. I insist we accompany you. It is not so far from my parents' home. Perhaps we shall stop in for our evening meal."

The boy appeared not at all relieved. Timothy supposed stumbling upon a troop of the earl's guards, pointing arrows his way while he was stealing berries would undo any child. Timothy draped his arm over the lad's shoulder and led him back toward the horses. The boy would be happy enough once safely reunited with his mother in Bryndenbury.

The thieves would have to wait . . . for now.

Chapter 5

Darkness had fallen, and still no sign of Gilbert. Although nary a sound had echoed from the forest for many hours, Merry and her band remained huddled and quiet in their makeshift fort. She attempted to keep Wren occupied playing a game with carved animals. In another corner of the room under a cross upon the wall, Allen led most of the children in whispered prayers as they knelt in a circle about him. He had long served as a spiritual advisor for the group.

Merry did not have the heart to inform them that as outlaws, they might well have been excommunicated from the church long ago. Of course, thanks to King John, all of England had been under an edict from the pope and forbidden to hold mass for several years during her childhood, and no one had paid that much mind.

Allen continued to pray in a sincere manner, with no pretense. Speaking to his heavenly Father, as he referred to God, in plain English, the most common language of all. Merry could not fathom where he had learned to pray thus. Yet she could not help believing that if God still sat upon His throne, if any prayer might reach His ears, it would be one from these devout children. Thieves or not.

As she recalled the stories she had read from her priest's copy of the Vulgate Bible, she supposed the Israelites had found themselves on the wrong side of the law a time or two. And, according to the biblical account, God had not forsaken them.

Not as He had forsaken Merry.

No, Merry could not partake in the children's prayers. She hugged Wren to her chest, thankful for the excuse to stay at a distance. She expected today's events would prod Allen to begin his Sunday services once again. She dreaded standing among them as they worshiped a God in whom she no longer believed. Her own fervor had been stripped away on that ill-fated night two years earlier.

But she had not the heart to strip them of their superstitions either. If thoughts of God brought them comfort, she would support their religious beliefs. And if by chance Allen and the others were correct, better she be responsible only for losing her own soul rather than affecting the souls of every person in this room.

Wren looked up from her play. She twisted in Merry's lap to study her in the dim glow of candlelight, then cupped Merry's face with her chubby hand. "No wo-wee, Ma-wee. Sunshine men take care."

Had Wren just admonished her not to worry? Merry chuckled.

She had heard of children creating imaginary friends before, but none so fanciful as Wrenny's collection of sunshine men. The tot often chased the invisible creatures about the camp in her own private game. Going so far as to clutch the illusive figures to herself and cry, "Got you!"

"So are your sunshine men strong?" asked Merry, tapping the child on her turned-up nose.

"Va-wee strong. And vaaa-weeee big!" The girl stood to her tiptoes and reached toward the ceiling.

"Are there many of your sunshine men?" Merry continued to humor her.

"So, so many. One, two, four, ten!" Wren raised her hands over her head, then plopped back down to the earthen floor and continued her play as if she had never ceased.

Merry envied her. How simple to be a babe. To live in the present. To think not of the past, nor the future. To exist in a singular perfect moment of romping wooden horses and sheep. Of flowers and butterflies dancing in the breeze. Of fleeting sunshine men and tumbles in the dirt. Contentment contained in the tip of her tiny thumb.

So unlike Merry's world. Her own mind ever brewed with haunting memories and troublesome worries.

Someday Wren would understand that her parents had been slaughtered, leaving her a nameless tyke, barely half a year old, to fend for herself in this merciless kingdom. Had it not been for the ingenuity of Merry and the other girls—along with a particularly cooperative nanny goat—Wrenny would have died, as so many children did in their early years.

Death always spiraled about them in this realm, brushing against their shoulders, reminding them they might be next. Like the rotting remains of criminals upon the town walls, and at every road crossing. So common that it had become the subject of humor and sport. But Merry would never grow accustomed to it.

An odd sound met her ears from just outside the door.

The call of a wood warbler . . . or rather a childish imitation of one.

"Thanks be to God," Allen said. "Our prayers have been answered."

Robert rushed to the door and opened it.

In tumbled Gilbert, red cheeked and panting for breath. "All . . . is clear." He collapsed against the wall. "But I lost . . . the berries."

Everyone laughed and cheered as they hugged him and thumped him upon the back. Jane offered Gilbert a ladle full of water, then chided him in her motherly way as he gulped it too quickly.

Once the fray settled, Merry sat down next to the boy. "So tell us your tale, Gilbert."

"Oh, 'tis a good one to be certain."

The children hushed and gave Gilbert their rapt attention.

He proceeded to tell his story of stepping through the bushes to find a nobleman and three giant soldiers pointing their arrows at his chest, his berries flying through the air, and the nobleman's unexpected kindness.

"I did just like you taught us, Lady Merry. I acted lost and scared. 'Twas easy, as I was frightened out of my wits. Except I couldn't remember the name of the village I was to tell them I lived, so I pointed to the west. I remembered it was the closest one in that direction. And I cried and told him my mum would beat me if she found me out. So he let me down before we got there, and I ran away and disappeared between the cottages."

"Excellent work, my good man." Merry ruffled his hair.

"That's what the nobleman done to me." Gilbert smiled his gaptoothed grin. "He mussed my hair just like you do, Lady Merry. And he was young, like us. That's when I knew everything would be fine. Said they were hunting, was all."

Merry dared not ask for a description of the nobleman. Nor his name. For all she had survived during the last two years, she feared her heart could not bear to hear if it had been Timothy Grey.

Young Gilbert tilted his head, as if an afterthought occurred to him. "Although one of the soldiers did ask if I'd seen any men in the forest, which was odd. But . . . no, they were hunting. They nearly shot me clean through."

Hunters indeed. But hunting deer . . . or ghosts? Her heart clenched.

Merry gathered together her courage. "Robert, please take some of the men to town and investigate on the morrow."

Robert's shrewd eyes assessed her gaze. "You can count on me, Lady Merry."

The following afternoon the children scratched their sticks into the dirt, practicing their letters and numbers beneath a cloudy sky. Writing. Another pursuit they would never have dreamed of in their former lives.

Merry scribbled her own dark thoughts upon a patch of cool, bare ground.

> Circling always, surrounding each day.
> Whisking my shoulder, death on the way.
> Acrid and screeching, afar off they burn.
> Crying and weeping, with nowhere to turn.

Hardly the typical love poem. Perhaps one might consider it a battle verse. A battle lost. She wrote the morbid words in her native English tongue. She rarely spoke French or Latin of late. Those languages were part of that other world. That world of love and family. Of safety and security.

> Ashes and dust, a bitter return.
> Longing for justice, oh, when shall I learn?
> The taste in my mouth, of char and of soot.
> The scream in my ear . . .

Soot. Soot. Why could she think of nothing to rhyme with *soot*? *Foot* simply would not suffice. Tears spilled onto her cheeks, and she brushed them away before anyone could notice.

Far! She could reverse the wording. *Far* would rhyme with *char.* But she could no longer gather her thoughts to finish the stanza.

Stupid poetry! Worthless words. She swiped her hand over the dirt, removing in a few quick strokes her feeble and dreary attempt of the day. An hour's worth of work gone in a heartbeat.

How fitting.

Instead she focused on the children—so industrious, so full of hope as they carved their short words into the dirt. As they practiced the spelling of their names. Christian names only. Peasants had no need of family names. Once upon a time these children might have been known as Abigail of Ellsworth or Henry son of Ilbert.

But no more. Perhaps she should devise a new surname for all of them. One that they could carry into some new sort of stable existence.

She dreaded the news Robert might bring at any moment. She feared they might not be able to stay in Wyndeshire—or for that matter, in England—much longer. King John might be busy in the north with his baronial rebellion, but eventually he would turn his mind to more minor issues. And hear of the Ghosts of Farthingale Forest. Assess that they might just be . . . the missing children of Ellsworth.

No, they could not stay forever. France seemed the most likely solution. The French would not be quick to turn over a wanted English noblewoman to King John. She supposed any enemy of the king would be a friend to France. Perhaps at the port she could declare herself Lady Merry Ellison and find safe passage for them all aboard a foreign ship. They had ample gold coin for passage. Perhaps they could buy their way into some sort of merchants' guild and open a business once settled.

French. She must teach the children French.

Though they had not come within a furlong of their camp, the nobleman—whether Timothy Grey or not—and his soldiers might yet grow suspicious of a stray child wandering the woods. So for now they would double the watch and be diligent to stay hidden.

Despite Wrenny's happy stories of sunshine men, this was no way to live. Merry needed to find a better solution, and soon. If it were not for her father's stubborn, reckless ways, these children would be beside their own hearths with their own parents.

"They're back. They're back," cried Henry from his watch point atop the hill.

Merry rushed to meet Robert, Allen, and Cedric at the rise.

"Tell me," she prompted. "What did you hear?"

Robert frowned and shook his head. "'Tis not good."

Merry bit her lip and braced for the news.

"Nothing conclusive," said Allen. "Rumors of a hunting party from the castle in the woods yesterday. Castle guards, though, not a typical hunting party."

"And other rumors as well," said Cedric.

Merry grabbed Cedric by the shoulders. "What other rumors?"

Robert answered for the stunned Cedric. "Rumors that the Ghosts of Farthingale Forest have come to Wyndeshire."

Merry steeled her heart. Steadied the racing beat. She would be strong. She must be. For all of them. Deep soothing breaths. In and out. In and out. The infusion of air did its job and cleared her spinning thoughts.

Somehow this felt so much worse than dangling from a branch as the king's own knights rode past upon warhorses. The children were at risk, not merely her own hide. The responsibility of it pressed down upon her, threatening to crush her into the ground. She rubbed her fingers and bade them to cease their trembling. "We will not panic. They are but rumors. Was there any talk of searching for the ghosts? Any reward offered?"

"None that we heard tell of." Allen gave Merry's shoulder a reassuring clasp.

It almost comforted her. "Then we shall stay still for now. Not stir matters further. And be ready to move if needed."

Robert surveyed the children, who had abandoned their studies and ran giggling about the circle. "It shall break their hearts if we have to leave so soon."

"It shall break mine as well," whispered Merry. But she allowed herself only the briefest moment of sorrow. She pulled herself to her full height, which was short for a noblewoman. Arranging her features into a mask of courage she did not feel, she turned to face her men. "But we shall survive this. We always do."

"Agreed." Allen stood taller as well. "Even if they find us, they shall never dream a band of children might be the notorious ghosts."

"No, of course not. That would be ridiculous." Although their being the survivors of Ellsworth would be enough to see them all hanged if King John had his way. Perhaps if he remained distracted by his war, at least the little ones might survive.

One could always hope.

Otherwise one was left with nothing but morbid poetry. Ashes and dust.

Chapter 6

People pressed in upon Timothy, clamoring for his attention, as they had again and again during the past days. Over top their heads, he stared at the blank grey walls of the castle in hopes of collecting his thoughts. An ache was developing in his right temple, and noon had not even arrived. No doubt it would grow into a throbbing headache by mealtime. But he would not be deterred from meeting his lordship's expectations. Not by noisy servants and most definitely not by the pain in his head.

"You have not approved the afternoon's wine." A kitchen servant thrust a flagon in his face.

Timothy pushed it away. "No doubt it is fine. His lordship shall not return for many days, and we have no special guests in the castle presently."

"As you wish, then." The man turned with such violence that he nearly splashed his precious wine and walked away in a huff.

"Now about those missives . . ." The scribe, Holstead, who had been hired to take Timothy's place when he had been given temporary responsibility for the castle, waved a stack of papers.

Timothy rubbed his temple. "Please place them on his lordship's desk. I shall deal with them this afternoon."

"As you wish, m'l . . . Mister Grey." The man offered a half bow, apparently unsure whether or not one was in order.

But his bumbling ways brought a smile to Timothy's face. The man performed his job impeccably. Perhaps he might keep it, and Timothy himself might rise to some sort of full-time advisory role. Now that he functioned in his lordship's stead, he clearly saw the need.

A castle guard shoved his way past the steward, who still awaited Timothy's attention. Timothy took a moment to seat himself upon a chair on the raised dais. If he must administer his lordship's duties, he might as well look the part. He rubbed his aching head.

Bradbury and Hadley dragged an emaciated man covered in rags to stand before Timothy. Their presence reminded Timothy that he needed to resume his hunt for the ghosts, if only he could escape the series of minor crises that he found himself buried beneath.

"Mister Grey," said Bradbury, "this man has been charged with thievery. And no petty thievery. Several weeks' wages worth of grain and vegetables."

One look into the man's desperate eyes told Timothy why. He sighed. "Have you a family, good man?"

"More like no-good man, this one here." Hadley shook the poor soul.

"Yes, sir. I have seven . . . no, now 'tis six children. I can hardly work my land since my foot went lame last year." He lifted the mangled appendage for inspection.

Timothy winced at the red and swollen appearance of it.

He turned to the guards. "Have you witnesses?"

"Aye," said Bradbury. "Witnesses aplenty to the crime."

"And has the accused anyone to speak on his behalf?"

"No, sir. I 'aven't a soul." The man stared down at the floor. Lord Wyndemere would no doubt demand the man look him in the eye when he spoke. But Timothy had not such a hardened heart. Having been granted the king's own authority, his lordship would likely schedule a hanging on the spot in such a situation. At least Timothy could be spared *that* duty. He would not take liberty with such a decision.

"Place the man in the gaol until his lordship returns."

"Yes, sir." Bradbury frowned, no doubt dismayed to miss the entertainment of an immediate hanging.

"And give the prisoner decent food and water while he awaits a proper trial." Was it his imagination, or did Hadley smirk as he gave the order?

Catching Timothy's gaze upon him, Hadley turned his lips into a full and open smile. He approached the dais and whispered, "You are doing an admirable job, Grey. Continue the fine work."

Timothy nodded his thanks.

His lordship's duties truly were enough to overwhelm a body. The village of Wyndbury had grown into a sizable community in recent years. The man needed an official assistant. Or perhaps a mayor to oversee the town and allow him to focus upon the remainder of the shire. A close friend to the king, Wyndemere was one of the few earls with any real power, and he held it tight to himself. But the man could not do everything alone.

As the son of a well-respected baron, Timothy might make a suitable mayor someday. But there was no sheriff's position in the offing for him—the morning's proceedings clearly indicated that he had not the stomach for law enforcement. He had always been the merciful sort. That characteristic, along with his small stature in his younger years and his thirst for learning, had set him on the academic path rather than the military route. The church still loomed as a possibility, but he was not yet ready to commit to a life of celibacy and a tonsured scalp.

Until two years ago, his path had been planned out for him. A surprisingly pleasant, fortuitous path for a youngest son. Then tragic events struck, swiping his future away like so much dust from a tabletop. The ache in his head magnified and traveled toward the region of his heart. Again, he rubbed it away. He would not allow himself to wallow in self-pity and sentimental recollections at a time like this.

Perhaps later tonight . . . in his quarters . . . alone.

Taking a deep breath, he surveyed the room again. Only Mister Bainard, the castle steward, a man as young for his position of authority as Timothy himself, rudely leaned against the wall. He eyed Timothy with disdain.

"Can I help you, Bainard?" Timothy forced pleasantness he did not feel into his voice.

"About time," the steward grumbled. "You've an important message from Lord Wyndemere. Arrived this morning."

"From Wyndemere?" Dread filled him. Had something gone awry? "Why did you not alert me sooner?"

Bainard stared down his nose at Timothy. No doubt the man hailed from some noble stock himself. Perhaps several generations removed, but his demeanor left no question that he would not treat Timothy as a superior. "You seemed to be enjoying your newfound popularity. I didn't wish to disturb you."

Timothy bit back a retort. "Bring it here. I will retire to his lordship's study to review it at once." Wasting no time, he stood and yanked the message from the man's hand. He strode across the great hall, down a dimly lit corridor, and up a stairway. Once to the study he tossed the sealed parchment upon the table.

Desperate for a quiet moment, he leaned against the open

window and gazed past the stinking, noisy town to the crisp, clean trees beyond the wall. So another day would pass without his return to the forest.

But he could not rid himself of the niggling feeling that the child might provide a clue.

The thought that things just didn't add up had followed him everywhere for days. That the boy had not known his own village, but chattered intelligently for much of the ride, asking questions of the soldiers. The story of a mother who beat him, although the boy bore nary a mark upon his healthy skin. The distance of the child from Bryndenbury.

No, the facts did not add up.

Upon the morrow he would let nothing deter him. He would return, alone and on foot, to the spot where he had found the boy. Stealth and anonymity were of the utmost importance. His brothers had taught him as much during childhood.

"'Tis just over here, Lady Merry."

Allen's voice hurried her up the hilltop and toward the highway beyond.

Merry's men had gone to great lengths over the past days to pull her from her gloomy state. Allen claimed he had found the perfect spot for raiding passing travelers, as they had in Farthingale. Although she doubted they should take such chances so soon, she could not deny that her chest thrummed with excitement at the thought.

Cedric looked like a little boy at play as they headed up the rise. He turned to grin at her. Comic Cedric, with his endearing crooked-tooth smile and over-large ears. She grinned in return.

They reached the top, and Merry struggled to hide her disappointment. Setting her face into a mask of placidity, she surveyed the terrain. To begin with, before her lay not so much a highway as a rough trail. She doubted royal wagons passed this way. And beyond that fact, the forest had been cleared for yards away from the road.

Indeed a long, nearly horizontal branch spread over the path, but it lacked the requisite cloak of oaks and maples surrounding it.

"I do not know, Allen. It is quite stark."

Allen's little-boy excitement had not dimmed—even though of all her "men," he most looked the part of an adult male. "Don't give up on me yet. Picture it first. Perhaps we shan't encounter magnificent equipages as we did at our old spot. But we could use the tree to attack the king's nobles on horseback."

He moved under the tree and gestured to the longest branch. "We swoop in out of the air—wearing masks to preserve our anonymity, of course—knock them to the ground, and before they know what we're about, we've taken their supplies and disappeared into the woods."

Cedric twisted his head from side to side as if weighing the concept upon a scale. "Could work. 'Tis different. Certainly not what one would expect from the Ghosts of Farthingale Forest. That stands in its favor."

Merry took a breath to disguise her frustration. "Yes, but in all these years we have never injured a soul. Someone could break a bone tumbling from a horse. And what if they are quick to their feet and fight back."

"We shan't be fools." Allen tapped his head. "We would choose our targets wisely. Besides which, do we train hours a day for nothing?"

As the one who demanded said training, Merry could hardly argue. "And what if they decide to give chase?"

"Ah!" Allen pointed a finger to the sky. "I've given that thought. We'll build a camouflaged lair just over the hilltop."

Thwarted again. Where was Robert when she needed him? Surely he would detect the flaws in this plan.

"Cedric," said Allen, "why don't you run down the road a bit and then come by as if you are a traveler."

Confusion washed over Cedric's face, turning his rather homely features even uglier. "But I have no horse."

Less skilled at disguising his frustration than Merry, Allen ran a hand down his cheek. "Then pretend."

A grin split Cedric's face once again. "Oh right, then." And he trotted down the lane, leaving Merry and Allen alone.

Merry scanned the area once more. It was by no means as perfect as their last attack point in Farthingale Forest, but no location would ever be. That spot had been all but magical. A highway often used by the royals and nobility. A long, curving road that they could watch from one side, then dash through the woods to the attack point. And the trees. The thick dense trees the local lord had failed to clear, creating a near cave-like effect. Not to mention the gossipy innkeeper in Farthingale who unwittingly kept the ghosts apprised of everyone's comings and goings.

That opportunity was long gone. They would never find such a place again, but at least they had not wasted the idyllic circumstances. A chest of gold lay buried in the woods near their camp. If their Masked Knight ruse was successful, they could start spending those coins and would not need to steal ever again.

Nonetheless, she followed Allen as he scurried up the tree like a squirrel. She had missed the feel of rough bark against her skin, the thrill of the hunt, the lure of danger—the surge of energy that came with fear. And she understood that her men did as well.

She perched herself close to Allen upon the branch. "We have no need to continue such perilous missions. I realize you miss them, but we have the little ones to consider. We should not expose them to King John, and with the gold, we now have no need to."

Allen turned to her, his warm hazel eyes only inches away. They flooded with compassion. That protective instinct she had always loved in him. He reached and stroked a short wisp of her brown hair behind her ear. His touch sent tickling shivers through her. Shivers, yet warmth to match his eyes. For a moment, she found herself floundering in their depths.

She shook her head and gathered her thoughts. "We have been whispering tales of the Masked Knight long enough. We shall send Red to town for provisions soon. You shall see. We no longer have need of raids. I would think you of all people should be glad to be relieved of such a morally questionable duty."

Allen smiled. A roguishly handsome smile that tipped to the right. With his hazel eyes, sandy hair, and strong features, he had always been her favorite of the men to gaze upon. Although she would never admit as much.

"You are right, Merry, as always. But I haven't seen such a smile upon your face in weeks. I'd say the mission has served its purpose. And just wait until you see what fun we shall have when we pounce upon Cedric."

Merry giggled, and Allen joined with his own hearty laugh. His warm breath brushed her cheek. Merry craned away from it and looked down the road. "Where is Cedric anyway?"

She turned back to Allen, and their gazes caught again.

"You know," whispered Allen, "sometimes I imagine what it would be like if you were not a great lady. Rather just Merry, a villager like the rest of us."

Merry gulped down a lump in her throat. "I am not a lady

anymore. I am an outlaw. A waif. The lowest of the low. We are the same now, Allen."

She watched his eyes. Lost in their swirl of brown and green like the forest, Merry did not pause to consider his intention. One moment he stared from a slight distance. In the very next instant, he pressed his lips against hers.

Though one instinct bade her to enjoy the sensation, a stronger one won out. All she could think about as Allen's lips caressed hers was a different set of lips from three years earlier.

"No!" she squealed against his mouth. Despite their close friendship, Allen's lips felt foreign upon her skin, causing her to draw back.

As she pulled away, she lost her balance. Her arms flailed, catching only air.

Before she could react, she tumbled from the branch. Not light and flexible like a cat. Rather, she landed hard upon her back—with a loud thump—at the base of the tree.

All air whooshed from her chest, and she struggled to pull in a breath.

"Merry, Lady Merry!" She heard Cedric's cry from a distance as the treetop seemed to spin above her head.

"Are you all right?" Allen flipped down from the branch and landed in a crouch beside her. At least someone had used their training properly this day. But she could not find the needed breath to reply.

"I'm so sorry," Allen said. "It was a mistake. It shall never happen again."

Fool! He berated himself. Allen had sworn to himself that he would undertake no such romantic nonsense with Merry. He knew the moment he leaned in for that kiss that it was wrong.

But the magic of sunlight filtering through the leaves, her stunning features so close, her beseeching brown eyes, her scent of honey and herbs, her enchanting smile . . . It had all proven too much for his resolve.

But it must never, ever happen again.

Merry pushed herself to an elbow, pain twisting her face. She drew in a ragged breath, which seemed not to reach her lungs. Staring at a point beyond his shoulder, she said, "It shall . . . never happen again. And it never . . . happened in the first place. Do I . . . make myself clear?"

"Yes, of course." Had he not told himself it must never happen again only moments earlier? 'Twas a mistake for certain. Yet to hear her deny that it ever happened cut straight to his heart. He clenched his jaw and steeled himself.

Merry was a lady—he a peasant. Those who fight and those who labor. Never the twain to meet. His father would be appalled with his behavior. Heat crept up his face at the awful thought, and he turned away from her.

Would God be appalled as well? He was not so certain anymore.

Cedric ran up to them and knelt beside Merry. "Whatever happened?"

Merry sat up now and rubbed her back, desperately sucking in air. "It was the oddest thing. A wave of . . . dizziness overtook me. That has never happened before. Perhaps I . . . have taken a slight fever."

She denied his kiss just as Peter denied his Christ. As if it had never happened. Somehow that hurt more than any other aspect of her rejection. It had happened, and in that single, priceless moment, it had split his world in two. He still felt her soft lips emblazoned upon his. Upon his very soul.

Pressing the back of his hand to Merry's forehead, Cedric

said, "You do feel a bit warm, and your cheeks are flushed. Perhaps that is the reason you've been so melancholy."

Allen shot Cedric a warning look.

"What? Is she not supposed to know she's been in a foul mood of late? 'Tis rather obvious." Cedric helped her to her feet and pulled her arm over his shoulder to support her weight. "We should not push you so, Lady Merry. We forget ourselves at times. You are not invincible."

"Not in the least." Merry found her footing. "But I think I shall be fine." She pulled herself away from Cedric and brushed the dirt from her backside, then bent to retrieve her bow and some scattered arrows from the ground. Allen turned his eyes away and focused them on a hawk soaring through the sky.

The three set out toward camp, Allen mentally chastising himself the entire way. Merry might never forgive him this misstep, and he would be the last to blame her. He knew better. Had known better since childhood.

Yet . . . what had she said? She wasn't a lady anymore, just an outlaw, like the rest of them. Were they truly so different now? And if not, might there yet be hope for them?

Ever since the rebellion started, Allen had dreamed of running off to fight. Suddenly, he could not fathom parting from Merry for even a moment.

He glanced at her out of the corner of his eye, limping along with determination, even as she held a hand to her side. How he wished to gather her lithe form into his arms and kiss away every hurt, every bruise, every heartache she had endured these last years. To feel her tremble and cry out her soul against his chest. She had lost as much as—perhaps more than—any of them. Yet she kept it all inside and maintained her strong façade for their sakes.

In that moment he pushed aside the voice of his dear father, which he'd heeded all his life. He silenced the voice of the parish priest, which he had treasured for years. He even hushed a still, small voice deep inside that warned Merry was not meant for the likes of him. Hadn't he learned to trust his own instincts in this new world?

Perhaps, just perhaps, he might gather his courage and win Merry Ellison for his own.

Chapter 7

As John perused the courtyard, his nemesis exited the great front portal of the castle. Anyone who did not so carefully watch Timothy Grey might have failed to notice his exit. Adorned in plain brown leggings and tunic rather than his typical bold velvets, he moved stealthily across the courtyard, his hood shielding much of his face and that appalling thatch of pale hair worthy of a woman.

But he could spot Timothy anywhere.

Had it not been bad enough when the earl promoted him to serve as an unofficial sort of assistant? Now he ran the entire castle in the earl's absence. Tiny Little Timmy. A man no older than himself.

A bitter taste filled his mouth. He spat upon the ground and rubbed it in with his booted toe.

What was the man about now, sneaking through the courtyard?

John watched Timothy exit the castle gate. He took note of the bow upon the man's back and the soft shoes upon his feet.

Timothy must be hunting the ghosts again. Alone this time. No doubt he longed to take all the credit for himself, could not even allow a few of the earl's guards to assist in the capture.

If he could escape his mundane duties, he would follow the man. But he was not his own master. He would forever be forced to serve the will of another. Not like Timothy, who set his own course, who aspired to power and greatness.

But he would never let that happen.

He would learn every habit, every secret of Timothy Grey, and he would bring the man down from his towering perch.

Timothy trekked through the forest in his oldest pair of soft-bottomed leather boots. Having been made years earlier, before he had grown his final four inches in a single spurt, they pinched at his toes, but they served their purpose for the day's mission.

"Stealth, anonymity, restraint," his older brothers had drilled into his head time and again as they played at war games in the woods. Some might find more honor in facing one's opponent in a direct and pompous manner. But the Grey boys did not play for pageantry. They played to win.

How he longed for those days. Days he had spent scampering through the forest with his brothers and . . . well, and other friends. No use in stirring up such poignant memories. He had wallowed long enough the previous evening over his lost love.

Stealth and silence—these were his allies. The ghosts embodied such traits, and he respected them for it. Someone had trained them well, as his brothers had trained him. Noble outlaws. The stuff of legends. Never had he dreamed of undertaking such a daunting mission. Daunting yet exhilarating. He would sneak up on the thieves, beginning where he had found the boy and following his trail to their lair.

Timothy moved through the forest with nary a sound. Ah, there it was, the clearing where the boy had nearly gotten himself shot clean through. Might he be a child of one of the thieves? Of course he would never arrest a child—or a woman, for that matter—but he must find a way to round up the thieves before Lord Wyndemere's return.

Searching the bushes where he first spied the boy, Timothy spotted a faint trail. Days had passed. Both rain and fog had rolled through the area yesterday. But he might be able to follow it.

The remnants of the trail took him meandering through the forest, past a berry bush, then several moments later another, and then another.

Hmm . . . it seemed the child knew his way about this section of land. The other day had not been the first time he strayed so far, as he claimed. Timothy smiled. His suspicions had proven correct.

However, two valleys later, the footprints disappeared into the same winding stream Timothy had crossed earlier. His senses piqued to high alert, and he hurried himself into a copse of trees.

Perhaps their camp lay nearby. The child might have traveled the closest portion to home by stream to disguise his trail. The thieves had not gained their title of ghosts without just cause. If he could peek a glimpse of them today, he might be the first to see them in the flesh.

Timothy remained still and quiet, and he waited. Waited, watched, and listened. Watched, listened, and offered up silent prayers until the sun had traveled a significant distance across the sky. Restraint. Another ally. He would not burst headlong onto the scene. Such tactics would have cost him the game as a child, but could cost him his very life today.

He sat against a tree and continued his patient examination.

As his eyes began to droop, he heard it. The giggle of a small child. He wove his way through the trees to the closest point and waited behind a particularly wide trunk.

The giggles grew closer. On the nearest hilltop, shadowed against the sun, toddled a little girl, still giggling as she attempted to run. He drew nearer, crouching into the thicket until he could make out the wispy tuft of baby hair upon her head, aglow with golden light like a halo.

"Sunshine man! Sunshine man! Wait me! Wait me!" she called, her giggles tinkling like chimes over the valley. A fairy of the forest. A petite tot in a fine pink tunic.

She made a mad dash straight toward him, and just when he thought she might tumble into the thicket where he hid, she embraced the air, grinning from cherubic cheek to cherubic cheek.

He dared not even breathe.

A voice trickled over the hillside. "Wrenny! Wrenny! Where are you? Come back here. I saw a sunshine man near the fort. Hurry!" Also that of a girl child, although much older than the one before him.

Timothy exhaled.

The tot turned and ran back up the hill, falling upon her hands and knees once along the way. "Sunshine man. I get you!"

Guilt flooded him. How could he justify using such a precious poppet to locate the ghosts? Yet, it seemed as if Providence himself had sent the child to lead the way. These were thieves he was dealing with, after all. No doubt that pretty tunic had been stolen from some nobleman's daughter.

Firming his resolve, he crept up the hill, watching for twigs that might snap and leaves that might crunch. Halfway up he spotted . . . a watchman? No, another child, this one a boy aged about ten or eleven years. With a bow and quiver of arrows slung over his shoulder and a sword at the ready upon his hip.

What in heaven and on earth?

Timothy flattened himself to the ground and remained stone-still, waiting again, glad he had worn the plain brown tunic and leggings.

The child approached, then turned and headed in the opposite direction.

Timothy searched for another watchman to his right, but he detected no one. He must hurry. There might not be much time. The Ghosts of Farthingale Forest could reside in the valley just beyond. This might be Timothy's gateway to all he had dreamed of this past year.

Using even more caution, he ascended to the hilltop and crouched behind a rock. Lifting up only so high that he might see, he stared down upon . . . a village? Children ran about, and he could now distinguish their squeals and laughter. Young females cut vegetables near a boiling pot. Two young males, perhaps fifteen years of age, practiced at swordplay in a relaxed and languid manner. It might be a manorial courtyard, except that he spied no animals, and in place of a large central home, several rounded constructions blended into the hillside. If not for the human habitation, one might miss the buildings entirely.

Still Timothy spotted no evidence of the grown men. The ghosts. Did they truly leave the camp to the protection of boys? Then another thought—a far worse thought—struck him. What if the children were the ghosts? Cold dread filled his chest at the possibility.

The idea seemed ludicrous. Yet he could not discount it entirely. According to the law, a child of seven might be hanged for thievery. He longed to win the earl's favor, but he could never hurt a child. His stomach churned even as he considered it.

Timothy scanned right and left again, but no guard approached.

He could make no decision now. He must take time to weigh the matter further before pursuing any action. As he was about to turn around and sneak back down the hill, a camouflaged door swung open in the largest structure. Out stepped another young man clad in a russet tunic. But something appeared wrong. Out of sorts.

His shape was too slight, even for a lad. And oddly curved. Then Timothy realized. This was a woman. But like no woman he had ever seen. He should be scandalized, but instead curiosity overtook him, and he remained bolted to his spot in the hopes her odd appearance might offer further clues to the identities of the ghosts.

She bent over to greet some of the children with her back to him.

"Ma-wee! Ma-wee!" called the happy tot who had led him to the camp.

No! Could it be!

He felt as if a spike plunged into his heart. But the size and shape of the figure were correct. As well as the short tumble of chestnut hair he had last seen as a waving curtain falling near to her waist.

And then she turned her face to him.

He swiveled, ducked, and pressed his back into the rock. The forest blurred around him. He squeezed his eyes closed, but her face remained emblazoned upon his mind.

Lady Merry Ellison. The woman he would have wed. The only woman he would ever love. In the forest with the ghosts.

And to his utter shock . . . very much alive!

Merry could not rid herself of the odd chill that had overtaken her as she greeted the children moments earlier. Now that they had resumed their play, she decided to investigate. She climbed up the hill and checked behind the rock that had given her pause. She would ask Big Charles to toss it in the stream when he awoke from his nap.

Surveying the valley below her, she spied nothing amiss. The last of the summertime wild flowers were dropping their blooms. Squirrels scampered about collecting nuts, as if undisturbed.

Perhaps she had been mistaken. Her mind had been filled with a riot of thoughts and emotions ever since the day she spotted Timothy Grey in town. Even more so since Allen's kiss, which had conjured in sharp detail the memory of Timothy's heart-stopping kiss over the distance of three years' time. Calling it to mind again and again, as if it happened yesterday. Leaving an echo of tingles to play across her lips.

She swiped at them even now.

It seemed Merry had been wrong about the single kiss to last a lifetime, but Allen's kiss had felt so different. So foreign. Whereas the kiss of three years ago had felt like coming home, had melded her heart to another. Perhaps for all eternity.

She may have been mistaken about the single kiss, but she had been correct about love and marriage. They could never have a place in her life—not with Allen, and most certainly not with Timothy. Although a secret part of her might long for them all of her days.

No, she had missed her chance with Timothy, but she had likely saved the lives of him and his entire family by hesitating at the thought of marriage, so she could not regret her choice.

It had been planned for years—Merry and Timothy would wed to join the families, and her father would grant him, her childhood friend, her ample dower lands and help him secure some minor appointment once political matters settled. And since her brother longed to visit the Holy Land before marrying, she could provide an heir, for the time being. The families could not fathom either of them marrying anyone else.

Yet no one had thought to inform her. They assumed she would be thrilled at the notion of marrying her childhood playmate, her best friend in the world. But she had never thought of him as more than that.

That part of her had never awakened until the kiss. . . . And after the kiss, after the certainty of her love settled upon her, she had waited impatiently throughout the fall for the ensuing summer when they would wed. But then came winter, when her father organized the failed assassination. And that summer, instead of celebrating her marriage, her family cowered, awaiting the king's return from Normandy along with his wrath. Then came autumn. The most horrible, ill-fated season of all.

Raking her hands down her face, she strove to bury deep all thoughts of handsome, charming Timothy Grey. She turned her attention back to the camp, where the children dashed about the clearing once again. The children she had put at risk when she stole the gold. She fancied herself their protector, but in fact, she needed them more than they needed her. Without Merry's well-known Ellison profile, might they not have slid into a new place in society by now, unknown and unnoticed?

Jane would have cared for the little ones. The men would have gathered food. Perhaps in the beginning they needed Merry to plan and to strategize, to lead with the confidence that the nobility were instilled with from birth, but they didn't need her anymore—not really.

Lately her thoughts had taken a new and disturbing turn. These English-born-and-bred children did not share her Norman blood, did not speak her French language. Perhaps she should use the gold to buy them apprenticeships and guild memberships in London, and she alone should slip off to France.

If only she were brave enough to let them go. These children had been her family for two years, and she loved them so. Did she love them enough to sacrifice her heart in order to offer them freedom?

She strode back down the hill to rejoin them, even as the question resounded in her mind.

Timothy stumbled toward his horse. Still in a trance. The forest falling in and out of focus about him. He pressed his face into Spartacus's warm neck, breathing in his scent of hay and oats. Drawing strength and comfort from the mammoth beast.

Merry lived!

Why had she not come to him?

But Timothy knew the answer to that question. Merry was an outlaw now, and any assistance he might offer her would put his life in jeopardy. Besides which, she had never loved him the way he had loved her. He had loved her with his whole heart and soul. When he thought she had been murdered, he vowed never to love again. Never to marry another. Would he have kept that pledge? Now he would never know.

After many dark months spent wallowing in the miry pit of his sorrows, he had dragged himself to Wyndbury and inquired after employment. His plans to wed Merry, to live upon her dower lands, had been dashed as a ship against the rocks. Splintered, devastated, until they floated away upon the tide of his despair.

He had since applied himself to his new station in life. He had contrived new hopes and goals. Shallow hopes and goals to be certain, but they had given him purpose and direction.

And now . . . Merry was still alive. He had no idea what this might mean to him. The stunning revelation might take him days to process. He could not yet grasp the ramifications.

Chapter 8

"Come," tempted Hadley, shaking the dice in his hand. "Come and play with us, Grey. You look as though you've lost your best friend in the world. Let us lift your spirits."

"We might allow you to win." Bradbury wiggled his brows.

"Or we might fleece his hide," said White.

Timothy managed a half grin. "I suppose."

He took his place at the long trestle table, which had been turned into a gaming table after supper. When his lordship entertained guests, they might enjoy minstrels, troubadours, even dancing in the evenings. But he would be away for at least another week. The message he sent mentioned a delay. King John had fallen ill, and his treasure—including the crown jewels—had somehow been lost while he traveled. Wyndemere must stay longer than expected.

As he shook the dice, Lady Merry Ellison's face floated through his mind once again.

Unfair! He had only once played dice in her presence. She had shaken them for good luck, and indeed he had won.

How those summers spent at their aunts' adjoining properties had haunted him the two days since he spotted her. And
the autumn when her family had visited his home, her father
wishing to convince him to join his plot.

He had not been able to escape her lovely face, nor the faces
of the children. The ghosts? Surely such ridiculousness could
not be true. He could never imprison them. Never order their
remains be hanged from the city walls.

Logic said they could not be the ghosts. A group so young
could not accomplish such notorious feats. Perhaps they were
only the rumored escapees of Ellsworth, living hand-to-mouth
in the woods. He had never before allowed himself to believe
the gossip true—not before seeing Merry with his own eyes.
Until then, he could not have afforded such hope.

"Throw the dice for goodness' sake, man," called Hadley.

Timothy let the dice fly, losing soundly, and moved for the
next man to take his spot. He leaned heavily upon the side of
the table, gripping its edge.

His circular thinking resumed as the other men cheered and
bickered.

But if he had found the lair of the ghosts, what could it mean?
Merry might be their prisoner—although she had not appeared
to be bound or in distress.

If they were the ghosts, perhaps he could administer justice to
the leaders alone. Help the women and children settle elsewhere.
But if they were the escapees of Ellsworth, nowhere within the
reign of King John would they be safe.

He could never imprison Merry for the crime of being her
father's daughter. His own father had been a breath away from
joining the rebellion, but after much prayer and soul-searching,
he decided to remain loyal to God's appointed king and seek
legal recourse instead. But for that one decision, it might have

been Timothy and his siblings killed rather than Merry's brother, Percivale. Where was the justice in that?

His father, Lord Greyham, now avoided all political intrigue and enjoyed his country home and grandchildren instead. He left the war to the barons in the north and east, only sending funds to King John for his mercenary soldiers. And Timothy sought favor and advancement with the king and his nobles. But what if Timothy were the one hiding in the woods, outside of the law?

Bradbury nudged him for his turn again. He took his place, shook the dice, and sent them skittering across the table, not even giving heed to the result.

"Ho!" shouted White to his left.

Timothy could not bring himself to care. The same thoughts had run a circuit in his mind over and again ever since he discovered the hideaway. The same questions plagued him day and night with no answer upon the horizon.

Only one person possessed the answers he sought. Though it might well prove the final death blow to his wounded heart, he must find a way to speak with Lady Merry Ellison.

And soon.

Merry grinned and clapped along with the children as Red emerged from the men's quarters fully bedecked in knight regalia and sword. A handsome lout indeed. Beneath his arm he held a flat-topped helmet with only a slit for the eyes and several holes for air. "Put it on and let us see."

Red tugged the helmet onto his head. Beneath it, his features were indistinguishable.

"Perfect," said Merry.

She crossed to him and straightened the collar of his blue-and-white surcoat—a design she had created to appear foreign and sewn herself. Smoothing it down over his chain mail and padded vest, she said, "I so wish I could see you astride your handsome destrier, my fine knight."

"I'm not certain I shall be seeing much of anything. 'Tis all I can do to breathe in this stifling contrivance." He removed the helmet.

"He shall strike a dashing figure," said Jane. "The women shall be swooning over you, Red. But remember who swooned for you first." Jane feigned a swoon, fanning herself, eyes rolling back as her knees buckled.

"Perhaps you should give me a kiss for good luck," teased Red.

Jane's cheeks flushed pink as her toe turned inward. The girl was bashful of a sudden?

Merry stood on tiptoes and planted a noisy kiss on Red's cheek. "Methinks that must do for today." The children broke into another round of cheering.

"That will be quite enough of that." Allen shot her a glare, no doubt recalling their own disastrous kiss.

This was precisely what she had been afraid of. The discomfort between them. That one thoughtless moment would forever affect the relaxed atmosphere of their little community. She should change the subject and shift attention away from her jesting kiss. "Be sure to listen for any rumors of the ghosts."

"I will, Mother Merry," said Red, using a title they employed only when she grew bossy and patronizing.

Merry laughed. "All right, then. I see you have matters in hand."

Robert and Cedric joined Red, although they were dressed in long brown cloaks rather than armor—with weapons, which were not permitted past the town gates, sewn and hidden throughout the coarse fabric. They would "sequester"—as Allen liked to say—a cart for transport once inside.

They headed over the hill, and Merry waved to them. "I bid you all Godspeed."

She bit her lip as the children returned to their chores and play. How she hated to send the men on a dangerous mission without her.

"No use borrowing trouble from the future, Lady Merry." Allen joined her at her side, nearly brushing against her. How kind of him to comfort her when she had upset him but moments earlier with her dramatic kiss on Red's cheek.

"I agree, yet I do not." She experienced a slight tingle at his nearness, but nothing like she had in the tree. Perhaps her response had only been the result of wishful thinking on behalf of that traitorous portion of herself that longed for love. "Worrying shall accomplish nothing. But we must be prepared for any contingency. I shall go into the forest to hunt and think today. Perhaps find a spot deeper in the woods to which we might move."

"I shall watch over the camp. Big Charles is here, and several of the younger men. You go ahead. And if you think of it, say a prayer while you're out in God's green forest. I find it the most effective place to offer petitions."

Merry shifted and mumbled, "A prayer, of course."

Dear, sweet Allen. In some ways he was too good for her. They would never be a match.

Allen gazed into Merry's haunting brown eyes, which contained a world of sorrow. Thoughts clearly spun through her mind at the mention of prayer, yet he could not discern what they might be. He would pray for her as well, fervently. Merry was wounded, and he suspected she might have turned her back on God, although she had never said as much. But surely her state of mind was only temporary. A reaction to the trauma she had suffered. It could not last forever.

She turned to him, and their gazes caught, much as they had in the tree.

He tugged at his tunic. She took a step back.

More than anything, he regretted this new unease between them. He must do something to alleviate the tension. Lifting his gaze to the clouds, he spoke without first considering. "I suppose I should apologize again. It was out of line. I didn't think. I just . . . well . . . in that moment . . . But you are a lady, and I had no right to kiss you." Did he mean that? Perhaps not quite anymore, but the words came so easily.

"Please do not apologize on account of my being a lady. I told you—we are the same now."

Her statement, along with her rich voice, warmed his heart. But a single beat later, the fickle organ turned cold again. If they were the same, why must she push him away?

"Then why?" Clearly she was not drawn to him, did not long for him in the same way he longed for her. But he had no desire to hear her say as much. He kicked at the dirt. "No, don't answer. It would be odd for us to forge a romance. We've been friends for too long. And it will affect the others. I understand. I didn't think. It simply happened." And since that moment he had dreamed of little other than kissing her again.

"Oh, Allen, it is right and natural that we both long for that sort of love. But it is not profitable. Until we establish a better life than that of outlaws, romance had best wait. Once we are back in society, you shall find someone to love. Someone wonderful, who deserves and suits you. Not just the best possibility in your little group of twenty-three members."

Not profitable? His eyes probed hers, but found no satisfactory answer. He could hardly believe that she thought of their relationship in such a cold and detached way. He would never find another like her. He was tempted to pull her into his arms then and there, and prove her wrong. But he respected her too much, and she had made her position clear.

He dropped his gaze in defeat. "But when will that happen? Will we ever have a normal life again? Sometimes I fear we might be outlaws forever."

"Matters are always changing. No one knows that more than we do." She bit her lip and gazed off at the sky for a moment. "And I have been thinking. Perhaps all of you could make a go of it in London. No one knows you there. Change your identities. Use the gold to buy apprenticeships and guild memberships."

Sick dread filled his stomach. "All of you? What about you, Merry?"

"I . . . I shall never be safe in England." She pressed her hands together, as if to prevent their trembling.

The forest blurred as frustration flooded him. He rubbed at his head. Was the woman crazy? She would just leave him, all of them, like that? "You want to leave us?" Allen shouted.

"Shh!" She glanced about at the children, but they continued at their play as though nothing were amiss.

Why must she always close him out? How he longed to soothe her soul. To find the rest in one another that they both sought.

"Leaving all of you is the last thing I want," she said. "It would tear my heart asunder. But we must do what is best for the children."

"Not a one of us would agree to that. We will never abandon you." He planted his feet more firmly into the ground.

She gazed into the forest. "Then France is our only other option."

"Then France it shall be." His voice filled with newfound hope. "But the northern barons might yet win their war and put Prince Louis on the throne right and proper. We must bide our time and see."

He would not admit to his true purpose. He was more determined than ever to head to battle. As much as he hated to leave Merry and the rest of the group, he needed to see this war won, lest she run off for good. And he would prove himself a hero worthy of a noble lady. He might have lost her for the moment, but he yet longed to win her for his own.

Today he had stayed behind, put aside his own desire to be a part of the action, as he so often did for the good of the group. But once Red and the others returned from their trip with supplies for the winter, he would finalize his plans. Soon he would be on his way north to war!

"All right, we will look toward France," Merry said, feeling uneasy at the oddly determined glint in Allen's eye, but she would not push him now that they had finally reestablished this tenuous peace. "We will wait in the forest for now. But we must be ready to move at a moment's notice. I will not sit idly and see these children captured." She turned her attention to them.

Little Wren was attempting her forward rolls again. Merry smiled a bittersweet smile. They filled her life with so much joy and laughter. If only they did not have to live with danger crouching behind every rock, around every corner. "We must find another location deeper in the forest."

"Go on with you, then." Allen offered a wry grin. "Go find us the perfect spot."

"I shall not be more than a few hours. I intend to relieve you from watch in the afternoon." She could not resist offering him a hug. They approached each other several times in an awkward dance before settling on a position, then both remained stiff for the quick embrace. "You are my rock, Allen. Despite all . . . this between us, that shall never change."

"I should not ask for more," he said. Although something in his eyes suggested he might. "But, Merry . . ."

"Yes?"

"Do not expect me to give up on you so quickly." He winked, relieving the tension but making his intent clear. "We have a long future ahead of us."

The searing gaze he sent her way caused pleasant butterflies to flurry in her stomach. She gave Allen's shoulder a final squeeze and without another word headed into the forest.

Once out of his line of sight, she grinned. Perhaps when they were settled in a safer life, she might grow to care for him after all. But not yet.

For today she must attempt to put everything behind her and find a moment of peace for her battered soul.

Time seemed to stand still as she immersed herself in the flow of nature's wonder. Her heartbeat aligned to the rhythms of the forest. Her ears attuned to the harmony of birdsong and the whisper of leaves. Her nose drank deeply the rich smells of moss and soil topped with a subtle floral bouquet.

She doubted she would actually hunt today. The mood seemed not right. And Red would be sure to return with ample supplies.

Instead she simply wandered through the woods, turned her face up to the warm, silken stroke of the sunshine, streaming through the leafy canopy in luminous ribbons, dappling the forest floor in a dance of light and shadow. She allowed its rays to sink into her skin, as she dreamed of a different time in a different patch of forest. The night she had sneaked away with Timothy Grey.

Within a grove of sweet-scented apple trees, she had stood upon her tiptoes and kissed his lips. Every bit as sweet and inviting as the fruit surrounding them. She felt the pressure of his lips against hers even now. After she finally pulled away, he had stared at her in wonder as her heart sped and her breath grew raspy.

He had clasped her shoulders in his strong grip. "This time next year, Merry. This time next year, I shall take you as my wife. I swear to you, I shall never love another."

Her mind skipped ahead to the sight of the grown man upon the horse in Wyndbury market. Taller and broader than she recalled, but with the same thatch of white-blond hair. The same full pink lips, pale eyes, and square chin.

Had he kept his vow to never love another? Of course not. How silly. He had been but a lad of sixteen when he made it. He had probably forgotten her soon after he thought her body cold in the ground. For certain, he must miss her dowry. But plenty of noblewomen would give up the opportunity of a title for such an attractive man. A kind man with humor and intelligence dancing in his eyes.

Or at least he had been. So why had she spied him traveling with the Earl of Wyndemere, a loyal subject to treacherous King John? Surely he did not serve the king.

Merry leaned against a tree and sighed. It seemed Timothy Grey had changed along with everything else. Perhaps even married another by now. She stroked her hand down the rough bark of the tree.

Merry again turned her face up to the sun.

And then her world went dark.

Chapter 9

What seemed like hours later, Merry thumped along in the incessant darkness, lying on her belly across a broad horse. When first captured, though without sight, she had fought and twisted until tiring, and her captor had bound her to a horse. Though it hindered her breath, at least the flaxen sack kept her from burying her nose directly into the sweating equine flesh.

The rope passing over the sack and looping through her mouth kept her from screaming out, as she wished to at that very moment. She attempted for the twentieth time to quell her panic, even as it wrapped around her chest and threatened to squeeze out what little air she had managed to gather into her lungs. Flickers of shining stars appeared and then disappeared against the back of her eyelids.

As she struggled against the ropes binding her hands and feet, she also struggled to make sense of the situation. She had no clue who had captured her or where they might be taking her, nor if they suspected she was one of the ghosts. Though firm and thorough, her captor had not been unduly harsh. He had been quick and sure as he secured her, but kind in straightening the hood for comfort and breathing purposes. And when he had slung her over the horse, he had done so more gently than she might have expected.

She assumed he had noticed her female form beneath her male clothing, but he had not touched her in an improper manner. The man had ample opportunity to violate her but had done nothing of the sort.

Surely her captor did not suspect her to be the Lady Merry Ellison. Most thought her long dead. She bade her heart to slow its frantic beating, wished to heaven that she could rub her bound hands to still their trembling. She must remain calm and in control of her senses. Therein lay her only chance.

Though gentle, the man could not be an ally. He had trussed her like a Michaelmas goose and said nary a word in the process. And was it only one person? She could not say for certain. It could be a son of the Baron Greyham. His lands lay the closest to the patch of forest they inhabited, and the man had raised them all to be chivalrous and kind. But most assuredly it could not be Timothy Grey. Timothy had loved her once upon a time.

King's man or not, he would never treat her thus.

So many crimes her captor might think her guilty of, and on so many counts he would be correct. The robberies weighed upon her conscience, but whoever had caught her could have no evidence to the crimes. The ghosts had not earned their mysterious reputation in vain.

Yet to the crime of being Lady Merry Ellison, she could plead no defense. Though it would be no crime in any sort of law-honoring nation, to the treacherous King John her existence was an unpardonable sin. He might well kill her. Kill them all. Hang their remains for the birds to pick clean upon the city walls. How young would he go? Would he stop at seven, the age of legal culpability? Or might even little Wrenny be in danger? Her mind could not bear the thought. She might have doomed them all.

Fear mounted in her chest again, squeezing tight. Her head, already light and hazy from its upside-down position, grew even dizzier. A buzzing began in her ears. No longer able to steady her heart or still her breathing, she panted against the rope, even as her blood grew cold. A bright tunnel appeared at the back of her eyelids.

Then the darkness enveloped her completely.

The sound of someone humming a happy tune pressed at the edges of Merry's consciousness. She awoke in a bright, airy room surrounded by grey stone walls. She lifted her still-buzzing head and pressed her unbound hands into . . . a feather mattress? What sort of prison could this be?

Fear welled again, but she would not give in to her instinct to squeal and jump to her feet. She would not so much as flinch a muscle but rather maintain her restraint. Assess the situation before anyone realized she had wakened.

A quick perusal of the room revealed a washbasin upon a stand and a colorful tapestry with a pastoral scene hanging on the wall. The humming had not been her imagination, but rather came from a plump serving woman with her back to Merry as she pulled gowns from a chest. Merry guessed her to be of middle years from the streaks of grey offsetting her reddish curls. She took out a gown in an apricot color and shook it before laying it over a nearby chair. Next came a slender velvet kirtle of cornflower blue. "Ah." The woman sighed. "This shall do nicely."

Still coming fully awake, Merry noticed the silken coverlet of purple and pink laid atop her. Whatever in heaven and on earth? She glanced about the room, searching every corner and crevice, but she and the woman were alone.

She eased herself to standing and moved stealthily toward the open window, her eyes trained upon the servant, but the woman did not so much as turn or cease her tune. Merry approached the window warily. No bars. Thus far the logistics appeared promising. She bounced lightly twice on her toes to prepare for a possible tumbling maneuver. Her body responded just as she wished. Her muscles strong and taut despite her recent ordeal, and her dizziness now fading.

With a bit of good fortune, she would hop out of this window, and all would be over as quickly as it started.

As she prepared herself to somersault, she paused for a breath to survey the exit. Then she slumped heavy against the window ledge as her stomach plummeted to her feet. Out the window was . . . nothing—nothing but air, clouds, and a single soaring hawk. Gazing downward she saw the castle courtyard far below her, and beyond that the bustling marketplace of Wyndbury. Her dizziness returned, and she gripped the window ledge tightly.

Having memorized the place so thoroughly not two weeks earlier, she understood exactly where she was being held. The north tower high over the town, attached to the castle wall. Behind her lay the forest and the only exit. She must have been brought in through that back entry, no one in the castle the wiser.

"Ah, there ye are, miss," said the maidservant. "I've been sent with clothing for ye, and a warm basin of water to wash. My master wished ye to have a bath, but the guards, they balked something fierce at the thought of toting water up so many stairs."

Merry sifted through the clues. The master of Castle Wyndemere held her captive. His guards at the ready. There would be no quick escape from this place. But a bath? Many people did not bathe more than a few times per year. Did the man yet wish to steal her virtue? She knew little of his reputation. A king's man, thus never a friend to her father. If a kindly knight had captured her, her true fate might still await.

But being fully upright and in control of her senses, she resolved not to faint into oblivion again. She rubbed her hands together. "So, am I a prisoner of the Earl of Wyndemere?" she inquired of the woman.

"Now, now." The woman winked. "Why don't we call ye a guest, m'lady?" Though her wary glance toward the door belied her words and told Merry that the guards stood just beyond.

And the woman had called her *m'lady*. Did the servant know Merry's true identity, or had her highborn speech given her away as a member of the upper class in those few words? She should have thought to disguise her voice, but it was too late now. "Then . . . a guest of the Earl of Wyndemere?" Merry persisted.

"So sorry, m'lady. I've been bid to tell ye nothing. But my master shall speak with ye before long. Let's get ye out of those grubby boy's clothes and into this fine kirtle." She held up the cornflower gown and shook it before her.

Merry approached it slowly and reached out to touch the smooth velvet. It would indeed look lovely against her skin. Although she had no clue as to whether the gown would prove an asset or a liability, a part of her longed to dress in fine velvet once again. No doubt that same traitorous portion that longed for love.

She gave one last look to the door. A sturdy door, indeed worthy of a prison, with guards just beyond. She brushed the back of her hand over her belt, but found her dagger—her last hope of escape—missing.

In that moment she decided, if she must face her fate, why not do so with dignity and style? This woman seemed to hold no ill will against her. Perhaps Merry's future had not yet been determined.

Before the sun traveled far across the sky, Merry stood bedecked in her noble finery. Her tight-laced blue gown swept to the floor with its long elegant sleeves hanging past her knees. As her hair was too short to pull into a braid or twist as befitted a maiden, it had been tucked beneath the scarves of a flowing ivory wimple and secured with a circlet of gold atop her head.

Although her rather benevolent captor had not spared a costly mirror for her tower prison, she could picture herself well enough. The old Lady Merry Ellison had risen from the dead—like a ghost, indeed. She waited at the window, although she could not see the tower entrance, which lay to the back, only the courtyard and market below. No doubt a strategic maneuver on the part of the castle designers.

Even if her men could ascertain her position, the circuitous route from the courtyard near her window to the entrance near the forest would complicate matters.

A scuffle upon the stairs outside her door alerted her that it would not be long now. Men exchanged low, gruff greetings. Then a key turned in the latch.

She braced herself for her first meeting with the famed Earl of Wyndemere.

The door opened, and a figure emerged from the shadows.

Not the broad figure topped with a balding head and greying beard that she expected. Rather, a more slender figure with pale hair and light eyes.

For the second time that day, Merry's world swirled and grew hazy.

Love, hope, fear, and confusion all battled to the forefront of her mind. Then in a moment of great clarity, the swirling sensations solidified and formed into a singular emotion. Her world seeped to red in a hot blaze of anger.

How dare he? The treachery! The betrayal! She balled her fists at her sides, as a desire to punch him in the jaw overtook her.

Two armed soldiers entered at his heels.

His eyes met hers, soft at first, then the look upon his face turned to stone. So it seemed he would side with the king against her after all.

"You!" she cried.

It had been Timothy Grey all along.

Chapter 10

They strode toward each other and stopped a mere yard apart. Though Timothy had stood eye to eye with her throughout much of their childhood, he now towered over her.

If for only one moment he had spotted love, even the warmth of friendship upon her determined features, Timothy might have surrendered and swept her into his arms. Instead Merry stood ready to pounce, anger ablaze in her eyes. Hard eyes, despite the soft gown that clung to her feminine curves. A part of him had wished to face her alone, in the woods, with no one the wiser. But she might have fought back, or escaped, or worse yet, talked him into one of her insane schemes.

They took slow steps, circling around each another like two animals poised to attack. Merry Ellison. Indeed a ghost from his past. Though his heart thrilled at the sight of her, she appeared to consider him an adversary. And a worthy adversary she was, a force to be reckoned with.

Merry managed to peer down her delightful slim nose at him.

It seemed an eternity passed before she spoke. "I should have known. You shall make your fortune from me yet."

Her comment struck his heart like a poleax. Surely she knew him better than that. But years had passed. What did they really know about each other anymore? He must convince her that he meant no harm, that his greatest hope was to protect her while still finding a way to administer justice to the ghosts.

She laughed, a low, bitter laugh, which stole the prettiness from her otherwise striking face. He would have sworn he had seen every emotion known to mankind flit through her doe-brown eyes at some point during their many summers of play. But never before had he seen such disdain. Such disgust.

"When I saw you with Wyndemere, I thought, surely not. Surely Timothy would never turn a king's man. But here you are, doing his bidding." She bowed low to the ground, sweeping her hand over her head in a mocking display. "Long live King John."

Her fear and rejection he had handled with grace all those years ago, but this was too much. He clenched his jaw and steeled his heart against her. He could not allow himself to be swayed toward her rebellion. He would not turn against the king, God's appointed ruler. Such choices ended in tragedy. Nor would he risk her spewing treason in the presence of Bradbury and White. "You may all wait outside. I would speak to our . . . guest in private."

Behind him, he heard his guards depart, but he never took his eyes off of the volatile Merry. She glanced to the doorway, then to the window, but even given her bizarre tumbling abilities he recalled from childhood, there was no means of escape.

The maid still sat discreetly in the corner.

"You may go as well," he instructed.

At that she stood, her plump face turning pink as she wrung

her hands. "Oh, I don't think 'tis proper. Our guest, she is a lady. No common trollop, this one here. Perhaps I should stay."

Timothy pressed his temple in frustration. He had brought Merry to the castle in hopes of exerting some sort of control over the situation. But perhaps he had made a mistake.

"You may go, Matilda." Merry crossed to the chair and took a seat—in that subtle and quiet way denying Timothy's authority over her. She waved a hand to the maid. "We shall be fine. No doubt your master wishes to question me in private. Off with you, before he rallies the king against us both."

The maid looked to Timothy and then to her newly assigned mistress and back again. She shot him a warning glare before walking out the door and closing it behind her.

He stalked toward Merry and dug his fists into his hips. "A king's man? Is that what you think me? But if you insist—better a king's man alive and well than a traitor dead in the grave."

She gasped. "How dare you speak of my father in that way? He was no traitor. No man loved England more than he." Tears brimmed in her eyes, and he regretted his rash words.

He rubbed his hand over his face, swiping away the fierce expression that no doubt covered it and allowing his confusion and concern to show instead. "I am sorry. I did not mean it that way. We all do the best we can in troubling times. This is not how I intended to greet you, Lady Merry."

She blinked back the moisture in her eyes and stared at the wall beyond him. "I am just plain Merry Ellison now."

So true, not unlike him.

Kneeling before her, he took her hands in his own. "If I had not seen you with my own eyes, I would have never believed you might be alive. I never dared to hope. I mourned you every day for two years. I do not wish to fight with you now."

So Timothy had decided to switch tactics. Turn sweet and conciliatory of a sudden. His warm skin upon her hands might give her a pleasant shiver, but he was fooling no one. This man had kidnapped her for his own selfish gain, had insulted her beloved papa on top of it. He had never loved her. He had merely seen her as a pleasant path to a bright future.

Though it might be the smarter maneuver, Merry was not ready to play at such games and niceties. Not while the flame of her anger still burned so bright. She snatched her hands away. "I should have guessed if anyone would find me, it would be you. You taught me every trick I know. A true friend to the end. Thank you ever so much."

He flinched at her words. "Must you choose to think so ill of me?"

"Did you never love another, as you promised? Or have you a wife and child awaiting you in the castle proper?" She willed her eyes to spit the fire from her chest and leave him singed.

"Of course not! I have loved no one else. I swear I have done nothing to earn your disdain. I have told no one your identity— only that I found a woman lost and confused in the woods. Where have you hidden for the past two years?"

Unwilling to give him any weapon to later turn against her, she merely glared down at him as he continued to kneel before her chair.

"Are you with the ghosts? Are you their prisoner?"

Ah, he offered her the perfect alibi, but she would not blame the children. Not ever. "If you thought me a prisoner, why did you come to me as captor rather than rescuer?"

He held his hands out toward her. "I did not know what to think. Only that we needed to speak, and that I wanted you safe here with me. I lost you once—I could not bear to lose you again."

Safe? Ha! She had never been in greater danger in her outrageously dangerous life. Surely he did not expect her to believe that. Although . . . something in his voice rang sincere.

"You are one of them, then?"

Still she did not deign to answer, merely crossed her arms over her chest.

"You fancy yourself a noble outlaw, but there is no nobility in thievery," he said.

She brushed a piece of lint from her gown, as if she had not a care in the world. "If I were an outlaw, although I admit to nothing of the sort, could you blame me? The very fact that I live and breathe has somehow become an offense in the realm of King John. Or should I say the realm of King Louis, for half of John's nobles are now outlawed and following a new king. Perhaps I am the loyal subject and you are the one outside of the law."

"Do not be ridiculous." Timothy raked his fingers through his hair. He sank to his haunches and turned his gaze to the window. A mask slipped over his features. "The pope stands by King John. He is God's anointed ruler."

She hardened her glare. "King John bought the pope."

Timothy's head fell forward. He shook it slowly from side to side. "And now you will speak against the church as well as the king."

"Someone must. I am no longer afraid of anything, leastwise the wrath of some fanciful God. I have suffered enough. I make my own way in the world now."

He returned his gaze to her, searching her eyes as if he longed to see her soul. "Merry. Turning against the king . . . that I admit to understanding. But turning against God . . . heresy atop of treason . . . I never would have guessed it of you."

She could not bear to witness the disappointment in his eyes. The eyes of the boy she had once loved. Looking beyond him again, she lifted her chin. He thought her an outlaw—fine, she was. He thought her a thief—fate had turned her such. And now he thought her a heretic as well—so be it.

"Tell me what to do," he pleaded. "Tell me how to help. You have been to hell and back, and no one understands that more than me." He stood to his feet and began to pace the room. "Though you were unaware, my heart has taken the journey with you. Help me to help you."

While she wished to hold on to her anger, her instincts bade her believe him. She swallowed hard as she digested the enormity of his statement, then whispered, "You cannot help me."

"Say that you were held prisoner by the Ghosts of Farthingale Forest. Assist me in finding their leaders and earn a pardon from the king for this favor. No harm shall come to the women or children, I swear to you."

She closed her eyes against his plea. If only matters were so simple, she might have been tempted, but she could never explain. Never tell him that the children were the ghosts and she their leader. Her men might yet rescue her, but Timothy could do nothing.

She would tell him not a word and at least protect him in his ignorance of the truth.

She braced her heart along with her nerves and tilted her head as if in confusion. "Of what ghosts do you speak?"

He worked his jaw from side to side, an action she recalled precipitated his full-fledged outburst of temper in the old days. But this new Timothy pulled himself under control and said through clenched teeth, "This is getting us nowhere. Think long and hard upon what I have asked you. When I return I hope to find you in a more . . . agreeable mood. I am your last chance."

And with that he strode out the door.

Back in his room, Timothy swiped a clay pitcher from his desk and sent it crashing to the floor. He could not bear the thought of letting her slip through his fingers once again. Much as his future slipped through his fingers even now. No, he had waited too long last time and let her out of his grasp when he might have married her. Might have saved her. He could never make such a mistake again. His heart twisted in his chest at the thought.

Merry! Merry! Why must she treat him so? Surely she must never have loved him. Not even the little bit he had convinced himself she did. Her kiss had meant nothing. Nothing but a thank you for saving her from marriage to his sorry self.

Ugh! He kicked the shards of the pitcher into the wall.

Had he made a dreadful mistake? This time he had moved quickly and decisively, but to little avail. He might have taken her to his family's home, but he dared not expose his parents to the danger of the thieves in their poorly defended manor, nor to the danger of King John thinking them subversive.

If Merry would not cooperate, would not allow him to help her, he knew not what he would do. Perhaps he could yet round up the ghosts if they had not guessed the reason for her disappearance and slipped deeper into the forest. But if she would not deny them, she would be hanged alongside the thieves.

No, he could not risk it. Lady Merry Ellison might indeed be the heartless chit she portrayed herself to be, but his own heart still beat warm in his chest. And he could not let her die.

Leastwise at his own hands.

He held those hands before him now, studying the fine lines and callouses from his feather pen. His hands were tied just as surely as hers had been earlier that day. He could not simply let her go only to put herself in jeopardy again. Wyndemere would not rest until he saw every last one of the ghosts hang.

Wherein lay justice in this situation? He could hardly tell anymore. Merry should not be a criminal, wanted by King John. If not for the ruthless man and his fickle proclamation, prompting the deaths of her family, she would be Timothy's wife of two years. Perhaps the mother of his child.

A knock sounded at the door.

Timothy gripped the edge of a table. "Who is it?"

"The steward. I need to clarify some issues with you."

He growled to himself. Surely he deserved a moment of peace. "Come in."

Bainard entered with his typical arrogant swagger and got directly to the point. "The . . . woman in the tower. What is to be done for her meals? Prisoner fare?"

Timothy strove to keep his temper steady. It was not as if this man knew how important Merry was to him. "Goodness no! She is to be treated as a guest. For now send meals of the best quality to her room. Perhaps in time, I shall persuade her down to supper."

"Then I assume she is of the noble class." The steward smirked.

"What business is it of yours?"

"'Tis just that Lord Wyndemere does not waste his best food on commoners. I would not want him to think I mishandled the situation. Your authority has limits, you know."

Timothy could not help but wonder in that moment if his authority might extend to knocking this fellow out cold upon the floor, but he reined in his anger once again and took a steadying breath. "I believe she is. Matilda has assessed that she must be from a noble background."

"Well enough, then," Bainard said with a sniff before walking out the door and slamming it behind him.

He had not even waited to be dismissed. But Timothy could not waste energy on the uppity fellow right now. Somehow he must find a way to convince Merry to trust him. Woo her back to his side. Remind her what a life of freedom and luxury could feel like.

He might even have considered running away with her, if he thought for one moment that she cared for him—which clearly she did not. There must be an answer. Somehow he must find a way to save her.

Chapter 11

As jangling and neighs heralded the return of the men from their mission, Allen's heart soared. He studied the shadowed figures cresting the closest hill against a backdrop of setting sun. Red, tall and broader than normal in his armor. Cedric, gangly and comical. Robert, wiry and leaning forward with purpose. They had dared not sequester an actual nobleman's destrier for the mission, but the hearty stallion they had found in a farmer's field near Endsworth bulged at the middle, where it was loaded down with ample provisions.

Barely able to breathe, Allen sent up a simple, *Please, God!* When no small fourth figure appeared, his heart plummeted.

He had all but convinced himself Merry had decided to meet the men along the trail. Why else might she stay away so much later than planned? But she was nowhere to be found, and he could no longer account for her delay.

"Ho!" shouted Cedric. "All hail the conquering heroes!"

"Come see what we brought you." Robert patted the horse.

From the clearing below, Gilbert gave a cheer. "We knew you could do it!"

Giggling children dashed up the hill to greet their champions. Cedric tossed apples, as shiny and pleasing as rubies, to each of the little ones. The young ladies left their dinner preparations to ooh and aah over the bags of nuts, dried fruit, flour, and spices.

"I can hardly believe it." Kate pushed her stringy hair from her eyes and rummaged through the sacks. "We shall eat like kings this winter."

Jane offered Red a smacking kiss on the cheek. "You've done well. I'm so proud of you."

Red's face turned the shade of his name. "Aw, 'twas nothing."

Allen struggled to push aside his mounting concerns and join the merriment. He thumped the men on their backs and offered the appropriate congratulations. He smiled at the children, but the expression felt strained upon his face. He nodded to Jane and Kate in response to their excited chattering but could no longer decipher a single word.

Merry was missing. Had it been any one of their group, he would have been concerned and distracted, but he would not have experienced the hollow ache that now filled his chest.

Robert wrapped an arm around Allen's shoulder and led him off to the side of the celebration. "What is it? Where is Merry?"

Thank goodness Robert missed nothing.

"I don't know. She went hunting, but I expected her back hours ago. I am going to search for her."

"Are the others aware?"

"I don't think so. I'm the only one who knew of her plans for the day. Let them enjoy their fun."

"Of course." Robert nodded and scanned the area. "Take the horse. You'll travel much faster."

"Excellent idea. Please ready him for me." Allen hurried to

his hut to gather weapons and a few supplies, in case he spent the night in the forest. By the time he returned, Robert had prepared the horse.

"'Tis not like Merry to get lost," Robert whispered beneath the continuing commotion.

Allen gave him a significant look. "No. 'Tis not."

Robert's keen eye shot to Allen's sword at his waist and the dagger poking from his boot. "Good, I see you've planned for any contingency."

"Like my father always said, 'Hope for the best, but plan for the worst.'"

"I'm certain it is nothing. Perhaps she turned her ankle." Robert sounded as if he wished to convince himself more so than Allen.

"Perhaps." Allen hopped onto the horse.

"Godspeed, then." Robert whacked the horse in the rump to send it on its way down the embankment toward the vast forest sprawling in all four directions.

Once a short distance from the others, Allen paused to breathe in the scent of the forest and turn his eyes heavenward. "Father God, please lead me in the right path. And please keep Lady Merry in your love and care."

He attuned to that place deep inside of him, to that still, small voice the parish priest had taught him to heed. Although Allen's father had not permitted him to learn reading or Latin, thinking such pursuits inappropriate for a peasant, the priest had helped Allen memorize Scriptures. Father Thomas had been a rare clergyman who concerned himself more with love and truth than with rules and appearances, or worse yet, power.

And the priest had been fascinated by the mystical connection to the Divine, by the work of the Holy Ghost, that oft-ignored member of the Trinity, in the lives of men.

Allen took a deep breath and sought to close his thoughts to all distractions, to seek the direction of God. Feeling drawn to the northeast, he turned the horse in that direction and proceeded. After a while, he sensed a need to shift slightly to his right, and the horse seemed eager to obey his lead.

The sun had fallen low in the sky. Before long, dusk would settle in, and shortly after, darkness would descend. He had no time to waste. His heart sped as he pondered what fate might have befallen Merry: injury, kidnapping, arrest, or worse. Within moments, he had lost his inner compass.

Taking more soothing breaths and chanting the words of David, he attuned to the Spirit again. *"The Lord is my shepherd; I shall not want."* A wash of peace and gentle anticipation kept him on course as he employed the technique that had helped him on many a frightening mission. *"He maketh me to lie down in green pastures: He leadeth me beside the still waters."* When Allen veered to the right or the left, that sense of rightness would leave him, until he corrected his direction once again. *"He restoreth my soul: he leadeth me in the paths of righteousness for his name's sake."*

Allen was getting close. He knew it. His eyes scanned the forest floor and the tree branches overhead for any clues. *"Yea, though I walk through the valley of the shadow of death, I will fear no evil: for thou art with me; thy rod and thy staff they comfort me."*

Father Thomas had faced that shadowy valley—as had Allen's father and brother, and his mother years earlier of a fever. They had been ushered into God's eternal arms, and no safer or more joyful place could they ever be.

Of course he missed them. Of course the pain still tore at him at times. He might never fully understand what happened on that fateful night when their village was destroyed, nor why it happened, but he would not allow that to dim his faith in God. Nor would he allow whatever he found at the end of this trail to destroy the most essential relationship of his life.

"Thou preparest a table before me in the presence of mine enemies: thou anointest my head with oil; my cup runneth over. Surely goodness and mercy will follow me all the days of my life: and I will dwell in the house of the Lord forever." Come what may, he would cling to God's goodness and mercy, and someday dwell in His most holy house forever.

Allen scanned the area again. And there it was just ahead—the clue he had looked for, yet dreaded. Merry's bow and several arrows lay scattered across the moist, leafy ground.

He kept his breathing calm and his wits about him as he slid off the horse and surveyed the area. A bare patch of earth with gashes and upturned clods of dirt gave evidence to a struggle. He picked up a clump and let it sift through his fingers. At least she'd been alive to fight.

From the area of attack, indentations indicating giant horse hooves headed off toward Castle Wyndemere. He would follow them to the end and find every piece of information he could.

Still quoting David, Allen dared not think what this might mean. Not until he had all the information. And he dared not think what it might mean for his heart if Merry had been taken from them for good.

The next day, Allen shuffled back toward camp, dreading the news he must share with the others. The midday sun trickling through the trees did little to lift his spirits. He kicked at a pile of leaves for the satisfaction of listening to them crunch and watching them scatter in the breeze. Then he stopped and closed his eyes, seeking to gather himself before facing the children.

The previous evening he had followed the tracks for hours, with only the moonlight to show the way. They led him to the north tower of the castle. From there he had camped in the woods until he could enter the town gates at sunrise and collect whatever gossip might be available.

Although he caught whispers of a mysterious guest at the castle, no one had any information beyond that, at least not for an outsider like him. The one bright spot in the morning was that the surprising description of *guest* indicated she was still alive—and likely not in prison. He had no idea which would be worse—for them to think her an outlawed noblewoman or a notorious thief. The situation seemed dire either way.

He'd left the horse in Endsworth, near its home, and trekked the long way back to camp alone, with far too much time to ponder. He longed to gather their forces to attack the tower, to save Merry and prove he was the hero she deserved. But he knew, once again, he needed to act in the best interest of the group, not himself.

And beyond all of that, he had been struck with the awful realization that he would not be departing to fight in the north anytime soon.

Opening his eyes again, he blinked until the forest came into focus, then he trudged over the rise and down the other side. Melancholy faces filled the clearing. No children dashed about or giggled today.

Red stood first and crossed to greet him. "The news is not good?"

"Not good. Gather the elders."

Red nodded soberly.

Allen tossed down his supplies near the main hut and splashed his face in the water barrel. A gentle touch whisked his shoulder. For a breath, he hoped against hope that it might be Merry.

116

"Can I get you some food?" asked Kate.

"I've no appetite, but thank you. Perhaps after the meeting."

"As you wish." She disappeared into the hut.

Allen glanced about. Most of the elders must already be inside. A few of the younger men had taken over the watch.

Red approached and nodded again. "I think we're ready for you." He looped an arm over Allen's shoulder and led him through the door, nudging him in the direction of Merry's stump.

All eyes focused on Allen, somehow begging him to fill the tragic void.

And every fiber within him longed to be the strong leader they craved. He situated himself on Merry's stump. Though the urge hit to sigh aloud, he pulled himself up regally instead, as Merry herself might do in such a situation. "I'm afraid I bring you dire news. To the best of my assessment, Merry has been abducted, perhaps arrested, and taken to Castle Wyndemere."

He shared his tale, from finding the bow and arrows in the woods to spying in the town.

"And you're certain she's alive?" asked Robert, his voice full of hope.

"In truth, I am certain of nothing, but it seems the reasonable conclusion."

"You're sure that there is no more information to be had?" Red ran a hand over his face in frustration.

"Not at the moment. Not in the time I allotted for the task." Should he have done more? Did he give up too soon? But he had to think of the well-being of the whole group. Not only Merry. Not only himself. No matter how much it might pain him.

"Well then. Let's gather the men." Cedric jumped to his feet. "We have to get her out of there."

James cheered in support, and they all began to stir, but when Allen held up a steadying hand, they settled back into their seats without question. "Not yet, Cedric. It is clear that our position has been compromised. As much as we will hate to do it, both Lady Merry and tactical wisdom would insist that we move camp first."

"But we can't just . . ." Jane's mouth gaped.

"Please." Kate pressed a hand to her stomach.

Robert stood now. "No, Allen is correct. We must see to the well-being of the children, of the whole group, first. We cannot undertake a dangerous mission in town if we're worried about your safety."

Now Allen truly wanted to sigh. In relief this time. Although he had not voiced it even to himself, a subtle fear had niggled at him all morning that they might not see things his way, that without Merry's confident leadership skills, the group might fall apart. So far matters had proven quite the opposite.

"But once we're settled, you'll fetch her, right? Everything will be fine—won't it?" Jane's eyes filled with tears.

Kate embraced her, clearly needing comfort as much as Jane.

"We will certainly go after her." Allen leaned forward on the stump, in a manner he hoped would reassure them that all was well. "Today we will pack and send a team to find a new location deeper in the woods. Tomorrow we shall move. The next step will be reconnaissance to plan our mission. Hopefully by that time she will have been there long enough that we will be able to gather more useful information from the castle servants."

Robert moved behind his sister, Kate, to offer her shoulder a reassuring squeeze.

Kate grabbed hold of Robert's hand but kept her gaze fixed on Allen. "But you didn't answer the other question. Will it all turn out well?"

Allen smiled at her with sympathy. "Kate, I will not make

empty assurances. But this I promise you—we shall all be praying night and day. I know that God will see us through this and give us strength."

Although he could not assure them of what they wished, his short speech seemed to rally the young women. They both sat up straighter and wiped off their faces.

Cedric stood. "I would like to volunteer to search for a new location. I always was the champion at hiding games."

Allen chuckled at the reminder that once upon a time they had all been happy, carefree children playing together. "That you were, my friend. Excellent idea. And Robert will go with you, of course."

"And take young Gilbert," Jane suggested. "He's clever as can be, and I've noticed how a child often sees the world with different eyes."

That familiar peace filled Allen's chest. "Perfect. That should do. The rest of us have a lot of work before us today."

"But can we not do anything at all for Merry?" James clenched his hands so hard that his knuckles turned white. "We have to try something."

"Pray and plan," Allen said. "My guess is we shall need to find a way into the castle without getting our necks wrung. We will never overtake the armed guards on brute strength."

"Ah," said Robert, "but let us not forget. We are the cunning Ghosts of Farthingale Forest. We will do this thing, for Merry's sake."

Cedric rubbed his palms together. His eyes sparkled. "I know who can get into the castle with little explanation."

"Do not say it," Jane warned, wagging a finger at him.

"Oh, I think I will." A grin spread across Cedric's face.

Allen felt that inner nudge of reassurance. "Cedric, I think you might finally get your wish. And I've been working on that new set of tumbling tricks with Sadie these past days. She's quite impressive."

"Ho!" Cedric stood and punched the air. "We will be a troupe of traveling performers at last."

The others began to buzz with the excitement of it all.

A lute in the corner of the room that Jane oft used to quiet the children caught Allen's gaze, and a plan began to form in his mind. For now they would make sure the children were safe and that Merry was indeed held prisoner in the castle.

But if all the pieces fell into place, his scheme just might work.

Chapter 12

Several days after her capture, Merry sat gazing out the window once again. Staring over the treetops on a dreary and overcast afternoon, wondering what mission her men might be on. Had they moved to a new hideaway deeper in the forest? Had the little girls cried when told they must leave their home yet again?

How she hated being helpless. She wanted to scream, punch something, smash something. . . . But she exercised restraint, as always.

Her life in the tower had fallen into a miserable sort of monotony. She looked about at the books, quills, and journal that Timothy had supplied her with. Bribes, or an attempt to keep her out of trouble? A weaving loom sat in the corner with a tapestry barely started, and a lute lay unused upon her bed. Most of the time she sat staring out this window, other than during her daily visit from Timothy, when he would lecture and cajole as she endured in stone-cold silence.

Matilda started up a tune again from the corner. A happy song of spring that Merry recalled from her childhood, when she still believed in new life and dreams of romance. The maid had proven to be the one comforting aspect of her otherwise maddening existence. Today she worked on resizing the apricot gown from the trunk, which had proven far too large for Merry's slight frame.

Perhaps her captors thought blood-drenched apricot silk would somehow look more shocking whipping in the wind than the blue velvet as she hung from a spike upon the city walls.

She peered down at the castle courtyard again, looking for any means by which she might escape. Any lapse in castle security. Any stranger who might come to her aid. So far, her only idea had been that, if she had a long enough rope together with a bow and arrow, she might shoot the arrow tied to the rope into a support beam of the building just beyond the wall. Given a firmly set arrow, complete darkness, and a lazy guard, she might be able to use the bow to slide down the rope and over the wall.

But she had none of those supplies.

She perused the guard staff again. That one by the gate never wavered, never closed his eyes. Unlike the young soldier near the entrance portal, who appeared to often wander off into his own dreams. But of the guards beyond her door, she knew little.

Then she heard it—the sound of a crested lark. A lone figure in a dun-colored mantle and hood stood beneath her. He had passed by her window three times now, but she had not dared to hope. The figure lifted his face and pushed back the hood only a bit.

Allen! His waving, sandy hair and handsome features had never appeared so precious to her. If he were not thirty feet beneath her, she might have kissed him right then and there.

They had found her! They were planning something. If anyone could plot a way to get her out of this place, the shrewd Ghosts of Farthingale Forest could. Hope swelled in her chest, a soft, warm tide battering against her cold stone of a heart. Melting it and reminding her not to give up while a chance yet remained.

She pressed a hand to her mouth to cover the smile she could not hold at bay.

He looked to and fro. The observant guard on the gate was occupied checking an entering cart. With the stealth of the legendary ghosts, he tossed a rock up to her. She reached out and snatched it in one neat, silent move, even as he pulled up his hood and slipped away.

Restraint, stealth, and anonymity had worked in their favor once again. They would prevail, and Merry would escape.

She tucked the rock—with note attached—into her sleeve and strolled to the bed, where she hid it behind an open book and read. *"Find a way to be at supper in the great hall tomorrow. We are coming. Never fear!!!"*

Supper in the great hall. Would Timothy let her out of this room? Surely not, considering the way she had been treating him. Perhaps the time had come to switch tactics.

She surveyed the room again. He had done everything in his power to make her comfortable. His provision of the comforts of home—her old home—had touched her. He seemed sincere in his desire to help her—even more sincere in his frustration over his inability to do so. Perhaps if she cooperated, used a bit of honey as bait, she might persuade him to take her to supper in the castle great hall. When he next visited, he would be met by a different Merry.

But for now, what she needed more than anything was tactical information. And she knew where she would get it.

After tucking the rock beneath her mattress, she sighed and twirled her hair about her finger, as if pining over a lover. "Matilda, what can you tell me of this Timothy Grey? Captor or not, he is a handsome man. Do you not think so?"

Matilda ceased her humming but continued sewing. "What of him, m'lady? Seems ye know him better than us all."

"Not so. I met him during childhood, but this man is not the boy I remember. What is his position here?" She sat forward on the bed, propping her chin upon her folded hands.

"I suppose there's no harm in telling ye. He began as a scribe, but m'lord took a fancy to him. He's in charge while Lord Wyndemere is gone, he is, and he's vowed to capture the ghosts in his absence."

Just as Merry hoped, three days and a bit of friendship had loosened the woman's tongue.

"Quite the ambitious young man, that one is," Matilda continued. "Ninth child was never good enough for him. Oh no. Everyone's been speaking of it. Sharp as a whip. Some say he planned to marry an heiress, but she died. I can see how that might confuse a body."

As she suspected. Timothy had wanted power, wealth, and position. Never Merry herself. And now he would use her in a different way to achieve them. She had been a fool to ever think he loved her. He loved only her dowry. But she would not make that mistake again.

Matilda returned to her humming, so Merry dared another question before she lost the woman entirely.

Merry tapped a finger to her temple. "So, does he believe I am one of the ghosts? Is that what people are saying? Is that why he has kept me here?"

Matilda stuck her needle into the dress and turned her full attention to Merry. "Well, now, they're not supposed to know anyone is here at all. Except of course everyone does—castle gossip and whatnot. Not from me, mind ye. They're saying ye were a prisoner of the ghosts, and Mister Grey done stole ye away. That ye're a lady, and he's keeping your name a secret to preserve your reputation. They've said a bit about how the ghosts must have used ye wrong, but I won't go into those particulars.

Somehow I suspect that part 'tis not true. Ye have such a sweet innocence about ye."

Matilda was astute, yet such rumors about the castle could earn Merry sympathy. She pondered how she might answer the woman. In this case, she could speak the truth.

Her maidenly virtue might not have been taken from her, but almost everything else that mattered had. "I have suffered much in my life, Matilda. Much has been stolen from me. Do not mistake a pretty face for a life of ease. Many never bother to look beyond a set of striking features to the haunted soul beneath. It is a curse at times."

Consternation twisted Matilda's pleasant face. She put down the gown and crossed to Merry, kneeling before her. She cupped Merry's chin in her palm and stared deep into her eyes.

Merry needed contrive no performance. She only thought for a moment upon her mother, upon her father and brother, upon the charred remains of the castle and village she had seen from a distant hilltop.

"Ye speak true, child." Tears filled Matilda's eyes to match the ones in Merry's. "I saw only your spitfire ways. And as ye said, your lovely face. I never paused to look further. I've spent much of my life envying those with more money, more power, more beauty, but I've suffered little enough pain. Have me a good husband, I do, and children and even my first grandbaby. I've lost less than many, I suppose."

"Pain and sorrow are no respecters of persons." Merry sighed. She had given this woman enough of a glimpse into her tormented soul to garner some sympathy. Now she must get ahold of herself before she fell to pieces. "Each morning I must gather every ounce of courage and strength within me, else I shall never make it. If I seem a spitfire, I cannot afford to be otherwise."

"I see that." Matilda cleared her throat and swiped at her

eyes. She moved back to her own chair and picked up the dress, but then crumpled it upon her lap and turned her attention to Merry again. "Tell me how I might ease your pain, m'lady."

Merry bit her lip, as if she must ponder for a moment. "I am going mad in this tower. I am going to beg Timothy Grey to let me attend supper in the great hall. If he asks your opinion, would you please support me in this?"

"Of course. I'll have a word with him myself, I will. He can't expect to keep ye locked up here forever." She eyed the door warily and dropped her voice. "I suspect he's wanting to use ye as bait for those ghosts. But I see no harm in a meal or two on that account."

Nor did Merry. If indeed he intended to use her as bait, he must know her men would never consider storming the tower. But they might take a chance in the crowded great hall.

This time she felt no need to hide her smile.

Timothy frowned and raked his fingers through his hair as he twisted his way up the spiraling staircase of the dimly lit tower. Merry Ellison! Had ever a more exasperating woman walked the face of God's green earth? Today would be his fourth day questioning her.

Somehow he must coax her down to the castle proper for supper tonight. Recalling well how Merry loved both physical activity and music, he had arranged for dancing, along with her favorite dishes. With some good food and wine in her, the right atmosphere about her, perhaps he could cajole her into a better mood and win her trust once again.

"Good day to you, Mister Grey," said White from his perch atop the stairs.

"And may God go with you." Bradbury chanced an impertinent wink.

"May He, indeed." Timothy sighed. "Say a prayer for me, if you will."

"She's a tough little filly." Bradbury grinned. "I've rather come to like her myself." He turned to unlock the door, and the guards parted to allow Timothy past.

Timothy squinted when he entered the bright room after the dark tower staircase. Thank goodness the guards stood at his back, lest Merry take this moment of weakness to attack.

But when his eyes cleared, she sat docilely by the window, embroidering a small kerchief, with the lute he had provided at her side. The Merry of his memories. The same soft brown hair he remembered. The strong cheekbones and stubborn chin. The delicate lips relaxed into a gentle upturn.

"God give you good day, my lady."

"I am not a lady, and well you know it."

The first words she had spoken to him in days! And she looked him directly in the eye with no malice, nor even with feigned innocence. Rather, this time, he spied resignation in her eyes.

He closed the door behind him. "So are you willing to speak with me today?"

"Yes. I am ready. You are right. I was never intended for that rough life in the forest."

He had been lecturing her so for days.

She brushed a finger over the shoulder of her velvet gown. "But please, do not leave me to rot in this tower another moment. I cannot bear it."

"She speaks true, m'lord," said the serving woman from the corner.

In his shock at Merry's cooperation this day, he had forgotten to excuse her maid.

"Everyone knows she's here," the servant continued. "A

mysterious noblewoman captured by the ghosts. No use hiding her away any longer."

Timothy rubbed his temple. He had intended to talk Merry into taking supper in the great hall, so why then did he feel as though he were being connived in some way?

"I . . . yes, well . . ." What were these two about? "Thank you for your opinion, Matilda. You are dismissed now, and please close the door on your way out."

"Yes, m'lord." The maid did as instructed, leaving Timothy alone in the room with the crafty, and potentially dangerous, little lady.

He studied her in her blue velvet dress upon her chair. She looked the perfect picture of domestic nobility, down to the embroidery loop in her hands.

"I see you have found something to occupy your time."

"Do you like it?" She stared up at him hopefully, holding the kerchief before him.

Upon the fabric was a rough outline of the Greyham coat of arms, featuring a falcon and a shield crossed by two swords. He smiled and reached to touch it. "You remembered."

"I thought it might be a peace offering between us, but I have not finished yet. Perhaps it shall be done by the time you take me down to supper?" She formed her mouth into a silly little smile, part entreaty and part jest, as she blinked her doe-like eyes at him.

He shook his head at her antics. "You are never dull, Merry. I concede to that."

"I shall wear a veil and remain your mysterious noblewoman, but I cannot abide another day locked in this tower."

"Perhaps we should deal with first matters first." He grabbed the maid's chair and swept it across the room, seating himself astride, as if it were a horse. Facing Merry, he leaned his chin upon the back of the chair. "Tell me of the ghosts."

"I want to trust you, Timothy. I do. But so much has changed. Can we not use supper tonight to become reacquainted? Can you not give me some time to adjust to this situation? I have little to gain and everything to lose." She bit her soft, peachy lip in the most charming manner.

His heart beat fast, and no amount of willpower would still it this time. He recalled the feel of that lip against his own and pressed his mouth tightly against the tingling sensation, sucking in a sharp breath through his nose. "I can give you some time. Lord Wyndemere has been delayed. But we must deal with this before he returns. Once he is back, the decisions shall no longer be mine. I long to keep you safe. Allow me to do so."

"Your Lord Wyndemere—is he a good man?"

Timothy had asked himself the same question time and again. He attempted to answer her as honestly as he could. "He is . . . a tough man, ruthless at times, but I have found him to be fair. He does not let his heart rule him, but he does have a strong sense of justice. The ghosts are thieves—there is no denying that—and he will show no mercy there. As for you, I cannot say. He is the king's man through and through. They have been friends since childhood. Yet I've seen him stand against the king's tantrums in the past and speak sense to the man."

A flash of intelligence flickered in her eyes, and then she returned to her sweet docility and licked her lip.

He braced himself against the impact of the simple gesture but still felt as if he were melting into a puddle upon his chair.

"So you will take me to supper tonight? Do you think it is safe?" She fluttered her lashes again.

Timothy must hie himself out of this room before he succumbed to her charms completely. "Of course. I shall return in the evening."

And with that, he hurried out the door.

Chapter 13

As suppertime approached, Merry sat upon her bed strumming her lute in the candlelight, remorseful that she had let her stubborn anger keep her from enjoying the luxuries that Timothy had provided for so many days. Her journal sat beside her ready for the next line she might compose.

Since entering the forest two years ago, Merry had rarely found free time to play music. And although they had once stumbled upon a stack of parchment during a raid, they guarded it like the king's own gold for special situations that might require it. She had turned over her own lute to Jane early on, along with a brief instructional session. Jane used it to play lullabies for the children and had even begged Merry to teach her some Scriptures so that she might sing those to them as well.

The tide of hope within her had grown to a flood over the past hours, and she had to admit, she looked forward to supper in the great hall with an excitement worthy of little Wren. She strummed a few more chords before dashing the accompanying words into the leather-bound book.

From the ashes sprouts a bud,
Standing strong despite the storm.
Small and green, it lifts its head,
Waiting for the drops so warm.

Would she be able to take the journal and lute with her when she escaped? She supposed it was unlikely if her men planned a rescue from the castle proper. But she would enjoy them while yet she could.

She wore the new apricot gown with delight, and that would no doubt go with her when she left. Its soft silken fabric and golden embellishments shimmered in the candlelight. She had not worn anything so fine since before . . . well, since before. She did not wish to dwell on tragic events this evening. Not in this gown so worthy of a celebration.

Her men had not forgotten her, and Timothy had not betrayed her. She finally believed it to be true. Her heart sang along with her lips as she practiced the lines of her new song. While his capturing her and bringing her to the castle had been foolish in the extreme, he indeed wished to help—though she knew not how he could. She had seen a new softness in his eyes as they talked that morning.

Might he have loved her after all?

She would leave any last vestiges of her anger in this tower tonight and enjoy the evening set before her. She would allow herself to flirt and savor the meal and see where that path might take her, though she would keep a careful eye out for her men. Timothy was her best ally within the castle, but she did not know if he would choose her or his lord if it came to that. He seemed to somehow wish to protect her while still pleasing the earl, and she saw no possibility in that.

While she had planned to charm Timothy this morning, once

she softened her demeanor and conceded to speak with him, her body had taken over with its own odd reactions. And since they seemed to please Timothy, she would allow her instincts to lead the way again tonight. Though she would remain cautious and alert, as always.

While she sang her new tune, more lines swirled in her head, and she paused to once more scribble them in her book.

> Fall, rain, so sweet upon me now,
> A hope of spring when flowers bloom,
> A chance to live, to breathe anew,
> A dream to wash away the gloom.

A dream. Precisely what she needed. A dream of freedom and a future. Hope, an odd entity for certain. So needed for survival, but so fleeting and tenuous. She must hope to get back to the children, lest she fall into despair, but she could never allow herself to hope of love with Timothy. No, false hope could only lead to disappointment, which could lead again back to despair. But surely she could afford one romantic evening in the firelight, if it might win him to her side.

A commotion beyond her door caught her attention, but she continued strumming her lute upon the bed, recalling Timothy had loved for her to play and sing to him in that other life. She switched from her new creation to a familiar song they both knew well. A song of a man and a maiden that might set the mood.

Matilda chuckled and offered a conspiratorial grin from her chair in the corner, where she worked at remaking another dress for Merry. It seemed Merry might have an unexpected ally in her maid.

The door swung open, and Timothy entered, resplendent in dark blue velvet. As he took in the picture of Merry upon the bed, his eyes lit with wonder. He cleared his throat and straightened himself. "We are ready for you, my lady."

She noted that he never said her name in the presence of the servants.

"Of course. Just a moment please." She laid her lute across her pillow, stood, and fluffed out her gown, knowing full well what a lovely portrait she must present. She smiled at Timothy, and he seemed to melt beneath her gaze.

Truth be told, she melted a bit herself. She played with fire—but she could not turn back now.

They remained locked in a stare completely different than the adversarial one they had shared mere days ago. A silent and heated exchange.

Matilda bustled over. "Let me fix you up right and proper, then, m'lady." She pulled one of the trailing veils of Merry's wimple across her face and fastened it with a brooch of twisted metal near her ear.

As Matilda worked, Merry's gaze did not leave Timothy's.

She watched him shake himself out of his trance. He lifted his gaze to the ceiling and rocked back and forth upon his toes, with his arms secured behind his back—a boyish position that caused her to grin and reminded her they had both been children not so long ago. This, of course, flooded her with memories of their happy times together. She closed her eyes as the recollections washed through her like warm rain.

She lifted the kerchief she had embroidered with his family crest from the bed and offered it to him. "My token for you, Mister Grey."

"Thank you, my lady. I will treasure it always." He tucked it into his tunic near his heart. "I have prepared a special evening for us."

"I cannot wait. Lead on, my handsome escort." Merry chanced a step toward him.

He sucked in a quick breath and swiveled to offer her his arm. She looped her hand through his elbow. As he looked down at her, she did not bother to still her heart, for this was the nicest sort of racing she had ever experienced. A racing heart devoid of fear, though perhaps she ought to be more afraid than ever.

Timothy wound her round and round the steep, dark steps of the tower. The torches on the wall flickered against his square jaw and full lips. A part of her longed to reach out her hand and touch him, run her fingers through his thatch of silky hair. But instead she focused on putting one slippered foot in front of the other. From the tower he led her to a side door and ushered her through a narrow passage in the castle wall.

She must focus. Sharpen her marksman's eye again and study every contingency, every angle, every strategic advantage this hallway might offer. She shushed her thrumming nerves and counted each guard along the path. Took note of their weapons and their demeanors.

Stealth, anonymity, and restraint, she reminded herself. She would need to call upon those traits tonight more than ever before.

But when they walked through an arched opening into the castle great hall, all thoughts of strategy fled her mind as the familiar tableau unfolded before her. The long rows of tables, the herb-strewn rushes upon the floor, the streaming red-and-gold banners lining the walls, lit by torch after torch. She surveyed the giant hearth near the raised dais where she and Timothy would sit. If one would simply replace the red with green, this place might have been the great hall in her very own home.

She crushed her heel against the rushes and twisted them into the stone floor. The scent of rosemary and lavender, so familiar, wafted up to greet her.

Her throat grew tight, and she tightened her grip upon Timothy's arm as well.

He looked down at her, concern etched across his handsome face.

"Until this moment," she whispered, "I did not realize how much I missed my home."

In the torchlight, tears shimmered in her beautiful doe eyes, and he knew this to be no act. Merry might connive and scheme with the best, but Timothy knew her true heart, and he saw it now displayed before him, wide open and wounded to the core. How horrible to lose one's family in such a manner.

He turned and clasped her hands in his. Lowering his voice, for no one could know her true identity, he whispered to her, "Merry, please forgive me. In all that has transpired between us, I have forgotten to offer my condolences. I am so deeply sorry about the loss of your family and your home. I wish I had been by your side to protect you, to help you through it all. I have not yet forgiven myself for letting you slip away when I might have taken you under my care."

She blinked back the moisture in her eyes and offered a small smile. "No, you did right. I was not ready to marry. I am glad that you and your family were spared the king's wrath. And as you can see, I have managed well enough."

He longed to drag her hands to his lips and burn his kiss upon them in a manner that might prove his sincerest regret. But he could never do so with so many watching. And as he turned to survey the great hall, he indeed saw every eye fastened upon them. So he patted her hand in a friendly gesture and hurried them to his table upon the dais.

Before he took his seat, he said in a resounding voice, "I welcome you all on behalf of the Earl of Wyndemere. Please make our guests feel at home this evening." He patted Merry's hand again, wishing to please her, perhaps more than he ever had before.

But as they sat and servants began placing trenchers upon the table, he paused to question his plan. All of Merry's favorite dishes spread before them, from the beef-and-vegetable pie, to the plum-glazed partridge, to the apple tarts for the sweet. Would they bring her joy, or would they wound her further? And he could not cancel the surprise he had arranged for later this evening. He must hope that once her initial shock faded, the familiarity of home might bring comfort.

She studied the table before her, even as he attempted to study her features through the gossamer of her ivory veil. But he could detect only the merest hint of her expression, which, if he must guess by her eyes, he would say to be wistful. Then she pressed a hand to her mouth and took several deep breaths.

Turning to him, at long last she spoke. "I cannot believe how thoughtful you have been. How could I have doubted you, Tiny Little Timmy Grey? I fear I owe you an apology."

Timothy chuckled, relieved by the humor in her voice. "I fear it is I who owe you an apology. Had I not been in such a panic to see you safely here, I might have concocted a plan to transport you in a more . . . hospitable manner. I know well your temper, and should have expected nothing less under the circumstances."

Her gentle giggle swept the air from his lungs. "I passed out upon your horse."

He placed his hand to his head in consternation. "I know! You gave me quite a scare."

"Nonetheless, I am sorry for how I treated you. I should have known you better than that. You have been so kind." She gestured to the spread before them. "And all of my favorite foods—I cannot believe you remembered."

"Ah, there is more."

She quirked a perfectly arched brow at him. "What is it?"

"You must wait and see." Though he was near to bursting with the news, he would not ruin the fun by telling her. He still could not believe the good fortune of the situation. Given her shift in mood, he now had no doubt she would enjoy his surprise entertainment that evening. "All I shall say is that, while you may doubt the existence of Providence, He has certainly smiled upon you this day."

"My, my, so cryptic, Timothy."

"Allow me to serve you." Timothy changed the subject, heaping all of her favorites onto their shared trencher of hardened bread. He sliced the partridge with his own dagger, offering her the choicest cuts.

She lifted her veil only an inch with her left hand as she took a taste of the meat pie. "Mmm . . ." She sighed, closing her eyes to savor the bite. She took several more before whispering, "In the forest we eat only simple fare. Roasted meats and vegetable stews. I have not had anything so delicious in years."

Timothy held back any response. This was the closest she had come to admitting she might be one of the ghosts. She was letting down her guard. But even as she did so, he realized he must not.

He must not enjoy this evening too much, nor allow himself to dream of the future. The best he dared hope for was to somehow keep Merry safe. No matter how he schemed or planned, he could devise no scenario in which he might make this delectable female his own. She was yet an outlaw wanted by the king. He must never let himself forget.

They could not have a future. Not based on dreams of what might have been and a racing pulse. Besides, she had given him no indication that she might return his feelings. He had invested too much in his position, earned too much favor with the earl to toss it to the wind.

Although, if he did not capture the ghosts, he might lose it all anyway.

He turned his attention back to the beautiful lady at his side. For just this one evening, he would enjoy her company all he could and then tuck that memory away in his heart to keep him warm on the many lonely nights ahead.

She took another bite of her partridge. "You know what this plum sauce brings to mind, do you not?" Her eyes sparkled with merriment.

"Do not remind me. Tell me you would not mention such a debacle on this pleasant evening."

"Oh, but indeed I would, Monsieur de le Grand Pied . . . or Sir Big Foot, if you prefer."

Timothy grabbed at his belly as if punched in the gut. "And whose bright idea was it to steal plums straight out of the kitchen, beneath the fat nose of the cook?"

She slapped down her fork. "It was a perfectly reasonable plan. I, as always, was stealthy as a cat. It was you, good sir, and your gigantic feet that got us into trouble."

He sensed, more than saw, her smile. "What do you expect? I was a thirteen-year-old boy, skinny and awkward as a colt. You should have planned for that contingency, O master schemer. 'Consider every contingency, Timothy,'" he mimicked in a sing-song voice. "Where was every contingency in that plan?"

"And should I have planned that for some unknown reason your thirteen-year-old eyes, eyes that could hit a target at fifty yards, would not spot the giant copper kettle?"

They both burst into laughter at that.

"Sir Big Foot or Tiny Little Timmy? Choose one, for you cannot have it both ways, cruel, cruel woman." Delight bubbled through him as he jested with her, so like the old days.

"I am cruel? You are the one who ordered apple tarts for the final course. The final course! However shall I wait so long? It is torture—torture, I tell you."

Timothy waved regally to the footman. "Apple tarts for my fair lady, with not a moment to spare."

The young footman gave a lopsided grin as he brought the treat to them.

Timothy stabbed one dramatically with his dagger. "You shall not escape me. I shall no longer permit you to torment my damsel in distress." He held the tart before her.

"Yes, well, perhaps you should not joke of such matters while you hold me captive in your tower."

"You wound me, my lady." He pressed his hand to his heart. "You are my esteemed guest. I only seek to protect you."

"Perhaps you shall yet redeem yourself." She lifted her veil, took one bite of the tart, and made as if she might faint. Her soft brown eyes closed. "Oh, Timothy, you must have a taste."

She held the tart toward him, and he took the edge into his mouth, purposely nipping her finger in the process. A little gasp escaped her. And as the sweet scent of the apples overtook him, another memory flooded him. Warmth rushed through him as his insides turned to pudding.

Her eyes grew wide. He knew she was remembering their kiss among the apple trees. The tart slipped from her fingers onto the table.

"Yes," Timothy whispered. "I remember it as well."

She turned her gaze down to the tart. Though he could not say for certain, he thought he spied a shadow of pink creeping across her veiled cheeks.

How he longed to pull her into his arms and never let her go. It took every ounce of his self-control not to do so then and there, in front of everyone.

This woman would drive him daft.

Chapter 14

Merry sipped at her warm, mulled cider, savoring the sweet spiciness. The evening in the great hall had all but overwhelmed her with sights, sounds, and tastes. Not to mention the fire that had flowed through her veins as Timothy brushed his teeth across her fingers. The cider was bold and robust rather than light and sweet like the tart earlier, yet the taste and smell of apples haunted her still. Reminding her again and again of their kiss in the fruit grove.

She knew she could not blame the cider, nor the blazing hearth, nor the fiddlers for the delightful bubbles that filled her head and chest. Timothy Grey bore the responsibility for that sensation. She would not let it overtake her, but if rescue was indeed imminent, she must treasure every moment she could steal with her childhood friend.

At the thought of rescue, she surveyed her surroundings. In addition to the two armed guards at the front portal, a full retinue of soldiers enjoyed their meals not three tables away from her. How could she ever hope to escape this place? She was not inconspicuous in her gown and veil. Rather, she was the focal point of the entire evening.

Scanning the tables, she spied no friendly faces. No one she remembered from her childhood. To the best of her knowledge, no noblemen or women at all, only castle staff, who had no doubt been instructed to pay close attention to her.

The man Timothy had pointed out as Mister Bainard, the steward, had been eying her all night, and as she perused the room, she caught another man watching her with an inscrutable expression in his eye.

"Who is that fellow at the far end of the back table?" she asked Timothy. "The one clad in brown leather and wool with curly hair?"

"Methinks you refer to the stable master, Greeves."

"Does he hold some manner of grudge against me?"

Timothy clasped her hand under the table. "Not you, my darling. It is me. I fear I am rather particular about the treatment of my horse."

"He is quite rude." She frowned toward the man, who had averted his gaze as she spoke to Timothy.

"Attaining a modicum of power at such a young age has won me no favors. The steward is hardly an admirer of mine either. I imagine Greeves expects I owe him some sort of special acknowledgment, since he grew up in our manor village, but he seems to forget that he rather picked on me as a child."

"You have done so well. Not yet twenty years of age and running a castle in your lord's absence. I suppose it must provide you with some consolation for . . . well, you know."

"No position, no amount of power can ever replace you, Merry."

She gulped down the lump that suddenly filled her throat.

At that moment, the castle steward gave Timothy a nod.

"It is time." Timothy grinned from ear to ear. "I still cannot believe my good fortune. I could never have arranged for this on my own. The good Lord gets all the thanks."

The tables in the center of the great hall had already been cleared, along with a path from the entryway beyond.

A flash of color spun into the room. At first, Merry's eyes could not gather the information fast enough. Her mind could not catch up with the motion. And then the color ceased to spin and coalesced into the image of Robert, festooned in the rainbow costume of a tumbler, kneeling before them. Next came Cedric, flipping sideways, like a spinning wheel, and then . . . Allen.

Heavens! Joy struggled with fright in her chest, and she steeled her heart, bade her breathing to slow, rubbed her hands together to quiet the trembling.

She sensed Timothy's gaze upon her and formed her face into a convincing expression of surprise and delight. The surprise came easily enough. But the delight? Was she ready to leave just yet? No matter. She would do what she must.

Young Sadie followed upon their heels, flipping with one arm and then the other. She took center stage as the troupe bowed and gestured to her. In a few short weeks, Sadie had mastered walking on her hands and forming graceful poses with her legs while upside down.

Merry drew her clasped hands to her mouth. She need not feign her delight. To see Sadie performing thus filled her with true joy.

Last to join the group came Jane, who accompanied them on her lute as they tumbled and cavorted for the audience. Cedric juggled colorful balls while the onlookers clapped and cheered. Merry made certain to clap and cheer along with them, as if she had not a care in the world. She should have known her brave band would contrive the perfect plan, right down to costumes and supplies. Cedric had finally gotten his wish. They were a band of traveling tumblers after all, with a minstrel to top it off!

As Cedric juggled, Allen finally had opportunity to scrutinize the room, for he had not found Merry as he glanced about earlier. His gaze swept every dark corner, near every guard, then finally the very last place he expected to find her.

Tucked against the side of the nobleman upon the raised dais.

Although a veil covered her face, he would know that form and those eagle-sharp eyes anywhere. She wore a silken gown, just like she had before they were outlawed, and she clapped her hands in delight at Cedric's performance.

He looked to Jane and nodded in Merry's direction. Jane caught his meaning, and her eyes grew wide with surprise. They would not be able to slip their gift to Merry unnoticed, as they had hoped, but they had planned for every contingency.

Though relieved to have found her, ecstatic that she was indeed safe and sound, his stomach slowly tied itself into a new sort of knot. She looked far too relaxed, far too at home in this place. This was where she belonged. Not with the likes of him. He had been a fool to ever dream otherwise, to dream of rescuing her and winning her heart for the favor.

Cedric took a bow, signaling the end of his act. Sadie stepped forward and smiled at Allen. Jane switched tunes.

At just the right moment, Sadie tumbled across the floor and Allen caught her midair, sweeping her over his head and around his shoulders. The crowd gasped, and warm satisfaction filled him. He might not be a nobleman, but he did possess some skills. After a quick drop to the floor, Sadie bounced back up with her hands upon his. He hoisted her until her feet were solidly upon his shoulder. She stood and waved to the crowd as planned before adjusting her weight onto one foot and lifting the other one high over her head.

The audience responded, chuckling and cheering. Sadie flipped down and Allen caught her, only to twist and twirl her around his body once more.

And now for the finale. Allen positioned himself on his back upon the floor and boosted his feet into the air. Using his feet to balance upon, Sadie pressed into a handstand position and formed shapes with her legs.

As she did so, Allen looked again to Merry. She leaned yet closer into the young nobleman and whispered something. The fellow wrapped his arm around her shoulder and nuzzled the soft brown hair that peeked from her wimple with his chin.

Had Allen not been flat upon his back, he might have stumbled. As it was, his knees nearly buckled and Sadie wobbled in her upside-down position. The crowd gasped again. Sadie gripped tighter to his feet and clenched her muscles to finish the final trick, as if it were all a part of the act.

But was Merry's flirting simply a part of the act, or might she be as happy as she seemed? Had all his worry been for naught? Did she even wish to be rescued?

He pushed the ridiculous thoughts from his mind and sprang to his feet, taking Sadie's hand in his own for their bow. They must save Merry. She could never be safe in a place like this, and he would never in a million years leave her in the clutches of that preening coxcomb on the dais.

Where had they learned such wonderful tricks? Merry recalled performing them herself as a child, but she had never taught her group such fanciful maneuvers. She turned to Timothy and

145

laughed. His eyes appeared as though they wished to drink her into his soul and never let her go.

That lump formed in her throat again, but she swallowed it back. Timothy would have to live without her. There remained no other choice. She poised herself. Tensed her muscles. At the ready. She noted Timothy's dagger lying idly upon the table between them. Surely at any moment her men would attack. She waited for some whistle, some gesture, any signal that it might be time.

Once Allen and Sadie cleared the floor, Jane took center stage. "We would like to close with a song."

Her soothing voice began a melody she often sang to the children at night to put them to sleep. A song of praise from a Scripture she loved to quote. A beautiful song of lush pastures and calm streams. Merry watched the gathered crowd as they fell under her spell. A hush pervaded the room, lulling some of them nearly to sleep.

Ah, the time must be soon.

But the song concluded, and still her men sat placidly beside Jane.

Jane alone stood and approached the raised dais. "A parting gift, for you, m'lady." She placed the lute upon the table before Merry.

Until that moment, Merry had not noticed anything amiss with the lute. Her eyes had been trained upon Robert, waiting for his cue for much of the performance. But this was not her old lute. The wooden neck extended longer, stretching both above and beneath the body of the stringed instrument. How odd.

"'Tis especially crafted by our troupe for its strong tones. I hope you will keep it to remember us by."

"Of course." Merry stood and clutched the instrument to her heart, hoping Timothy would not detect its thumping rhythm through the fabric of her dress. The lute must be a clue. The strange shape must indicate something inside. Timothy could never realize. Gathering every ounce of drama and control within her, she acted the role of lady. "How kind of you. Your graciousness shall be remembered in these halls for years to come."

With that, the entertainers departed as quickly as they came.

She gazed at Timothy and smiled through her veil, then lowered herself onto the chair, still clutching the priceless lute.

"Even I did not suspect they might give you a gift," he said. "I shall have to reward them in a fitting manner. I take it you enjoyed my surprise."

She ducked her head and giggled. "Oh, Timothy, it is too much. I can hardly believe it. I shall sleep well tonight for certain."

"Truly, was it not providential? They showed up on the castle doorstep this very morning looking for work."

If only he knew how providential . . . but he seemed not in the least suspicious. Perhaps, just this once, a God in heaven did smile upon her.

"We are not finished yet." He clapped his hands and the fiddlers reemerged, striking up a lively dance tune.

Merry glanced skeptically at his feet. "Should I be afraid?"

"Very afraid, my darling, but not on account of my feet. I promise you they are proportionate to the rest of me these days." He held up one booted foot for her inspection.

She nodded. Yes, everything about his form fit together quite nicely. "So why am I afraid?"

"Of my prowess on the dance floor. Not to mention my incredible charm and powers of persuasion."

"Oh please, you do not intimidate me, Timothy Grey, for I have seen you swimming in your breeches."

"And I you in your shift." He held out his hand. "Come."

Merry hesitated a moment as she considered the precious lute in her hands, but she could think of no excuse to avoid the dancing, nor to take the instrument along with her. So she tucked it under her seat and for the first time in years, dared to offer a brief prayer to whatever divine being might have shown her favor this day.

Timothy tugged her to the dance space and spun her in a circle. Between the dizziness the spin invoked and the comfort of his nearness, Merry soon found herself relaxing. She memorized every detail of him while yet she could: his warm, spicy scent and the manner in which his light hair curved over his smooth forehead, highlighting pale greyish-blue eyes with a boyish sparkle, the ruddiness of his cheeks. She reveled in the touch of his calloused fingers against hers, and the tingles they sent flowing through her arm.

Fortunately, the dance required them to move no closer, for even with her veil, she feared he would see too plainly the growing admiration upon her face. They stepped forward and back, shuffled side to side, and spiraled about one another. When the time came for them to run through a tunnel of the castle dwellers' outstretched arms, Timothy clasped her at the waist and drew her near.

She giggled again in spite of herself.

Chapter 15

John could not fathom the audacity of Timothy Grey. How dare the man bring this chit to the great hall and expect none of them to question her identity? The man was not an earl, not a baron, nor even a sheriff. Merely an assistant, and a bumbling one at that. Such arrogance must come of being raised in a manor home, ninth child or not.

But Timothy had always been a pompous fool, even when they were young. Strutting through the forest as if he owned the place. Perhaps he thought he did, but John had always been of the opinion that neither nobles nor kings could possess the earth, only God himself—and the people He had created to enjoy it. All of His people, not merely those of the highborn class.

Most of these castle dwellers would never dare to question the man. These worker bees who functioned on some primal instinct to serve and obey their "betters," accepting the divine right of kings and nobles without a moment's pause.

But he understood—matters were not so simple.

And this woman, might she hold a key to finding the ghosts?

To his knowledge, Timothy had not gone back into the woods in many days. John must find a way to speak to her. If he captured the ghosts himself, perhaps he could at long last win some favor with the earl. Favor he had long deserved but never received, unlike Timothy Grey, who had danced into this castle on a whim and found himself in charge not two years later.

He noted that the woman kept glancing back toward the lute. Timothy thought himself so wise, but he seemed not to notice her obsession with the instrument. Nor its odd shape, though John had also failed to notice it while the minstrel played. He must keep a close watch on this mysterious woman, no matter who she might be.

One thing he knew for certain, this woman was a chink in the armor of Timothy Grey. Whoever she was, he held some special affection for her. John had seen the look in his eye as they chatted over supper. He recognized the mannerisms of a man in love. The way Timothy leaned in close, found reasons to brush her arm. And now, the look of rapture upon his face as he danced. The man should not be so foolish as to expose his weakness.

Yes, John must find a way to speak to her. Perhaps he would spirit her away and demand she take him to the ghosts. He hoped she would put up a fight and give him a reason to rough her up a bit, for he could think of no more intoxicating way to harm Timothy Grey.

"Oh no," Merry whispered to Timothy as a romping country dance concluded.

Greeves, the stable master, headed straight toward them with determination displayed upon his rather plain face. What might he want with her?

"It will be all right." Timothy reassured her with a squeeze to her arm.

Greeves halted mere inches from them. "May I dance with the lady?"

She scanned her mind for a reason to deny him, looking up to Timothy in desperation.

Though Timothy seemed to register her plea, he shrugged his shoulders as if to signal he could think of no excuse. He frowned and then collected himself. "Of course, my man. Please take good care of our guest."

"Right," Greeves mumbled, grasping Merry's arm and dragging her back to the center of the floor.

The fiddlers began a more sedate song, signaling a courtly dance. Merry wondered if this uncouth man would even know the steps, but it seemed he had lived in the castle for some time, as he fell into the patterns with ease, leading her with slight pressure upon her left hand.

Several lines of music passed before the man spoke. "I like horses," he declared in a gruff tone.

How was she to respond to that? "Right, then. You are the stable master, I hear."

"Are you fond of horses?" He led her in a circling pattern.

Thankful that he could not see the confusion upon her face, Merry replied. "I am . . . I recall them to be a sturdy and faithful species, although I have not owned one for some time." Was the man testing her to ascertain her supposed status as a noblewoman?

"Nothing better than galloping through a field with the wind in your hair." He seemed to be warming to her, his speech sounded less stilted now. Perhaps the man was merely awkward in social situations.

And Merry did recall some lovely horseback jaunts from

her childhood, although she had been more one to traverse the forest by foot.

She had grown too suspicious over the years, could no longer even manage a polite exchange while dancing. Giving one last glance to her lute, Merry let down her guard and engaged fully in the conversation.

Timothy watched from a rear table near several of the guards. As Merry danced and conversed with Greeves, his blood began to boil. Whatever could the odd man be thinking, to ask a noblewoman to dance? Perhaps a soldier or a squire—maybe even a scribe or a steward—might ask a lady to dance, but not a common stable master. However, once he had inquired, Timothy could think of no good reason to cause a scene and turn him down.

He pounded the table before him with his fist.

"Get her back, if you're so riled up," said Hadley from his right.

"I cannot cut between them before even one dance has concluded. 'Tis not mannerly."

Hadley shrugged. "I have no manners of which to speak. I'll do it." Given his tall stature and broad shoulders, the man appeared intimidating even without his chain mail and armor.

"Yes, that might just be the thing. Thank you, my friend." Timothy thumped the man on the back.

"At your service," Hadley tapped his head in a deferential manner, although he wore his dark hair cropped too close to pull a forelock as the peasant folk did.

He strode across the floor and towered over poor Greeves. The man backed away in an instant, and Hadley took over the dance.

Merry glanced at the soldier with admiration and thanks in

those eyes Timothy could easily lose himself within. He wished he had been the one to take her away from Greeves. But he had pushed matters to the limits merely by bringing her to the great hall this evening. He did not wish to arouse suspicions further with unusual behavior.

She laughed at something Hadley said and swatted him on his huge arm.

Timothy's blood continued its slow boil on a different account now. Why had he not paused to consider how handsome a young woman might find Hadley? His closely cropped dark hair and whiskers surrounded a face that even Timothy could not miss as attractive.

Hadley flashed a flirtatious grin Merry's way.

But Timothy held himself still and endured until the dance finished. He pressed his fingers to the place on his chest where he had tucked her token of a kerchief. A token she had sewn for him and no one else. Hadley escorted Merry back to Timothy and handed her over with a bow.

Timothy sniffed back any resentment. Hadley had never been other than a faithful companion to him. He should not let jealousy sneak upon him so. The man had only been trying to help.

"Come, my lady," said Timothy. "That is enough merriment for one evening."

"I have not danced so much in years, and my feet could use a rest."

Timothy turned Merry toward the exit, but she pulled away. "Wait, my lute."

"Of course." He watched as she hastened to the table and retrieved it, then returned to him at a more sedate pace. His mission had been fulfilled. At least for one evening, he had brought a bit of joy into her life.

"Ready." She hugged the gift to her chest.

Timothy offered his elbow and, as she tucked her tiny hand into it, could barely believe the wave of protectiveness that overwhelmed him. He must find a way to keep her safe. But how, if she would not tell him the truth?

He led her back through the dark passageway toward the tower. "Has the time come, Merry? Can we talk now? Discuss the details of the past two years?"

She remained silent for a moment. Then said, "Can we do so in the morning? I am exhausted after this lovely evening."

Though he wished she would not put him off, neither could he force her to speak. "Of course."

As they exited the passageway and entered the base of the tower, Timothy noticed that they were briefly away from the watchful eyes of the earl's many guards. And at last he allowed himself to give way to his desires.

He dragged Merry's slight frame into his arms, wishing he could shield her from the world forever. Only the lute between them kept him from crushing her to himself. Resting his chin upon her head, he sucked in the intoxicating lavender scent of her hair. He closed his eyes, savoring this brief moment.

Believing for just a moment that his topside-turvy world might be made right with Merry back where she belonged.

Setting her a few inches away from him before he gave in to even greater desires he might regret, Timothy pulled her hand to his mouth and pressed his lips against the delicate flesh, as he had wished to all evening.

Merry cleared her throat. "I think . . ." She wavered upon her feet, then straightened herself and tugged her hand free of his.

He watched as she seemed to gather her resolve and tense her body to match.

She tried again. "I think you should escort me to my room now. Matilda shall be wondering at my long absence."

Of course she was correct. Neither of them could afford to lose their hearts, nor to give in to their passions at such a volatile time.

He led her back up the twisting stairway. So much had transpired. So much had changed in the less than two hours since he had ushered her down. She remained silent at his side until they reached the top and White unlocked the door.

"Thank you for this evening, Timothy. I shall remember it for the rest of my life."

And with that, she slipped into the room.

If only he could hold her in his arms, keep her for himself forever, but he feared their time together would end all too soon.

Chapter 16

The next morning Timothy awoke with a start. He bolted upright in bed in his small room at the far end of the castle from
Merry. Though he could not recall the particulars of his dream,
he remembered grieving the loss of her. Regret and sadness clung
to him as his dream world faded into the ether.

The dream might be a warning. Merry, together with the better portion of his heart, could have escaped during the night. He
jumped up and jammed his limbs into his tunic and leggings as
he scanned the occurrences of the previous evening for anything
out of the ordinary. The tumblers, perhaps. He had thought them
a godsend, but upon further consideration, a group rumored
to be ghosts might possess just such lightness upon their feet.

He dashed out of his room and through the castle, needing
to see Merry at once. Needing to soothe his fears and that ache
in the center of his chest that felt as if someone had thrust a
dagger into him and continued to twist. Nothing but the sight
of Merry would fill that hole and staunch the sense that his life
drained right out of him.

Reaching the tower, he pounded up the stairs, causing a stir

157

at the top. Two guards, the night watch, blocked his path with swords drawn.

"It is I, Timothy Grey," he panted. "I must see the prisoner at once. I fear she has escaped in the night."

"Not on our watch," said one of the burly fellows, unlocking the door.

Timothy pushed him aside and tumbled through.

Merry gasped, sitting up in her bed and pulling the covers over her shift.

Timothy could hardly believe his eyes. She remained, safe and sound. Sleeping like a babe with her tousled hair and flushed cheeks. The knife withdrew from his chest, and his breathing slowed.

"What do ye think ye're about?" Matilda had hoisted her large frame from the pallet on the floor with surprising haste. "Get out of here, I say. Ye don't come barging into a lady's room while yet she sleeps." She slapped at him, chasing him back toward the door.

Timothy shielded himself with both hands. "Stop that, Matilda. I had a dream and feared some harm had come to the lady."

Matilda rubbed her sleepy eyes and seemed to come more into her right mind. "Don't ye worry, Mister Grey. I'm keeping a close watch on your lady guest, just as ye instructed."

Merry swiveled about in her bed and placed her feet on the floor. "Everything is fine, Matilda. I promised Timothy I would speak with him in the morning. Perhaps 'tis best if we get this done with."

Still, he could not accept that her sleepy form sat here before his eyes. Might this be a dream as well?

"Not in your shift, ye won't be. Not while I draw breath." Matilda swatted him toward the door again. "Out with ye until she's dressed right and proper."

He chuckled as he submitted to the matron's stern will. No, no dream. Matilda's slaps were all too real. Once he was outside the door, Matilda slammed it shut.

The larger of the two guards raised a brow. "All is well, Mister Grey?"

"Yes." Timothy bade himself to believe it. "Methinks all is well. I shall speak with our . . . guest in a moment."

He had worried for naught. His fear of losing her had overcome his reason. Still, he could not shake this sense that something was amiss. He scanned the details of last night again. Greeves's odd behavior? Perhaps that was the source of his concern. Might he wish her ill? Next he recalled the lute crammed between them as he embraced Merry. She had seemed rather too attached to her gift from the tumblers. Again he wondered at the timing of their arrival.

Once he had spoken with Merry, he would find an opportunity to examine the instrument, but he dare not risk her trust by asking for it now.

The door opened, and Matilda strutted out. "All right, then. Ye may have a bit of time with her ladyship. But I will be checking on ye, I will." She pointed to her eye and then to him in a threatening manner that he found amusing on the small, round woman with her mop of curling hair.

Timothy entered Merry's chamber for the second time that morning. She sat upon a chair and tidied her hair with her fingers. He pulled the other chair across from her and sat as well, taking in the room as he did so. On the far side, the new lute leaned against the wall in a nonthreatening manner, partially hidden behind the one he had lent her. Though a bit longer than the other, it otherwise appeared normal. He presumed such instruments must vary in size.

Merry sighed, and he turned his attention back to the beautiful young lady.

"I am sorry you were troubled this morning," she said. "I will keep you waiting no longer for the truth. That is, if you are certain you wish to know it. For I promise, you shall not thank me for telling you."

"You must, Merry. It is the only chance for . . . you." He wished to say *for us,* but he did not want to give her false hope. Nor give himself false hope, for that matter. "Tell me what has transpired these past two years."

She wrung her hands in her lap. "On the night that King John's men murdered my father, we knew they were on their way. All of the adults from the castle and village were armed. But they sent the children, including me, away to a cave in the forest under Percivale's care. My father wanted, more than anything else, that his heirs would survive the imminent slaughter."

Merry paused and closed her eyes, biting her lip and taking several deep breaths.

No longer able to restrain himself, he scooted his chair closer to hers and took her hands in his own.

She gripped them hard and seemed to draw strength from them. Opening her eyes, she looked directly into his. "But when we heard the screams and smelled the smoke, Percivale could stand it no longer. He bade the village boys to watch over me and took off toward the fray. I never saw him again."

She fought back her tears and continued. "In the morning we all ventured to a hillside, where we witnessed the ruins. Days passed. We survived on spring water and berries, and finally we realized there was no one alive to rescue us. And so . . . I did what I had to. What anyone in my position would do."

Her doe eyes pleaded with him to put the pieces together, to not make her speak the awful truth, and he could indeed pick up the story from there. He saw it displayed clearly in her expression. Merry knew the forest. She had been trained in fighting. She would never allow those children to die. They must have found the ghosts in the woods and somehow banded together with them.

His mind continued sorting through facts he must have known on some level all along. No one was as stealthy, as sneaky, as cunning as Lady Merry Ellison. She might well be an integral part of their band. But whatever else might be true, he no longer wished to know.

He would have sworn the tower walls crumbled before his eyes. But it was not the sturdy castle tower but rather his own world that fell apart.

He had made a tragic error. She had been better off in the forest.

Many moments passed as Merry waited. She watched while Timothy's mind sorted through what must have happened. He had not wished to believe her one of the ghosts, but he of all people must have known she possessed the skills, having taught many of them to her himself.

He had played at war games in the woods with his brothers throughout his childhood, but as the youngest, his playmates had outgrown him too soon for his liking. And so, at their aunts' adjoining properties during the summers, he had drawn her and Percivale into the fun, teaching them strategy and battle maneuvers. Add to that her tumbling prowess, a prowess he had long envied, and what other conclusion could he arrive at?

He stood and pulled at his hair, causing the pale blond strands to stick out at odd angles. "Do not say it, Merry. Do not say another word. I cannot charge you for what I do not know. How? Why?"

But she knew he desired no answer.

He roared his frustration at the ceiling. "Where is justice? Where is mercy in this land? There must be a way. I will not rest until I see you safe."

Of all Merry had endured in the last two years, nothing since the death of her family had pained her quite as much as the tortured expression upon Timothy's face. She longed to tell him that her rescue was imminent, but she could not make him responsible for such information. Despite the feelings writhing inside her, she must keep her wits. Make use of restraint, her ally, as she always reminded her men.

Timothy appeared to be having difficulty drawing breath again. "I need . . . a plan. I need . . . to talk to someone."

And Merry *needed* him far from her, lest he disturb whatever plot Robert had concocted. "Your father, Timothy. Your father has always been a fair and just man. A wise man who considers both the law and mercy. Go to him. He will know what to do."

"Yes, my father. I will go to my father." Timothy seemed to clutch to the idea like a rope thrown to a drowning man. "You are correct. Only my father has managed to live his convictions without displeasing the king. He never wanted me to come here and work. I should have listened. But I was so . . ."

He stopped pacing and knelt before Merry, taking her hands in his. "When I believed you were dead, I nearly died myself. I had to find something new to live for. And so I chose ambition. A stupid, shallow goal. A goal that put me at odds with the Ghosts of Farthingale Forest. A goal I will ever regret."

"But why a king's man?" She whispered the words.

For a moment he bowed his head. Merry's eyes filled with tears as she witnessed his inner torment. "I thought . . . I convinced myself your father was to blame. Told myself that one cannot go about plotting murder and not expect retaliation. I never wanted to find myself on the wrong side of King John again. I never wanted him to take anything else away from me. But I swear to you I would not have worked for the man himself. I do not trust him nor believe him to be in the right. The Earl of Wyndemere is a just ruler, yet never at odds with the king. Can you understand? Can you ever forgive me?"

In light of that reasoning, she supposed she could. The trauma of thinking he lost her had clouded his judgment. And he always had been a strong proponent of the divine right of kings. But she could not endorse his decision, so she merely nodded.

He still held her hands in his, and he pressed a kiss upon them as he had last night. Another searing kiss that left her dizzy and confused.

Raising his head, he said, "I fear I might never have another chance to tell you. But I love you, Merry. I have always loved you, and I shall never stop loving you."

Merry said nothing. She should not allow herself to be ruled by fickle emotions. By tingles and kisses.

He searched her eyes, and despite her resolve, she could not pull her gaze from his. Silence stretched between them, but he must have spied something within her that gave him courage. Timothy leaned forward. His warm breath tickled her face.

Her lips cried out to meet his, but she fought the urge, wavering toward him and back again. Just when she thought she might lose the war and relent, the door burst open.

"Ah ha! So that's how it is."

Matilda thrust her considerable girth into the room, and Timothy's head drooped forward, leaving Merry's lips alone and cold.

"I suspected as much, I did. The earl's assistant or not, you'll not be laying your grubby hands upon that maiden unless you marry her properly, Timothy Grey. Now out with ye!"

Timothy rose to his feet, even as that traitorous portion of Merry longed to reach out and pull him to her breast. He shuffled toward the door with a defeated stance. "I will get help. I will find an answer, and I will return by suppertime."

Still without words, Merry nodded again.

Matilda harped at him as he walked out the door.

Hopefully by supper the issue would be settled, and Timothy would be free of the problem of Merry Ellison for good. She blinked back tears at the thought.

Later that evening, in his office strewn with papers and ink, Timothy scanned the missive for the tenth time. He and his father had spent most of the afternoon crafting each and every word. Now that he was back to the castle, he no longer felt certain they had gotten it right.

To His Majesty, King John of England,

May God grant you good health, prosperity, and success in all of your endeavors. I consider it my great honor to serve you and this marvelous kingdom.

It has recently come to my attention that Merry Ellison, daughter of the former Baron of Ellsworth, along with a number of children from their village, might still be alive. I knew that you would want to be alerted to this situation immediately.

However, I also feel a need to beg for your mercy on their behalf. Merry Ellison was a young girl of only fifteen at the time of her father's indiscretion, and I believe the children to be as young and younger. I will personally vouch for Merry Ellison's innocence in this matter, as her father always protected her from such issues. Two

*years have passed, and I beg you to forgive them for
the misfortune of their births and a sin that was never
their own.*

*You have demonstrated your power and your justice
in this situation, as a wise king such as yourself must.
However, at this time I believe your cause could be best
served and your wisdom best conveyed by tempering your
justice with mercy. Many in England have not yet chosen
sides in this war between Your Majesty and the traitorous
barons to the north. Demonstrating your generosity might
go far in encouraging the goodwill of the English people
and win many to your side.*

*Again I beg you to declare a decree of clemency for
Merry Ellison and these children, that they might come
out of hiding and find a place of refuge.*

May God preserve the King!

> *Your loyal servant,*
> *Timothy Grey, ninth child*
> *of the Baron of Greyham,*
> *and assistant to the Earl of*
> *Wyndemere*

Every word was in order, each sentence designed to appeal to
the king's considerable pride, but Timothy remained uncertain.
His father had promised this was the best course of action.
However, his father thought only of his family's best interest,
while Timothy's heart bade him to consider Merry's interests
above his own.

All that remained was for Timothy to seal the parchment
with wax and hand it over to the courier along with other correspondence meant for the king. But he could not bring himself

to do it. He needed to talk to Merry further. The letter did not take into account her involvement with the ghosts. His father had urged him not to mention that possibility, as nothing was definite.

But he could not stand the thought of Merry coming out of hiding only to face a new round of accusations. He had hoped that she might assist him in capturing the ghosts and earn the king's favor in that manner, but now he realized that would never be possible.

What if the king did not relent and turned against Timothy instead? Hopefully the earl could protect him. But if the king felt driven to search out Merry and the children, neither he nor the earl could stop him.

Timothy crossed the room to the fire blazing in the hearth. A nip of autumn now filled the air as the sun set outside his window. He held his hands to the fire and watched its glow through the thin parchment. Perhaps he should toss the missive into the flames and watch it burn. Be done with it. But he could not bring himself to do that either. He needed time to think and to pray. And to talk to Merry once more.

For now, he placed the parchment at the bottom of a trunk that sat in the corner of the room. He would enjoy another supper with Merry tonight, and he would decide what to do with the missive come morning. But first he would return to his room to change his clothes and wash off the smell of his long day of travel.

Chapter 17

Merry could hardly believe another day had passed, and still no sign of her men. She stared out her tower window but could only detect shifting shadows in the hazy glow of torches from the dark courtyard below. They must have decided that she looked well enough, and therefore they needed not rush. Or perhaps they planned to come again in the evening all along, now that she was armed and could assist them.

In the middle of the previous night, while Matilda snored, Merry had dared to investigate the lute they had given her. As she suspected, the head of the instrument popped off the wooden neck near the top, where the strings were secured. When she withdrew it, being careful of the strings, she discovered a sword hidden within the overly long neck, although she had not yet determined the reason for the portion that stretched below the lute. She had only seen one similar instrument before, an unusual shape to be certain.

Merry supposed she must find an excuse to bring it to supper again tonight. When Timothy came to fetch her, she would offer to play for the castle folk.

Timothy. She twisted her lips in consternation. Merry knew not what to think of him anymore. His kisses upon her hands and that embrace at the foot of the stairs had left her trembling, confused, and somehow more alive than ever before.

If Merry had been the romantic sort, like Jane, she might say something silly such as *last night was magical* or *the stuff of dreams.* And while she might be impatient for her men to move, since she was in no immediate danger, she would savor one more evening with the handsome and charming Timothy Grey.

She crossed her arms upon the window frame and rested her head on them.

To think that he might have been her husband these two years. Perhaps the father . . . She cut off her wandering thoughts. They would do her no good. No use in pining after what could never be.

At that moment, she heard a dull thud against the window's open shutter. She glanced to Matilda, but the woman sewed placidly in the corner, this time adding some embroidered touches to the collar of a yellow gown.

Merry knelt upon her chair and leaned her head out the window only a bit. There, with its point buried deep in the shutter, stuck an arrow. Her eyes darted about the courtyard. The night was particularly dark and foggy. Still, she could detect no stir of the guards caused by the thump.

She reached out to the arrow and felt a rope attached to the end. In that moment, she understood the purpose of the lute. Just as she had thought to use her bow to slide down a rope, the neck of the lute reinforced by the sword would provide a strong, flat surface for such a purpose. Her men had designed the long neck extending past the body for her to grip as she sailed down the rope and safely over the castle wall.

Their plan was perfect, except for one small contingency. She looked to Matilda once again. This time, Matilda looked her directly in the eye.

"The time has come now, has it? I take it ye shall be leaving us."

Merry's tongue tangled in her mouth. She could overpower Matilda, with or without the sword, but she would hate to do so. She should move before Matilda could rouse the guard, yet she could not bring her body to launch into action.

"You'll be needing this, then." Matilda took a bundle of twine from her basket and held it before her. "And perhaps this as well." She grabbed a kerchief with her other hand.

Merry stared at her, still frozen in place, kneeling upon her chair, partway in and partway out of the window. Her mind struggled to make sense of Matilda's words.

"Tie me up, girl. Right good and tight. I'll not be losing my job or worse for ye."

Merry let out a breath she had not realized she had been holding. "Oh, Matilda, you are the truest friend a girl could have." She dashed toward the woman and hugged her plump form.

Matilda swatted her away. "No time to waste on sentiment. Get on with it, then." She reached her hands behind the chair.

Merry smiled as she tied them with twine. Then she picked up the kerchief. She looped it about Matilda's chin. "Here, I will tie it right below your mouth. Once I am gone, you can call for the guard as if you just got it loose."

"Godspeed, Lady Merry."

Merry spied a sparkle of tears in Matilda's eyes. "And may God richly bless you for your kindness, dear Matilda. You shall be rewarded." She would see to it. An entire deer, at the very least.

Merry grabbed up her lute and ran for the window. She tugged at the rope until her men gave her some slack, and wrapped the excess about the heavy bed frame. She tested the rope's tautness to ensure it was tied tight on the other end. She perched on the ledge and crossed the lute over the rope.

Then she slid away into the night, silent as a feather on the breeze.

Timothy bounded up the tower stairs with a spring in his step. He felt good about his decision not to send the letter and looked forward to another evening in Lady Merry's fine company. He reached the top and nodded to Bradbury and White, but at that moment, a stir came from within.

"Help . . . escape . . ." came Matilda's muffled voice through the door.

"Dear God, no," Timothy whispered under his breath.

Bradbury, usually the picture of composure, fumbled with the keys as he hollered back, "We're coming. Hold tight. We're almost there."

At last, he opened the door, and the two guards rushed inside with Timothy close behind. For a heartbeat he could see nothing but their broad backs. Then the men parted, and revealed the form of the plump Matilda, tied upon the chair.

So many thoughts swirled through his head. First of which was that he never suspected Merry might be so heartless as to bind her maidservant. But then again, she had survived two years as an outlaw, a fact he still struggled to accept. His second thought was that he had lost her again. His stomach tied in knots as a long future without her spread before him.

One final thought surfaced—Merry was safe. Beyond the immediate reach of King John. Outside of the authority of the Earl of Wyndemere. He would no longer have to struggle with how to handle the matter. Though the rational part of him thought it for the best, a more elemental instinct bade him to run after her without delay.

Only then did he remember that in his shock at her admission, he had failed to examine the lute that morning. And assuredly, it was missing from its place against the wall. His gaze next fell to the rope tied about the bed frame, now hanging slack.

"Shall we go after her?" asked White, shuffling in the direction of the window, then back toward the door again in confusion.

Bradbury scratched his head. "How on earth? Is she long gone, Matilda?"

"Aye. Took me a terribly long time to work the kerchief from my mouth," she said. "I'm so sorry, I am, Mister Grey."

Timothy shook himself out of his dazed stupor and removed the kerchief from her chin. "No, not at all. I apologize, Matilda. I did not intend to put you in any danger. I did not think her capable of this." He pulled out his dagger and released her hands from the twine.

"Don't blame the child. She was frightened, 'twas all. And who wouldn't be? Being held against her will."

"I liked the girl," said Bradbury. "She had spunk. And she was nice to look at too."

Timothy chuckled softly. "I liked her as well. What of you, White?"

"I suppose as she was a guest, she might have departed anytime she wished. We were here only to protect her, were we not? It looks as if she left fully of her own accord."

Timothy raked his hair from his eyes. "I am glad to see we are of one mind on this. Truly, I never wished to imprison her.

The situation was . . . delicate. Can we all agree to say that she departed quietly for home?"

"'Tis true enough. She flew out of that window like a phantom in the night. I've never seen such a thing." Matilda stood and rubbed at her wrists, which appeared only slightly chafed from the rough twine. Merry must have been as gentle as she could.

"How did she do it?" Timothy asked. He went to the window and found the arrow outside. The ghosts must have come to the rescue.

"Someone shot that arrow, and after she tied me up, she slid down using her lute for support."

As he suspected, the lute had been the key. The tumblers must have been her band of thieves. He supposed he need not concern himself over whether they would return to entertain at supper this evening.

"But what of Lord Wyndemere?" asked White. "I would not wish to mislead him."

"Never fear." Timothy looked out the window but saw little in the dark, fog-filled night. "I shall explain everything. I intend to hide nothing from our lord, only from the castle gossips."

"Right, then," said White.

"We shall support you," agreed Bradbury.

Matilda reached up to tousle Timothy's hair. "It will all be fine, my boy. Ye shall see."

Timothy forced a wry grin and shook his head. They would be fine. Perhaps Merry would be fine. He might even find a way to convince Lord Wyndemere not to send him packing for his failure with the ghosts.

But as for Timothy himself—he might never be *fine* again. Fine had flown out the window that night, never to return.

Merry and her men made their way through the shadowy forest toward the new camp, a league deeper in the woods. The leaves had begun to change their colors, offsetting the lush green scenery with flecks of red and gold. They now crackled more than rustled as they danced in the breeze, and hints of autumn scented the air.

She rubbed at the crick in her back from sleeping on the ground last night, surprised that the activity of their hike had not loosened it. How had she grown so pampered and spoiled in mere days at the castle? Once her men had whisked her safely into the forest, they found shelter for the evening, well shielded in a dense copse of trees. The air had been unusually chilly, but they dared not build a fire.

No doubt her straw tick would feel good to her tonight, although she would miss the fluffy feather mattress for many weeks to come. At least she was back in her preferred leggings and hooded tunic once again.

"Not much farther now," said Robert. He had stuck close to her side the entire journey.

"I am so glad you took time to move camp before coming after me."

"It was a hard decision." Robert swiped at a bush as he walked past it, no doubt reliving the frustration of that day she disappeared. "But we all knew you would wish us to put the safety of the children first."

"Wait until you see it, Lady Merry. I found it myself." Cedric skipped at her other side like a child.

Young James jogged just ahead of them, excited to reach their new home as well. "I thought Gilbert spotted it first."

Cedric's mood did not dim. "We saw it together, but I investigated and deemed it fitting."

"Good for you, Cedric. I think you all underestimate how capable you are without me."

"Be that as it may," Allen grumbled from behind, "we wish never to suffer through that again."

Merry detected a note of anger in his voice, and slowed her pace to walk with him. "I am so sorry to have upset you, Allen. And to have put you to all this trouble."

"That is not the point. You aren't any trouble, and you know it." He seemed upset with her nonetheless.

"You were all quite brave to rescue me. Your plan was exquisite."

"It was our pleasure to serve you, Lady Merry." He jerked back his head, tossing his waving, sandy hair from his eyes.

Lady Merry? Had not the fellow kissed her in a tree? But she would not challenge him while he was in such a foul mood. "And you looked quite dashing in your tumbling attire. I enjoyed seeing you bedecked thus."

"Jane and Kate's idea, but I'm surprised you noticed me for all you were mooning over his lordship."

Ah, therein lay the problem. "Timothy Grey is not a lord, merely assistant to the earl."

"He looked lordly enough." Allen kicked at the dirt of the forest floor.

"I suppose he did. Please do not be upset, Allen. He was a childhood friend. I needed him to trust me." Though she wished to tell Allen that she had merely curried Timothy's favor, she knew that would not be the entire truth. Still, she wished to diffuse this tension. "The situation at the castle was challenging to say the least."

"'Tis just . . ." Allen lowered his voice and made sure the other men were not listening. "'Tis just a harsh reminder. You weren't meant for a life like this, nor a fellow like me. The sooner I accept it, the better."

Dina L. Sleiman

Merry reached out and gave Allen's shoulder a squeeze as
they continued down the trail. She considered his words. For
the past two years she had immersed herself in this new life, in
the weighty responsibility of caring for the children. But being
at the castle with Timothy had brought to mind her old dreams
and desires, had rekindled a small hope that she might yet be
free someday. She found herself too confused to say more.

A ripping sensation pulled at her chest. Her heart felt tugged
in two—between her old life and her new. Between ease and
struggle. Between castle and forest. Between a love lost with
Timothy and the possibility of new love with Allen, which she
had chosen to deny.

They emerged from another thick copse into a more sparsely
treed area, leading to a hillside. There sunlight streamed through
the branches and hit the ground in a patchwork pattern.

"This is it!" Robert swept his hand, indicating the area.

"What is it?" asked Merry, seeing nothing noteworthy.

"Watch this." Cedric whistled the call of the wood warbler.

The steep hillside shifted a bit, sending leaves and branches
astir. Then it slid to the side, revealing the narrow mouth of a
cave behind it. The children burst forth with giggles and shouts.

"Merry, Merry, we've missed you so." Abigail threw her arms
around Merry's waist.

"I knew you'd make it back, Lady Merry. I never doubted
you." Sadie's voice sounded of bravery, yet she hugged her with
all her strength and buried her head in Merry's shoulder.

The children descended upon her and wrapped themselves
about her, their joint hug growing into one large mass of bodies.

A small figure pushed her way through, shoving the larger
children out of her path. Before Merry stood little Wren, arms
crossed over her chest and a frown upon her face.

175

The group cleared a broader opening for her, all curious to witness her antics.

Merry stooped down to Wren's eye level. "What is it, sweetheart? Whatever could be wrong?"

Wren scrunched her face into the most threatening expression she could manage. She shook her pudgy little finger in Merry's face. "Don't you never go way gin! Hear me, Ma-wee?"

Everyone burst into laughter as Merry scooped the child into her arms and stood up straight. "I promise, Wrenny. I will never disappear like that again."

Wren sniffled and popped a thumb in her mouth to calm herself.

Merry took in the faces of the children around her. A poignant mix of joy and fear. No, she could never leave them. She had been mistaken to even consider the possibility. They might be able to function without her, but it was clear that they loved her dearly. She was an integral part of this group. Despite all that had gone wrong in the last two years, she must remember to be thankful for this gift. She must put fancy gowns, delicious meals, elegant castles, feather mattresses, and most of all Timothy Grey far from her mind.

"Well then." Merry gathered hold of herself. "Show me our new home."

"'Tis quite comfy," said Jane.

Kate nodded her agreement. "When I first saw it, I thought it would be horrible, but wait until you get inside."

"These lovely ladies could make a home of anything." Red took Jane's hand in his, and she looked up at him with pride and admiration in her eyes.

Goodness, whatever had happened in Merry's absence? She struggled to maintain a pleasant expression despite the twinge of concern niggling at her belly. No point fighting the inevitable.

She had known this day would come, no matter what trouble it might cause. To think that not a week ago, Jane had been too shy to kiss Red upon his cheek. "Red! Your trip to town. In all the excitement I forgot about it. Was it a success?"

"You should have seen him," said Cedric. "A fine knight indeed. No one questioned him for a moment."

"Especially not when he tossed shillings at them," added Robert.

Jane pressed to Red's side as they ducked beneath the rocky outcropping.

Merry followed suit, being sure to protect Wren's head. But once she passed the entrance, the cave opened into a spacious room. Her band had set up this main area for cooking and playing, as they had used the clearing in their old camp.

"Over there are the supplies I brought you, Merry." Red gestured to sacks of grains, nuts, dried fruits, and root vegetables along the wall, as well as a fresh supply of candles and oil. Enough to last a good part of the winter.

"He purchased those apples I wanted." Cedric's grin spread across his face. "And we've plenty of small coins now, so any of us might purchase supplies in the future."

"Very good," said Merry.

"Look over here." Jane tugged at her arm, and Merry took note of a passageway extending off to the left. "The girls and little ones sleep back in that room, and there's another one to the rear where the boys sleep."

"Aye," said Cedric, "and the smoke from the fires filters into a hole hundreds of feet from the opening. A gift sent from God, don't you think?"

Merry did not answer, although she was more open to the possibility than she would have been two weeks earlier.

Allen came beside her. "We have tightened security. The

children play inside much of the time now, and we keep the camouflage up all day. We will go out for sunshine and military training during the afternoon, but the guard will be doubled at that time. And only the oldest will be sent away from the camp to collect water and provisions."

Merry's muscles, which had been knotted since the moment the arrow thudded against her windowsill, began to unwind. She had held so tight to her control for so long. Perhaps she could give more responsibility over to the men. "You all have done so well. I feared we would have to run away immediately."

This new plan might buy them some time to recoup. Lord Wyndemere would not likely give up his search for the ghosts, but even Timothy Grey would be hard-pressed to find this hideaway.

Wren now cuddled peacefully in her arms. This was all that mattered. Keeping these children safe. They must take advantage of this respite now while they could, but they would remain at the ready. No doubt new threats would emerge soon enough.

Chapter 18

Timothy could barely restrain himself from fidgeting in his chair across the desk from Lord Wyndemere. The earl perused the accounts he had meticulously kept during the man's absence. Although Timothy knew the earl could not read or write well, he had a shrewd eye for numbers. And while Timothy felt confident that his lord would find not one pence amiss, he felt not at all confident about how to proceed in accounting for Merry Ellison's short stay in the castle.

During the past week, Timothy had thrown himself into the job of managing the earl's holdings with excellence. He could think of no other way to numb the ache in his heart, although he met with little success on that matter.

Somehow, he still hoped to please his lord and maintain his position, but he could not completely decide why it was so important. For both moral and professional reasons, he did not want to deceive the man. But did he not have a moral obligation to protect women and children as well? Women and children who, were it not for the fickle whims of a ruthless king, would be guilty of no crimes whatsoever? He must tread with care when stating his case.

The earl turned his attention from the pages back to Timothy. A random glint of sunlight from the window bounced with a sharp shard of light off the lord's bald pate. Timothy was struck, as he had been on multiple occasions, by the fact that he found this phenomenon intimidating rather than amusing. But thus was the demeanor of the earl.

Lord Wyndemere folded his hands and tapped his pointer fingers together. Timothy recognized the gesture. Matters were about to get serious. The earl's eyes hardened, and a smirk covered his face. "I believe all is in order. That leaves only one more issue to discuss. The ghosts. I must say, I was quite disappointed to find no rotting remains to greet me upon my return to the castle. Then I thought to myself, no, Timothy would not kill them. He would merely imprison them—leave the hanging to me. But alas, I found only a lone cripple in my dungeons. Nary a ghost at all."

Timothy's throat constricted. "Um . . . yes . . . well." He attempted to clear his voice and try again. "It seems that it might be a more tangled situation than we first anticipated."

"Tangled, you say. How so?" The earl drew his dagger from his belt, and turned it to and fro in his hand, examining the blade.

Timothy took a deep breath and steeled his courage in the same manner he had taught Merry years ago. He must find his strength. For both of their sakes. "I caught sight of a few young women and children who seemed to be living in the forest, but not anyone who might fit the description of the ghosts."

"I daresay ghosts are rather ethereal and difficult to describe. One should not presume to guess at their appearance." The earl ran his thumb over the blade of the knife.

"But I assumed we were searching for adult men of some strength and skill."

"Most likely," the earl agreed. "Although not for certain." He scraped at his teeth with the blade.

"But would you truly wish to see women and small children hanging from the castle walls?"

The earl paused from cleaning his teeth and gave Timothy his full attention. His features softened as he considered Timothy's question. "I confess, that would bring me no joy. Justice is justice and I would do my duty to the king, but methinks such a sight would rather spoil my dinner for days."

"Precisely as I feel, my lord. And I do need to tell you something rather important in relation to this matter. I most sincerely hope it will not displease you overmuch. I did my best to serve both your interests and justice, but I fear my inexperience might have led me astray."

"Go on, my boy. Spit it out."

"I recognized one of the young women from my childhood. Not wanting the ghosts to notice me, I captured her and brought her back to the castle for questioning. I kept her under house arrest, but in a manner befitting her station."

"And what was her station?" the earl asked slowly, enunciating each word.

"She was . . . rather is . . . Merry Ellison, daughter of the former Baron of Ellsworth."

He studied Timothy for a moment and then the wall beyond him as he pursed his lips. Placing his dagger back in its sheath, Lord Wyndemere said, "Ellsworth. Quite a bloody mess that was. You know I do not speak against the king, but that affair never did sit well with me. To wipe out an entire village for their baron's sins? That is not justice. It is revenge pure and simple. Between you and me, I believe it was the final blow that precipitated this rebellion." He shook his head and closed his eyes for a moment. Then they flashed open once again. "But you say his daughter, Lady Merry Ellison, might still be alive."

"The title no longer applies, but yes, Merry is very much alive. She was here in this castle not a week ago."

"So where is she now?"

"That, I am sorry to report, is where matters went amiss. She disappeared. She was in the north tower and well-guarded. It must have been the ghosts. I can think of no other possibility."

"Did you learn anything from the girl?"

"I am afraid I could coax no helpful information from her." Timothy sought for words that might protect her without being false. "My suspicion was that she, along with a few other escaped children from Ellsworth, might be prisoners of the ghosts. But she never did confirm that."

"And you say she was a childhood friend of yours."

"Yes." He did not wish to cloud the situation by mentioning she was his intended. Still very carefully choosing his words, Timothy said, "But I surmised at some point that she feared for the safety of the children. Despite our past relationship, she was unwilling to trust me with any details. These ghosts might have threatened her, but I had no wish to resort to such tactics myself. She seemed rather wounded."

"Hmm . . . if they knew you had her, they must realize we were searching for them. Have there been any further reports of thievery?"

"A horse went missing a day after you left, but he has since found his way home, which means no mysterious thefts in several weeks. And oddly, the herbalist found three shillings on his shelf the same day that Merry disappeared."

Lord Wyndemere sighed in relief. "I do feel rather sorry for those children. On the other hand, they might be with the ghosts of their own will . . . " The earl drummed his fingers upon the desk. "One could hardly blame them if they did so to survive."

"I considered that as well," said Timothy.

"Merry Ellison alive—that is a tricky situation. I must admit, I am glad to be spared any difficult decisions on that count. I would hate to be forced to execute her."

Timothy unclenched his hands from the edges of his seat, although he did not recall grabbing it in the first place, and the muscles of his shoulders relaxed. The earl would not go after Merry. "My father suggested we might beg King John for clemency on behalf of Merry and the children. I penned the missive but could not bring myself to send it."

"Well, on that one matter you acted wisely. The king is in an outrage over his treasure that sank in that estuary and the barons' rebellion. Not to mention quite sickly at the moment. I have never seen the man in such a foul temper, and that is saying much."

Timothy did not know how to respond. It seemed even the earl's loyalty to the king might be wavering, but he dared not speak his opinion on the matter.

The earl continued the conversation, sparing Timothy a reply. "I agree that the situation should have been handled better. However, I recognize that you attempted to do right. Even brought your father into the conversation. That shows wisdom to ask for help when needed. Perhaps I heaped too much responsibility upon you too early."

Timothy's nerves shot to high alert. The earl might regret his decision and return him to lowly scribe. Or dismiss him entirely. However, with Merry and the children still weighing heavy upon his heart, he could not bring himself to care much. Perhaps the earl was correct, and he had not been ready for the responsibility. He had acted rashly, largely out of his fear of losing Merry again. Now he had failed at his mission and lost her in the process anyway.

"It was indeed a challenge." Timothy filled the silence gaping between them. "But I hope that in all other matters I fulfilled your expectations."

"Yes, everything else seems to be in order." The earl patted the stack of parchments before him. Then something in his demeanor shifted, and a chilling smirk crossed his face. "Know that I do not doubt your faithfulness, my boy. However, I must maintain certain standards and expectations."

"Of course, my lord." Although he did not know where the earl might be going with this, by his expression, the direction could not be good.

Wyndemere pounded the table before him. "Then you understand that you still owe me several bodies to hang from my walls. You *will* capture the ghosts if you wish to remain in my employ. Though I imagine you have made the challenge considerably harder on yourself by spooking them deeper into the forest. Let the women and children go, but find the leaders and deliver them to me." He stood now and stared down at Timothy.

Dread ran cold through Timothy's veins at the thought of undertaking such a task, at the thought of chasing Merry even farther away. "Shall I take a troop of guards with me?"

"No, that opportunity has passed. You shall do it alone."

Timothy stared down at his hands to avoid the lord's icy glare. He took a calming breath and rallied his courage. "I see."

"Fail me, and you are dismissed from my service. Beyond that, if I should discover that you did not allot this mission your full effort and attention, I will see to it that no one in this kingdom shall hire you again, not even as a scribe, not even as a scullery maid. Do I make myself clear?"

Forcing himself to meet the earl's stare, he said, "Abundantly, my lord." He fought back a shiver at the intensity of the man's hard brown eyes.

"Well, what are you waiting for? Off with you, then. Do not return without at least three bodies in tow, unless it is to pack your belongings."

Timothy stood and held his head high. He would not cower before the earl. Such men feasted on weakness. "Good-bye, then. For now." The next words came from his mouth before fully forming in his head. "I will not fail you."

As he pivoted to exit and pack for his journey, he contemplated if he had meant that last statement. He tortured himself with the question as he passed through the shadowy hallways of the castle, and by the time he reached his room, the answer grew clear.

Yes, he would capture the leaders of the ghosts. He had worked too hard and too long for his position to give it all up now. Merry had not confessed love, nor even any particular like for him. Certainly not any loyalty. Perhaps she had dallied with him to win his favor, but she had made it clear she did not want him. He had witnessed the harsh truth of that with his own eyes time and again, and he must accept it.

Beneficial anger simmered in his chest. She had used him, played him wrong. There would be no dishonor in bringing her fellow thieves to justice. Of course, he would still do everything in his power to keep her safe. Despite her shoddy treatment of him, his heart would not permit otherwise.

But he would capture the ghosts!

Before long, Timothy made his way through the congested courtyard to the wooden stable beyond. He ducked into the shadowy, hay-scented place and called to the stable master, "Greeves, fetch my saddle."

Greeves ceased brushing one of the horses, eyed him shift-
ily—no doubt biting back some rude retort—and finally turned
to obey. Timothy would not bother himself with the man's
attitude, for he had far weightier issues on his mind at the moment—like how to capture the ghosts and what Merry might
think when he did.

Greeves returned a few moments later with the saddle and
carried it to Spartacus's stall. He handed it over to Timothy and
stroked the horse on its nose as Timothy worked at saddling it.

"Where are you off to, if you don't mind me asking?" It seemed
Greeves had straightened his attitude, for the words sounded
properly respectful.

Timothy could not confess to chasing the ghosts. "Going
to visit the family for a time." As he would be in their area, he
would likely sleep at the manor when possible. In that moment
the realization struck him that he had no idea how far his search
might take him, nor how long he might be gone.

"Haven't seen me mum in months. I don't get many days off,
you know. Tell her hello for me, if you would," said Greeves.

"Of course, my good man." As Greeves seemed to be warming to him, Timothy decided to address an issue which had
troubled him these last days. "I did not know you were such
a dancer. You rather surprised me last week. What . . ." He
thought to say *possessed you* but realized that would not win
him an honest answer. "What made you decide to ask the lady
to dance with you?"

Greeves continued stroking the horse and nickering to him.
The man did much better with horses than people. Perhaps he
ought to stick to them.

After a moment, Greeves answered. "I thought I might have
recognized her. I wanted a closer look."

Timothy froze in his spot beneath the horse, securing the

saddle. He paused to erase the shock from his face before standing to address the man. Why had he not considered that Greeves might remember the Lady Merry from her visits? They had been all about the village that autumn. "And did you? Recognize her?"

"No. Couldn't tell much past those veils."

Greeves walked away, seeming unaware of the gruff manner of his departure.

Timothy was merely glad the conversation was finished and that Greeves had not recognized Merry. He needed no more complications in this situation. Hopping onto his horse, he headed out. He had ghosts to capture and a future to secure.

Merry ran, flipped sideways, and then threw her body backward, catching herself on her hands, then feet, and repeating the pattern as she skimmed the ground with a springing motion. She finished with nary a thump in the newly fallen leaves. By the end of the combination, she was breathless and exhilarated. She held her hands overhead and turned to smile at her audience of one.

"Teach me how, Lady Merry. I know that I can manage it." Sadie hopped from foot to foot and clapped.

Merry moved through the clearing toward the girl. "You begin with a single backward flip. Come here, and I shall help you."

The girl looked ready to burst out of her skin.

Merry recalled that feeling from her own childhood—that inner knowing that your body was made to perform such feats. "Stand here beside me, facing that tree."

Sadie obliged.

"Now, hold your arms over your head, elbows tucked tight by your ears, and sit down and back like this." Merry demonstrated. How much better to focus on Sadie and tumbling than to torture herself with memories of Timothy Grey.

Sadie bent as instructed, testing her weight and how far she could go without falling over.

"Excellent. Now, from that position, you shall spring back onto your hands, passing through the arched shape. There shall be a moment you feel unsafe, but don't worry—I shall be right here to catch you if matters go amiss."

"All right." Sadie looked a bit frightened, but then set her face with determination.

Merry smiled. She and the girl were so much alike.

"On my count then. One, two, three!"

Sadie launched herself backward and slightly to the side. Merry adjusted her body midair, allowing Sadie to catch herself on her own strong arms and flip her legs over to the ground.

"I did it!" Sadie squealed, hugging Merry and jumping up and down.

Merry's heart warmed as she shared in the child's success. From a slight distance came the sounds of children giggling and the clink of practice swords. The rich scent of roasting meat wafted from the cave. All was right in their little corner of the world. For once. She was so happy to be back where she belonged. And if she might miss Timothy Grey a bit, she could manage that.

"Very good start, Sadie. But you must be careful to throw yourself straight backward and not to the side. Let us try again."

Sadie positioned herself, arms overhead, and wiggled her small rear as she tested her balance to ensure that she solidly shared the weight between her two feet. Just as she was about to toss herself backward again, the sharp *pook, pook, pook* alarm of the blackbird met their ears.

Both of them straightened to attention to see if it would repeat three times with pauses in between. And most assuredly it did, alerting them to intruders in the area.

Chapter 19

"To the cave," Merry whispered, her heart thumping in her chest.

Sadie did not waste words answering, and they both dashed over the hillside and into the sparsely treed area in front of the cave. By the time they arrived, the little ones already hid inside, as the older members of the group brushed away footprints and other signs of life.

"In!" She practically shoved Sadie through the entrance.

"Who is on watch?" she whispered to Allen as she helped the men toss leaves about the clearing before the cave.

"Robert and James," he whispered back.

Good. Robert would know what to do. Surely it must only be hunters. Why would anyone else have cause to enter so deep into the forest? They could not still search for the ghosts. Surely Timothy would find a way to prevent that.

Or would he?

Once everyone but Robert and James were safe inside the cave, they pulled the camouflaged door closed.

"Take the children to the back room, and keep them quiet," she ordered Jane. "Only the battle-trained men will stay here to guard the opening. Prepare the weapons. And, girls, be sure you have your daggers at the ready as well. You are a second line of defense to protect our little ones. Big Charles, guard them by the passageway."

Everyone jumped to obey, like a well-trained battalion of soldiers. The fire was already out, but there would be no way to disguise the smell of the venison.

"No talking above a whisper, and keep that to a minimum until further notice. I will sound the call of the partridge if silence is required," said Merry. Robert would use their whistling signals to keep them apprised of the situation.

"And pray that God stops up the noses of our guests," added Allen.

Merry prepared her bow and arrow and wrapped her belt and sword around her waist. Had she not been tumbling about, she would have been prepared for battle, but thank goodness she had time to ready herself now.

All her senses sharpened. That odd blend of excitement and fear filled her. She should be terrified for the children, and no doubt later she would sink into sobs as she recalled this moment, but right now her racing heart and tingling nerves bade her to fight. To fight with all her might, with the ferocity of a mother wolf, and never surrender. She would protect these children if she must do so with her own life.

Peering through the slight gaps in the woven wall of branches and leaves, she could see nothing of concern. Just more leaves, grass, and trees. A rabbit scampered past. It stopped to twitch its nose and look about, then hopped along its way as though nothing were amiss.

Taking note that she was panting, Merry slowed her breathing with deep, cleansing breaths. She looked down to her hands, and they trembled with her nervous energy.

Allen tucked in close at her side. "Let me do that for you, Merry." He proceeded to take her hands in his larger, stronger ones and rub the trembling from them.

The action so caught her unawares that she failed to draw back immediately, as she should have. The heat of his skin permeated something cold and fierce that had settled inside of her at the first alarm.

"I can't tell you how many times I've watched you do this before a mission and longed to ease your tension." Allen offered a shy smile. "No need worrying yet. I'm certain Robert has the situation well in hand. And I do think, of all of us, he could kill if needed."

Though she realized her body had been ready to commit murder only moments ago, Merry's stomach knotted when she heard it put into words. She pulled her hands away and settled them upon her sword. Her warrior spirit battled with her nurturing side once again. "But what if the person is innocent? Oh, Allen, we have gone all this time and never hurt a soul."

Or worse, what if Timothy had come searching for her once again?

"Robert will act with wisdom and restraint. You can trust him," Allen said. He placed his arm about her shoulder and pulled her to him. Though that traitorous portion of herself longed to sink into his strength, she tensed and backed away. "We must stay alert, Allen." Against all sorts of things.

What trick of nature caused a woman to long to be watched over by a man? Even a woman such as herself, who could best every male in their band at the bow and hold her own with a sword. Perhaps it was force of habit from being protected by her father and his knights for so long. Two years ago her "men" could barely care for themselves, let alone anyone else, but they had grown strong and capable.

Moving away from Allen, she checked the view from a different angle. She must take care not to mislead him. Though he might stir warm, soft feelings within her, they were nothing compared to the fire and thrill Timothy evoked. She dragged her mind from feminine musings and back into battle mode.

Wait! What was that? Merry pressed her ear closer to the opening. Although far away, she detected the faint call of the wood warbler.

"Did you hear that?" whispered Allen.

"Shh!" Merry attuned her ears. This time she heard it more clearly, followed by the sound of the crested lark, and the wood warbler again.

"All is well, be at the ready?" Cedric came up behind her and closed one eye to peer through the crack in the wall. "What do they mean by that?"

"I suppose not to worry, but to stay alert," said Allen.

Merry drew out an arrow and nocked it to her bowstring just in case. Now that her nervous energy had waned, she longed for a quiet afternoon teaching reading to the little ones rather than this constant danger. Again she considered France, but she hoped it would not come to that. Though plagued with a ruthless monarch, England was their home.

It seemed eons passed in those few moments as she waited with Allen, Cedric, Red, and the younger men, peering through the entryway. Finally Robert and James crested the nearby hill and entered the little valley that led to their cave.

Over Robert's shoulder hung the long, lifeless form of a man. Merry now understood the signal. Had he killed for them? She closed her eyes against the awful thought but used that moment to dig up her resolve. At a time like this, she must think as a leader. Powerful. Tough. Heartless, if need be. But oh, she was glad it had been Robert and not her.

At the call of the wood warbler, they slid through a hole in the entryway, and Merry emerged to greet the men, willing her heart to turn to ice.

She gulped down any stray vestiges of emotion. "Robert, James, I am so glad you are safe."

"The situation has been dealt with for the moment. But I wanted you to remain on the alert, for I had no idea what I should do with him."

Robert turned to the side, revealing the back and head of the person he had killed.

Even as the thatch of pale hair came into view, Merry's vision blurred. The world spun around her. One of the men caught her from behind and righted her on her feet. She could not see through the tears filling her eyes to know whether or not they had somehow deceived her.

"Dear God in heaven!" she said, covering her mouth with her hand. For once, she dared to wish He might be listening. "Please say it is not true."

"I thought I recognized this one from the castle. 'Tis the fellow you said you knew, is it not?" Robert hoisted the body higher upon his shoulder. "I doubted you'd want him dead, but I thought you might wish to question him."

Allen blew out a breath. He had recognized the fellow as well, and for a moment feared that Robert had killed him. In addition to the fact that they'd gone so long without harming a single soul, Timothy Grey—much as Allen might detest the cur—was Merry's friend. He turned to study Merry's reaction.

Her face grew deathly pale. She teetered upon her feet. "He's not . . . you didn't . . ."

Allen caught her for a second time and clutched her to his chest. "'Tis all right, Merry. His lordship is merely knocked unconscious." And for that, Allen felt some small sense of satisfaction. Though he hated to see her obvious affection for the fellow, he yet longed to soothe her anguish. "Look, no blood. No arrows. All is fine."

Her tense body sagged against him, and he treasured this moment to comfort and hold her. How he wished she would let him do so more often. But something about her reaction to this Timothy fellow warned him it might never happen again.

"What shall I do with him?" asked Robert. "I could take him back to his horse and smack them in the direction of the castle. Or deliver him there myself. Or, if we all agree 'tis wisest . . ." He let the sentence trail off.

In other circumstances Allen might agree, but Merry must make this decision. Not him. He knew little of the unconscious man, and Merry clearly had a history with him.

She pulled herself up straight, steeling herself as he'd seen her do on so many occasions, although she did not yet disentangle herself from his arms. "I did not think he would come after me. Was he alone?" Her voice sounded wispy rather than strong and confident like it usually did.

"As far as we could tell." James appeared in control of the situation and not at all afraid.

Why would this Timothy have come? Did he wish to have Merry back for himself, or did he yet seek the ghosts?

"Maybe he wished to warn us of something," said Cedric.

"Yes." Merry clutched to that idea. "I believe we should keep him here for now, until I can speak with him. We must know why he has come. How close did he get?"

"Not close enough that I would have shot him," said Robert, shifting Timothy's considerable weight upon his wiry shoulder. "But close enough to follow the scent of dinner. I feared he had reached the point of no turning back. I'd say about a furlong away."

Allen watched as Merry calculated the facts.

"Very good," she said, finally stepping free of Allen's support. "Then he does not know the precise location of the camp. Take him to the room to the rear of the cave. Red, guard him so that Robert might take some refreshment."

Her act seemed to convince the others, but Allen still feared she might collapse at any moment. She strode determinedly toward the cave and disappeared in the direction of the sleeping chambers. He hoped she would take a moment alone to process the situation.

He stared at the form of Timothy Grey as Robert passed by. He noticed again how tall and strong the man was, and how pleasing a woman might find his features and boyish thatch of hair. Without meaning to, he clenched his fists tight, then he opened his hands and shook them out.

These last days he'd been doubting if he'd ever get the opportunity to support the rebels and prove himself a warrior. Now that Timothy had come, Allen longed to leave more than ever, but the danger was greater than ever as well. He had no choice but to stay until this matter was concluded and the children were safe once and for all.

If that day ever came.

John approached the hill over which the unconscious form of Timothy Grey had disappeared. At the sound of voices on the other side, he paused to assess the situation, ducking behind a broad tree trunk.

Over that next rise might lay the camp of the ghosts. And those ghosts might just do the dirty work for him and dispatch one arrogant, insufferable Timothy Grey. Either way, John would soon lead a party of soldiers back to this place and finally prove himself a hero. Prove himself worthy of his father's love and acceptance after all these years. Not Timothy Grey. Him!

Timothy thought himself so smart, so resourceful, such an expert on this forest, but he had never seen the wiry little fellow coming up behind him. John cackled as he relived the moment when the blunt edge of the young man's sword had come crashing down upon Timothy's head.

No, Timothy was not the only one who knew his way around this forest. John recalled wandering this very area, starving and alone. Looking for anything edible he might bring home to his sick mother—for the good Lord knew his father had never bothered providing for them.

Before long John had learned to fashion a slingshot and became quite adept with it. He mastered the sounds and rhythms of the forest and could move silently through it. He supposed some might call what he had done poaching, as only noblemen such as that had the right to hunt. But he had never believed such nonsense.

Besides, were it not for a cruel twist of fate, he might have been a nobleman himself. He would never forgive Timothy for having what he deserved. Timothy deserved whatever pain and suffering the ghosts might inflict upon him this day.

John shuffled a few feet closer to the hillside, but a dark dread came over him. A sense of danger and fear he rarely experienced. He had learned to trust his intuition in these woods. Perhaps these ghosts were more of a threat, or even more "ghostly" than he had supposed.

Studying the hillside once again, he thought he detected the shapes of some hulking men. They seemed to flit and flicker through the shadows. He could not say for certain, but of a sudden he felt like the Israelites facing the Philistine camp. Like a mere grasshopper.

He shook off his fright, but he would go no closer. Not today. Not alone. He now knew where the camp lay. He would await the perfect moment, and then he would bring down the ghosts. And if they had not killed Timothy Grey, he just might have to find a way to do it himself.

Glancing at the sun, he realized it was time for him to hurry back. He must get to his horse and return to the castle to work his shift. Not everyone could laze about in the woods like Timothy.

As he headed toward the castle, he recalled Timothy's cherished horse tethered not a furlong from his. Ha! Poor fancy horse might just die in the woods with no water to drink. More the pity that.

Timothy awoke to utter darkness. A searing pain in the back of his head thumped in rhythm, like that of a blacksmith's anvil. Had he died and missed the path to paradise? He attempted to rub at his head but found he could not move his arms. As his senses came back to him, he realized he was in a cool, damp place with his hands tied together behind his back.

At least his first suspicion had not been correct. He struggled against the ropes and determined that someone had propped him against a wall with a cushion behind him and placed a blanket over his chest. Either he had been taken to some benevolent sort of dungeon, or he had gone blind, for he still could not see a thing.

He fought to recall how he had come to this place. What had he last been doing? Then it came back to him. He had thought to do some reconnaissance, to find the ghosts and assess their numbers before requesting assistance from his family. After all, he had located the ghosts undetected once. Why not again?

At their former camp, he had discovered only the empty structures. But he followed a faint, sporadic trail another league deeper into the forest. He should have paused to consider that if they remained, the ghosts would have increased security. But between the earl's threats and his unfortunate longing to look into Merry's eyes once again, he might not have been thinking straight.

One moment he had listened to a blackbird calling a warning to its mate, and the next a splitting pain had struck his head from behind as all went dark. This must have been how Merry felt when he captured her—although she had, thankfully, been spared the pounding head.

Wherever he was, whoever held him captive, he must at least try to escape. He could not just sit waiting to see what would happen next. The ghosts might kill him, send his body back as a warning. Or it might not be the ghosts at all. Surely this forest crawled with other violent criminals. Between King John's insane demands and outrageous taxes, it would not be long before half of England would be outlawed.

No, he should not think such thoughts against God's appointed king. Render unto Caesar his due, and all of that.

Stop it! He needed to pull his rambling thoughts—no doubt the result of his injury—under control and escape this place. He searched his surroundings again, and saw a faint light now shown through an opening, and he could make out the shadows of irregularly shaped walls. Struggling to his knees, he stroked his tied hands along the damp, rough surface behind him. It must be a cave. He dragged his feet beneath him but stumbled about, bouncing off the hard rock before sinking back against it.

Rustling to his left alerted him that someone stood watch, and his bumbling had given him away. But for now he fought merely to stay conscious. The shadows swirled around him. Bright light burst against the back of his eyelids. But he maintained his awareness of the cold, damp room.

Stay awake, Timothy, he silently coaxed himself. This could be a matter of life and death. He saw the faces of ghosts swirling before him. Ghoulish, twisted faces with gaping mouths. *They cannot be real.*

He was not given to superstitions. His head must be playing tricks on him, playing with his worst fears and nightmares. Blending them with thoughts of the ghosts.

He opened his eyes to find a brighter flickering orange glow emanating from a passageway to his left. Soft, padding footsteps approached.

Chapter 20

A torch emerged first through the opening. He could not see the figure holding it for the bright light now blinding his unaccustomed eyes. But someone reached up to fasten it on a holder in the wall.

As his vision cleared, he thought he might not be in hell but rather in heaven. The face he had longed to see—the face that haunted him, floating in the back of his mind night and day—stared down at him in the warm glow of the firelight.

"Timothy, do not struggle. I am here now." Merry knelt beside him and wiped his face with a cool cloth.

"Merry, I . . ."

"Shh. Relax. Let me attend to you." She placed a cushion behind his head and sliced the rope with her dagger, setting free his hands.

"Your . . . fond . . . tying people." To his alarm, his words came out garbled. Now with the torch illuminating the room, he realized just how dizzy and injured he was. The walls spun about him. Merry's intriguing face faded in and out of focus.

201

He strove to remind himself he was angry with her, but the thought would not stick in his head. Not while she continued with her gentle ministrations.

He rubbed his hand over the back of his skull and found a large egg-shaped bump. Though he had no chance of capturing the ghosts in this condition, perhaps he could convince Merry to let him go. Later he could return with reinforcements.

Merry covered him with the blanket again. "The men insisted we tie you up."

Of course her men wanted him bound. They were wise to demand as much. He could not fathom why no one stopped her from releasing him now. "Head . . . hurts," he managed as an answer.

"I imagine it does. Whatever were you thinking? That a band of renowned criminals would simply allow you to skip into their camp? If one of the guards had not recognized you from the castle, I assure you, you would be feeling no pain right now, for you would be dead. So in a manner of speaking, that bump saved your life."

"I . . . did not think. Wanted to find you. Make sure you were well." The words flowed more easily now, although each one cost him a deeper-pounding spike to the head. There was some truth to the words, yet his conscience niggled at him over his glaring omissions.

"Here." Merry pressed the cool cloth directly to the wound, and it brought him a bit of relief. She offered him a flask filled with an herbal concoction, and as he sipped, he began to feel somewhat human again.

Blinking his eyes, he brought them into clearer focus.

She sat back on her heels, pressed her hands to her hips, and smiled down at him. "So let me see if I have this straight. *You* wanted to make sure that *I* was all right."

"Looking back, it seems rather silly, I admit. But you never did tell me the nature of your relationship with the ghosts. You seemed rather frightened as you told me about them." Yes, that was true enough. Though he seemed unable to maintain his anger now that he gazed into her gentle eyes.

"Ah, I was frightened for their safety—not mine."

"*Their* safety?" Merry always had been a strange one, but perhaps his befuddled mind yet played tricks on him. "Merry, you make no sense. Allow me to take you away from here. I will find somewhere safe for you to hide. "

She brushed his hair from his brow, and for once he did not feel a child at the action. Rather, her fingers upon his skin along with the look in her eye stirred him and made him feel a man.

"Timothy, Timothy, why must you always complicate matters? Why can you not leave things be? First kidnapping me. Now chasing down the ghosts. Perhaps you should stick to your quill pen and books."

"Hey!" He leaned toward her, but pain sliced through his head, and he sat back.

"After all, if one cannot beat a mere girl, why bother with war games to begin with?"

"Oh." He chuckled. She repeated verbatim an argument from their childhood. He recalled his answer. "Because men are men, and we shall always be so. God has ordained it. Women should stay in kitchens and solars."

She continued with her line from their past. "Then I suppose you should find someone else to play with. I shall be in the kitchen baking a pie. What shall I make, apple or cherry? Or even better . . ."

They repeated the last line together. "A mud pie!" And both broke into laughter.

She had shoved him into the mud when she said it, and they

had both wound up tossing off their tunics and continuing their tussle in the stream. He recalled looking down at her in her shift, with her wet hair pooling like chestnut silk. That was the first day the impulse had struck him to press his lips against hers, but she was still a child. He had resisted the urge, mumbling something about being too old to swim in their underclothes.

Now, here, in the cave with torchlight playing along the curves of her face, he reached out to stroke her cheek. "If I recall, you won that argument soundly. I am just glad that I found you."

She cleared her throat and leaned away. "What shall I do with you? I cannot put the safety of my band in jeopardy."

He could not bid her trust him, though in this moment, he almost wished she could. "I did not intend to make matters difficult for you."

She eyed him warily. "I want to trust you. But you must swear to it. By the oath from our childhood."

"The holy Scripture says let your yes be yes and let your no be no."

"But I no longer live by the holy Scripture." She crossed her arms over her chest. "The code of thieves says trust no one who is not loyal to you."

He sighed and rubbed at his wrist. How could he get around this complication? He had little choice but to do as she wished. The ghosts could torture or kill him. Merry alone stood between him and disaster. He would simply have to find a way around his oath at a later time. "Fine."

"Then repeat after me." She lifted her right hand. "I hereby swear an oath upon my blood, and the blood of my parents, and the blood of my siblings, that I shall not utter a word about the identities nor the whereabouts of the ghosts."

Strong words, those. His head continued to pound as he repeated the oath. "I shall not utter a word . . ." *Hmm* . . . Then he must think of a different plan. A plan to lure them into the open. Get the herbalist to identify the man in his shop.

Merry surveyed him. "Do you think you can walk a few paces?"

How he hated to betray her. But he had no choice. He simply must see the ghosts brought to justice. The law was the law, and he should not shirk his duties in administering it. The choice had been stripped from his hands. "With a little help, I can manage it."

"All jesting of childhood aside, I am about to reveal to you my most precious treasures. I am placing them in your hands. Please, I beg of you, be worthy of this honor."

Timothy could think of no fitting reply.

He gained his feet with Merry's help, his arm around her shoulder. He could grow accustomed to this. Smiling to himself, he leaned heavily against her slight, though surprisingly taut, form. Taut, yet soft in the right places. He quickly swiped the grin from his face. She seemed even stronger than he remembered and would no doubt be happy to plant his face in the mud once again for such thoughts.

The throb in his head had lessened since drinking her herbal potion, and he managed to continue putting one foot in front of the other until the low, narrow passageway opened into a huge room.

Before him spread the scene from the clearing in the last camp all over again, except now lit by firelight and encased in stone and branches. Young women cut vegetables around a pot as children played nearby and some older boys dueled with practice swords. But no sign of the rough sort of criminals he had expected.

He spied, at the far end at a table, some young men closer to his own age and size. Two strapping fellows, one with sandy hair and the other with red. But they appeared more the pleasant farming sort than hardened outlaws as they laughed affably, playing at a wooden board game. Another gangly fellow with a huge grin and floppy ears sat beside them. Timothy remembered him as a tumbler, and now that he thought of it, the sandy-haired fellow looked familiar as well.

Glancing about he found the girl who had been the focal point of the show, and then the woman who had sung and played the lute. He even spotted little, lost Gilbert among the children at play. Timothy caught the boy's eye and shot him a questioning glare. The boy just shrugged his shoulders, smiled, and waved to him.

But where were the fellows with the scars, grubby faces, and tangled beards that one would expect to find at an outlaw camp? A big, burly man sat near the low wall of twisted branches and leaves, which Timothy concluded must be the exit to the forest. He would have appeared more the outlaw sort, except for the rather dim-witted, childlike expression upon his face.

Timothy nearly jumped when Merry let loose a shrill bird call that sliced through his aching head. He blinked his eyes and rubbed at the pain. "But where are the ghosts? I still do not understand."

Merry seemed to be waiting for something before she answered.

The branch wall shifted and slid to the side. Two more small-ish young men, one with a fresh, innocent face and the other with a wary look of caution, entered the cave and then slid the door closed behind them. Timothy recalled the wary one to be yet another tumbler.

"Well," Timothy repeated louder this time, "where are they? Where are the ghosts?"

Everyone in the room turned their attention to him. Right down to the tot in the pink dress who had led him to their camp. She ran to one of the young women and tucked herself into her skirt, sticking her thumb in her mouth.

Still Merry did not answer.

"Please, Merry." He shifted toward her.

Taking a step away from him, she gestured to the occupants of the room. "Timothy Grey, I would like you to meet the Ghosts of Farthingale Forest."

"But . . . what . . . ? Who is your . . . ?" But then the answer came clear in his mind.

"Who is our *leader*?" She said the words for him. "I take sole responsibility for that."

"Oh, Merry! How could you?"

The two strapping fellows stood from the table and approached him with their arms crossed over their chests. The red-haired one spoke. "Make no mistake. We are all in this together. We've done what we needed to keep ourselves and these children alive, and we make no apologies. We've injured no one in the process and stolen only from those who could spare it."

"But," said the sandy-haired fellow, "we aren't above hurting the likes of you if you cause so much as a scratch on one of these little ones."

Timothy's gaze darted about the dim room. These young people were fiercely devoted to Merry and to one another. He would be wise not to rile them. He rubbed the back of his head. "So let me guess. I have you two fellows to thank for my hospitable welcome to your camp."

A few of the children snickered at that.

"That would be me," said the wary young man who had come in last. He watched Timothy even now through squinting eyes. "Be thankful it was a thump to the head and not an arrow to the heart."

"All right. Enough of that," said Merry. "So you can see, Timothy, I am well loved and well cared for. And as for all of you . . . " She directed her attention to the group. "Timothy is here now, like it or not, so let us make him feel welcome for the time. He wishes only to see to my safety and happiness. As some of you are aware, he was a close friend during my child-hood. Let us show him who the Ghosts of Farthingale Forest really are."

Already Timothy was forming a picture. They were good-hearted young people who only did what was necessary to survive. Beyond that, he suspected they had become family to one another. He felt the need to say something, to further alleviate the tension. "I know that I cannot ask you to trust me. But let me assure you of this. No one in this room loves the Lady Merry Ellison more than I do. I will do nothing to endanger her."

All eyes remained focused on him, but postures seemed to relax. The strapping fellows dropped their arms from over their chests. A child began rolling a ball in the corner, and the russet-haired tot came out from the protective skirt to eye him with curiosity.

The redhead spoke first. "In that case"—he moved to Timothy and offered his hand—"welcome."

Several of the other young men greeted him and shook his hand. Guilt washed over Timothy in a heavy wave, along with an accompanying wave of doubt as to whether or not he could achieve his mission. The girl in the pink toddled over. He bent down to her height.

"You one of us?" she asked.

His heart ached. Under no circumstances could he breathe even a whisper of untruth to this poppet. "Would you like me to be?"

"Maybe. Sunshine man say you nice."

Timothy turned to Merry in confusion.

Merry bent down next to them. "Wrenny's sunshine men are very special, magical sorts of creatures." She gave the tot a gentle poke on her plump belly. "If they say you are nice, that is the best compliment a person could receive."

Timothy just shook his head. How had he won the approval of this tot's imaginary friends when he had come here to capture the leaders of her band? Rather, now that he knew Merry led the ghosts, he must focus upon the men. Of course he considered himself a nice person, but he also believed in justice. He had no doubt those gathered around him would not consider his intentions to be "nice" on any level.

After spending only a few moments among them, however, the game had changed. He would not merely betray Merry if he went through with his plan—he would betray every person surrounding him. He had managed to muck up matters in record time. Perhaps Merry was right, and he should stick to his books and quills.

Chapter 21

Merry perched herself on a stool in the corner and observed from a distance as Timothy interacted with the group after supper. Wren cuddled upon his lap as he told stories of their childhood adventures in the forest. Hopefully Wren's acceptance, and even more so the acceptance of her sunshine men, signaled that Timothy would not betray them. Though he had roused Merry's sympathy earlier, she remained uncertain as to his motives.

Even as he told his dramatic tale with wild hand gestures and accompanying voices, his eyes wandered and caught hers across the dim room. Those eyes shone fully of something she had only seen in part when he kissed her three years earlier. Infatuation? Lust? Deep inside she knew neither of those were correct. Yet she dared not put the true emotion into words.

Timothy should accept facts and let her go on her way. She recalled him preaching to her again and again, *"Never undertake a battle you cannot win."* So why did his eyes shout across the room that he would do anything, give his very life, to be with her?

The fool! He would indeed lose his life if he insisted on such a path. If not his actual life, at the least his family, his position, his very identity. No, she would not let him risk it.

"Merry, come join us," called Jane from the group surrounding Timothy.

She could think of no excuse.

As she settled on the floor in the space they cleared for her, the children stared at Timothy with dreamy-eyed expectation. He had always been a mesmerizing storyteller. Perhaps he could add to their group of tumblers and minstrels a troubadour. She smiled despite her annoyance with him. Whether she liked it or not, he did seem to fit right in.

Her band of criminals had accepted this outsider all too readily. Even Robert sat at the table with a relaxed posture and smiled in Timothy's direction. Perhaps she must add a new trait to their list of outlaw virtues. Stealth, anonymity, restraint, and *wariness*.

Abigail yanked at Merry's sleeve in excitement. "He's about to tell us the tale of Robyn of the Hode."

Over Wren's head, Timothy wiggled his brows at Merry.

"Give the little one to me," she offered. "If I recall correctly, you might need two hands for this story."

He chuckled and passed the child to her. "Indeed."

Wren snuggled into Merry's lap. "Love you, Ma-wee."

Merry took a deep inhale of the tyke's hair. "I love you too, Wren." If she allowed herself, she could easily imagine Timothy as her husband and Wren as their own daughter. But she refused to let her errant thoughts wander in that direction. Timothy might yet be up to no good.

With a flourish of his hand, Timothy began his tale. "Once upon a time, not so long ago, during the reign of King Richard, a nobleman by the name of Robyn of the Hode returned a hero from the crusades to his manor home, only to find his country in the midst of turmoil."

Merry buried her face against Wren's head, not wishing Timothy to see the emotion clouding her features as he continued. This had always been one of his favorite stories. He should not be surprised that she had turned a criminal. And he should most assuredly not serve an earl faithful to John, the villain of the story.

Did the death of Richard turn a villain into a king? She did not believe so. But Timothy had always been sanctimonious. Always cautious to follow the law to the letter. Did he consider her own murdered father a villain?

Merry closed her eyes and willed her battling emotions to quiet. Images of Timothy as a gentle sweetheart, a faithful friend, a potential husband and father struggled against a portrait of captor, betrayer, and pursuer in her mind. Wren and the children might have come to their own conclusions about him, but Merry was determined to withhold her final verdict.

As she stilled herself and focused upon the precious child in her lap, Merry noticed a subtle rattle and rasp to Wren's breathing. Why must they deal with this malady every autumn? They had nearly lost her twice in the last two years. She could not bear to go through that again.

Timothy had reached the place in the story where Robyn battled Little John with a staff. He acted it out with flair and drama, dancing about in front of them, sparring and parrying as he played the role of Little John.

He bellowed in a deep voice, "I pray, good fellow, where are you now?" Laughing outrageously, he held his belly with one hand as he brandished his imaginary staff in the other.

Falling to the ground and switching to the role of Robyn, Timothy swiped at his face. "Good faith, in the stream, and floating along with the current."

Then changing back to Little John, he continued. "I acknowledge you are a brave soul. With you I shall no longer contend."

As entertaining as this story was, Merry could no longer sit and watch Timothy act out this tale of thieves. Thieves not unlike the ones he had recently sought—or perhaps still sought—to capture. She slid Wren onto Jane's lap and whispered into her ear, "Her breathing has gone awry again. I will go prepare a remedy."

With that most excellent excuse, she left Timothy and his playacting behind. She fetched the needed herbs along with a mortar and pestle and situated herself on a bench at their long table to grind them for a draught.

As she worked, Allen thumped down beside her. "I care not for his ridiculous stories. I still do not like nor trust the fellow one whit."

Ah, at least one of her men remained wary. Good for him. "I doubt he means any harm."

"But do you trust him?"

She had been asking herself that question all evening. "Not entirely. Make sure the men keep a close eye on him. I do not wish him to know the specific location of our hideaway."

He huffed. "Thank goodness you have not lost all of your good sense."

With a quelling glare, Merry reminded him who was leader of their band.

Allen's face mottled pink, and he turned his head downward. "I'm sorry. That Timothy just irritates me like a bad rash. If you don't trust him, why did you release him?"

"I know not Timothy's true purpose for being here. He might yet seek to capture the ghosts. But . . ." She sent Allen a shrewd glance.

"What?"

She lowered her voice a notch. "This I do know, that man has a soft heart. If anyone can win him to our side, the children can."

"Ah, so it is a strategic maneuver." Allen grinned. "You never cease to amaze me, O fearless leader."

Merry smiled in return. She loved that epithet. A leader must never show fear. Especially not a female leader. Queen Eleanor of Aquitaine, King John's own mother, served as her role model in this. Well-educated and a duchess in her own right, the woman never quavered, simply took charge and led with confidence, even taking her own troop of crusaders to the Holy Land.

Merry returned to her grinding as Allen watched Timothy's performance, shaking his head in disbelief. "He thinks he is so funny."

"Well," said Merry, "trustworthy or not, his comic abilities speak for themselves."

"Then perhaps he should be a jester for a king, somewhere far away—perhaps Rome." Allen swept his hand toward Timothy in disgust.

Merry wished to tease and ask if he were jealous, but she knew the answer. No need to bring up the tension between them again. She offered him a wink in support of his amusing comment, however.

Evidently reading too much into the gesture, Allen reached for her hand. She jumped back as though burned by his skin. "Cease at once, Allen," she hissed. "You would not wish for Timothy to target you specifically. Not until we know his true motive for coming."

"Why would he . . . ? Oh, so there is something between you."

Merry sensed a warm flush rising up her neck and toward her cheeks. She slammed her pestle harder into the mortar to fend off her embarrassment. "Was. Not is."

"When he said he loved you more than all of us . . ."

Merry shot Allen a glare.

"Why didn't you just say as much?"

"Well, now you know!" she snapped.

Good-natured Allen just chuckled his low, rumbling laugh at her display of temper, and she relaxed at the soothing sound. She turned her gaze from Timothy to Allen and back again. Though Timothy stirred her heart like no other, Allen had admirable qualities as well. Stalwart, faithful, every bit as handsome, in a more rugged sort of way. In fact, she preferred Allen's simple brown apparel to Timothy's embellished tunic of red velvet she had found in their supplies for him to wear.

She stood, gathered a pot, filled it with water, and hung it over the fire in the center of the large room. Then she sprinkled her ground herbs into the pot. A blend of hyssop, peppermint, and chamomile. These should do the trick.

Staring into the water as she waited for it to bubble, her mind wandered back to the two men in her life. Allen had proven strong and dependable time and again. This new Timothy seemed to stir up trouble at every turn. Though she longed to trust him, her gut told her she should not. Still, his surprise visit had proven a blessing in disguise, allowing her to examine and compare them in close proximity.

Once she rid herself of Timothy for good, perhaps she should turn her mind toward building something lasting with Allen after all. Not right away, but slowly over time, once they settled somewhere safe. Jane and Red seemed to be faring well enough, with no ill consequences so far for the group.

Since she could not seem to rid herself of this appalling girlish need for love, she would at the very least steer the direction of her heart. *Restraint,* she reminded herself. Merry was nothing if not determined, and she was determined to remove Timothy from her affections once and for all.

Catching Allen's glance, she shot him a warm smile. His eyes lit with wonder.

In that moment, the performance fell silent. Timothy ceased reciting his story and stood gaping in their direction before recovering himself. Merry shook off a chill of concern. She had no proof that Timothy still sought the ghosts. Perhaps she should not worry herself so on Allen's behalf. But again, the clench in her gut told her she should not trust Timothy entirely.

At least not yet.

Chapter 22

Timothy dodged to the left, then moved in for the strike.

Young James met him with a defensive maneuver as Henry urged him on.

Timothy wiped at his brow, surprised at the heat in the forest on this sunny day, or perhaps the sun was not to blame so much as the challenge offered by this young man before him.

Their swords clashed over and again. Timothy had not practiced in years, but the technique returned to him as they battled. He had never received the intensive training of a knight, but all noblemen knew basic swordsmanship. For that matter, many a feisty noblewoman knew how to handle weapons in self-defense—though few took matters to the extreme of Lady Merry Ellison. He smiled as he ducked and struck again.

He must admit that Merry had put her skill to good use. Either of these young men would make a worthy squire. He feinted right. James turned his sword to an odd angle, and Timothy saw his opportunity. In a flash, he sent James's sword sailing into the forest.

"Ho!" shouted Henry, as he ran to retrieve it.

James leaned forward with hands on his knees. "I concede. You are a worthy opponent, Timothy Grey."

"You held your own. But watch the angle of that sword. You cannot afford a lapse in form." Nor a lapse in judgment. Though the blunted practice swords would not do any terrible damage, the boys should not have been so quick to let their prisoner play with one. He could have used the weapon to get away.

"Right. Got it," huffed James.

Henry returned, offered James his sword, and turned to Timothy. "Me again!"

"No," Sadie interjected, approaching them from across the clearing. "You have had Timothy long enough. 'Tis our turn." Wren and Abigail followed her with stern expressions on their faces. These girls were nearly as tough as their male counterparts.

"We're not finished. I still need to best him." Henry crouched low with his sword.

"Give him us!" Wren wagged her finger at Henry.

"Oh fine, then." Henry turned to James. "I guess it is you and me, as usual."

Abigail squealed in delight. "Come, Timothy. We're working on our tumbling. Know you any tricks?"

"I must confess, I have never been very good. Merry showed me a headstand once, but I never did conquer it."

"Oh, 'tis easy," said Sadie. "Give it a try."

He should probably take more care with his borrowed—rather, stolen—tunic than to tumble in the dirt. He wondered where, or whom, it had come from. Not that they would ever get it back. "I suppose I can try, if you insist."

"Indeed, I do." Sadie crossed her arms over her chest and stood by to observe.

Timothy lowered himself to his knees, pressed his head into

the dirt, and attempted to hoist his legs in the air. They flailed about for only a moment before he toppled to the ground. Familiar ground he had played on as a child, though Merry must not know he recognized the area. He was surprised she had allowed him outside, giving him opportunity to survey the surroundings—but he certainly was not going to point out her tactical error.

"Get up and try again," said Sadie.

The blood had rushed to his head while upside down and caused the world to go dark and shadowy. He rolled over but could not make out her features. However, he could tell by her outline that the miniature tyrant towered over him with hands upon her hips. He rubbed his eyes with his fists until his vision grew clear and her frown apparent.

Wren and Abigail sat nearby, giggling at his attempt.

"You think it is funny, do you?"

"Very," said Abigail. "Watch. Like this." She flipped onto her head and balanced there with little effort.

"This," mimicked Wren, placing her head on the ground and turning a circle around it.

Timothy propped himself on an elbow and grinned, though Merry's remedy had relieved the pain significantly, his head was beginning to thump again. It seemed he would go to rather ridiculous lengths to please these children. A twinge of guilt tugged at his gut, but he tamped it down. He had never had any intention of harming the little ones.

"I am telling you all, it is no use. Merry tried to teach me years ago. I am hopeless."

Sadie bent over and placed a hand on his arm. "Forget your past failures. Listen and observe closely."

She knelt down in front of him. "Place your hands sturdily upon the ground, shoulder-width apart, pressing all five fingers into it. Form a triangle of your head and your hands." Shaking a finger at him, she said, "But don't throw your legs into the air willy-nilly. Watch what I do. 'Tis simple."

The girl made the triangle of hands and head, then propped her knees upon her elbows. Still upside down, she said, "Now, very slowly, using the muscles in your belly, lift your legs." She did so, only a few inches. "Along the way up, adjust your weight between your fingers and your head as you progress, always keeping those stomach muscles tight."

Merry had never explained the process to him so thoroughly. She merely did the trick and expected him to imitate.

From the headstand position, Sadie pressed up into a handstand, formed an arch with her back, and flipped over and stood to her feet. Timothy, Abigail, and Wren all clapped.

"Now your turn." Sadie returned her hands to her hips.

"All right, then." He formed the triangle shape with head and hands. "You are an admirable teacher, but I hope you shall not be disappointed if I fail once again."

"You will not fail. Determine to do it," came Sadie's shrill young voice from above him. She sounded just like Merry.

"Do it!" shouted Wren.

"Dooo it, dooo it, dooo it." Abigail began the chant and the other girls joined her.

Timothy supposed under these circumstances, he could not let them down. He did his best to recall the instructions. He propped his knees on his elbows—a step he had never attempted before—found his balance, and controlled the motion from his stomach. As he raised his legs, he sensed just how to shift his weight to maintain control. And instantly, he was standing upon his head.

"I did it!" he shouted. His upside-down heart thrummed with excitement.

"Don't topple yourself. Stay steady," said Sadie. "Now straighten your legs and point your toes. Tighter still in the belly."

He made the adjustments.

"Perfect."

The girls cheered and clapped.

Still under control, he lowered his knees to the ground. As he sat and lifted his head, things went shadowy again but cleared quickly. "I finally did it."

"We never doubted you, Timothy." Abigail smiled her gap-toothed grin and took his hand.

"Good job." Wren patted him on his head, and he hugged her to himself.

He was becoming more and more entrenched with this band of thieves with every passing moment. The little bundle in his arms felt so warm and wonderful that he could not resist. Before long he would be a full-fledged ghost. He snickered at the thought. This trip had proven a monumental detour along his path to political success. How could he betray the ghosts now?

Wren took a turn attempting the trick as they all stood by and watched.

Now he understood why Merry needed to get back to these children so urgently. They were delightful. And she had taken such good care of them. So many times he had dreamed of rearing a family with Merry. But he must find a way to rid himself of that dream.

Only when seeking to win his favor in the castle had she ever looked at him as she looked at that surly Allen fellow last night. Timothy had nearly choked when he saw the two of them tucked so close together. Surely he had misread the situation. Merry would never lower herself to engage in a romance with a mere peasant. The idea was ludicrous.

Not wishing to pursue that line of thinking, he stood and

brushed the dirt from the knees of his leggings. "May I return to sparring with the boys? I am much better at that." He longed to send another sword streaking into the trees.

"Absolutely not," said Sadie. "We taught you something, now you must teach us something."

"What sort of things do you wish to learn?" He scratched at his head, scanning his mind for ideas. "The history of England?"

"You mean the history of invading royals and nobles, seizing our lands from far-off France?" Sadie scowled. "No thank you."

Timothy had no comment for that unexpected tirade and dared not hazard another guess. Again that twinge of guilt bit at him. If Sadie learned his true intent for coming here, she would never forgive him.

"Perhaps something that you do every day at the castle," suggested Abigail with a shrug of her shoulders. "We've never lived in a castle."

Timothy scanned his mind for an activity to entertain the children. "Ah!" He held up a finger as the perfect plan came to him. "I now serve the earl in a variety of capacities, but in the beginning, I was a simple scribe. I will teach you a letter or two."

Abigail laughed. "You're silly."

Sadie pressed a hand to her mouth, as if she wished to giggle as well but realized it would not be polite.

"What is so silly about it? You are intelligent young ladies. Reading and writing need not be reserved to the priestly class, as so many believe. We can begin with the first letter in each of your names." If they could learn their names—which he imagined they could if they were willing to apply the effort—it would be helpful for signing documents in the future. The country turned more toward a system of proper legal paperwork each day.

Abigail laughed so hard that tears streamed from her eyes. She slapped at her knee.

"Somebody please explain to me what is so blasted funny."
He frowned at them with false ferocity.

"You needn't teach us 'a letter or two,' for we know all of
them," said Sadie with a roll of her eyes. "And how to form
words with them as well."

"All of you?" Timothy did not understand. Even among the
nobles, many were not literate.

"Wren, tell Timothy your letters." Abigail pushed the little
one forward.

"A . . . B . . . C!" said Wren, jumping in delight.

"She doesn't know the rest of them yet, but she will." Sadie's
chest puffed with pride. "Lady Merry wants us to be prepared
for whatever life might bring us next. We cannot remain outlaws forever, you know. She hopes that someday we might be
merchants or craftsmen."

"Cedric thinks we should be a troupe of tumblers, but Merry
won't have it." Abigail did a forward roll and bounced back up
to her feet with a flourish of her hands.

Timothy studied the children now with different eyes. Literate. All of them. Amazing. "And the young men?"

"They are often busy with hunting and raids, but they study
when they can," said Sadie.

He turned to contemplate the men as they continued at their
swordplay. His head swam in confusion. But he sought to bring
one idea to the forefront. These men were thieves. Thieves who
must be brought to justice.

"Let's gather some sticks and show him." Sadie rallied the
other girls, and they dashed off.

Timothy barely registered the comment. He could not draw
his gaze away from the group of young males. The dark wiry one
with the sharp eyes, Robert, battled against the larger Allen, the
suspected object of Merry's affections. They were both quick

and light on their feet. Robert made up with agility for what he might lack in brute strength. Both appeared cunning, calculating, and well-trained. No, he need not feel guilt on their accounts. They could fend for themselves.

Henry and James had been adequate swordsmen, given their young ages, but these two skilled warriors truly deserved his admiration. As Robert struck low, Allen dove over his sword, rolling upon the ground, swiveling on one foot, and landing in a crouch, ready to attack again.

If he must capture three token ghosts, Robert, Allen, and Red would be his preferences. At least they could offer a fair fight.

An inspiration sparked to life in his head. Perhaps he could arrange for a tournament at the castle and allow common folk to compete. That might well draw these trained warriors out of hiding. Especially if the earl offered a large monetary prize. There must be a way to capture them without breaking the specifics of his oath to Merry. And a part of him—albeit an ever shrinking part—remained determined to find it.

Timothy glared in Allen's direction.

To think this former peasant could read and write and fight like a knight. Timothy ran his hands over his face, struggling to collect his thoughts. Considering those facts, along with Allen's broad shoulders, admirable height, and pleasant features, Merry might just be in love with this fellow after all.

Though he had spent significant time of late convincing himself that he no longer loved Merry, Timothy's heart plummeted to his boots. He had just found her after three long years apart. For her to reject him was harsh enough. He could not bear the thought that he might somehow lose her to . . . a peasant.

But if he captured Allen, Merry would think him vindictive and add that to his ever-increasing list of sins, for which she would assuredly never forgive him.

A rustling behind him caught his attention.

"There, Timothy," called Abigail. "You see?"

She pointed to the dirt by her feet. Upon it she had scratched with a stick, *Abigail can read!*

He raked his fingers through his hair. "I see, Abigail. I see far more than I ever imagined."

And unfortunately, he saw that his goal of capturing the ghosts grew more and more impossible by the moment.

Allen dodged around Robert, arcing his sword in the process, and managed to catch him from behind, holding the dull edge against Robert's throat.

Henry and James whooped their approval.

Allen let him go and rested his hands on his knees as he struggled to catch his breath.

"Good fight," said Robert, panting as well. He rubbed at his neck a bit, but Allen had not injured him in any lasting sort of way.

"Good fight yourself—right up to the moment when you died." Allen chuckled. He wiped his brow with his sleeve, and the moisture soaked through.

Looking up, he spied that arrogant Timothy Grey glaring directly at him.

"Think you can do better, Grey?"

Timothy shrugged and lifted his nose into the air. "Perhaps."

Timothy need not be so smug. Merry had been particularly warm to Allen these past days—he might yet win her affection and best Timothy in love as well as swords. "Well, if you're done playing with children, let's have a real go at it."

Allen grabbed Robert's sword and tossed it to Timothy.

Timothy smiled as he snatched it from the air. Allen had thought to thrash him outright, but this might prove interesting.

Timothy danced around a bit, testing the weight and sharpness of his sword.

"Sure you want to risk those fine clothes of yours?" Allen jerked his chin to the man's ridiculous red velvet tunic with its gold embellishments. Although he had arrived in hunting clothes, Merry had found him something "suitable to his station" in their stores.

"I'm not afraid of a little dirt. Perhaps you are the one having second thoughts."

"Not at all."

Allen moved in and made the first strike. They clashed swords several times, testing each other. "Must be nice growing up in a castle. Training to be a knight. Gives one a certain unfair advantage in most situations. But this is not most situations."

"As a matter of fact, I serve Lord Wyndemere as a scribe. So when I beat you, be sure to keep your story straight."

Red snickered. "Come now, Allen. The Ghosts of Farthingale Forest cannot be bested by a scribe. We have a reputation to uphold."

They circled around each other, swords poised, both crouching low to the ground.

Allen's blood heated. This man rubbed him in all the wrong ways. "Never fear, I will not suffer to lose to a filthy king's man."

"Ah, so Merry has turned you a traitor as well."

"I have my own mind." Allen struck harder, just for the satisfaction of watching Timothy wince as the metal clanged. Though he hated to admit it, Timothy had good form. He had yet to spot a weakness. "And I like to think of King Louis as the rightful ruler and you the traitor."

"Nice delusion." Timothy faked several times before striking, but Allen deflected his blow nonetheless.

"I might join the fight, once you're dead and can no longer

betray us. I long to be part of an honorable cause and support a just king," Allen said, intentionally attempting to bait the man.

Timothy took a step back and lowered his sword, staring Allen straight in the eye. "And the delusions continue. Think you Louis is a good ruler? The entire French court is corrupt. Power never fails to corrupt. At least John is English. Louis is naught but a pompous Frenchman who wishes to lord it over us. And who on earth told you the rebel cause was noble? The northern barons are a greedy and unscrupulous lot, FitzWalter more than any of them."

Allen's blood roared to a boil now. His heart thumped hard in his chest. He would not for one moment believe such lies. "Less chatting and more fighting, pretty fellow."

Timothy's face hardened, and a scowl twisted his features. From then on, there was no time to talk. Swords clashed over and again. Allen attempted a tumbling maneuver, only to find Timothy ready to meet his blow. Their swords tangled to the hilts, and they stood face-to-face, pressing upon one another.

Allen could feel Timothy's hot breath on his face. "I will defeat you."

Timothy shoved him away. "Not with that slovenly technique."

Now he just hated the man. He'd have to repent later. Not everyone could be trained by skilled knights. Allen came hard again, losing his focus in his anger.

Before Allen realized what his opponent intended, Timothy swiped in from the left, landing a crushing blow against Allen's ribs and winning the match. Pain seared his side. He would carry a bruise for a very long time. To his pride as well as his ribs.

The other men watched in silence. No one had beaten Allen in months.

Timothy stepped away and grinned. "I lied. You are skilled, my good man. But you let me rattle you, and you favor your right. Keep your focus and never let your guard down. You will be a fine warrior yet."

He offered Allen his hand.

Allen could think of no recourse but to shake it. "I underestimated my opponent."

"No worries. In a few years, I shall not stand a chance against you. Keep at it."

Allen's hatred melted into grudging respect. "Then you lied about the northern barons as well."

Timothy's expression turned apologetic. "Sadly, I did not. I will concede that King John has many faults, but I believe he is the lesser of two evils. Perhaps someday true justice shall prevail, but it will not happen at the hand of Prince Louis. Although . . . I imagine he might pardon Merry and the rest of you, and for that reason I would not stand against him." He tossed his sword back to Red and returned to the girls.

Now what on earth was Allen to make of that? His mind swirled as he struggled with this new information. He did not wish to believe Timothy, but he seemed so sincere. Perhaps the man was merely misinformed. Allen supposed he could take his time considering the matter. It was not as if he was free to leave anytime soon.

Chapter 23

Later that evening, after a supper of savory venison stew as fine as any served at the castle, Timothy sat cross-legged on the floor of the cave. He held his hands to the fire. The air smelled of woodsmoke but had a chilly nip to it, and he was no longer as accustomed to life out of doors as he had been as a child. Wren toddled up. With nary a word, she plopped herself onto his lap and stuck her thumb in her mouth. She leaned back against him and sighed.

Merry, wearing a surprisingly pleasant expression on her face, came and situated herself next to them. She clearly had a soft spot for the little girl. "It seems you have made a friend for life," she said.

He stroked Wren's soft head. "It seems so." He had not intended to grow so attached to the ghosts as he had in the past twenty-four hours. "She reminds me of my niece."

"Which one?" Merry laughed. "You must have twenty of them by now."

"Only twelve nieces. And fifteen nephews, plus another child . . . no, two more children on the way."

231

Merry brushed at her sleeve and stared into the flickering dance of flames before them. "I can hardly fathom such a large family. It is just me now."

"It seems you have all formed a large, warm family here." He nodded to the youngsters filling the cave. "And do you not still have your aunt near Bristol?"

"Yes, but I have not wished to saddle her with an outlawed relative. If it were only me, I might consider it. She might be able to hide me away, but . . ." She curled her knees to her chest, wrapping her arms around them.

"You do not wish to leave them," Timothy supplied.

"I do not. I have considered it a hundred times. But none of us, least of all me, could bear it."

He so badly wished to get her far away to a safe place, separate from the ghosts, but how could he ever convince her to leave this precious poppet now cuddling upon his lap? Truth be told, he himself would have difficulty leaving these children when the moment came.

He should make haste to get on with the ghosts' capture, but he needed more time to determine his thoughts on the issue. As the day had passed, his doubts over this mission had continued to grow. But he was as yet unsure that he could abandon his position with the earl either.

He focused upon Merry's face, relaxed and open for once, in the fire's glow. Though he wished to reach out and stroke her cheek, he resisted the urge. "You have done amazing things with these children. I understand now, Merry."

She turned her head toward him and rested that silken cheek on her knees. A half smile curved her peachy lips. He longed to brush them with his own, but he dared not.

"Do you?"

"I think so." The fire crackled and a spark snapped into

the air. But it did not compare to the sparks he sensed flying between them as he melted into her soft brown eyes. Did she feel it too? Or was the stalwart Merry Ellison impervious to such emotions?

She shivered. Then something flashed and hardened in her brown eyes. She jerked away from him and sprang to standing. "It is my turn at watch soon. I do not have time to laze about the fire. I am a noblewoman no longer, as you might recall."

Though he had expected something of the sort, nonetheless, her rebuff pierced straight to his heart. He moved to chase after her, and then remembered Wren upon his lap.

"Merry, wait!" He struggled to his feet, scooped Wren to his chest, and jogged to where Jane sat weaving in a corner of the cave with the other girls. "Could you take her for me, please?"

"Of course." Jane held out her arms. "'Tis nearly time for bed, Wrenny."

"Wonderful," he said, though distracted and already searching out Merry among the group.

He found her shrugging on her quiver and bow. She tucked a dagger and circle of rope into her belt, then turned toward the exit. Timothy moved to block her path.

From the table where the young men played a game with wooden pieces Allen called, "Stay warm, Merry."

"I will." She smiled his way with a notable degree of affection, which Allen clearly reciprocated. Brotherly? Timothy suspected not.

Heat built in his chest, a very different kind of heat than the one he had experienced by the fire moments earlier.

Finally she approached but paid him no attention. He stood firm in her path.

Merry shoved him aside with her shoulder. "If you do not mind."

But he grabbed her by the forearm and halted her progress. "But I do mind. Very much."

She smacked at his hand and tugged away. "Must I thrash you in front of the children? Would you not be embarrassed to be bested by a girl yet again?"

"You are not going anywhere until we talk."

She glared at him. "You are always talking, Timothy. Have you not run out of words? I grow sick to death of your words, for they mean little. Now, if you do not mind, I must relieve Robert."

"Then I am coming with you."

"Suit yourself." She stormed out of the cave, but he slid the door closed and followed.

He fell into step beside her but did not want to open the conversation until they had some privacy. Instead he took in the blustery twilight, already glimmering with stars through the rustling canopy of leaves. Little puffs of fog escaped his mouth. As the cold settled into his bones, he rubbed at his arms.

His coat remained with his horse, which Robert reported he had loosed and slapped in the direction of the castle yesterday afternoon. Spartacus had no doubt found his way home and was fine, but Timothy wished he would have thought to fetch a blanket for himself. He might well freeze to death in this forest.

Merry stalked up the hill to the lookout point. She wore a thick woolen over-tunic and seemed not at all fazed by the cold. Perhaps her boiling blood kept her warm as well. Timothy did not understand why she turned so angry of a sudden, unless she did indeed have some tender feelings for him, which she had determined to fight.

He would get to the bottom of this issue with Allen.

"There you are," said Robert, chafing his hands together and blowing upon them. "I've never been so ready to see a fire as I am right now."

"The temperature dropped rather suddenly." Merry took off her bow and struck the end into the ground. "Go warm up."

Robert ran down the hill without so much as a farewell, but Timothy could not blame him. And he was thankful to be alone. "So what is this with you and that Allen fellow?"

"Allen? He has been my right-hand man since we were chased from our village."

"Really, for it appeared to be far more than that. Must I remind you that he is a peasant? A pauper? You are the daughter of a baron."

"Not anymore." She pulled out an arrow and tested its tip against her finger. "And I will not tolerate you speaking ill of my men. I trust them with my life. *They* would never desert me. *They* would never betray me."

The unspoken *like you* hung in the air between them, piercing his heart far more than her rebuff moments earlier. Ignoring his current motives, motives she knew nothing about, he chose to focus on the past to which she referred. "I thought you were dead! The moment I learned you were alive, I began plotting to rescue you. I never meant to betray you. I meant only to protect you." That still held true.

"You dragged me off to a castle friendly to the king. A king who wishes me dead." Her words rang as cold as the air around them.

"Do you truly believe that I would intentionally hurt you?" He peered at her in the dim light, but her features gave nothing away.

"I believe that you wanted to capture the ghosts and curry favor with the earl. Perhaps the king himself." She jabbed her finger at his chest. "And I was your ticket to do so. You lost a fortune once by not marrying me, and you did—or perhaps still do—not want to miss such an opportunity for advancement again." Snatching up her bow, she marched a few paces away from him.

How dare she think him so mercenary? She would not get away so easily this time. "Do not level an indictment against me and then turn your back."

He pulled her around and caught her arms in his two hands. She gasped, but he did not relent. "You cannot just dismiss me when I am inconvenient. I am not one of your men. I was meant to be your husband. Not because I wanted your money. Because I wanted *you*. Because I love you, try as I might to stop. You are a part of me. We belong together." He shook her, hoping it might jar some sense into her stubborn head.

She wilted in his grip. Her voice dropped to a whisper. "Love is not enough. Not when I am wanted by the king."

He dropped her arms and turned to rake his fingers through his hair, unable to argue with that statement. *And love is not enough when I must capture your friends or lose my position,* he added to himself.

Before he could consider his response, he spoke. "Then allow me to take you away from here. To France, perhaps. I have family there." Where were these words coming from? "The ghosts will make it on their own. Your rescue proved that. They are well capable."

"Do you not understand? England. France. It matters little. France shall provide a haven for a time, but unless good men like you stand up against injustice, no place on earth shall be safe."

"Please, Merry." He reached toward her again, but at the sight of her with feet planted resolutely in the ground, he let his arm drop to his side.

"I will not leave the children. Sadie and Abigail, Wren and

all the little ones. They need me." Determination sparked in her eyes.

He dared to take a step closer. "Have you never paused to consider that they might be better off without you? That your presence might lure the king to the group?"

Her eyes dropped to the ground at that. His words appeared to pain her. "I . . . I have. But they do not wish to be without me. I made a promise to Wren, and I will not break it. We have provisions enough for the winter. Come spring, if the rebels still have not prevailed, we will consider traveling to France. Together."

She fiddled with her bowstring. No longer looking as tough or confident as she had moments ago. "Who knows, by spring, King Louis might sit upon the throne. You might well be the outlaw, and I the Baroness of Ellsworth. I might have to rescue you. Have you paused to consider that?" Though her words were brave, her voice sounded frail.

He cupped her cheek in his palm. She turned into it, softening at last, and his breath caught in his chest.

"Merry," he said in as gentle a tone as possible, "I beg of you to accept that John is king. There is nothing we can do about that."

Merry wrenched herself away from Timothy's hand, putting several feet of cold night air between them. Twice this evening she had nearly succumbed to his spell, to the tingles and shivers that plagued her each time he was near. She should have known better than to let him comfort her beneath the starlit sky, even for a moment. He would never change. And she would never, ever accept John—the man who had ordered the murder of her family—as king.

"Nothing we can do about it? For a time last summer the Great Charter reigned supreme in this land, and we were under the rule of law, not the fickle whims of the king. Your own father supported it. Perhaps the possibilities that document offered spoiled me for a ruthless monarch." She widened her stance and crossed her arms over her chest. Enough of that ridiculous, girlish weakness. She poised herself to win this battle.

"The charter did not work. It is not the way of this world. King John is too powerful, and he is still God's chosen sovereign."

"God's chosen sovereign? How do you know this?"

He pressed a hand to his forehead. "The pope decreed it."

"The pope! Some stranger far off on the continent? He decreed it, then undecreed it, then magically decreed it again once he had something to gain." She snorted at his ridiculous reasoning.

"Do not speak sacrilege." He shook his hands toward her. "The pope is God's ordained oracle. He has chosen King John. It is God's will."

"It is not! It is certainly not the will of any sort of God I wish to serve."

"Please, Merry, do not—"

"No, let me finish." She uncrossed her arms and rested her hand upon the handle of her dagger. "If God does indeed exist, then He is good, and He is just, and He stands upon the side of right. You would have me believe in the divine right of a king who would wipe out an entire village, including children. Including Wren. Perhaps my father made a mistake, but at least he lived his convictions. What about you?" She spat the final question at him.

He took a deep breath and blew it out slowly. "I do live my convictions. You just do not like them."

"You are right. I despise your convictions that God ordains ruthless kings. Do you truly believe God creates some people to bask in luxury while he creates others, others—like Robert and Sadie and Gilbert—to be the underlings who slave for them? What sort of God is that?" Her hand gripped tighter to the handle of her dagger of its own accord.

"It is not like that. There is simply a divine order to things. Why can you not accept it?"

He disgusted her, pure and simple! She clenched her jaw and ground out her answer. "Because I have stopped listening to drivel and begun to think for myself. Why can you not do the same? How can you see these children—their wit and intelligence, their raw humanity—and believe for one moment that they were designed to be your chattel?"

Timothy bowed his head. "That is not what I meant. That is never what I meant."

"The beliefs all tie together. You cannot accept one and deny the other. There is no logic to it. It does not work."

Timothy remained silent. He leaned heavily against a nearby tree.

"I knew you were not to be trusted," she said. "Childhood friendships count for little in times like these. We did not understand the chasm of philosophy between us. I do not trust you, and furthermore, I do not even like you. I will not tolerate you one more moment in my camp."

Her heart thumped in her chest, as if it might explode. Her blood pumped hard and hot through her veins. Before Timothy knew what she was about or could even think to fight, Merry whipped him around and twisted his arms behind his back. She grabbed the rope from her belt, wrapped it around his wrists, and tied it tight.

"You must be joking," he sputtered.

"Yes, I am quite the jester." She yanked him behind her and headed toward the cave.

"Merry, please!"

But she did not falter in her course. She would not waver. Her questions had been resolved. She knew what needed to be done.

"Robert, Allen," she barked, knowing she sounded like a female dog and caring not one whit.

Familiar with her tone, they hurried out to meet her.

"Blindfold the prisoner. Leave him bound on the outskirts of the village near Greyham Manor. If he is lucky, they will find him before the elements take him."

Robert's jaw dropped. He looked at her, clearly mystified. "I don't understand."

"You know well that I do not like the fellow," said Allen, slapping his fist against his open palm. She sensed a *but* coming. "I shall be happy to remove him far from here and even pop him in the jaw a time or two, if you like. But . . . Merry, he's done nothing to deserve being left bound and helpless in the cold."

And there it was. He would indeed question her authority.

Robert scratched his head. "Do you mean now? 'Tis nearly dark."

"Take him!" She shoved him toward them and began to pace back and forth. The evening had taken on a red tinge in her fury. She felt like a kettle about to bubble over, steam escaping from the lid. "Ugh!" she shouted to no one in particular.

Robert and Allen stared. They knew her temper, but rarely did she seethe out of control like this. She must pull herself together.

"Fine," she relented. "Take him to the rear of the cave. In the morning, deliver him home and wait and see that he is safely found. But I mean it about the bindings and the blindfold. I do not want him to be able to locate this camp. I do not trust him."

"There must be some mistake." Timothy's eyes pleaded with

her more so than his words, but her heart had turned to cold stone as she had listened to his ridiculous arguments about the king.

"Oh no, there is no mistake. The next time you come looking for me . . . the next time you come within two furlongs of this camp, the last sight to meet your eyes will be an arrow through your chest."

She turned her back to him and ignored his final words, stomping off toward the women's quarters. Timothy Grey had no place in her life. She had deceived herself to ever consider that he might.

Now he must leave for good.

Chapter 24

Timothy sighed as he tucked his personal items into a sack. He paused to glance around the small stone room that had been his home at Castle Wyndemere for over a year. A cell, really. How had he never seen it before? He removed a tapestry of greens and browns, handmade for him by his mother and sister Ellen, from the wall. A forest scene that reminded him far too much of his recent bittersweet time in that verdant world.

For three days he had hidden at Greyham Manor, pondering his next step. But he could not betray the ghosts. Especially not after seeing the remains of the crippled thief he had sent to prison hanging from the castle walls upon his return to Wyndemere—God rest the poor man's soul. He could not betray Robert or Allen, who had given him little but trouble yet defended him in the end. Nor even Merry, who had turned on him so cruelly.

Though her betrayal stung deep, he had seen the torment in her eyes. The girl had been through too much. She no longer knew how to trust. Not that he fully deserved her trust. And in the end, she had allowed him to walk into Greyham unbound, not wishing to draw attention to his capture.

Though he still burned at the threat against his life, he should never have underestimated her considerable instincts. Regret hung heavy on him, like a coat of chain mail. He should never have gone after the ghosts once he knew the truth. He should never have put his career before the well-being of the children of Ellsworth.

Nothing remained for him now but to pack his bags, burn that ill-advised missive to the king, and head home in defeat. Tiny Little Timmy, runt of the family, back in the fold once again.

He shoved several tunics into his sack, although he now realized he had little of his own in this place. Through the window, the forest beyond the village—a patchwork of green, gold, and amber—drew his eye.

Somehow, someway, he would find a new path for himself. Perhaps as castle steward for a relative, though he had so longed to make it on his own. And while his parents thought marriage to a young lady with an inheritance his best course of action, given what his mother called his "adorable face"—ugh!—the prospect held even less appeal for him than it had for the last two years. If he could not have Merry Ellison, he desired no woman in his life.

As much as he longed for her, he understood her drive to protect the children. Would his father do anything less for his own family? Would Timothy? As he had played with his nieces and nephews, he had been struck by the truth that he would without a doubt turn an outlaw to save any one of their lives. But still he did not understand Merry's anger toward him. He had only spoken the truth. Truth they had both grown up believing.

He swiped his hair comb and a few other trinkets from his stand into the sack.

Merry's words had haunted him for days. *"Unless good men like you stand up against injustice, no place on earth shall be safe."* He had initially rejected them out of long-held habit, but they rang true somewhere deep within him.

And her stinging indictment. *"Do you truly believe that God creates some people to bask in luxury while he creates others—like Robert and Sadie and Gilbert—to be the underlings who slave for them?"*

He had not held to that reasoning in any sort of conscious or intentional way, but she was correct. His acceptance of the divine rights of kings tied to just such a philosophy. Her opinions challenged him to question everything he held dear.

Taking his iron crucifix from the wall, he studied it a moment before tucking it into his sack with his other belongings.

Most of all, he had been struck by Merry's assertion about the nature of God. *"If God does indeed exist, then He is good, and He is just, and He stands upon the side of right."* He had not sorted out how such a statement could be balanced with biblical respect for the ruling authorities, yet he could not deny a word of it. The very survival of the escaped children of Ellsworth attested to its truth. That they had lasted two years as outlaws in the forest, not losing even a single soul to illness, illustrated clearly God's favor shining on them.

Might not Wren's sunshine men be God's very angelic hosts?

As much as his heart ached over Merry's rejection, he had been even more stunned by her vehement rejection of God. The Merry he knew as a child had revered Scripture—had even studied Latin so that she might read and copy the Holy Book herself. At one point she had spoken of being a nun in a scriptorium to preserve the Bible for generations to come.

Now she rejected both God and His Word. Perhaps thinking such as his had jaded her—and perhaps the loss of her beloved

3222222222

family. How he longed to return to her and convince her of God's love and faithfulness.

But she had made matters clear, had pounded the final nail in the coffin of their friendship when she threatened his life. He would pray for her soul. That would have to suffice.

With another sigh he slung the sack, containing surprisingly little, over his shoulder and headed through the dim, echoing hallways, smelling of pitch from the torches, to the room that had served as his office since becoming Lord Wyndemere's unofficial assistant.

The room stood empty, except for the parchment upon the table. He sat in his chair for a moment. Lifted the quill into his hand one last time. Scratched it over the crinkly parchment just to savor the sensation.

With a creak of the door, Lord Wyndemere swept into the room. The scribe, Holstead, scurried like a mouse at his heels.

Timothy jumped to his feet as his stomach clenched. He had hoped he might slip out unnoticed and send his apologies later in a missive. "My lord, greetings."

"There you are, my boy. Good to see you back to work." The earl reached up and ruffled Timothy's hair.

Whatever in heaven and on earth? He had delivered no ghosts for the castle walls. The earl should be shouting and ranting to find him here at his post. He tensed lest a blow to the head might be coming next.

"I hear you stopped by your home."

Wonderful, now his prospects would be ruined throughout England, not only in Wyndeshire. Timothy held his breath and awaited his due berating.

Wyndemere chuckled. "I suppose anyone would be ready to return after a few days at that manor crawling with screaming brats."

What was this? Though he dared not relax, Timothy decided to ride out this odd turn in the impulsive earl's mood and see where it might take him. "It was not so bad as all that. They are rather a cheerful lot."

"Hmm. If you insist." The earl smacked him on the back and took a seat by the window. "You may sit, Grey."

Timothy turned his chair from the table to face the earl as Holstead stood patiently by. He might never understand the earl.

Lord Wyndemere crossed his legs and wrapped his hands around his knee. "I must say, you are looking a bit peaked. Is all well at home?"

Though his head spun at the odd turn of events, Timothy managed to answer with grace. "Indeed. My father sends his felicitations."

"Interesting. And you are feeling well?" The earl observed Timothy quizzically.

Timothy did not feel well. He had lost the love of his life along with his employment for good this time. He had managed to bumble everything. And now the earl made no sense. "Perhaps . . . perhaps I caught a chill in the forest," was the best he could come up with as an answer.

"I see." The earl frowned.

Here it came. Perhaps in all his responsibilities the man had forgotten for a time, but surely he would remember and punish Timothy now.

"So, any sign of the ghosts? Any rumors of them flying about Greyham?" Wyndemere flapped his hands like wings.

Timothy chose his words with discretion and looked the earl in the eye as he made his confession. "Nothing recent, I am afraid." He pressed his lips together tightly as he considered what to say next.

He must do something to keep Merry and the children safe.

Yet despite his shift in thinking, he could not bring himself to speak an outright falsehood to his lord. "Based upon the rumors, I would surmise they have moved camp and are no longer within our jurisdiction." That was the best he could do for them.

Dropping his head, Timothy continued, "I am sorry to have failed you in this. I have packed my bags as instructed and will be leaving once I have finalized a few last matters of business."

"Nonsense. I can hardly do without you." Wyndemere flicked at the air as though his previous threats had been naught but an annoying insect. "Search the area one more time, and we shall call this issue closed. It simply would not do to lose my best advisor over some illusory ghosts who may or may not even exist."

That was it? All of these days spent dreading his decision, and the earl had only been utilizing fear tactics to get his way? Although Timothy knew not if he wished to keep his employment under such a man, he would do nothing rash. Instead, he would exhibit the stalwart faithfulness and discretion he was known for until he could consider the matter further.

"Then I am at your service, my lord." But his muscles did not unwind, as he did not trust the fickle whims of the earl.

"And all is well here?" Wyndemere pointed to the table covered with parchments.

"It appears that Holstead has done an admirable job in my absence." Timothy eyed the earl with caution.

"Good then." Wyndemere patted his knees and stood. "I will leave the two of you to catch up on issues of business. Methinks I will be moving you officially into an administrative capacity in the coming months. Holstead can handle the scribe position."

A mere week ago, Timothy's heart would have leapt with excitement at that statement. But the words fell flat in his ears. Too much had changed. Beyond which, he feared this might yet be some sort of test. He responded as expected nonetheless.

"Thank you, my lord. You are most gracious. I will be happy to relieve you of some of your duties. I understand how taxing they can be."

"Indeed they are." The earl yawned and stretched. "And my evening activities have been quite taxing of late as well." He left the room without explanation.

Timothy turned his attention to Holstead and shrugged at the unfinished innuendo.

"New serving maid." Holstead completed the earl's insinuation.

Interesting. Timothy had not taken Holstead for a gossip, but perhaps it was not gossip, only honesty. Lord Wyndemere's exploits were hardly a secret. And perhaps the new serving maid explained the earl's sudden shift in mood. Despite Timothy's swirling thoughts over the morning's unexpected occurrences, he strove to give Holstead his full attention for the moment.

"Have a seat." Timothy indicated to the chair the earl had just vacated.

"Thank you." Holstead wrung his hands together. Unlike Timothy, he wore the more typical black hood and tunic of a scribe. His large brown eyes looked as though they might pop out of his rather narrow head at any moment. And his protruding teeth reinforced the mouse image his scurrying often brought to mind.

Timothy smiled. He could not help liking the earnest fellow.

Holstead situated himself. "I hope you found everything done to your satisfaction, sir . . . rather, Mister Grey."

The man's needless nervousness did much to ease Timothy's own tension as he strove to calm the man by creating a peaceful environment. "Yes, I have found your work to be quite organized and efficient. I really have no questions for you, other than, are you happy working here at the castle?"

If possible, Holstead's eyes grew even wider. "Why, of course."

"Good. And are your quarters satisfactory?" Timothy leaned back in his chair.

"I, well . . . Rather, that is it . . ." But Holstead seemed unable to finish his thought, so flustered he was by the personal question.

Timothy attempted a different approach. "Do you have any inquiries or reports for me?"

"No, sir. Only, sir . . . I hope you will not be terribly troubled, but I fear your missive to the king went out a day later than intended. I do not know how I missed it upon my desk that first day you were gone. But I sent it out straightaway the following day, as soon as I discovered it." He ducked his head and cowered, as if waiting for someone to strike him.

Timothy had no idea why the man might be worried. He could not even recall such a missive. "I am sorry. I do not understand."

Holstead dared to peek up at him. He clenched his hands in his lap. "The missive from you to the king. With your personal seal. You left it for me before your trip."

Timothy rubbed his chin and scanned his memory. He could recall no . . . No! It could not be. He had penned only one missive to the king. The missive safely tucked at the bottom of his chest. The very missive he now intended to burn. Though his own hands began to tremble at the possibility, he strove to maintain his composure. It would help nothing for him to fall to pieces before Holstead, nor to rant at the poor man.

He closed his eyes. Took several calming breaths, pressing his hands into his thighs to steady them. "Um . . . thank you, then."

"My pleasure."

A sharp pain dug into Timothy's head, nearly causing him to gasp. His fingers clawed deeper into his thighs. He had to know the truth. To search his chest and hold the volatile missive in his hands once again. He must be rid of this fellow. "You know, Holstead, his lordship was correct. I am feeling rather peaked. Would you mind if we continued this later?"

"Not at all. God give you good day, Mister Grey."

"And you as well," Timothy managed.

With an expression of relief, Holstead scurried from the room.

As soon as the door closed, Timothy rushed to the chest. He tossed books and parchments willy-nilly about the room in his need to reach the bottom. But he found nothing. The grey walls threatened to close in upon him. The ceiling seemed to press down and retreat several times in quick succession.

He scrubbed his hands about the sturdy wooden bottom of the chest, as if it might magically appear. But the missive begging Merry's pardon was not there. He pounded his fist against the chest and searched every document one more time. Words swam before his eyes as he read through parchment after parchment.

Nothing.

Timothy slumped onto the floor and buried his face in his hands. His head pounded like the anvil of the Viking's Thor, God of Thunder. He could barely find his breath. Gone! The missive was gone. He stared into his empty palms. What had he done?

The king would know that Merry still lived. And it was entirely his fault. She had been correct. He had indeed betrayed her. If Merry had not already put a death warrant upon his head, she would surely strangle him if she learned of this. And he would not for one moment blame her.

He struggled to calm himself. The king might grant the pardon, he reasoned. Perhaps he had done Merry a favor after all. Though given her new crimes, it might not serve much good in the end.

And given the earl's assessment of the king's recent mood . . .

Timothy dug his fingers into his throbbing temples in vain hope of relieving the pressure and the pain. He forced himself to finish the thought. Given the earl's assessment of the king's recent mood, he would most likely demand her found and hung.

There—that was the truth of it. Timothy slapped his palm against his head. What had he put into motion? And how had this happened? Someone in this castle must wish him ill, though he could not fathom who or why.

Holstead's nervousness had surpassed even his norm today. Timothy had never considered the man capable of foul play. But perhaps he had been desperate for work and fearful that Timothy would reclaim his scribe position. Or perhaps just plain jealous and spiteful, like the steward.

Bainard! He seemed the more likely suspect than the meek and gentle Holstead. But Timothy could not afford taking time to investigate who his enemy might be. He must get to Merry before tragedy struck. He would tell Lord Wyndemere he would soon leave for his final search. He must maintain his position in the hopes he might be able to use it to help Merry and the children in any way. Even if she ordered him killed, he must risk it.

An oath slipped from John's mouth. Whatever was Timothy Grey doing rushing off once again? How sickness had welled in his stomach when the man pranced into the castle—not at all dead. But now as he watched Timothy dash into the stable, a suspicion . . . or rather a hope, sparked within him.

Timothy's casual return followed by his quick departure could only mean one thing. His enemy must be in league with the ghosts. Else how could he have survived their camp? Though the fact that he'd entered the camp unconscious suggested he must have struck a deal with them while there, that perhaps they had offered him a cut of that chest of gold coin they were rumored to have stolen. His heart soared as he pondered the ramifications. He would see to it that the man was not only killed, but also disgraced. A much better fate than he had dared to hope for.

He waited, and moments later, Timothy emerged on his mammoth horse and galloped out the castle gates. To the ghosts, no doubt. Perhaps to warn them of something he had learned since his return.

But no amount of warning would suffice. John had set matters into motion that could not be undone. He had known in his gut that the mysterious young woman must hold a key, and when he had searched Timothy's office after his departure, he discovered just how right he had been. John held back his laughter in this public place.

No doubt Timothy thought him an uneducated fool, but he was not. John's mother had seen him instructed by their parish priest, hoping that someday his father might relent and claim his illegitimate son. After all, the man had no legal heir of his own body. She had wanted John to be prepared to impress his father with his wit and capabilities, but matters had not turned out that way. Instead, he'd been forced to survive on brute strength while Timothy Grey enjoyed the luxuries of the castle.

He had, however, studied his namesake, the king, his entire life. No one knew better than King John of England how ruthless determination and a bit of time could turn matters around. The man had not let the misfortune of birth order stop him. No, he allowed nothing to stand in his path as he strove toward greatness. And John would not let his own illegitimate birth stand in his way.

A bitter taste filled his mouth, and he spat upon the ground. When he'd spotted the missive to the king he had nearly fainted in delight, but he managed to gather himself, seal it with the stamp Timothy had left behind, and place it on Holstead's desk. Though he had been tempted to add a postscript that this same Merry Ellison might have some link to the nefarious Ghosts of Farthingale Forest, he refrained. No, he would hold some leverage for the future.

Soon the king would know that Timothy had harbored the fugitive Merry Ellison. It would not take long before the king discovered Timothy had let her go and began unraveling other clues about Timothy's attachment to the woman—and his involvement with the ghosts.

And who would be the hero in it all? When the time was right, John would lead them to the ghosts and win his father's favor. With any luck, Merry would be put to death before Timothy, so his enemy might suffer the ultimate heartache of losing the woman he loved due to his own blundering actions.

But until then, John would wait, and plan, and revel in his imminent most perfect revenge.

Chapter 25

In the shadowy sleeping chamber at the rear of the cave, Merry found herself completely alone for the first time in weeks. And she was not at all certain that she liked the sensation. How much better to keep herself busy. Senses on the alert as she guarded the camp or tended to the little ones.

Being alone in nature was different. The sunshine, the breeze, the scurry of animals, and the avian symphony filled her to overflowing and kept her company. Here, in this dark and quiet room, nothing but empty silence—without even a trickle of water or a distinctive scent—surrounded her.

But she must take advantage of this rare moment. Use it to face the demons that threatened her day and night, that she held at bay with busyness. In the corner near her pallet lay a sack she rarely opened. A sack of items her mother had packed for her on that horrible night. It felt as if it weighed a thousand pounds as she tugged it into the open. The drawstring seemed to fight against her fingers.

She reached her hand in as though a snake might bite her.

First, she withdrew a tiny piece of white linen, embroidered with scrollwork. Her christening gown. Once upon a time, this meant something to her—proof of her identity. She was a Christian. Baptized into the holy church. She had strived to make her life an act of worship in the eyes of her Creator.

Merry ran her fingers across the linen and sighed. But what did it mean now? Would the church even welcome her? Thank goodness the king had no proof of her survival. To her knowledge he had not yet had them excommunicated. She might doubt the existence of God, but if for some reason He did exist, she was not convinced she wished to be cut off from Him for eternity.

Gathering her courage, Merry reached even deeper into the bag. She pulled out a stack of parchments bound in leather. The book of Matthew, which she had copied in her own hand. Though she held tight to the book, she could not bring herself to open it and read the Latin words. Words that had once radiated so vibrant and precious to her that she had dealt with the torture of sitting still long enough to write them down. She could not bear to watch them lying flat and lifeless on the page now.

With a deep breath she stilled her racing heart and sent her hand into the gaping chasm of the sack one last time. She brushed about the bottom of the velvet bag until she found it. Her fingers rubbed over the raised metal, pressed into the biting edges. Though they had spent the coins and sold several pieces of jewelry from the sack early on, she could not bring herself to part with this final memento from her mother.

She drew it slowly, cautiously from the sack. As her eyes fell upon it, she made the sign of the cross despite herself. Jesus—battered and bloody, pinned to the crucifix—stared up at her from her palm. Whether he had been a deity or not, surely the man had known suffering and pain. More than she could imagine.

Unable to resist, she pressed the crucifix to her lips, recalled the rugged feel and the sharp taste from the many times she had done so in her childhood as it dangled over her mother's soft and comforting bosom. And in that moment, she could almost sense her mother smiling down at her from heaven.

Merry placed the book and the gown back in the sack, but she could not bring herself to part with the cross. Though its matching gold chain was long gone, she found a piece of twine and hung it from her neck, buried it deep beneath her tunic.

She needed her mother's strength. For finding Timothy again, feeling those sensations all over, then hardening her heart to send him away, had sapped her of her last reserves. She had never felt so weak. So vulnerable. She did not like it one whit.

Curling into her pallet, she pressed both hands against her tunic to experience the impression of the cross upon her belly. She thought that perhaps, if nothing else, the memory of her mother's death would remind her of what was at stake. King John was not above killing them all. Timothy did not understand this—therefore he could never be trusted.

A scuffle near the entryway wakened her from that introspective place and turned her attention to the issues at hand. Sniffling met her ears.

Heavens, one of the children might be hurt.

"You tell her." Sadie's words were followed by a sob.

"No—you. She likes you better," said a voice Merry suspected to be Sadie's brother, Henry, along with a loud sniff. "I can't bear to speak the words."

Merry jumped up and ran to them. Almost to the end of the passageway, lit by sunshine filtering through the door of leaves and branches beyond, stood Sadie and Henry with muddy, tear-streaked faces.

When Sadie spotted her, her confession tumbled from her mouth. "We tried to, Merry. We did. We both did. We meant to, but . . ." She dissolved into uncontrollable sobs and could say no more.

Merry hugged the girl to her. "Henry, what could you not do? Please tell me."

"We couldn't kill him. We knew it was the right thing to do. We both pulled back our arrows and aimed them straight for his heart, like you said. But neither of us could let go. 'You do it,' Sadie says. 'No you,' says I. Then we both started crying and ran straight to you."

"Who?" asked Merry, although she suspected, nay dreaded, the answer.

"Timothy Grey."

Her heart thudded to her feet. How had he found them? Never mind that now. "Where?"

"Coming . . ." Henry hesitated as if he did not wish to answer but finally continued. "From the south."

"He was kind . . . and funny . . . and . . ." Sadie sputtered the words against Merry's soon to be drenched tunic.

"Where are the men?" Merry reached and offered Henry's head a reassuring pat.

"Still out hunting."

"'Tis all right, children. We should not have left you on watch alone. It was too much to ask. I will take care of this."

"Don't kill him. Don't!" Sadie shrieked, clawing at Merry's tunic.

With that, Jane, cooking at the far side of the room, hurried toward them.

Merry handed off the wailing child. "Tend to her, please. Timothy Grey has returned."

"Must you kill him? Truly?" Jane hugged Sadie to her chest. A bevy of little ones and young women behind her whimpered and gasped.

Merry steeled her heart to a degree she did not know possible. She gulped down a lump from her throat, and it landed with a sick thud in her stomach. She struggled to keep down her morning meal. "Please do not make this any harder than it already is," she whispered to Jane.

She sensed no less than twenty eyes digging into her as she took her bow and quiver from the wall, but no one uttered a word. She dared not look into those eyes. Dared not witness the horror upon their faces.

The time had come. She must do what she must do. She must not question.

Like a ghost, she floated from the room, out the door, and up the hillside. She watched as though outside of her body as she pulled an arrow from her quiver and nocked it to the bowstring. Scanning the countryside, she found him, though she wished she had not.

Daring not to look too close, she lifted her bow and stared down the shaft of the arrow, pointing directly to the center of his blue velvet tunic. She would not focus upon his face. She would not look into his eyes. He must remain an object. An enemy. A weapon of destruction. And in just a moment, when she finally let the arrow fly free, the danger would be eliminated.

Eliminated. Danger. Not Timothy. Not the boy she had loved and kissed. Never her best friend. *He is the enemy.* She fought to convince herself as her finger trembled against the bowstring, as she stared at the deep blue velvet.

"Merry!" he called.

In a moment of great weakness, she lifted her eyes to his. Those beautiful blue-grey eyes. That face she had adored for much of her life. The flopping thatch of hair. And all was lost.

She dropped the bow and arrow to the ground, as the air deflated from her lungs. Collapsing next to her discarded weapons, she pressed a hand to her chest. No one would ever know how close she had come. How hard her heart had grown, that she could nearly kill her best friend.

Her sickened stomach cast up its accounts upon the grass beside her, and her hands clutched her aching belly. Then she felt it beneath her tunic. The cross. A picture of her mother with soft brown hair and love-filled eyes flashed through her mind.

No, her mother would never wish to see her as cold and callous as this. Merry had nearly gone too far this time.

"Merry, Merry." Timothy ran up beside her, dropped to his knees, and gathered her into his arms. "Are you all right?"

"I . . ." She struggled to find her breath. "I . . . I almost did it." Then she sagged against him and began to cry. Deep body-wrenching sobs. Wails to put Sadie's to shame. Years' worth of tears, pouring onto his chest.

His lips pressed against her forehead, but he said not a word. Rather, he allowed her to spend her pent-up heartache within his arms. All this time she had remained so strong. Now Timothy could be strong for her. Strong enough to hold her and comfort her. Strong enough to share the heavy load of her pain. Shushing and snuggling her like the broken child she was.

When Allen and Red entered the dim cave after a long morning of hunting, a passel of crying children met them.

Abigail threw herself against Allen dramatically. "Merry is killing Timothy!" She shrieked and commenced sobbing upon his tunic. Allen had little choice but to pat her back and offer soothing shushing sounds. Good thing they had deposited the rabbit carcasses outside the door. Red was likewise entangled with Sadie. Allen scanned the room and shot a questioning look at Jane where she cuddled Wren along with several of the other youngsters.

Her horrified nod said everything.

Merry kill Timothy? Surely she would never. He and the other men had discussed and dismissed her kill order days ago, each of them convinced that she would despise anyone who carried it through. She would never forgive them. But what if she carried it through herself?

A dull ache filled Allen's stomach at the thought. He must find her. He must stop her. Timothy did not deserve death, and Merry's heart would never survive if she murdered him.

Red stared at Allen with dread written across his face. "What shall we do?"

"Which way did she go?" Allen asked.

Between hiccups, Sadie pointed to the south.

Henry stood from where he had huddled in the corner and wiped at his grimy, tear-streaked face. "'Tis all my fault. I saw him first. I should have warned him away when I had the chance. But I could never shoot him, and I didn't believe Lady Merry would either."

"You did right, Henry. Never fear, Red and I will see to this." He pried Abigail from his waist. "You all stay put. And pray with all your strength."

Allen thrust aside the many emotions warring within him. Sympathy, dread, fear, jealousy, anger. Why must this Timothy forever stir up trouble? But Allen could not afford the luxury of emotions. He grabbed his sword and shield from the wall, and noticed Red doing likewise. They still wore their quivers and bows from the morning hunt.

Together they dashed through the doorway and toward the south.

He gripped his sword, knowing not what might lie over the

rise. Not that a weapon would help. Who did he think to fight? Timothy's ghost? Merry's devastation? Yet the feel of the molded hilt in his palm gave him strength.

Which he would need. The sound of Merry's wailing met his ears, a soul-crushing sound the likes of which he had never heard before. Again he quelled those churning emotions. As they crested the second hill, the sight that met his eyes comforted him yet shook him to the core all in the same instant.

Timothy held Merry in his arms as she keened with abandon against his chest. Her thin body convulsed with each sob. Merry was safe. Timothy was alive. Yet that moment brought death nonetheless. The final death blow to Allen's dreams of a life with Merry. How many times had he wished to soothe Merry, to comfort her, to share her burden. But she would not allow him. Not him, only Timothy, the man who held her heart.

Before his eyes he saw proof of what he had known deep down all along. Merry was not meant for him. She belonged to another.

His sword arm sagged as the truth struck him in the gut like a battering ram. Timothy took note of Allen and Red and nodded their way, as if to say all was well. But nothing might ever be well again.

Red must have sensed the significance of the moment. For he wrapped a sturdy arm around Allen's shoulder and turned him in the direction of camp.

A camp that might never feel like home to Allen again.

Timothy watched the sun travel a goodly distance across the sky before Merry cried the last of her tears upon his sodden chest. How wonderful to hold her in his arms. Warm despite the cool breeze. To see the soft, vulnerable girl he remembered.

To cuddle her close and wipe tears from her silken cheeks with his thumbs. He must treasure every moment, for it could not last much longer.

She hiccupped and spoke for the first time in the better part of an hour. "I nearly killed you. Oh, Timothy, why did you risk it? Can you ever forgive me?" Her doe eyes begged him to understand.

The moment that had filled him with dark, sickening dread had arrived. He could put it off no longer. "Do not apologize, for once I explain why I have come, you might kill me yet."

Merry struggled as if to sit up but then collapsed into him again. "What do you mean?"

"You were right. I did not intend to, but I have proven a danger to you. I had to warn you at once."

She covered her face with her hands. "This sounds dire. Do I even want to know?"

"I am afraid you must hear it. Before you left the castle my father convinced me to write a missive to the king begging him to forgive you."

"Tell me you did not."

"I did, but I never sent it. I had no peace about it. Instead I buried it deep in a chest of documents. Once Lord Wyndemere returned, he confirmed my decision, saying he had never seen the king in such a foul mood."

"Why do I sense a horrible *but* is coming?" She peeked between her fingers.

"But . . . I fear I have an enemy in the castle. Just this morning as I planned to burn it, I discovered that someone sent it while I was here."

He closed his eyes and winced. He tensed himself to receive the brunt of her fury. The glaring flame of her anger. But nothing. He cracked open one eye. If anything, she sank even deeper into his chest. It seemed her tears had drained her of all fight. She did not speak nor even flinch. A dazed expression crossed her face.

He opened the other eye and dared to proceed. "By now the king knows that you are alive. And some of the children as well."

She shivered and seemed to grow smaller in his arms. "What should I do?" Her voice rang frail.

Moments earlier he had been enraptured to see her so soft and open, but this broken girl had no emotional armor to face his news. He sat her up gently and wiped the new influx of tears from her cheeks. "Merry, you must snap out of this. You and the children are safe for the moment. No one knows where you are. I am safe. You did not hurt me. You must let that go."

With a shake of her head, she ran her hands over her face, and appeared to come back into herself. "You are right. I cannot afford such weakness." He watched as a hardness fell back over her features, as her muscles firmed and her eyes grew sharp. "Do you have a plan?" she asked.

"I must return to the castle before dark. My guess is, we will hear something very soon. The missive went out the day after you captured me. Nearly a week has passed, and the king's retinue is a mere three days journey away."

"We must pack. We must be ready to move."

"Precisely, but go nowhere yet. We must not assume the worst. It could be good news. I will return tomorrow evening, to this spot, and bring you word. Either you will be free at long last, and I shall take you all to Greyham Manor, or if need be, I shall see you safely to France, and we shall live together there."

She disentangled herself from his arms. "Do not speak madness. You cannot leave your home, your family, for us. It is too much to ask. Trust me—I know. You would resent me for the rest of our lives."

He pressed his forehead to hers. "No, Merry. I will love you for the rest of my life."

She pushed him away, a spark of anger finally flaring in her eyes. "Stop it! I insist. Stop it this instant. I will not allow you to make matters worse than they are."

He sighed and raked his fingers through his hair. "Let us not fight about this now. At least wait until we have a reason. We know not what the future will hold. And we have been through enough upheaval this day. We can fight on the morrow."

Her shoulders sagged. "Agreed. Go. Wait for word from the king."

He brushed his fingers along her cheek and swiped her hair behind her ear. "But I meant what I said. I do love you." He pressed his lips to her cheek, then turned and dashed into the woods before she could argue with him again.

Chapter 26

The next day, Lord Wyndemere came up behind Timothy as he traversed the dim hallway en route to the great hall for the nooning meal. "There you are, my boy." The earl clamped a hand onto Timothy's shoulder. "When I told you to check for the ghosts one last time, I did not expect you to run off straightaway."

Timothy cleared his throat. He had hoped to avoid this conversation. "I . . . well that is . . ." He must not betray the children. "I am afraid I received some rather disturbing news. I thought to clear my head in the forest."

"I see. Female troubles? Not about to be a father, are you? Heavens, do I know that awful feeling." The earl squeezed his shoulder and chuckled in a suggestive manner.

Timothy shook off the unwanted information. "No, not quite. The news just caught me off guard. 'Tis nothing, really." Nothing other than betraying the woman he loved to the king. He fought back a sigh of weariness. And now he must await the ramifications of his actions.

"So no ghosts, I take it."

Again, Timothy searched for an answer. "Nary a haunt nor a spirit in sight."

"Good. Good, then."

They entered the noisy great hall together, and the earl ushered him to the front table upon the dais. "Sit with me. We have matters of business to discuss."

"Of course, my lord." Timothy situated himself upon the bench to the right of the earl.

As the lord greeted the steward to his left, Timothy battled his troubling thoughts. His fears that Merry might die as a result of his carelessness and stupidity. No, he must not give in to despair. Like Merry herself, he must gather his fighting spirit. Either the news would be good, and they would rejoice together, or it would be bad, and he would get her out of the country.

He would need to leave at meal's end if he wished to make his appointed rendezvous with Merry. Though sadly, he would have nothing to report. It seemed they would have to wait yet another day for word from the king.

The steward glared at him over Lord Wyndemere's shoulder. Timothy still did not understand why the man despised him so. He quirked a questioning brow in return, wondering again if the steward might have been the one to find his missive for the king. Until Timothy uncovered his enemy, neither he nor his loved ones would be safe. He must take the man aside and question him soon.

A messenger dashed up to the table, panting and out of breath. "My lord, an urgent missive from the king."

Timothy tensed. This might be the one.

Wyndemere frowned to have his meal disturbed before it even started but reached for the parchment and broke the seal. He unrolled the scroll and perused it, but likely could not decipher much. The steward peered over the earl's shoulder, and the earl shot him a glare in return. "Timothy, could you please take a look at this and see if I must abandon my meal over it?"

Timothy took the parchment with trembling hands and forced himself to read the words.

My Dear Robbie,

Are you aware of this mess with Merry Ellison? I thought the chit long dead. I assumed the rumors of her survival to be greatly exaggerated, but your man, a Timothy Grey, informs me otherwise. The fellow begged for her forgiveness. He seemed a goodhearted, if addle-brained, sort. But as you and I well know, we cannot show weakness in such situations.

As I am still ill, I shall leave this matter to you. The girl is to be captured and hung at once. I imagine she shall make a pretty sight upon the city walls. This act shall finally strike fear in the hearts of the rebels—convince them once and for all that I am entirely without mercy. I will try to visit while she rots, as it would bring me great pleasure to do so. Her father was the one to start this blasted rebellion after all.

No weakness. Never surrender. I know I can trust you with this matter.

King John of England

Timothy's stomach grew sicker and sicker as he read. A familiar thumping began in his head. "My lord, I must speak to you alone, at once."

"Dear, dear, just as I feared." He turned to the steward. "Await serving the meal until I return."

Timothy tucked the scroll under his arm, and he and Lord Wyndemere walked to the hallway.

The earl dismissed the guards from the area and sent them to their meal. Once they were alone, he said, "Well, spit it out. No use putting off bad news."

He attempted to straighten his thoughts between the rhythmic thumping of his head. "Do you recall the situation with Merry Ellison?"

"I thought we were in agreement that we were glad she had left."

"Yes, and I never sent the missive to the king." Timothy rubbed at his temple. "But it seems someone else did while I was gone."

"Good heavens. Why?"

"I know not. Perhaps I have an enemy at the castle. Holstead informed me he found it on his desk and dispatched it, but I swear to you that I never put it there."

The earl tapped a finger against his cheek. "And this is the king's response, I take it."

"Yes." Timothy dropped his head. "He bids you to find her and hang her."

The earl growled. "This is precisely what I did not wish to happen."

"I know, my lord." Timothy's eyes remained downcast.

"Look at me when I speak to you."

Timothy returned his gaze to the earl's red face, though all the blood now drained from his own face, and an icy coldness overtook him. He had ruined everything.

A vein throbbed near the man's balding temple. "I shall have to put up wanted posters and send out a search team by tomorrow. You have left me no choice."

"I understand." Timothy fought to maintain his composure. He wanted nothing more than to dash off and warn Merry.

"Where do you suggest I start the search?"

Here was his chance to help them. "I suppose you should sweep the area near the castle and work slowly outward."

"Hmm . . . I will do as you suggest." The earl shrugged his shoulders and gestured toward the castle exit. "So what are you waiting for? I assume you must go and do a precursory examination of the area. Why are you just standing about? I can put this off no longer than the morrow."

Timothy shook his head. Surely he had not heard correctly. "Go on, my boy. Quickly." The earl shoved him by the shoulder.

The earl knew. He was allowing them a head start. Timothy wasted not another moment but took off toward the stables.

After being rather rudely dismissed from the hallway, John joined the other castle guards in the great hall. Whispers filled the place that the earl had received a missive from the king. This must be it, the moment he had been waiting for. The king would never forgive Merry Ellison. John knew his type. John was his type. His very namesake. His own mother had named him after his father's best friend while Richard still lived, and had been delighted when John became a king.

She thought for certain that the Earl of Wyndemere would relent in time and accept his only son, legitimate or not. An educated, strong son, named for the king himself. No such luck. The best the earl would do was give him work as a guard in his castle, but the man never so much as nodded in his direction. Every time the earl ignored him, he felt the betrayal like a stab to the gut all over again.

And when he favored that wretched Timothy Grey in his stead, John just wanted to wrap his hands about the man's throat and watch his eyes bulge out as he breathed his last.

Timothy had always thought himself so much better, so much

higher. But John would bring him down. He sidled his way closer to the hallway.

The earl returned alone and did not so much as glance in John's direction. Where had Timothy gone? Why had he not heard the earl berating him? He waited to see if the man would make an announcement, but he merely gestured to the steward to begin the meal.

Duties be hanged! John could not allow Timothy to slip off into the forest without him once again. Surely he was headed back to the ghosts. John could not afford to let them get away.

Making a mad dash for the courtyard, he spied Timothy slipping through the castle gates upon his horse. Without pausing even to pack a sack, he hurried to the stables. His weapons and the forest would suffice for his needs. He would not follow his enemy too closely, but he had been raised in those woods as well, and he would have no problem trailing the man.

He must see Merry and her outlaw band hanged. He would destroy his enemy in the most painful, most humiliating manner he could possibly devise.

After a day of frantic activity, a sort of despondent lethargy had fallen over the camp. Merry settled under a tree on the hillside, pressing herself into the cool, moist earth, wishing she could become one with it and somehow stay in this beautiful land of her birth.

Though the older members of the group tried to convince the little ones otherwise, no one believed that King John would pardon them. And the tears of the youngest children as they packed had just about torn Merry's heart from her chest. "Me like me cave house!" Wren had protested. She had said it with that rasp in her voice that Merry dreaded so much.

At least the packing had gone quickly. With each move they had traveled with less and less. This time they would take only clothing, personal effects, and some food supplies. Whether enough to travel to Greyham Manor or to the port in Bristol was still to be determined, but Merry braced herself for the latter.

The camp lay still and inconspicuous at the bottom of the hill. Smells of rabbit stew with vegetables wafted up to Merry, but she had no stomach for food. Worn out after all their tears, many of the little ones had napped about the fire when she left. Merry understood. Exhaustion from yesterday's torrential outburst still niggled at her. But she must not give in to it.

She had no anger left to waste on Timothy. He had meant well, and he had merely hastened the inevitable. Soon Merry's life would return to some sort of normalcy, whether in England or in France. Just another day, or week, or fortnight at the most as a battle-hardened thief. Then what would she be? Just a girl again.

The memory of Timothy's chest in her sights blasted into her mind, and she shuddered. No one would ever know how close she had come to committing the unthinkable, how hard her heart had grown. But those tears had torn down her defenses. Somehow she must find a balance. A way to be strong and stand firm without growing bitter and heartless. She must never allow herself to do that again.

Rubbing her hand over her tunic and the rough outline of the crucifix, she realized, even worse, she had hardened her heart toward God. But she did not know what to do about that. If He did indeed exist, where had He been all these years? These years when she had turned a criminal, no doubt earning even more of His wrath.

Surely she would not be pardoned by the king, but in the spirit of considering every contingency, she must at least think through the possibility. She could barely imagine a free life in England, so long ago had she given up on the idea. But forced to ponder the issue, she realized that a small chance existed that she might still marry Timothy Grey and raise a family with him.

Her heart clenched so tight at the thought, she could not endure it. Nor could she find her breath for a moment. Love was a daunting prospect indeed. Her hands began to tremble. But Merry knew how to deal with such weakness of the flesh. Before long, she had herself under control and the idea pushed far from her mind once again.

A lone figure slipped out of the cave and headed toward her. Allen, with his big open heart and a big smile covering his face to match. He waved to her. She did not understand how he had kept his faith in God throughout all they had endured. How had he kept his heart gentle and hopeful, even as he accompanied her on mission after mission?

If Merry were a gambling woman, she would lay huge stakes on Allen being the more likely man in her future, for she would never allow Timothy to follow her to France. It would seem a romantic gesture at the first, but he would resent her for it before long—grow bitter, as she had, at the loss of family, home, and country. Besides, if their band was forced to make a new life in a new country, they must do so together, without dragging outsiders along.

Allen plopped down beside her and picked at the grass by his feet. "So, I guess we're ready, whatever might come our way."

Merry turned her gaze to the hazy sky above them. "I guess we are."

He shifted toward her, but she continued to focus on the sky, which appeared ready to unleash rain. She hoped Timothy would make it with an answer before the storm. "How do you do it, Allen?"

"Do what?"

"You have no guilt. You steal one day and approach God so boldly the next."

He picked up a stone and threw it. "God judges the heart. My heart is clean. I do it for the children, not my own selfish gain. And the laws of this country are so turned upon their heads, who could ever be innocent according to them? No, God's laws prevail."

"And the Ten Commandments say 'Thou shalt not steal,'" Merry reminded him.

"And Jesus says to love God with all your heart, and love your neighbor as yourself." He yanked a few more pieces of grass from the ground. "You were right in that tree. We got a bit carried away in our theft from the herbalist. So I paid him back the day we rescued you."

"You did not!" Good Allen with his good heart. Hers was not so clean.

"I did."

So much for stealth and anonymity, but she would not fault him for following his conscience.

"Merry . . . ?" Allen waited quietly for her response.

The tenor in his voice made her wary. Nonetheless, she looked him in the eye. "Yes."

"Are you going to tell me what happened yesterday?"

"I already did. I almost shot Timothy, but I could not." She steeled herself against a chilling wave of regret.

"What if one of us had done it? Would you have forgiven us?"

Merry tucked her knees to her chest. "I suppose I would have had to. It was my order, after all."

"And what was the scene with you crying in his arms?" Allen poked at the ground with a stick.

"You saw that, did you?"

"We checked on you, to make sure you were all right. Were you?"

That exhaustion niggled at Merry again. How she longed to close her eyes and curl into the moist ground for a long nap like the little ones enjoyed by the fire.

"Were you all right?" Allen persisted.

"I nearly killed my best friend. I was not all right. And once I started crying . . . well . . ." She could not bring herself to finish the statement. Her heart ached too badly at the memory.

"I understand. You cried all the tears you have been holding back for years. You felt safe with him. Someone from your childhood. But, Merry . . ." He lifted her chin and turned her toward him. "I could have been strong for you."

She wrapped her arm through his and rested her head upon his firm shoulder. "I know you could have. I just . . . 'Tis force of habit, I suppose, to be strong with all of you. Being with Timothy brings me back to a time when I was a girl. Tough and strong to be certain, but with a feminine side and gentle heart as well."

"I should like to see that side."

She smiled up at him. "Perhaps someday you shall. Perhaps once we are settled in France."

He bent down to place a kiss upon her hooded head. A brotherly gesture, and she realized she still thought of him thus. As a brother. But with time and a bit of determination, he might be more.

"Would you like me to stay with you?" Allen squeezed the hand tucked into his arm.

"Honestly, I would like to be alone. Once we start our journey, I might not get much time to think."

"As you wish."

He left her and made his way back to the camp.

Merry picked up the stick he had stuck into the ground. She had not written a word since her time in the castle. An urge hit her to fetch writing supplies, but she could not indulge in such silliness at a time like this. What would she say if she held a quill pen in her hand?

> This fertile ground, so moist with tears.
> Once hard with bitterness and strife,
> Once bound to hold in pain and fears,
> Now broken by the trials of life.
>
> How to beat, to pump anew?
> This heart so fragile waits in me.
> How to send warm blood, renew?
> Face the truth and set me free.

Chapter 27

Timothy had galloped most of the way through the rugged forest terrain to get word to Merry as quickly as possible. And there she sat, just ahead, a slender shadow on the next rise, waiting for him against the setting gold-and-orange ball of sunshine. She expected him this time, and no one had reason to follow him . . . yet.

He dismounted and took the last ten yards on foot. She did not move but awaited him with chin resting on her knees. Somewhere during the long ride, his tension and sickness had turned to numb dread. He must rally himself to face the awful task of telling her.

"It is not good news," she said, without so much as flinching from her position, sparing him from speaking the words.

"Did my face give me away?" He had hoped to break it to her gently, but so much for that.

"It did not have to. I know King John better than I wish."

Timothy slumped to the ground beside her. There was not much left to say. "Are you ready to move?"

"Yes. But I will not allow you to come with us. You may as well accept it. I have always had the stronger will."

Though she was right, he could not let her win so easily. "Or so I let you think."

A gentle smile crossed her face, the likes of which he had not seen since he found her again.

It gave him courage. "Before we argue logistics, there is something I must say to you. I was wrong. I see that now. You are correct. God stands upon the side of right. Upon the side of the poor and oppressed. One need look no further than Jesus' Sermon on the Mount to see it."

She rubbed a hand against her stomach, though he did not understand why. "Or perhaps God is merely a figment of our hopeful imaginations." But her words did not contain the bitterness he had sensed last time.

"I do not believe so. I believe He is real. And if I truly believe that, then I must live my convictions. I made a grave error in supporting a ruthless monarch, but I will do so no longer. You were right—if good men will not stand against injustice, we have no hope."

She ducked her head between her arms, where they rested on her knees. "Or perhaps therein lies the real truth. We have no hope. We live out our lives upon this evil earth, then we die and go to nothingness. Perhaps life is a cruel joke. A game of illusions and shadows."

Though tempted to do so himself, he must not let her give up her fight so easily. He must find strength for both of them. He sat up straighter and leaned toward her. "Merry, it wounds me to hear you speak this way. I know that I have let you down, but I will do so no longer. The government has let you down. The church has let you down. But God has not. Look at what you have built here." He gestured to their camp.

"Exactly. Look at what *I* have built. I did this. I took charge. I educated them. Where was God in all of that?" Her voice sounded of a sad little child.

"You think yourself that smart. That resourceful. What of Wren's sunshine men?"

She looked up with shock in her eyes. "They are not real."

He stroked a knuckle over her finely chiseled cheekbone. "What if they are? What if God has been here, providing and protecting all along?"

Confusion clouded her face. "But . . . I . . . you cannot begin to think that . . ." She pressed her hands to her temples.

He merely quirked a brow at her. The thought that the sunshine men might be God's heavenly hosts had not left him since those mystical men led Wren his way in the forest.

"We are thieves, Timothy. Have you lost your mind?"

"You were unjustly outlawed. You did your best under trying circumstances. God forgives, and He looks to the heart. You have a good heart, Merry. Loving, protecting—under normal circumstances, even forgiving. You have allowed your heart to grow hard. Your true heart is still there, though, underneath it all. You are simply afraid to let it out."

She bit her lip. "You know me too well." Shifting uncomfortably, she restored some distance between them. "I hope you are right. About everything. Oh, Timothy, I am so afraid. Afraid for all of us. Terrified I will make a mistake and let them down."

"Shh." He reached to stroke her back. "You are not alone. I will stand for justice. I will stand for you. And I believe with all my heart that God has been here as well. Though you did not wish to see it."

She sighed. "Perhaps you are right."

He sent up a silent prayer that she might accept the truth, and in that truth be set free.

Merry gazed at the handsome face of Timothy Grey. The sun had sunk during their brief exchange, the warm golden glow seeping to the harsher tones of silver moonlight. It played along his pale brows and lashes, created an enticing shimmer along his plump lower lip.

For only a moment today she had allowed herself to consider the possibility of a future with him, and somehow in that moment she had lost her resolve to shut him out. Her body trembled at his nearness. Her cheek and back still tingled from his touches.

Love shone from his eyes as clear and bright as the moonlight above them. He would never leave her willingly, but she would find a way to escape him. She would not rob him of his birthright as she had been so cruelly stripped of hers. And she could not give him what he wished for. Neither her promise of love nor a declaration of belief in God. So she said nothing.

She could no longer avoid his intense stare, though. Nor did she wish to. She allowed him to gaze deep into her soul. This one last time.

When he reached for her and wrapped his hand about that vulnerable place at the nape of her neck, it felt as natural as the tides ebbing or seasons changing. As he lowered his lips, nothing could have seemed more right, more true. His lips touched hers, warm and gentle at first, like that kiss so long ago. But they were no longer youngsters at play.

Something shifted, and their lips moved in a hungry dance. He pressed her body to his with a fervor she had never dared imagine. Too many years, too much distance, too many lost dreams all spilled into that kiss, as for one brief moment, they drank deep of each other's souls.

Merry found the resolve to break off first, and she leaned her forehead against his.

"I love you, Merry," he whispered.

She attempted to slow her panting breath. Now *that* was one perfect kiss to last a lifetime. But she could not let him hear the farewell in her voice, lest he never allow her out of his sight. "We have so much to plan. You must return to the castle. Collect your belongings. Write to your family."

"As much as I hate to part from you, even for a time, I agree." She held back her sigh of relief.

He straightened to full alert and scanned the darkening forest. "And if at all possible, I must find my enemy. I hate to leave an unknown threat behind."

Merry stood and brushed herself off. "Yes, and you will travel much faster on horseback than I shall on foot with all these children."

He stood, smiled, and took her by the shoulders. "So you will let me come after all."

"I cannot waste time arguing otherwise." She hoped he would not detect the strain in her answering smile nor the careful wording of her statement.

"Let us go and map your journey to Bristol. You can wait there with my Aunt Isabel if I do not find you first along the way. She will have plenty of room for us all."

"Your aunt? Are you certain?" Merry did not wish to put the woman in danger, not that she had any real plans to stop there. No, they would make their way straight to the port before Timothy could find them.

He placed another quick kiss on the tip of her nose. "She has been a secret rebel for years. She and my uncle have ample guards at their castle to protect you." Unlike Merry's nearby widowed aunt, who oversaw only a small manor home.

Timothy's plan held merit, but she would stick to her own. She would not allow him to throw his life into the rubbish heap.

"You must keep to the woods, of course, but I shall point you to a village halfway called Farmingham that supports the rebels." Timothy led her down the hill toward camp. "You can get supplies there, if needed. I do not think they will betray you to the king, though the Earl of Wyndemere will send out wanted posters tomorrow, so you must exercise caution. Send one of your men in your stead."

What had he just said? Merry halted her downhill progression as her mind digested the strange words. "The earl has not acted yet?"

Timothy's grin spread even wider across his face. "No. It seems the world is not as harsh and hopeless as you imagine it. The king placed your arrest in the Earl of Wyndemere's hands. And he has given us a one-day head start."

That warmth of hope blossomed in her chest again. Not everyone wished to see her dead. Perhaps somehow, against all odds, they would make it safely to France. But they would do so without Timothy Grey—she would not ruin his life.

Merry moved through the early morning shadows. Though dawn broke over the horizon, thick clouds held the emerging sunlight at bay. As she turned back to the camouflaged camp one last time, the story of Lot's wife came to mind. How hard it was to leave one's home, even a temporary one. She had had such hope for this place. But no choice remained. They must leave England for good.

She attempted to distract Wren, who dangled from her back, with a happy song. Merry did not think she could take more tears from the child this morning. She feared she might break down herself.

> "Summer is a coming.
> Loudly sing, cuckoo.
> Seeds grow and meadows blossom.
> Sing again, cuckoo!"

As she sang the words, her eyes adjusted to the dim morning light, and she kept close watch over their departure. Each person over six carried his own pack. The young women took care of their own belongings, plus one child apiece. And the men carried supplies. The gold coins, which would buy their passage aboard the ship and launch their new life in France, had been split among the elders. Merry also toted her weapons and a small stock of herbs, which had decreased rapidly in the last weeks.

Wren's chest still rattled against her back, and most of Merry's breathing remedies were gone. They would need to stop at Farmingham, the village Timothy suggested, for more. Surely he would not catch up that quickly. He had too much to accomplish before following them. But after that stop they would veer off his prescribed path and head straight toward the port without him.

She arrived at the chorus of the song, and Wren joined in with her raspy voice.

> "Cuckoo, cuckoo, loudly sing, cuckoo
> Cuckoo, cuckoo, gladly sing, cuckoo."

As they left the serene valley behind, Robert and Allen surrounded her on either side. She was the most obvious target, though they had no reason to believe anyone would be after them just yet. According to Timothy, the only name on the arrest warrant would be Merry Ellison. She suspected the men surrounded her as much to keep her from escaping them as to protect her. But she would not try to leave them behind, not after seeing how heartbroken they all had been by her kidnapping. She had made Wren a promise, and she would keep it.

They were a family. Families must stick together and face together whatever dangers might lie ahead.

Allen reached over to rub her arm. "'Tis not your fault, Merry. We are in this together."

She forced a grin. The dear, sweet man. He knew her almost as well as Timothy Grey. Again she hoped that once they reached France, her feelings for Allen might grow.

For the first time in his life, John wished Timothy Grey stood beside him, so that he might witness this handsome peasant flirting with Merry. He laughed quietly. Ahh, how delightful his revenge would be.

Timothy's trail had been all too easy to follow, especially as John rightly assumed he headed back to this place. He had almost given himself away by getting too close, but Timothy and his woman had been too enthralled with one another to notice. When they slipped into the hillside through a hidden passage, John had been left to wait and wonder in the soggy, storm-ridden night for far too long. Wait and wonder and stew in his hatred for Timothy Grey.

And when Timothy mounted his horse and galloped off toward the castle in the wee hours of the night, John had been torn. But it seemed the bigger treasure would be in capturing Merry Ellison, as surely the king would announce her a wanted criminal at any moment. Knowing not what might lie within that hidden cave, he decided to wait for her to emerge.

At dawn, she exited the cave with a motley assortment of

young people. Though the children appeared decently fed and clothed, he recognized something about them. They were children of the forest, as he had once been, surviving by cunning and wit.

Only ten years ago, John had poached in these woods to feed himself and his mother. And on an autumn day, not so different than this one, he had encountered that arrogant Timothy Grey, who threatened to have him whipped for thievery, but John had outsmarted him and gotten away. And he would outsmart him again, by capturing Merry Ellison and seeing her hanged.

Due to the strapping young men surrounding the chit, he would wait until he could capture her alone. Preferably nearer to a village. At least he spied no sign of the hulking fellows he had noted on his previous visit. For now he would follow silently, a skill he had mastered long ago, leaving both horse and clinking chain mail behind.

As the young people filed past his hiding place, he tapped his finger to his head in grudging respect. The Ghosts of Farthingale Forest. Though he had no real desire to hurt them, he might need to kidnap one or two for leverage if they maintained the guard so tightly about Merry. He took note of the tiny one in pink dangling from her back. The tot would pull at her girlish heartstrings quite nicely.

John did not ascribe to having a heart. Emotions served only to weaken a person. He would stick to power, pride, and determination. Much more loyal companions. He would yet prove to his father, the Earl of Wyndemere, that he was worthy of the man's respect. Once Timothy Grey was arrested for aiding a traitor, John could finally rise to power as his father's successor.

Oh, how sweet it would be!

Chapter 28

"I say, Grey! I did not expect to see you back so soon. Have you completed your search already?" The Earl of Wyndemere straddled a warhorse before a line of guards in the castle courtyard. Looking more threatening than ever, covered in chain mail and fully armed, he eyed Timothy warily.

Timothy trotted Spartacus to his side. "Yes, my lord. Since I began the search earlier, I had only a few more locations to secure. It looks as if you are ready to begin the full-scale mission."

"We shall leave no stone unearthed. I will have to call for reinforcements from your father, as I shall be sending many of the soldiers into the villages, and the largest contingent to scour the forest. We shall not have much protection left here at home. Fine time for that sluggard Hadley to disappear."

Alarm bells sounded in Timothy's head. His stomach clenched tight. "Hadley is missing?"

"The good-for-nothing bastard," grumbled the earl. "Never should have wasted my time on him. Should have known better."

Harsh language, that. From Timothy's perspective, Lord

Wyndemere had never given Hadley a moment of his time other than to bark orders at the fellow. Timothy would be glad to be out of the fickle earl's control. He could no longer fathom how he had justified working for this man and thereby indirectly for his ruthless king. "How long has Hadley been missing?"

"Since yesterday's nooning meal. Or so says this one here." The earl pointed to Bradbury.

If anyone knew of Hadley's whereabouts, it would be his close companion.

"Is this true, Bradbury?"

"Yes, Mister Grey. He dashed off shortly after his lordship received the missive."

Those alarm bells in Timothy's head increased in volume. He should have stayed with Merry to protect her, but he had no way to know that last night. "And have you any idea why he left?" He patted at Spartacus's mane, although he was the one in need of soothing.

"No." Bradbury pulled at his reins to steady his mount. "Although his mother lives nearby. Perhaps she has taken ill."

"Worthless, the both of them." The annoyed earl slapped at his sword. "The sot could have at least told someone before he left us shorthanded."

Though Timothy's mind reeled, he managed to keep his composure. "I will go to my father for you. We shall get those troops here in no time." And then he must find Merry before Hadley could do any more damage.

"Hmm . . ." The earl tapped his chin. "Timothy, I must speak to you privately for a moment."

He hated to spare the time, but he could hardly disobey the earl. They guided their horses in the direction of the stable. "Yes, my lord?"

"I have given you every opportunity here. But if this goes

badly, I will deny you to the king. You understand this, do you not?" He studied Timothy with a hard gleam in his eye.

It pained him to hear the earl voice the words aloud. "Of course. You have gone above and beyond in your fairness to me. I understand that your loyalties lie with the king."

Within a week, Timothy would leave this mess of England behind and head for France. There he would begin a new life with Merry and the children, and the Earl of Wyndemere's tenuous relationship would no longer matter. Likely should not have mattered in the first place.

"And so you will be taking off again shortly." The man frowned.

But Timothy did not waver under his stare. Yes, he was more than ready to leave this corrupt place behind. He nodded. "I will. But I will deliver your message to my father first, as I promised."

"And when shall you return?" The earl adjusted his helmet.

"I cannot answer that, my lord."

Wyndemere huffed. "I see. Tell me no more. Godspeed to you, my boy."

At that Timothy turned his horse and galloped back out the city gates. He had thought to gather his supplies and send a few letters, but now he must hurry to his father en route to Merry. If he took the highway to Farmingham, their meeting point, Greyham Manor would lie directly on the path. There he could rally help, for both himself and the earl.

He had no time to spare.

Hadley might be tracking Merry even now, trailing the group as they headed for Bristol. The man must have followed him yesterday. Why else would he have left at the same time? Could he have somehow overheard what was in the missive and wished to earn a reward? Surely the man bore Merry no ill will. He had danced and laughed with her just a few weeks earlier. Flirted with her, for heaven's sake.

Could Hadley be the one who put his letter to the king on Holstead's desk? Timothy had not even known the man could read. And he had always been so pleasant. But then Timothy recalled a soulless, arrogant glint that had flashed through the man's eye on several occasions. If Hadley had followed him into the woods, he must be the one.

Once past the edge of town, Timothy kicked his horse into a full gallop. He clutched to the mane of the mammoth Spartacus. As the forest blended into a blur of golds, reds, and browns to either side of the road, Timothy focused straight ahead. He must get to his father. Then he must get to Merry and far away from this godforsaken country.

"How much farther to Farmingham?" Merry shifted the lethargic Wren in her arms as they emerged from the dense forest into an inviting clearing of moss, grass, and piles of newly fallen leaves. The child wheezed, and she cradled her closer.

Allen held up the map Timothy had drawn for them. "Not far now, methinks. We just crossed this stream here." He pointed to it. "And it looks to lead straight to the village."

"Thank goodness. Then we must make camp for the evening. You and Robert continue into the village for the herbs. And do hurry. She is struggling so." Her shoulders sagged with weariness from her burden. Both physical and emotional weariness. Thoughts of Timothy Grey and even of the evil King John had been pushed by the wayside for the moment. She would have to struggle with those later. For now, she could focus only upon the immediate issue: Wren, withering away in her arms.

Allen stopped and gazed at her. "Indeed, you need to rest.

Red, Cedric, James," he called, "guard Merry while Robert and I head into the village."

"Remember, hyssop, peppermint, and chamomile." She hoped the children would not detect the frantic edge to her voice.

"I know, Mother Merry." Allen patted her back and offered a reassuring smile. "All will be fine. Try to relax." Then he and Robert headed off.

Merry collapsed against a large boulder as the men gathered round her. "Start a fire, at once. As soon as they return, I must set the remedy to boiling. James, fetch the pot. And get some of the boys to gather water and wood."

Over the past two days she had used the last of the herbs, feeling certain that if she increased the dosage Wren would rally. But the child had fallen deeper and deeper into her raspy breathing.

Wren cupped Merry's cheek as she sucked in breath after body-wracking breath. "I . . . be . . . all right, Ma-wee. No wo-wee."

Merry hugged the precious girl tighter, breathing deeply herself and hoping to somehow pass the air along to the child, that the in and out of her own chest would will the girl's to work. "All will be well soon enough, my sweet."

Robert and Allen had already disappeared over the next rise, and she noted Gilbert and Henry gathering firewood. All would be well soon. She must continue telling herself that, for making it safely to France without Wren would seem no victory at all. Merry had lost too much in her life. She could not bear one more blow. Without Wren, she might not wish to go on at all.

Pressing down her fear, Merry conjured a smile and began to sing the song of summer to Wren once again. Yes, summer, full of life and sunshine. Not autumn—with crackling leaves and woodsmoke in the air—when Wren's breathing grew brittle and crackly to match. Not autumn, when everything seemed to die, when Wren's lips tinged blue.

Please, God, no.

Unable to look at the child's sickly coloring, Merry buried her face in Wren's neck, her song becoming a desperate cry, but this time the child did not join in. Wren merely struggled to continue taking one breath after the other.

Merry's focus on the child was pulled away as Robert dashed back over the hillside waving frantically and shouting in a whisper, "Go! Go! Deeper into the forest. Someone is following us. We cannot be caught so close to the village. Go! Now!"

As they had only begun to unpack, it took but a moment for everyone to pick up their belongings and head into the forest. Cedric took the lead, and Merry counted them off one by one until they were all safely on their way. Then still clutching Wren, Merry ran alongside Robert into the thicket. Her senses sharpened as her sluggish blood began to flow fast through her veins. Her feet pounded in time with her quickening pulse. "But we must get the herbs," she said, wanting to scream the words, as they raced through the forest.

"We cannot now. Allen is watching the man. He will hold him off if needed, but we must get away while he thinks us setting up camp." Robert spoke without so much as a hitch in his breathing, even as they sped along.

If only Merry could pour some of his life's breath into Wren. If only she could will the child's lungs to function. But now a more imminent danger threatened. "Who is it?"

"He wears the livery of a guard from the Castle Wyndemere."

"Blast it all!" They had traveled too slowly. It seemed their day's head start had mattered little. But why would the guard be alone? Surely more lurked nearby.

Robert was correct. They must head deeper into the forest. Stay away from the villages and roads.

Wren shuddered against her chest.

Merry could not afford to consider what this detour might cost them. She continued placing foot in front of foot, heading farther and farther away from any possible help for Wren. Branches and thorns clawed at her, as if they would thrust her back toward the village, where surely some herbalist lived, but she paid them no heed and pressed forward. Though her heart cried otherwise, she had twenty-three people to think of, not just one.

Even if by some miracle they could outrun the earl's men, they could never outrun the malady gripping Wren's little lungs.

Allen observed the castle guard through an overgrown patch of bushes. The man stripped off his Wyndemere surcoat of red and gold with a wolf motif and his leggings as well. He must have forgone his chain mail the entire journey—otherwise they would have heard him long ago. Wearing only his braies, the man stepped into the stream and sighed. He splashed off his dark hair and his well-muscled torso. A thin, pinkish line streaked across his chest. Drops of water clung to his short beard.

The fellow must be several years Allen's senior, and Allen had dreamed of someday being a true soldier just like him. To be scarred and battle-hardened the way this man was. He was no taller than Allen, but his bulging arms bespoke more intense training than Allen had received. Someday—hopefully, someday soon—Allen would prove himself on the battlefield and earn a commission in a castle or perhaps on a crusade to the Holy Land.

His world had expanded in the past two years. Before their village was destroyed he'd never traveled beyond the neighboring town, and had not even bothered dreaming of distant realms. But now he'd seen castles and cities. Soon he would see a port and the foreign kingdom of France.

The man continued to wash in the stream, never suspecting Allen lurked nearby. Since he appeared to be settling in for a rest, Allen turned and, silent as a ghost, took off in the direction he and Robert had agreed upon. Once past the clearing, he noticed a few crumpled twigs that helped him better discern their path. He would catch up soon enough.

As he hurried through the woods pushing aside branches, only then did he recall the medicines for Wren. But they could not turn back now. The danger was too great. Her wracking breath had concerned him during the journey, but he trusted their heavenly Father would care for her, as he had done these past two years.

And He would care for them even after Allen's inevitable departure.

Soon he would put his broken heart far behind him and be off to see the world. He would not stay long in France, despite his growing familiarity with the language. His place was not with Merry Ellison and her ghosts anymore. Once they were settled, he and Red planned to sail back across the channel to the rebel-held capital of London.

And from there on to wherever they were needed.

Timothy might well be correct about Prince Louis and the rebel barons, but if they succeeded in their quest, Merry and the children could return home where they belonged. That made it a worthy enough cause for Allen to pursue. And pursue it he would. As soon as possible.

"Curse them!" John kicked at the pile of wood in the empty clearing. He had thought only to refresh himself in the cool stream after two long days of tracking Merry Ellison. Tonight, so near Farmingham, would have been the perfect time to capture her. "Curse them all!"

He had planned to steal her after dark, when she went to relieve herself for the night. A habit he had noted she followed routinely. One of the only times she would not suffer her guard dogs to follow along.

Now they were gone. All of them. Disappeared into the air, as ghosts were wont to do. Such a large group could not be hard to track, but they had a significant head start. They might have moved too far from the village for his plan to remain feasible.

Someone would pay for this. Forget his grudging respect for the ghosts, for the children of the forest—they had foiled his plans, and now someone must die. He growled and kicked the wood again, stomped the closest log into splinters, as he longed to do to them. He would snap the neck of one of those insufferable young men just to see the pain and fear in his eyes.

Fury flowed through him, but he must calm himself and form a plan. Though he suspected many rebels dwelt in Farmingham, the local baron remained loyal to King John. Perhaps he should rally the man, but he knew not if he was even in residence. Nor if he would believe his story. Besides which, the manor home lay to the far side of the village, and John could waste no more time. The sun had already sunk well below the treetops. He must find the ghosts before darkness concealed them for the night.

Spying a broken branch on the outskirts of the forest to his left, he headed that direction. He would think of a way to make Merry Ellison and her band pay for this. The chit was becoming more trouble than she seemed worth. But when at long last he watched Timothy Grey's face while the girl writhed from a rope, all would indeed be worthwhile.

When he learned the villagers of Farmingham had seen no sign of Merry or her group, Timothy searched the forest to the west while the sun dipped toward the horizon once again. They could not have traveled farther than this village in the past two days. Surely they would be camping somewhere nearby for the evening.

He must find them soon, must protect them from that underhanded Hadley. He still had no idea why the man had turned on him. Knew only that Merry and her band were in danger, and it was his fault.

By the time he arrived at his father's manor, he had discovered only the women of the family. His male relatives and all the troops had already been summoned by the king himself. He could find no one to send to the earl or to assist him in his own mission. Timothy could only hope they had been sent north to help with the rebellion and were not searching for Merry even now.

Whatever the circumstances, he was left to do this thing alone. And he must succeed. Too much was at stake this time. He must save Merry and the children. Must for once in his life do something truly honorable and important. Ninth child or not. He had wasted too much time playing at politics.

The good-bye kisses he had given his mother and sisters might have to hold him for many years, but all would be worthwhile once he escorted Merry and the children safely to France.

Except that he still could spot no sign of them.

Timothy crossed over a stream, and there he spied some crumpled leaves along the bank, then noticed a clearing with what appeared to be firewood smashed and strewn about. Ahead, he heard a crackle of branches, and he rushed in that direction.

A bold flash of red and gold gleamed through the dense, darkening forest.

Hadley!

He must draw the man back. He must keep him far away from Merry.

Chapter 29

Timothy hopped down from Spartacus and landed with a thud in the clearing.

He could not risk stealth or anonymity. No time remained. He must protect them at all costs.

"John Hadley, you coward. Is that you skulking about in the woods?" He shouted to the retreating back in the Wyndemere coat of arms. "Come here and face me like a man."

Once the words were out and the hulking fellow turned back his way, Timothy questioned the wisdom of his decision. Hadley thundered toward him enraged, as Timothy had intended. But what now? Should he draw an arrow on the man? He as yet had no proof of his betrayal, so he clutched the hilt of his sword instead.

John Hadley broke through the branches and snarled in Timothy's direction. "Who is the coward? Certainly not I. I would say you, Timothy Grey. You, who made a pact with the ghosts in exchange for freedom. Have you shared that tidbit with my father?"

"With your . . ." Timothy could not recall who John Hadley's father might be. Nonetheless, he would not tolerate such slander against his character. "You have it all wrong."

"I'm sure my dear Papa Wyndemere would love to hear about it. And once I've captured Merry Ellison, I will tell him and ruin your good name. I had hoped to see you hanged, of course, but no time for that now."

Timothy's mind reeled, unsure which information to process first. "Wyndemere is your father?"

Hadley chuckled as he drew his sword. "I'm his bastard, truth be told, but still, not so far beneath you as you always imagined."

Although the man spoke nonsense, Timothy clasped his sword and pulled it from its sheath. "I made no assumptions about you. We got along well enough. What did I do to earn your disdain? Why in heaven did you send that missive to the king?"

Hadley moved two steps closer with a menacing tread. "Ah, you liked that, did you? Thought me an illiterate fool, no doubt, but you couldn't have been more wrong."

And Hadley no doubt thought Timothy a weakling, but he knew nothing of the training Timothy's brothers had drilled into him. He would taunt the man no further though—he had his evidence.

Restraint, his remaining ally.

His opponent brandished his sword as a wry grin spread across his bearded face. "I suppose you have no recollection of threatening a boy in the woods, who did nothing more than catch his dinner. Do not recall stepping on his throat and calling him a worm. Declaring the entire forest yours. But you let him get away—that was your mistake. You are weak, Timothy Grey, and now you must pay."

Memories flashed through Timothy's mind. A boy in the forest.

Timothy had thought himself so tough and noble capturing the poacher, until the boy flipped free of his foot, bounded up, and punched him in the gut. It was then that he spied the hungry, wounded look in the boy's eyes. Hadley's deep brown eyes. Compassion had washed over Timothy, and he had let the fellow, so close to his own age, run away into the forest with the contraband boar in his hand.

And here that boy stood before him, intent upon revenge, with murder simmering in those same brown eyes.

"That was you? I am so . . ." But before Timothy could get out another word, the man lunged toward him.

A sword flashed toward his face, and Timothy ducked aside just in time.

Hadley regained his footing and thrust his sword several times in Timothy's direction, toying with him. "So what? So pathetic?"

"Sorry." Timothy lowered his sword, hoping that his words might be enough. "I am so sorry. I misjudged you, but once I understood, I let you go."

"And that was your mistake." Hadley swung his sword at Timothy again.

Timothy swiveled out of its path. This time he assumed a crouch and prepared to fight.

"You misjudged many things, Timothy Grey. My goodwill, for one. And I can't say much for your timing either. I had dreamed of making you watch your sweetheart die, and now I must kill you before you get the chance. More the pity, that." Bitterness dripped from every word.

Hadley circled Timothy, hatred seething in his eyes. Had he been resenting Timothy, plotting against him all this time? Timothy could not fathom such bitterness. But then the realization hit him—Lord Wyndemere treated Hadley like a pesky insect while honoring Timothy at his right hand. Little wonder the man detested him.

Hadley struck, but Timothy deflected his blow.

He must gather his thoughts. Recall his training. Again and again their swords clashed. Timothy's arm reverberated with the shattering strikes, even as his mind attempted to sort the situation.

This man was after Merry. He must stop him!

Hadley's sword slashed his left arm and sent fire shooting through it. In that moment, fire flowed through Timothy's veins to match the burning in his arm. He dove at Hadley. "Leave her alone! Whatever you believe I have done to you, leave Merry and the children out of this."

He slashed at his enemy again and again, but Hadley matched each strike. He ducked to the ground and rolled away from Timothy's attack.

Staring up at him, Hadley laughed, low and evil. "Never. I will never let them get away."

He bounced back to his feet and came at Timothy again. This time Timothy stood poised and ready. Something about the angle of Hadley's swing drew Timothy's eye. In a flash, he struck back, sending Hadley's sword flying in a streak of silver toward the bushes. He wrapped his foot around Hadley's leg, pushed him to the ground, and pressed the tip of his blade into Hadley's neck.

The man stared up at him, red-faced and panting. Panic seized his features. Hadley held his hands before his face. "I didn't mean it. Any of it. He just makes me so crazy. You don't understand. Your father always accepted you." Hurt and desperation flashed through Hadley's eyes. Not unlike the moment when Timothy had let him go ten years earlier.

Emotions warred within Timothy. Anger fought compassion

with the same ferocity of the battle moments ago. He pushed against his sword. Felt the spongy resistance of Hadley's flesh against the tip.

Choking back the awful sensation, he instead pictured Merry, hanging dead from the castle walls, in hopes of fueling his hatred to the point that he could administer the final thrust. Drive home the deathblow to this scoundrel.

But Timothy could not.

He pinned his gaze to Hadley's—this man who had been so hurt, so wounded. He saw no more hatred in his eyes. Only fear. He pulled back his sword an inch.

And in that moment, Hadley's eyes flashed and hardened. "Weak!" he shouted as he shoved the sword aside with his arm.

Timothy was so caught off guard, he flew to the side with his sword and crashed to the ground. In that brief moment, Hadley leaped to his feet and dove at Timothy. Timothy raised his arms to fend the man off. The air swooshed from Timothy as Hadley slammed atop him.

Then nothing.

Even as Timothy tensed himself for the scuffle, the man barely moved. He lay atop Timothy, moaning. A heavy weight. Timothy rolled him off and knelt over him. Saw his sword caught between them, plunged into Hadley's side.

The man twitched and groaned for breath as Timothy withdrew his sword. He watched a puddle of blood form.

Timothy's stomach soured at the sight. "This didn't have to happen. Your hatred did this." His sword felt weighty in his hand. He knew he should strike a final blow and ensure the man's death—stab him straight through his hard, dark heart. But this day had seen enough violence, and Timothy's heart had not the capacity for murder.

As a chill surged through him, Timothy glanced down to

his left arm. Blood flowed from a burning wound and coated his sleeve. The warm sticky stuff dripped over his hand, and he held it before him in the twilight.

Through his fingers, he again spotted the trail leading into the woods, though darkness had nearly fallen. Merry's or merely Hadley's? His face buzzed and pulsed in an unfamiliar manner. He could not follow. He must seek medical attention, or he would be no help to them at all. And so Timothy pressed his hand against his wound and stumbled in the direction of the village while he still could, with faithful Spartacus following at his heels.

"Weak," the single, garbled word called out to him from Hadley's dying form.

"Better than hateful." He called over his shoulder. *Better than dead,* he thought but did not say. Although by the ringing in his head, Timothy assessed he might not be long behind the man. He would have no life with Merry in France if he could not get this bleeding stopped in time.

Chapter 30

Merry held the gasping, blue-tinged Wren upon her lap in the corner of a strange cottage. The scent of dust and mold pushed in upon her, but at least they had found a place to stop, undetected, for the moment. Allen had joined them not long after their escape, and they had run directly east through much of the night toward the port at Bristol.

As a fog rolled in, Wren's breathing had eased for a short time, but by midday her malady had flared once again. At long last Cedric had discovered this cottage in the forest, and hope had blossomed for a moment—but only until they entered the dank, abandoned place.

They had outrun their enemy for the time being, but how could they outrun this more insidious threat? Merry's herbs were long gone. She held the child near a steaming pot of water, but there was nothing else she could do. Weariness enveloped her. Between running, lack of sleep, and so much worry, she had no more reserve of strength from which to draw. With whatever last drops might be left within her, she willed herself not to collapse crying on the wee child.

Between her loud, wheezing breaths, Wren managed, "No wo-wee . . . Ma-wee." Another rasping intake of air, and then, "Sunshine men . . . here."

If only that were enough. Merry forced a smile as the image of the child in her lap quavered through her unshed tears. She swiped at them, hoping Wren did not notice.

Wren wrapped her arms around Merry's neck. Before Merry knew what she was about, the small hands pulled the string from her tunic and clutched onto her crucifix. Merry had nearly forgotten it was there.

"He . . . love you." Wren wheezed. "He . . . here."

The chant of prayers reached to Merry from where Allen led the huddled mass in the corner of the crumbling cottage, and she felt compelled to join them. "Father God," she whispered. The words were oddly comforting against her tongue. Tears that she could no longer hold at bay rolled down her face. "If ever you loved me . . . if ever you cared, if indeed you are even there, please, heal this child."

Wren cuddled the crucifix against her cheek and a beatific smile crossed her face. The girl took a deep wracking breath in. Did not release it. Her eyes rolled back in her head. Her lips faded to an alarming shade of grey.

Merry's breath stuck in her chest as well, as if the life would seep right out of her along with Wren's. Pain ripped through her. As her stomach tied into sick, aching knots, she took several attempts to find her voice, then shrieked, "Wren! No!"

Allen rushed to her and tore the child from her arms. Lifting her lifeless body high over his head he shouted. "In the name of Jesus. By His power, by His blood—child, live!"

The group banded round and reached to where she lay in

Allen's two strong hands, raised almost to the ceiling. Prayers poured from their mouths.

Merry collapsed in the corner, pressing her feet away from the awful scene, which she could barely see now through the downpour of tears marring her vision. She shoved her fist into her mouth to stifle her screams. Somehow she must find a way to be strong for them once they realized the truth.

Helpless. Powerless. Hopeless. The words bellowed in her head.

She could do nothing for Wren. Just like she could do nothing to save her family on that awful night two years ago.

Then, not fully understanding how or why, she sensed more than saw flashes of white-hot light swirling around Wren's limp body.

Merry gaped. Did she hallucinate? Had it come to that? The swirling energy formed into a thick streak and entered Wren's body, where it coalesced into a tight, bright, shining star before shattering into a million sparkling diamonds shimmering about her.

Then all went silent and still.

Merry watched and waited in awe.

With a sharp intake of breath, Wren stirred to life high above them. She pulled up her dangling head and bent her limp body, as if attempting to sit and look around.

Allen brought her to his chest and hugged her tight, as the children crashed in upon them in one huge embrace.

"What wrong?" asked Wren, confused, with not a hint of rasp to her squeaky little voice.

The children cheered, laughed, and cried as they enfolded her again in a massive hug.

"My dear Wren, Jesus has healed you." Tears streamed down Allen's face now, and he did nothing to hide them.

"I tell Ma-wee Jesus here," said Wren.

Robert leaned over to kiss her baby head. "Yes, poppet. Jesus is here. Like I've never felt Him before."

Wren laughed. "He a sunshine man."

The knots in Merry's stomach finally released. Forcing herself from her hideout in the corner, she stood and joined the group, resting her chin upon Sadie's head from behind and wrapping her arms around a clump of children.

She had witnessed a miracle, but she did not understand, was not ready to put the pieces together. Surely such a monumental event must mean something. Did it mean God lived and dwelt among them after all? But she could not reconcile that concept with the shattered remnants of her life.

The next afternoon, Merry trudged through the alleyways of Bristol, Wren dangling merrily from her back once again. But the closer they came to their destination, the more Merry struggled. This journey had sapped her of so much, yet it had given her so much in return. She should have been rejoicing at the sight of the water in the distance, rejoicing at the weight of Wren hanging from her back, but still she wrestled with thoughts of leaving her home, and perhaps even worse, of leaving Timothy Grey.

She could not falter in her plan, though. Somehow she and the children would slip away without him. And when he arrived at his aunt's home and found them gone, no doubt the wise woman would speak reason to his befuddled mind. As befuddled as Merry's own.

Wren sang the happy cuckoo song over Merry's shoulder, but Merry's heart could not catch the mood. She had witnessed a miracle on this trip, no doubt, but it raised so many questions.

Where had God been when she had needed Him most—two years ago when her family perished? She still could not understand, but it seemed, perhaps, Timothy was right. God had been with her and the children all along.

Scanning their innocent, healthy faces, she could almost make sense of it. If God dwelt in heaven, He would want to protect these children, oppressed on every side but full of joy. It almost made sense . . . for a moment. And then she thought of her mother's kind, beautiful face gone from her these two years, and the logic of it flitted away on the wind.

They continued weaving through dim, narrow passageways between the homes and shops, toward the fresh breeze and the squawk of gulls. For now, they must stay out of sight. But upon the open sea, they could breathe more easily once again.

"Look," shouted Abigail. "Boats just ahead." Everyone shushed her, but her excitement proved contagious among the younger children as they pressed about her, gazing into the distance.

Henry sniffed at the air. "I smell fish."

"We're close. Let us prepare ourselves," said Allen, lowering Gilbert to the ground from his back.

Merry handed Wren to Sadie and took off her sack and weapons. The thatched roofs of two homes stretched over the alleyway, nearly touching over their heads, creating a dark tunnel for their transformation.

They had worked out their plan along the way. The older girls huddled about Merry, concealing her as she pulled on the apricot gown. She fingered the embroidered collar with a wistful smile. God bless Matilda. They would never have gotten this far without her assistance.

Meanwhile, Allen pulled on the rich, fur-trimmed tunic and finely woven leggings they had stolen long ago for just such a purpose. Since she could not introduce herself to a ship's captain as Lady Merry Ellison, they would assume the identities of Lord and Lady Gilly, escaping the fighting in the north with a contingent of servants in tow. Hopefully they would be far out to sea before the captain took note of the unusual number of children in their entourage.

Out to sea. Her stomach churned at the thought of leaving England. Timothy must be scouring the forests between Farmingham and his aunt's castle even now. She hated to have deceived him so, but truly, it was for the best.

Then she recalled last night in the cottage, when she had been so sure Wren had died in her arms. She could do nothing on her own. Her strength had run out. Yet some mysterious entity—she could only assume God—had seen them safely through that awful time. Perhaps she had not been the guiding and protecting force that she assumed herself to be all along. Perhaps it had been the prayers of Allen and the children upholding them through their entire perilous journey.

Such reasoning still felt unfamiliar, but she could no longer deny the very real possibility of it. Did such thinking mean she should let Timothy in, let him help her, take risks for her, as well?

"Let us do this thing," said Allen, offering her his elbow. He looked like a nobleman born. This life had changed him, given him confidence and leadership skills. And he had always been so strong in spirit. A truly rare young man. Perhaps someday they would lead their odd family side by side.

Merry slipped her hand through the crook of his arm. "I am ready."

"I'll chat with some fishermen and see if word of your arrest order has reached them or not." Robert took off his weapons and handed them to James, although he no doubt wore a dagger in his boot. "We shall meet back here shortly." He headed down the lane to the left, toward the fishmongers.

The time for turning back had passed. She must move forward into the future. Allen led her down the alleyway and toward the ships.

Chapter 31

Images flashed before Timothy. Merry along the seaside. Aboard a ship. Her face loomed large before him as her words, *"I cannot waste time arguing otherwise,"* echoed through his head. He heard them again and again, as the pitch dropped lower and lower.

He bolted upright on his pallet in the corner of the healer's cottage. Though he had little memory of how he arrived here, he had an awareness that he had spent several days under the care of the wrinkled and stooped old lady with the wise eyes and gentle hands. Drinking broth and gaining strength. And even if he had not vaguely remembered, the permeating scent of herbs would have given him a clue.

"I cannot waste time arguing otherwise." The words sounded again. Merry had no plan to wait for him. Why had he not realized it sooner? She just had not wished to fight with him. What had she said earlier that night in the woods? That she would not let him give up his family, his home, and his country. Pain

shot through his head. Of course she would not. She had lost every one of those.

But he was willing to give them all up, to give up anything to be with her. He must convince her. Sitting up, he held his clanging head between his hands.

"Now, now. You just lie back down." The old lady shuffled toward him. "Lost too much blood, you did. Might be days before you build up your strength."

She pushed him back onto the pallet with surprising force.

Timothy tried to resist but failed in even that small task. Lying upon his back, he pleaded with the craggy woman, who now hovered over him against a backdrop of drying plants hanging from the ceiling. "I must go. You do not understand. I lost her once. I cannot lose her again."

"Lost who?" The woman placed her hands upon her hips over her loose black tunic.

"My true love. Please, let me go." He pressed a hand to his chest, where he had worn Merry's embroidered token every day since her stay at the castle, and he found it still safely nestled in its spot.

The woman tsked. "True love, you say. Well, that I shan't dismiss so easily." She quirked her mouth to the side, creating even more wrinkles upon her weathered face. "You know this for certain, do you?"

He took a deep breath. He must convince her. "She is indeed the love of my life. I would have married her long ago, but I thought her dead. Then I found her alive. Now she will leave the country without me if I do not go immediately. I must catch her before it is too late."

The woman offered him her hand and helped him sit. "Then I suppose you must. But you won't be running off without proper supplies and some broth to build your blood. I didn't go to all this hard work of saving you for naught. You owe it to me to stay alive, young man."

"I have every intention of doing so." Timothy offered a grin. He must stay alive, and he must get to Merry—although, he felt much like death at the moment. Somehow he would summon the strength to find her.

The woman bustled about gathering supplies and packing them in a sack. "I suggest you tie yourself atop that fine horse of yours. You have barely stayed awake these past days."

"Yes, of course, Dame Wipple." *Dame Wipple?* Yes, that was her name. He now recalled several drowsy conversations with the woman. "My horse, how is he? How long have I been here?" He rubbed at his head, which seemed to be clearing now that he had remained in the seated position for several moments.

"Nigh on two days. That horse of yours, he made a terrible ruckus night before last—until the townsfolk found you passed out on the street and brought you to me. Once I had you in my care, he seemed to sense everything would be fine. He's been camped out front of my cottage ever since."

Timothy struggled to his feet and shuffled to the window. Spartacus neighed to him and shook his silky mane. "There you are, boy. I suppose I owe you a debt of gratitude." He turned back in. "And you as well. I shall leave a coin with you now and ask my father to send more later."

"You just keep yourself alive, like I said." The woman reached up to tousle his hair. "And find that true love of yours."

He hoped—nay, offered up a prayer then and there—that he could find Merry before she slipped off to God only knew where.

"And while you're about it," the kindly woman said, "you might want to keep an eye open for a Lady Merry Ellison and a group of young people. The king's offered a fine reward for her, he has. You just might earn yourself a boon to win your lady love."

Dread filled him at that. Though he had bested the man at swords, it seemed John Hadley would yet reach out from the grave and strive to destroy them all.

Merry held tightly to Allen's arm as she headed with heavy steps back toward the alleyway. From the opposite direction, an equally dejected Robert headed toward them. They met near the entrance and stood staring at one another for a moment.

"Well, get in here and tell us what happened," came Cedric's voice from the shadows.

Merry sighed and turned toward them.

"You first," said Allen, kicking at a rotten apple core at his feet.

"No, you, please," answered Robert, his shoulders slumping.

"I will tell them." Merry braced herself and faced the group. As her eyes adjusted to the dark crevice between the shops, her band's hopeful faces came into view and she nearly faltered. But as always, she steeled herself to do as she must. "Because we are such a large group, there is no quick passage available to us. The only ship that can accommodate us will not be leaving port for six more days. When it does, it can take us to Southampton, and from there we will need to find a different ship to France."

They all moaned at the prospect.

"I wanna go boat," cried Wren.

"Shh." Abigail hushed the child and ruffled her hair.

"'Tis not a disaster." Jane lifted her chin with determination worthy of Merry herself. "We will find a room in town and remain hidden. We can do this."

"Yes, of course. Thank you, Jane. It will be fine. Just a delay." A delay long enough for Timothy to locate them. Merry's emotions warred within her yet again. She could not decide whether she wished him to find them or not. "We will figure this out."

"I'm afraid it won't be so easy as that." Robert stared at the ground as he said it.

Apprehension seized her. What else could go wrong? "Please, Robert. Look at me. Tell us."

He lifted his eyes to her. The eagle-sharp glint that usually resided there was gone, and in its place . . . fear? "Not only Merry Ellison, but also the missing villagers of Ellsworth are wanted, dead or alive. And their captors will be rewarded with a fortune of twenty gold coins."

"Twenty gold coins," Cedric shouted, clearly forgetting his oath of stealth. "That's more than most folks see in a lifetime. My own mum might have turned me in for that."

Merry's chest clutched tight. "I do not suppose anyone will believe me to be Lady Gilly for long. I visited here too often as a child." Unseen enemies pressed in on them from every side, and for now their best hope for escape had been ripped from them as well.

"We must leave at once." Allen gripped both her hands in his. "I know you did not wish to, Merry, and the good Lord knows it is the last place I want to go, but we must hurry to Timothy's aunt. He said she will protect us."

The sad light in Allen's eye spoke clearly that he knew what this might mean. They had almost left Timothy Grey far behind, thereby increasing Allen's chances with Merry tenfold. But Allen would offer any sacrifice for these children, as would Merry.

Robert leaned out of the alley and peeked around the corner. He turned back and swallowed hard. "Nobody panic, but . . . soldiers heading this way."

And they dashed as one massive entity back toward the forest. Thoughts of Timothy Grey would have to wait.

Chapter 32

Timothy continued pushing Spartacus to the horse's considerable limits. He drove his heels deeper into the flanks of the mammoth beast, then leaned down and clutched the reins as they maneuvered around a tight corner in the path. A low-lying branch speckled with brown and gold leaves smacked him in the face, but he paid it little heed.

He must get to Merry and her group before they left the shores of England. Already he had managed nearly a two-day journey in less than one. Even if they headed directly through the forest rather than taking the more circuitous route near roadways and villages, if they traveled at a walking speed and stopped for appropriate rests for the children, they should only be arriving there now. Surely it would take them at least a few hours to secure a passage. He still had a chance.

And if for some reason he did not find them there, he had determined he would take the first ship to France and hope to catch them before they melted into that foreign land for good.

He had another ten miles to cover before reaching the port. In his childhood, the trip to Bristol from this area where his aunt's home lay could have taken nearly half the day as they dallied along the route. But today he intended to make it in record time.

"Whoa!" Timothy pulled up Spartacus to a canter as the village of Linham spread before them. He must not trample any innocent children in the streets. It would defeat his whole purpose.

For once, he would be the hero. He would not be overshadowed by the accomplishments of his older siblings. Nor would he be thwarted by Merry's incessant stubbornness. This time, he would win the day and prove himself worthy of her.

He sped past shops and taverns as quickly as he dared, but the side street leading to his aunt's castle caught his eye. It would only be a brief detour of a few furlongs to her home. Was there any chance Merry and her band waited for him there? No, he knew to the core of his being that Merry planned to leave England without him. He had seen her intention in her eyes as he dreamed in the healer's cottage.

Yet something like a lodestone still pulled him in that direction. He could only account it to his wishful thinking that Merry would not abandon him. Fighting the draw, he maintained his course toward Bristol. He would not let rash emotion sway him. He must at last learn to balance decisive action with caution. He could not lose her this time.

He must get to the port to find them. And if he could not, he must catch the swiftest boat to France and never look back!

Still his body swayed to the right, though he had passed the turnoff. He did the only thing he could think of. "Lord," he whispered up to heaven, "if I am making a mistake, please stop me. Please make your plan clear."

A few brief moments later, a tiny, giggling girl streaked onto the road in front of him from seemingly nowhere.

Timothy pulled hard on the reins as he shouted, "Look out!"

Spartacus reared, with his mighty front hooves flailing in the air over the child's head.

The girl dressed in pink, so like little Wren, froze and gaped as she stared up at the beast.

Timothy jerked the reins sharply to the right, and the horse managed to shift position and land a couple feet from the girl rather than on top of her small head.

At once the child began to wail. A woman dashed through an open doorway Timothy had not previously noted and snatched up the child. She held her tight while comforting her.

Turning to Timothy, she gasped. "I saw it all clear as the sun in the sky. Thought my Beatrix a goner for sure. Thank you, sir. Thank you for protecting her."

Timothy blinked several times. Though the woman had called the child Beatrix, he still strove to convince himself that she was not Wren. Those children from Merry's band had entrenched themselves in his soul. "I am just glad she is well."

Blood coursed fast through his veins. He blew out a breath and raked his fingers through his hair, whispering up a word of thanks that tragedy had not struck this day. Then he scanned the village streets, unsure of his next move. Though he needed to hurry on, manners said he should stay and comfort the shaking woman and wailing child.

Unable to come to any logical sort of conclusion, he followed his heart and slid off his horse, offering the mother a pat on the arm and the child a kiss on the head. "All is well now. All is well."

For some reason he could not bring himself to move along his way.

The woman began to settle. "Could I offer you some refreshment? 'Tis the least I can do. I should have never let her dash into a busy street like that."

"Oh no. Please do not give it another thought. I am on a dire mission to the port at Bristol. I apologize. I slowed a bit on my way through the village. But not enough, I now see."

"Just enough, I should say. But go on, if you must. We shall be fine."

Still torn, Timothy looked to his horse. The faces of Merry and the children flashed before him. "I really must."

"Go!" The woman gave him a gentle shove.

As he turned to Spartacus, a hooded figure exiting the shop to the far side of the street caught his eye. Something about the form appeared familiar. Peering closer, he noticed a tuft of red hair escaping. Unable to stop himself, he ran and caught the man by the forearms.

Joy flooded him at the sight of the familiar face, chasing away all the dread and worry of the past days. Though he longed to push back the hood and shout the man's name, instead he settled for an embrace, and a whispered, "Red, I thought I might never see you again."

Alarm spread over Red's face as he looked around, but he quickly caught up with the situation. "Get your horse and meet me on the lane to your aunt's home."

Timothy gathered Spartacus by the reins and followed Red up the road and around the bend. Relief coursed through him, as strong as the flood of joy moments earlier. Thankfulness soared to the surface as well, as he recalled his prayer and realized the little girl had been God's shockingly timely answer. He might have passed through Linham and never looked back. Once they had a bit of privacy, Red waved him over to talk.

Embracing Red a second time, Timothy sagged against the sturdy fellow and strove to hold back his tears. No need to collapse into a complete ninny.

Red chuckled as he patted Timothy's back. "Well, well, Timothy Grey. I knew not you loved me quite so much."

Timothy pulled away and punched him on the arm, laughing as well, even as his face heated. "I love you not nearly so much as your mistress. But truly, I feared I would never see you again. I had the strongest premonition that she meant to leave England without me. I can still hardly fathom I was wrong, though I am glad I was."

Red dragged Timothy deeper into the shadows and glanced about. "I came to the village for some herbs. We are here, nearby your aunt. She helped us, just as you said. But I fear you were right in your premonition." He tugged uncomfortably at his hood.

"Explain," Timothy demanded.

Red grimaced. "We did go straight to Bristol, but we could not book passage as quickly as we hoped. Merry did not wish for you to follow us. We have all lost far too much, and she did not wish the same for you."

Despite his fear of losing her, or perhaps because of it, anger now flared at Red's words. "I knew it! She had no right to take the decision from me. When I see that girl, I ought to . . ." He shook his hands before him as if he might choke the stubborn chit.

"Kiss her? Marry her?" Red supplied with a wiggle of his brows.

Timothy's anger ebbed at that, and he laughed. "I had meant to say throttle her, but perhaps you have the right of it."

"Let's go, then." Red looped his arm over Timothy's shoulder and led him down the road. "Though I doubt she will admit it, she will be happy to see you."

Timothy, still somewhat in a daze over all the sudden occurrences and dizzying gamut of emotions that had washed over him since learning Merry was near, allowed the man to steer him along. So he had found her. But she had meant to leave him.

Once he caught up to her, whatever would he do with her?

Merry sat in the shade of a rickety old manor home as the children played an unusually quiet game of hoodman's blind in what had once been the village center of a hamlet called Lindy. Weeds now grew through the lanes, and sapling trees encroached upon the area.

According to Timothy's Aunt Isabel and Uncle Frederick, the hamlet had been wiped out by a harsh round of the pox some thirty years earlier. They never had the heart to fill it with new tenants and so left it a shrine to their former inhabitants—until yesterday, when she dubbed it the perfect hiding place for the outlawed Lady Merry Ellison and the Ghosts of Farthingale Forest.

And perfect it had proven, tucked deep into the woods. The path had overgrown long ago, and Merry doubted even most of the locals recalled the place. Though she had played in these woods as a child, somehow even she had never stumbled upon it.

She could almost imagine living here. Making a life with the children. Turning that patch of weeds near that dangling shutter into a fresh flower garden come spring. A rainbow profusion of bright, budding color. Turning over the fields to yield new life of vegetables and grains.

Her heart could almost burst forth in a new song as well. Or perhaps an old song this time. The one from the Scriptures about beauty for ashes that Jane often sang the children. If only King John had not decreed her arrest. If only they had come here long ago, before she stole that chest of gold and matters began to fall apart.

But she would never have thought to trouble Timothy's aunt rather than her own—who, as the matter had turned out, was not currently in residence anyway. Merry must cease troubling herself with these *if only* scenarios.

Then she looked up to witness her most dreaded, most dreamed of, *if only* scenario of all. Timothy heading toward her.

The children ceased their play to welcome him. He handed off his horse to Red and gave them their expected hugs and pats, all the while watching her over their heads. Then one by one, the children glanced in her direction and slipped away.

Leaving only Timothy. Leaving only Merry.

Only Timothy, gazing at her with love-filled eyes across the overgrown lane, yet with pain resounding within them. His handsome face she could never shake from her thoughts, that drew her despite every bit of logic and will within her.

Only her, looking back with a mixture of trepidation and longing.

He took the final steps to meet her, and she stood.

"I know not what to say," he began.

"Nor do I."

"You tried to leave me."

"I tried to protect you."

"Let *me* protect *you*."

She shifted to a broader, more determined stance. "I can take care of myself." Her gut twinged at the statement, but while she could not control everything, she still would not let Timothy be punished for her father's crimes.

For a moment, he closed his eyes and pressed his lips together. Then he looked at her again and spoke. "But, Merry, I love you. No one should have to make it on their own. Please do not reject me again."

Those words, along with the shimmer in his eyes, broke through the cold, hard place remaining in her heart. She could not leave him behind thinking she did not want him. She reached out and stroked his arm, took his hand in her own. "Timothy, it is not rejection. I will not steal you away from your parents, from your nieces and nephews. From your whole life."

"Do not treat me like a child. I can make my own decisions, and I choose you." He reached out with his free hand to cup her cheek. "Do not stop me from following my heart. I beg you to let me go to France with you."

"I know you are not a child. But you cannot begin to fathom our lives. You have not been a part of our hardships." She dropped his hand and moved away. "We could still be captured. Still be killed. If you turn back now, you might never be linked to us. Go back to your home, resume your station. Do not take the risk."

His eyes sparked. "You might not even be here today had I not taken the risk and dispatched Hadley for you."

"Hadley?" Though the name sounded familiar, she struggled to recall the face. "The guard I danced with? What has he to do with anything?"

"He followed you. And he is the one who sent the missive to the king."

"Why? What happened?"

Timothy's shoulders slumped. "He hated me since childhood, though I am sad to admit I did not even remember him until he reminded me. But he is dead now. So you need no longer fear that threat."

That must be why their pursuer did not give chase into the forest. Timothy had protected her, and she had not even known it. Had this gentle, bookish man killed for her? "Did you . . . ?"

He shrugged and pushed his thatch of pale blond hair behind his ears. "He was wounded in the fray. As much his fault as mine. I never understood that such hatred existed in the world." He said nothing else, only continued to stare at her with that same mix of love and pain.

She longed to pull him to her. To wipe the sadness from his face. To kiss away his hurt. But she would not let her heart sway her to foolishness. Nothing had changed.

What else could be said? She would not permit him to travel with them, though truth be told, she could not prevent him from following. Perhaps his family could talk sense to the man.

"Go find your aunt and uncle. They have been waiting for you."

He swiveled to follow her command, then turned back. "This is not over, Merry."

Chapter 33

Timothy refused to retreat, but for the moment, he would withdraw and recoup. Once the surge of energy from his chase had quieted and the initial shock at finding Merry had worn off, he had sensed the strength ebbing from his body. He still needed to rebuild his blood supply. He must get to his aunt's home before he collapsed right in front of Merry and proved her right—that he could not handle their journey, should not follow them to France.

He winced at the throbbing in his arm as he gathered Spartacus from Red and continued up the overgrown path. However, a few steps later, a strapping figure fell in step beside him. Allen, of all people.

Timothy braced himself for the lecture—for the command to leave, the threat to stay away from Merry—but Allen just kept walking beside him. If possible, in what seemed to be . . . a show of support?

They passed through the decrepit hamlet and over the rise toward Aunt Isabel's castle on the outskirts of Linham. Allen pushed aside weeds and branches for Timothy. Before long, he could take the silence no more. "Is everything all right?"

"Everything but you," said Allen. The words could have been construed as a threat, but his voice held no intimidation. "You look rather pale. I thought I should see you safely to the castle."

Timothy did not wish the man to assume him weak. "I was wounded battling off your pursuer. If you think I look pale, you should see the other man."

"How does he look?" asked Allen.

"Dead."

"I see." Allen nodded in respect. "And did he appear in any way heartbroken?"

Timothy cleared his throat. "That, my good man, is none of your concern."

"I've been there, you know."

So Merry had turned him down as well. Timothy expected to feel some satisfaction in that, but Allen had grown on him. Must Merry turn every prospect away? Did the girl no longer possess a heart at all?

"She's frightened," Allen offered with no prompting.

"Then why will she not let me help?"

"I suppose she does not wish to open her heart." Allen stepped on a tall weed to allow Timothy easier passage.

"Does she not understand I would give up everything for her? Power, position. It means nothing now. I would give it all up for love of her."

Allen paused and turned to him. "Honorable as that sounds— forgive me for saying so—something seems not quite right. Sounds like that new courtly love nonsense to me. I would say the more important issue is, is this God's path for your life?"

Timothy's blood might have heated at that, had it not already gone cold. Lethargy filled his veins. Sluggishness weighed down his muscles. He needed to get to bed and let his aunt tend to him. He felt far too tired to rail at the fellow and call him the pious interloper that he was.

So he continued plodding along. And as he did, he considered again his prayer in Linham for direction, and God's quick, stunning answer. He supposed this must be God's path for him. And he had credited God for leading him to Wren in the forest.

Another flash of pain struck his arm. He clutched it and wavered on his feet.

Allen jogged over to catch him. "Come along. We can talk later." He took charge of Spartacus and slung Timothy's good arm over his shoulder. Thus with Allen supporting him, they stepped onto the road that led to the castle.

Before they had gone far, jangling behind them caught Timothy's ear. He managed to disentangle himself and stand on his own strength as a retinue of the king's blue-and-red-clad soldiers rode his way. He recognized Niles Thoroughgood, son of Baron Thoroughgood and distant cousin to the king, at the lead.

To his credit, Allen remained still and quiet, doing nothing to give himself away. In fact, he seemed almost to shrink in upon himself, until he achieved a servile sort of anonymity.

"Ho, Timothy Grey!" shouted Niles. "My old friend. Am I glad to see you. Have you heard the news of Merry Ellison and the missing children of Ellsworth?"

Children of Ellsworth, drat! So the authorities were after the children too. The king had only mentioned Merry in the missive he had read. Again, the legacy of John Hadley came back to haunt him. Timothy managed to remain calm nonetheless. *Restraint.* He must keep his wits about him.

Allen remained in ghost mode as he studied the nobleman and his retinue. If Timothy were in full form, they might have

333

been able to take them, but not with him so close to collapsing from loss of blood.

Yet from the moment the intruders had rounded the bend, Timothy managed to stand firm and proud without wavering. In the flash of an eye, he had switched from a vulnerable human being into as arrogant a coxcomb as Allen had ever witnessed. The man belonged in a performance troupe.

Timothy chuckled. "Think I would give you *my* twenty gold coins so easily? No, I shall capture the girl. I know a bit about her. We used to play in these forests as children, which is why I came directly here."

"And . . . ?" questioned Niles, leaning forward over his horse, his chain mail clinking.

"Alas, nothing." Timothy sounded properly dejected. He jerked his chin toward Allen. "My man and I questioned the locals quite thoroughly and scoured every inch of this area. I am thinking to head toward the port."

In spite of his mixed feelings about the fellow, Allen was impressed with Timothy's quick thinking.

Niles frowned. "We just came from that direction."

"Then, perhaps to her home," Timothy said. "She might return to the familiar."

And Timothy might have a promising future as an outlaw if he kept up such proficient storytelling.

"Good point." Niles nodded. "Once I have informed the nobles along my appointed route, I shall loop back that way. I was headed to your aunt and uncle just now, but I assume you have told them."

"Of course. They have been aware and on the alert for days." Timothy took a step closer and lowered his voice. "Although I must say, I am surprised the king is spending such effort on this minor issue with the rebellion still under way."

Niles sat up straight and surveyed the area. "You know King John—once he gets something in his head, he rarely lets go. He sees Lady Merry as a symbol, thinks killing her will break the spirit of the rebels."

Allen's heart sank, but he kept his eyes vacant and did not twitch a muscle. He hadn't realized King John took such a personal stake in Merry's death.

"True indeed," said Timothy. "I will not rest until this matter is resolved."

"Nor I. Men, let us go." Niles waved the men back toward the village and thankfully away from Merry.

"Whew!" Allen still stood frozen in his spot. "That was close."

"Too close." Timothy wobbled on his feet and clutched at Allen. "I suppose I am all in this now, right along with the rest of you."

Allen smiled. "I suppose you are. Welcome to our world of intrigue and danger. Try not to get yourself killed."

Timothy had woven an elaborate fabrication on their behalf. The sort of fabrication that could indeed cost him his life. All along Allen had remained uncertain as to whether he trusted the man, but in that moment his doubts melted away and a new camaraderie formed in their place.

"So tell me true." Allen gathered his courage to ask the question that had pressed on his mind for many days. "Is FitzWalter really a scoundrel? I'd been planning to join his troops, but you've given me pause."

"He has been causing trouble for as long as I have been alive. But who is to say? Perhaps Louis will prove a strong king and take the reins. Perhaps he will grow to love England and care for its people. Stranger things have happened, I suppose."

"But you cannot support King John?"

"In truth, no. But I try to keep my head low and stay away

from trouble, which shall surely come no matter who is king. That is where Merry's father made his tragic error, I am afraid. He committed treason alone. One cannot expect a king to forgive such a trespass."

Allen had not expected Timothy's answer to tread on so sensitive an area. He winced at the pain that sliced through his chest. "He killed my family too."

"I know. And there is no excuse." Timothy patted Allen's arm. "But one thing I have learned. The enemy of my enemy is not necessarily my friend. Oft as not, he is just another enemy waiting to be discovered."

The statement struck a chord and resonated deep within Allen.

Timothy turned to look him in the eye. "I think I shall take this opportunity to turn your words back upon you, my man. Is this God's path for your life? Has He called you to take up this battle?"

Without even pausing to ponder, Allen knew the answer. How had he never seen it before? God had not called him to this battle. His own pride, his ambition, his heartache, and—worst of all—his need for revenge had led him this way.

"Hmph," Allen grumbled. "I was just starting to like you. Must you ruin it?"

Timothy chuckled as they rounded the bend and the beige stone castle came into view. "The enemy of my enemy might not be my friend, Allen of Ellsworth. But the friend of my friend is most certainly my friend as well. There is nothing you can do about that."

True enough, although Allen did not wish to concede at the moment. "So is there a just cause anywhere on this earth? Any kingdom, any crusade where righteousness reigns supreme?"

"I have yet to find one. Although . . . I have heard tell of a small dukedom almost to Scotland. A North Brittania. Legend has it they built a society based on justice and Christian principles. It is probably only a myth."

Something warm, bright, and hopeful flickered in Allen's chest. "But what if it is not?"

Timothy scratched his head. "It would be a wonder indeed. I have heard that any man of wisdom and good character can make his way there. Might be just the place for a warrior like you."

"Trying to get me as far away from Merry as possible?" Allen jostled Timothy's good shoulder. "I don't blame you." Although he jested, Allen wondered if this place might be just the answer he had been looking for all along.

"Where have you been? I was worried." Merry dashed to greet Allen as he entered the manor house.

"I took Timothy to his aunt. He's wounded, you know." Allen moved to the fire and warmed his hands before it.

They could not afford to give off much smoke, but evening had fallen. A chill had filled the air, so they had built this one fire in the main manor house for everyone to gather round.

"I did not know that." Merry scanned the faces of the smaller children. Perhaps they did not need to hear the specifics of Timothy's battle, nor the results. "Come. Talk to me in private."

She led Allen through the great hall. Yesterday the place had barely been fit for human habitation, but after Jane and Kate's hard work, it would do as sleeping quarters for the week. Merry could almost imagine it as it had once been. Filled with banners, tapestries, and torches. Perhaps a cat roaming the place or a dog curled up by the stone hearth. A home, the likes of which she had not known for several years.

She pulled him into a small side chamber, illuminated by a single candle. "What happened?"

"Much. He has a nasty gash in his arm. Says he lost a lot of blood. A healer in Farmingham found him and tended him. She did not want him to leave, but he insisted he had to find you."

Merry shuffled her toe. "We owe him a debt of gratitude. I will thank him in the morning."

"For more than you think. Merry, you admitted to me once that he loved you, but tell me true, do you love him as well?"

She steeled her heart against the question and looked away from Allen's probing gaze. "I cannot. I should not. Why do you wish to know?"

He laid a hand on her arm. "Because I want the best for you. You must open your heart. Open it to God. And if you cannot open it to me, then open it to this Timothy Grey. He is a good man, and he loves you."

"I do open my heart. I love every person in this group."

"You love downward to those you feel responsible for. But you do not allow yourself to be vulnerable. Open your full heart again, Merry. 'Tis time."

She reached out to touch his shoulder. "What about you? I thought you wished to pursue me."

He offered a rueful grin. "You are not meant for me, Merry. I realized that the moment I saw you crying in Timothy's arms. Besides which, I saw a terribly pretty maiden selling wares in Bristol. You were right. There is a whole world of possibilities. I should open myself to them, just as you should open your heart to Timothy."

Not wishing to deal with the truth contained in his speech, Merry laughed and turned to brush some dust off a nearby chest. "I thought you did not like the fellow. He is not one of us."

"He is now," Allen said with quiet assurance.

Merry's gaze shot back to him. "What do you mean?"

"He lied to the king's men for us. Sent them away. I would say he is as much a part of us as anyone now. He has taken huge risks for you, from the beginning. You can trust him."

Merry wished she could. Wished she remembered how. But too much danger yet loomed about them. While a part of her, that admittedly traitorous part, wished to try, she remained unsure that she had the courage to open her heart and risk having it crushed to pieces all over again.

Chapter 34

Merry threw herself into a tumbling combination, gliding across the newly worn path in a series of flips and spins. Exhilaration surging through her. At the end she planted her feet firmly into the cool English soil. She pressed her bare toes into it, relishing the sensation. Soon she might never feel this treasured piece of earth again. Both excitement and dread filled her at the thought.

"You see, Sadie. Not long now, and you will master it."

Sadie, also barefoot and stripped of weapons as they practiced the highest-level agility skills, approximated the forms as she worked through the series in her head.

On the other side of the overgrown village clearing, Allen instructed the younger children at their balance upon the board. Most of the older men, even Big Charles for once, had headed out on a final hunting foray, no doubt wanting to enjoy this land of their birth while yet they could. Only two more days now.

Young Henry and James stood watch at the obscured path, as any soldiers looking for them would surely take the direct route. And the castle guards watched over the lane beyond. But since the king's men had been sent away by Timothy and their remote location was nearly impossible to find, Merry dared to hope they just might make it out of England alive. She checked her bow lying nearby nonetheless.

"Could you show me one more time?" said Sadie.

"Of course." With pleasure. Anything to keep her mind busy and away from the many concerns that pressed at her.

Merry jogged to the far end of the clearing, then turned and prepared herself. How she loved the weightless sensation of soaring through the air. A jolt of energy flowed through her. She leaned forward into a pounding run and threw her hands to the ground. Hands, feet, hands, feet—spinning freely through space, she landed solidly back to her feet.

Sadie cheered. "I think I have it now."

A low, slow clap met Merry's ears. A whistle followed. A familiar whistle she had not heard since childhood. Timothy's whistle.

"Then again," said Sadie, "it can wait until later." She slipped away in the direction of the balancing board.

For a moment, the childish urge struck to run into the manor house and lock the door. She had not seen Timothy since his arrival, though she had chided herself again and again that she should visit his aunt's home and thank him. Her heart at once tugged her in that direction and pushed her away.

She had been able to convince herself that the risk of detection was too great, though it should have been her by his bedside. She was the one he had been protecting when he was injured. She was the one he loved.

But did she love him as well? The fluttering in her heart and butterflies in her stomach must have some significance. More importantly, that sense of rightness and coming home that she always felt in his presence seemed to indicate love. But could she choose to trust him, to commit to him with all her heart?

Finally she turned her gaze to the full impact of his striking face. A smile flashed across his lips. Hope flickered in his warm eyes. He tossed back that thatch of silky blond hair her fingers ached to run through.

She took a bracing breath. "I should have come to you. I meant to."

"No worries. Auntie took good care of me, and you are safest here."

"Come." She motioned him closer. "Let us sit and talk for a moment."

They settled themselves upon the drooping front steps to the manor house.

Merry clasped her hands tightly together to prevent their trembling and stared down at them. "I owe you much thanks. Not just for dispatching of Hadley, not just for turning away the soldiers, but for your kindness and faithfulness all along. You are my best friend in the world. I should never have turned you away."

"Hmm. Best friend. I suppose that shall have to do for now."

She ignored the insinuation and continued kneading her hands. "It is hard for me to accept help. I have been doing this so long on my own. I apologize."

He reached his hand around the back of her neck, tucked it beneath her short-cropped hair, and rubbed his thumb against that sensitive spot, sending shivers of delight through her. "I apologize as well. You were right not to trust me at the first. After I thought you dead, I threw myself into becoming a success. I fixated upon making my place in the world, upon being as good as my older brothers. And because of that I made some poor decisions."

"Like?"

"When I came to your camp, I yet wished to capture some of the men."

"Timothy!" She pulled away from his hand, despite the lovely shivers.

"But I quickly realized I never could."

"Oh." She relaxed and took his hand in hers to examine it, wondering how simple human flesh could evoke such magical sensations. She experienced that warm, shivering surge again.

He flipped his hand over and gripped hers. "Allen showed me that it is not about me or my pride or my ambitions. It is about God's plan."

She gazed deep into his eyes. "I see."

"Do you? I believe that Wren's sunshine men led me to your camp. And I know beyond all doubt that when I nearly passed you by and headed straight to France, God placed a runaway tyke in my path to stop me before I made a dreadful error."

He reached to her cheek and brushed his fingers across it.

She swallowed hard. In that moment she could almost imagine letting him into her heart completely and utterly.

Why had he said all of that? Timothy immediately regretted his words. He should not confess so much so fast. But he could not cease stroking her cheek, and for once she did not pull away. "You probably think me foolish," he said. "I know you doubt God and certainly do not believe in sunshine men."

She attempted speaking several times before she got out the words. "I . . . no . . ." She sighed and leaned her face into his palm. "I saw them. The flashes of light. Wren would have died without them."

So many thoughts flew through his mind. Did she understand

now? Might she believe? Might she be ready to accept him? "Does this mean . . . ?"

Merry offered a shy grin. "I think it means you had best get to practicing your agility skills. Cedric still insists we should be a tumbling troupe in France."

And in that moment none of his questions mattered. Though he longed to press his lips to hers and whisper proclamations of love and forever, he resisted. Hesitation lingered in her eyes. He should not push her. She would let him go to France. That was enough for now. He had the rest of their lives to woo her.

"You know you need not live on your tumbling expertise. I have family in France. We could stay with them."

Merry winked. "But where is the fun in that?"

"Then shall we test out my aunt's most excellent nursing skills with a few tumbling exercises?"

"A marvelous idea." She stood and brushed off her boy's leggings and tunic. He dreamed to see her in a beautiful flowing gown with hair streaming over her shoulders once again. Although, he had grown accustomed to this look as well and found her charming either way.

"Let me see your rolls," she instructed. "I recall you at least mastered those when we were young."

"Ah, and Sadie has taught me to stand on my head. Watch!"

He knew he must be grinning like a fool as he executed the trick. With caution, he perched himself into the upside-down position, held it to the count of ten, and lowered himself back down.

When he rose to standing, Merry rushed to hug him and nearly knocked him over in the process. He caught her against him before they both toppled to the ground.

"I always knew you could do it," she said, then she seemed to realize what she had done, and stepped away. "Now, those rolls."

He would roll for her. Forward, backward, sideways, from here to the moon. And once they made it safely out of England and away from their ever-threatening enemies, he would spend the rest of his life with this woman.

John Hadley slunk toward the decrepit old village as giggles drifted through the forest. Though his side still burned like thunder and lightning, he would not abandon his quest until he saw both Merry Ellison and Timothy Grey hanging from the gallows. He no longer cared in which order, as long as they both rotted in hell where they belonged.

Pressing his hand to his wound, he felt the warm, sticky blood seeping through. He had no idea how he had stayed alive so long, except by the pure hatred flowing through his veins. A surgeon along his route had confirmed that the sword had not struck any vital organs. But the infection would do him in before long. He had feared he would never make it, never find them. But that same hatred had fueled his determination. Just a few more hours, and he could turn them over to the sheriff in Linham and peacefully breathe his last knowing his father would finally admire him, finally praise him, and finally regret that he had turned him away so cruelly in favor of Timothy Grey.

He peered past a boulder and studied the children at play in the center of the ancient, overgrown hamlet. The fools. *Ghosts of Farthingale Forest.* Hah! They had left a trail from Bristol to this place that even an idiot could have followed, let alone an expert tracker like himself. Where were those hulking guards who had once scared him away? Only a few soldiers watched the lane from the castle and two scrawny boys stood at the entrance to the hamlet.

Ah, there! His searching gaze landed upon Timothy and Merry

as they tumbled about like a set of court jesters. Now that was just too easy. They would strip all the fun from his revenge. He might be able to take them out now with bow and arrow, but again, too easy. Besides, he did not trust his aim. The pain in his side might throw him off. No, he had enough strength and bitterness remaining to see them safely to prison. He would do this properly.

He crept in closer and hid behind a barrel between two crumbling cottages. Taking a moment, he checked his sword and bow. All was ready. He drew his dagger from his boot, ran his thumb across the razor-sharp blade, and grinned in satisfaction as a thin line of blood formed across it. Perfect.

Glancing past the barrel, he sought out his first target. The one that would force them to do his bidding without complaint. Like puppets on a string. Power surged through him and filled his chest near to bursting at the thought. There she was. The tiny girl dressed in pink toddled toward him, as if the gods of vengeance and justice smiled down upon him at long last.

He tiptoed from his hiding place to the edge of the clearing, glancing around to ensure he remained undetected.

Just as he was about to snatch the girl, she hollered, "Sunshine man!" and dashed in the opposite direction.

Chapter 35

As Timothy rolled to standing, the sight that met his eyes caused his stomach to lurch. Merry must have seen it at the same time, for she froze beside him, agony twisting upon her face.

A pale and grubby John Hadley grabbed for Wren but missed her by inches and fell onto his face. He stumbled back to his feet and grabbed Sadie from midair as she flew by in a tumbling combination.

"Don't move!" he called. "Nobody move an inch."

As if they could. Fear glued Timothy in place. Hadley had indeed come back from the grave to ruin everything. Timothy should have finished him off while he had the chance. "Do not hurt the child," he managed, slowly raising his hands over his head. "We will give you whatever you want."

Hadley hooted in delight. Pure evil shone from his eyes. A madness of the soul. "I want you and your despicable chit swinging from a noose." Tightening his grip on Sadie, he jerked his head to young Gilbert. "You, fetch a rope."

Gilbert's eyes grew large.

"To tie them up. I won't hang them here and now, unless they give me too much trouble."

The boy took two shrinking steps away from Hadley.

"Now!" he hollered, shaking the knife. "Or you shall see your friend's head roll."

Gilbert shrieked and ran into the manor house.

Sadie clutched to Hadley's wrist where he held the knife to her throat.

"No, no!" screamed Abigail, streaking directly at them, but Jane caught her back.

Timothy took the opportunity to survey the yard and spied Merry's bow and quiver a mere ten feet from him, lying on the ground. If only he could reach them.

Hadley seemed confused by Abigail's outburst. No doubt unwilling to kill his hostage and render her useless so soon, he shouted, "Shut the brat up!"

And in that moment as he turned his attention to snarl at Jane, Sadie caught Timothy's eye.

Timothy nodded. The time had come.

Sadie picked up her feet and sent her weight shooting to the ground, moving away from the knife at her throat and tucking in her chin at the same instant. As her back made contact with the grass, she sprang in one neat move—up and away from Hadley and to her feet.

As she flipped back toward him, sending the knife shooting from his hand with her foot, Timothy ran and dove upon the quiver and bow.

The next moment seemed to last a lifetime. He gripped the cool, curved wood in his hand and snatched up the quiver. How he longed to stand to his feet and shoot an arrow directly through Hadley's black heart. To be the hero. To at long last prove to Merry that he deserved her. But Merry was the better marksman and had the straighter trajectory. He had no time to debate his decision.

"Merry!" Timothy's voice drew her from her stupor even as she caught sight of the bow and quiver flying her way out of the corner of her eye. Instinct took over. In a flash she caught them, whipped out an arrow, and nocked it in the bowstring, even as Hadley still stood in confusion, gaping at his empty hand.

Aligning the tip with the man's chest, she sent the arrow flying straight and sure, deep into his heart.

Hadley looked down at the red stain seeping over the gold of his Wyndemere surcoat. He stared at the arrow, as if he could not believe it real, then he wrapped his hand around it. "I only wanted him to love me," he said, crumpling to the ground. Allen dashed over, brandishing his sword above the man, and made certain Hadley would not rise from the dead again.

Emotions crashed in upon Merry. Elation, regret, victory, and sadness, all at once. The world wavered about her.

Timothy caught her just when she might have fallen and lowered her gently to the ground. "Merry, are you all right?"

"You did it! You saved us. You and Sadie." She clutched his tunic and buried her face in his neck. "I needed you all along. How did I ever convince myself otherwise?"

"We did it?" He stroked her hair, confusion apparent in his voice. "You did it. I feared I could not make the shot."

"No, I froze. I could not move. Seeing the children in such immediate danger proved too much. If you had not rallied me . . ." She let the thought trail off, unable to speak the awful words. "But you did."

"I shall not argue with you but to say we all did it together. You, Sadie, Allen, and me. And we must credit the sunshine men with protecting Wren from Hadley's grasp. She could not have fought so admirably as Sadie."

"Sadie!" Merry's gaze shot to where the girl had finished her flip, which had so neatly disarmed their enemy, and she found her in the center of a crush of young women and children.

Gilbert emerged from the manor house, rope in hand. Surveying the scene, he threw it to the ground, whooped, and skipped to join the hug.

Wishing to join them as well, Merry said, "Help me up, please."

Timothy pulled her to her feet.

Still a bit wobbly, she stumbled against his strong chest and grabbed at his tunic. Once there, within his magnetic pull, she could not bring herself to let go. How she had needed him all this time. She had just been too afraid to admit it.

"Oh, Timothy, I will never let you leave me again. I love you!" Merry would no longer be a coward concerning love. From this day forward her love would be dauntless.

He crushed his lips to hers, sealing that promise for all eternity.

Timothy looped his arm over Merry's shoulder in a manner that had become pleasingly familiar in the last two days. To his great satisfaction, she wore the lovely apricot gown he had asked Matilda to alter for her back in Wyndeshire. With her hair tucked beneath gauzy white veils, she looked every inch a noblewoman. He could hardly believe that after all these years, they were back together, as they belonged.

They gathered with the rest of the group in front of his aunt's castle. She had insisted she would see them safely to the port, bedecked in finery, and declare them her passel of Grey nieces and nephews departing for France. With her guard along, no one would dare question them. It seemed they would be safe at long last.

A surge of melancholy passed through Timothy as his aunt and uncle exited the castle portal to lead them on their way. How he would miss his family and his country. His gaze crossed over the courtyard filled with children dressed in a bright array of colors. But he had a new family, and he would make a new life far from the ruthless King John. Though he knew not what rank or title he might hold, he knew he was where he belonged.

He leaned down to kiss Merry atop her head. "Are you ready?"

She turned her adorable face up to him and hugged him around the waist. "I have never been more ready for anything in my entire life."

Unable to resist, he deposited one more kiss on the tip of her nose.

The moment had come. His aunt and uncle climbed onto their horses, and the group fell into step behind them, soldiers bringing up the rear. How regal his aunt looked perched atop her mount, tall and steady despite her twists of silver hair. How honorable she and his uncle were, willing to stand up for the innocent and oppressed against their own ruler.

Allen pressed toward the front of the crowd and fell into step beside Lord Linden. He had no wish to watch Timothy snuggle with Merry the entire journey to Bristol. Though he knew things had turned out as they should, the sight of them together tore at his heart nonetheless.

At least he had had the satisfaction of dispatching of that awful Hadley for good. Had he known the future, he would have put an end to the man when he'd first seen him outside of Farmingham. Allen could hardly wait to face down the next villain in his path. To fight for justice and protect the innocent. The more he pondered Timothy's question about God's path for him, the more he realized that was his calling in life.

Lord Linden swiveled upon his horse to face him. "Are you ready for France . . . Allen, is it?"

"Yes, m'lord. I'm surprised you remembered." They had only met once—when he'd brought Timothy to the castle. Lord Ellison had never bothered to learn his name in the fifteen years that he lived in the man's village. "I doubt I shall stay long, though. Once the children are settled, it will be time for me to find my own place in the world. I had thought to fight with the rebels, but perhaps I shall give a try to North Brittania instead. Have you heard of it?"

Lord Linden raised his brows. "I have indeed. If I were a young lad, I would be tempted to join you. But alas, my responsibilities are here."

"Is it true? A man such as I might make my way there?"

"Possibly. Timothy speaks highly of your character, and I have heard amazing stories about your band of ghosts. Can you handle a sword?"

"Quite well." Allen's confidence swelled.

"And a lance?"

Just as quickly, it deflated. "I'm afraid not. I've not even held one."

"Then I suppose you shall have to return here and train with my men before you head north. My captain of the guard has a reputation for turning out the finest knights." Lord Linden chuckled and winked at Allen.

But Allen could barely catch his breath, and he saw no humor in the situation. "Would you do that for me? Truly?"

"Why, of course."

Upon hearing those words, Allen knew for a certainty that God's favor smiled upon this new path. He had chosen well.

Chapter 36

Perfect. Everything was finally perfect. Merry lifted Wren into her arms and leaned closer to Timothy as they headed toward the port, well guarded and well disguised. The children fluttered about her in a bright rainbow of silks and satins. The Ghosts of Farthingale Forest could at last be retired to the legends of England, where they belonged. And she no longer needed dream of rescue. Whatever might come their way, she and Timothy could face it together.

Then the jangle of chain mail called out to Merry from down the lane. So like the jangle that had once alerted her to the approach of royal horsemen before her missions. Yet this time it rang somehow deep and awful in its pitch. Nervous energy flashed through her. They had come so close. Though she no longer desired to steel her heart, she steadied its beating and clutched her hands together nonetheless.

An almost palpable wave of fear flooded the group. Everyone froze, but before they could panic and dash into the woods,

Timothy's uncle held up his hand with understated authority. "Hold tight. Stick with the plan. Merry, into the woods."

Merry handed Wren to Timothy, and she alone melted into the woods as the king's soldiers cantered into sight. Her apricot gown blended fortuitously with the golds and oranges of autumn. Though one instinct bade her to scurry up a tree, her gown would not allow, so she stood ready to fly like the wind deeper into the forest. Stealthy like a cat, she peered between the branches.

"My Lord Baron Linden," the soldier in the lead called out to Timothy's uncle.

"Yes," the man answered with a sniff of disdain.

The soldier nodded deferentially. "So sorry to disturb your journey. But I have come with important news. King John has passed from this earth—God rest his soul."

Merry nearly gasped but managed to restrain herself. She dared to take a step closer.

"I see. I am sorry to hear it. All of England shall mourn the loss of our great king." The baron somehow managed to keep a straight face as he said it.

As if anyone would regret seeing the awful king gone. But death was death, and Merry had witnessed too much of it. Her heart did not rejoice at the news, although the tension across her back eased considerably and the roiling in her stomach ceased.

"And who will succeed him?" asked the baron.

"There seems to be some dispute. Officially, the boy Henry III has been declared king and Marshal his protector. The barons in the north still insist Louis is their rightful leader. I imagine the battle will wage on for some time."

And so politics continued as usual. But at least the soldiers seemed not at all interested in her and the ghosts. Her band could yet make their way to France.

"Thank you, my boy. You may go, then." The baron waved the soldiers off dismissively.

"But wait." Timothy took a step forward, and the king's soldiers reined in their horses. "Thoroughgood, what of Merry Ellison and the children of Ellsworth? I have not given up my search nor my ambition to win those twenty gold coins."

Her stomach twisted at that. But no. She would trust Timothy. He seemed to know the soldier. He must have a good reason for speaking so.

The soldier chuckled. "Nobody cares now, I am afraid. She was John's enemy, not Henry's. Marshal wishes to start fresh and leave King John's policies far behind. Prove to the northern barons that this is a new era. Sorry about that."

Timothy frowned. "I suppose I will survive. I have my family after all." He swept his hand to include every one of the young people around him.

"So you do," said the soldier. With a click of his tongue, he and his men turned and continued on their way.

The immensity of the moment hit her. Now her heart did soar. She was free! Free, free, free! Though she beat her feet excitedly against the ground, she managed to hold in her celebration until the soldiers' horses turned the bend. Then she danced out onto the lane cheering, "We are free!"

Chaos erupted as the children crowded in around her, dancing and cheering as well.

Timothy grabbed her and swooped her in a broad circle, her feet flying weightless through the air. "We are free," he echoed, as if he had been one of them all along.

After a time of raucous celebration, Allen struck up a song of thanks to God. The Scripture that Jane had set to music long ago about beauty for ashes.

Tears stroked Merry's cheeks as she joined them. Timothy

tucked her under his arm again and stared down at her, love
shimmering so bright and clear in his eyes. He took up the tune
in his strong, rich voice, then shook his head as if he could not
believe it.

Merry could not believe it. God had indeed been there all
along. His love as clear and true as Timothy's.

The song concluded and lingered, whispering upon the air.

"But whatever shall we do now?" Cedric broke the silence
with the all important question.

"Funny you should ask." The baron slid from his horse. "It
seems I have an entire hamlet with no one to fill it. I would say
it has stood empty for far too long. What say you, dearest?"

Timothy's aunt clapped her hands together. "Oh, splendid
idea! I have never heard better. But where on earth shall we find
a group of able-bodied workers, not to mention a man and
woman of noble birth to manage the place?"

Then she hopped down as well and ran with surprising speed
to embrace Timothy and Merry. "Welcome home. Welcome
everyone."

For a moment, they all stood in quiet reverie, drinking in
the wonder of it. Merry closed her eyes and breathed deep the
scent of the English countryside. For just that instant, the earth
seemed to stand still. The tension of the last two years floated
away from her. Lightness washed over her from head to toe.

Then she opened her eyes and surveyed her faithful band.
The men—Allen, Red, Cedric, and Robert. The young women
and boys. The girls—Sadie, Abigail, and Wren.

Again the earth held its breath as Allen took a knee before
Timothy and Merry. He pulled off his hat and held it to his
heart. Then Robert. Then one by one all the children joined
him upon their knees in a pledge of fealty.

Timothy motioned them to stand, gently taking charge of

his new people, as if he had been born to do so, ninth child or not. "Come. Let us go home."

He offered his hand to Merry.

"And what of the gold?" she whispered.

"Perhaps someday we shall be able to return it to a true and rightful king."

As he took her hand in his, Merry's heart filled to the brim and burst over with love. She might never be able to close it again. Together, just plain Merry Ellison and just plain Timothy Grey led the way into a future more perfect than she would have ever dared to dream.

Historical Notes

I should begin by mentioning that the least plausible scene in this entire novel is the very first one. According to English law, all trees along the highway should have been cleared, but I imagine some nobleman might have failed to keep up with that law. In addition, I have no evidence that the English loaded luggage on the top of their traveling wagons at this time. However, this is the scene that popped into my head and sparked my imagination for the entire story, so I hope you will forgive my fanciful daydreaming.

I do believe that a strong medieval heroine such as Merry Ellison would not only be possible, but probable, given the circumstances. The 1100s and 1200s in England were a time when females were strong and full of spunk, many holding land and titles of their own. One need look no further than King John's mother, Eleanor of Aquitaine, to find an excellent example. According to *Medieval Lives,* by Terry Jones, the popular "damsel in distress" motif was an invention of later times. An actual medieval woman was often left to protect her castle and lands while her husband was off to battle.

The noble outlaw is also a well-established part of English history, and goes much farther than Robin Hood legends. From the time of the Norman invasion, many Englishmen found themselves outside of the law of the local rulers. These outlaws often banded together and lived in the forest. They were dissidents and guerrilla warriors as often as actual criminals.

While legend often portrays King Richard as good and his usurping brother, Prince John (later the King John of this story), as evil, the truth was more complicated. Richard was not a particularly good king. He never actually lived in England, and he taxed his people excessively to support his crusades in the Holy Land. Some historians view John as a strong king who advanced the English cause, but he was also cruel, unfair, and fickle. At one point the pope excommunicated him, and in the end, half his kingdom turned against him. I have found no direct evidence that King John would have burnt an entire village, including women and children, to punish one man, but since the BBC came up with a similar scenario in their Robin Hood series, and since he did destroy villages in his fight against the rebels, I would say it is a plausible idea.

In fact, King John's unjust practices proved pivotal to the history of England by provoking the signing of the Charter of Liberties, later known as the Great Charter or Magna Carta, in 1215 to ensure certain rights for its inhabitants. Although John did not honor the charter, the document became foundational to both English and American law. This year celebrates the 800th anniversary of its signing.

The language of this time is complicated. The common English person spoke Middle English, a language we would barely recognize today. The nobles spoke Norman French, and all official communication throughout Europe was written in Latin. While I allude to this at some points in the story, for the sake of an enjoyable read, I chose a slightly archaic, slightly British version of English for the story.

In addition, at this time in history the Bible would have been read in Latin, and mostly only by priests and other churchmen, but I used the King James Version since it is the earliest English version that is familiar to contemporary readers. I would like to believe there were nobles, like Merry, who took the time to learn Latin and study Scriptures—and pass the knowledge of those Scriptures on to others.

Farthingale Forest, Ellsworth, Wyndeshire, the accompanying titles, and many of the towns and villages are my own invention. I kept the names of the noblemen, their titles, and their holdings similar for ease of reading. Beyond that, I tried to be as accurate to my understanding of the time period as I could. Historians themselves often disagree about the particulars of the Middle Ages, but I did my best, and I hope you enjoy the results.

Acknowledgments

Thanks so much to everyone who has helped me along my writing journey! I am blessed to have a family and church that support me, as well as affiliations with wonderful writers groups like my local ACFW, the ladies of Inkwell Inspirations, and my medieval group, Wenches Writing for Christ. Thank you to my agent, Tamela Hancock Murray, who has stuck with me during ups and downs, and to the wonderful team at Bethany House Publishers, who gave me this incredible opportunity.

A special thanks to all the ladies who had a hand in critiquing this book, including Roseanna White, Christine Lindsay, Gina Welborn, Susan Diane Johnson, Niki Turner, Debra Marvin, Angela Andrews, and Kim Upperman. And the biggest thanks of all to my wonderful teen beta readers—Megan Maurer, Amalie Andrews, Christi Sleiman, Jerah Welborn, and Rhyinn Welborn. You girls rock!

Finally, I am forever grateful to God and to the whispers of the Holy Spirit in my heart. In you I live and move and have my being. I could never do this alone.

Dina Sleiman holds an MA in professional writing from Regent University and a BA in communications with a minor in English from Oral Roberts University. Over the past twenty years, she has had opportunities to teach college writing and literature, as well as high-school and elementary classes in English, humanities, and fine arts. She lives in Virginia with her husband and three children. She can be found online at www.dinasleiman.com.

More Fiction You May Enjoy